SEBASTIAN FITZEK

TRANSLATED BY JOHN BROWNJOHN

First published in trade paperback in Great Britain in 2012 by Corvus,
an imprint of Atlantic Books Ltd.

This paperback edition published in Great Britain in 2013 by Corvus,
an imprint of Atlantic Books Ltd.

Originally published in German as *Der Augensammler* in 2010 by Droemer Knaur.

10 9 8 7 6 5 4 3 2 1

A CIP catalogue record for this book is available from the British Library.

Paperback ISBN: 978 0 85789 371 0
E-book ISBN: 978 0 85789 370 3

Printed and bound by CPI Group (UK) Ltd, Croydon, CR0 4YY

Corvus
An imprint of Atlantic Books Ltd
Ormond House
26–27 Boswell Street
London
WC1N 3JZ

www.corvus-books.co.uk

In memory of Rüdiger Kreklau.
It's the fantasists who change the world,
not the bean counters.

Playing is experimenting with chance.
Novalis

It's the end where I begin.
The Script

EPILOGUE

ALEXANDER ZORBACH

Some stories are like fish hooks, prickly with lethal barbs that embed themselves ever deeper and more inextricably in the minds of the audience, compelling them to keep listening. My name for such a tale is *perpetuum morbile,* a narrative with no beginning or end because it tells of death everlasting.

Stories of this kind are sometimes recounted by unscrupulous souls who revel in the look of horror in their listeners' eyes and the nightmarish visions that will haunt them later on, leaving them staring up at the ceiling and unable to sleep.

A *perpetuum morbile* can occasionally be found between the covers of a book, in which case it can be avoided by shutting the volume in question. And that's my advice to you right now: Don't read on!

I've no idea how you got hold of this story. I only know that it wasn't meant for you. An account of such horrors should not be allowed to fall into the hands of anyone. Not even your own worst enemy.

Believe me, I speak from experience. I couldn't shut my eyes or lay the book aside. Why not? Because the story of a man whose tears oozed down his cheeks like drops of blood – the story of a man who embraced a contorted lump of human flesh that had breathed and lived and loved only minutes earlier – is no novel or film script. It it not a figment of the imagination.

It is my destiny.

My life.

There is a man in this tale who was forced to realize, just when the agony within his mind reached its peak, that the process of dying had only just begun. And that man is me.

FINAL CHAPTER

THE END

> *'Rock a bye baby on the tree top,*
> *when the wind blows the cradle will rock...'*

'Tell her to put a sock in it!'

> *'When the bough breaks, the cradle will fall,*
> *and down will come baby, cradle, and all.'*

'Tell her to stop singing that goddamned song at once!'

'Yes, yes, I know what I'm doing,' I told the commander of the mobile police unit, via a tiny radio mic that the technician had pinned to my shirt a few minutes earlier. 'Keep yelling at me like that and I'll dump the goddamned earpiece, understand?'

I was nearing the middle of the bridge over the A100. The city expressway was eleven metres below us. It had been shut in both directions to safeguard passing motorists, rather than for the sake of the mentally disturbed woman standing several metres from me.

'Angélique?' I called. I knew from the quick briefing I'd received at our temporary command post that she was thirty-seven years old, had twice been convicted of attempted baby-snatching, and had spent at least seven of the last ten years in a secure mental institution. A month ago, unfortunately, some sympathetic psychologist had decided that, in his expert opinion, she should be reintegrated into society.

And dropped us in the shit. Thanks a bunch, doctor!

'I'll come a bit closer if you don't mind,' I said, raising my arms. No reaction. She was leaning against the rusty railing with her arms cradled across her chest. Now and then she swayed far enough forwards for her elbows to briefly hang over the edge.

I was trembling with cold as well as tension. Although the temperature was surprisingly mild for December, the wind chill made Berlin feel like Yakutsk. Three minutes' exposure to that icy blast and my ears were almost falling off.

'Hello? Angélique?'

Gravel crunched beneath my boots. She turned her head and looked at me for the first time. By degrees, as if in slow motion.

'My name is Alexander Zorbach. I'd like a word with you.'

Because it's my job. I'm the police negotiator on duty today.

'Isn't he lovely?' she said in the same sing-song voice she'd used for the lullaby. *Rock a bye baby...* 'Isn't my baby adorable?'

I nodded, although I was too far away to make out

what she was clasping to her scrawny chest. It could have been a bolster or a rag doll, but no such luck. Our thermal imaging camera had confirmed that the thing in her arms was warm and alive. I still couldn't see it, but I could hear it.

The six-month-old baby was crying. Rather feebly, but crying nonetheless.

That was the good news.

The bad news was, it had only minutes to live.

Even if this mentally deranged creature didn't throw it off the bridge.

Damn it, Angélique, you picked the wrong baby this time – in every possible way.

I made another attempt to engage her in conversation. 'What's the little mite's name?' I asked.

A bungled abortion had left her unable to have children. It had also robbed her of her reason. This was the third time she'd taken someone else's baby and tried to pass it off as her own, only to be discovered not far from the hospital. Today it had taken only half an hour for the barefooted woman with a whimpering baby to be spotted on the bridge by a motorcycle courier.

'He doesn't have a name yet,' she said. Her self-delusion was so far advanced that she firmly believed the child in her arms to be her own flesh and blood. I knew it was pointless to try to disabuse her. I certainly wouldn't achieve in seven minutes what seven years of intensive therapy had failed to do. But that wasn't what I had in mind.

'How about "Hans"?' I suggested. I was now no more than ten metres away.

'Hans?' She withdrew one arm from the bundle and folded back the blanket. To my relief, the baby started to cry again. 'Hans sounds nice,' she said absently, stepping back a little. She wasn't as near the rail now. 'Like Lucky Hans in the fairy tale.'

'Yes,' I said, taking another cautious step towards her.

Nine metres.

'Or,' I added, 'like the Hans in the other fairy tale.'

She turned to me with an enquiring look. 'What other fairy tale?'

'The one about the nymph called Undine.'

It was more of a saga than a fairy tale, actually, but that was irrelevant under the circumstances.

'Undine?' The corners of her mouth turned down. 'I don't know it.'

'No? I'll tell you it, then. It's a great story.'

'What the hell are you playing at?' the unit commander bellowed in my right ear. I ignored him.

Eight metres. I was edging into the penalty area step by step.

'Undine was a godlike creature, a water nymph more beautiful than any woman alive. She fell hopelessly in love with a knight named Hans.'

'Hear that, my pet? You're a knight!'

The baby responded with a loud cry.

So he's still breathing. Thank God for that.

'Yes,' I went on, 'but Sir Hans was so handsome that

all the women ran after him. Sadly, he fell in love with someone else and left Undine in the lurch.'

Seven metres.

I waited until I heard the baby give another cry. 'Undine's father, the sea-god Poseidon, was so angry with Hans that he laid a curse on him.'

Angélique stopped rocking the baby. 'A curse?'

'Yes. From then on, Hans could no longer breathe without thinking. He had to concentrate all the time.'

I drew cold air into my lungs and expelled it noisily as I spoke.

'He had to breathe in, breathe out, breathe in, breathe out.'

My chest rose and fell demonstratively.

'If he forgot to do this, even for a moment, he would die.'

Six metres.

'How does the story end?' Angélique asked suspiciously, when I'd got to within a car's length of her. She seemed less put out by my proximity than by the turn the story had taken.

'Hans made every effort to avoid falling asleep. He struggled with his weariness, but in the end he couldn't keep his eyes open.'

'He died?' she asked dully. Every spark of joy had left her haggard face.

'Yes, because by falling asleep he'd automatically forgotten to breathe. And that signed his death warrant.'

There was a click in my ear, but this time the unit

commander kept his mouth shut. There was nothing to be heard but a distant hum of traffic. A flock of big, black birds soared over us, heading east.

'That's not a nice fairy tale.' Angélique edged forwards a little, clutching the baby tightly to her and rocking it with her entire body.

I put out my hand and came closer still.

'No, it isn't. And it isn't really a fairy tale, either.'

'What do you mean?'

I paused, waiting for some sign of life from the baby, but there was nothing to be heard. Just silence. My mouth had gone dry.

'It's true,' I told her.

'True?'

She shook her head – vigorously, as if she already guessed what was coming.

'Angélique, please listen to me. The baby in your arms is suffering from Undine's Curse, a disease named after the story I just told you.'

'No!'

Yes.

The tragic thing was, I hadn't told her a tactical lie. Undine's Curse was a rare disorder of the central nervous system. Children suffering from it died of asphyxia unless they deliberately concentrated on breathing. It was a grave, life-threatening illness. In Tim's case (the baby's real name) his respiratory activity when awake was sufficient to supply his body with oxygen. He needed ventilating only when asleep.

'But he's *my* baby,' Angélique protested in her lullaby voice.

Rock a bye baby...

'See how peacefully he's sleeping in my arms.'

Oh God, no. She was right. The baby wasn't making a sound.

... on the tree top...

'Yes, he's your baby, Angélique,' I said urgently, taking another step towards her. 'No one disputes that, but he mustn't fall asleep, you hear? If he does, he'll die like Sir Hans in the fairy tale.'

'No, no, no!' She shook her head defiantly. 'My baby hasn't been naughty. He isn't under a curse.'

'Of course not, but he's sick. Please give me your little boy so the doctors can make him well.'

I was now so close to her, I caught the rank, sweetish smell of her unwashed hair and the effluvium of mental and physical decay that clung to every thread of her cheap tracksuit.

She turned towards me, giving me my first good view of the baby. Of its tiny, slightly flushed, *sleeping* face. I stared at Angélique in alarm. And that was when I lost my head.

'Jesus. No. Don't!' the unit commander's voice yelled in my ear, but by then I was past listening to him. 'Put it away!'

I'm citing his words and the ones that follow from the transcript sitting before me, written by the chairman of the board of inquiry.

At this remove, seven years after the day that wrecked my life, I'm no longer certain I really saw it.

It.

That *something* in her expression. A look of unadulterated, despairing self-knowledge. I was sure of it at the time, though.

Call it premonition. Intuition. Clairvoyance. Whatever it was, I sensed it with every fibre of my being. The moment Angélique turned towards me, she became aware of her mental disorder. She recognized herself. Knew that she was sick. Knew that the baby wasn't hers. Knew that, once I got hold of it, I would never give it back.

'Don't, man! Don't do anything stupid!'

I'd had enough experience as an amateur boxer to know what to focus on in order to guess what an opponent would do next: the shoulders. And Angélique's shoulders moved in a direction that allowed only one interpretation, confirmed by the fact that she slowly opened her arms at the same time.

Three metres. Only another three fucking metres.

She was going to throw the baby off the bridge.

'Drop your gun. I repeat: Drop it at once.'

That was why I ignored the voice in my ear and aimed straight at her forehead.

And squeezed the trigger.

Usually, that's the moment when I wake up yelling. Then comes a fleeting, euphoric sense of relief that it was just a bad dream. It lasts only until I put out my hand and feel that the other half of the bed is empty – until it occurs to me that this chain of events actually happened. It deprived me of my job, my family, and my ability to sleep through the night without being woken by nightmares.

Since firing that shot I have lived in fear. A cold, clear, all-pervading kind of fear: the concentrate from which my dreams derive their sustenance.

I killed a human being on that bridge.

Much as I try to convince myself that I saved another life by so doing, the equation doesn't add up. What if I was wrong? What if Angélique never meant to harm the child? What if she opened her arms in order to hand it over – opened them at the very instant my bullet pierced her skull so swiftly that her brain had no time to transmit an impulse to her arms and open them still wider? So swiftly that I was able to catch the baby before it fell from her lifeless grasp?

In other words, what if I killed an innocent woman on that bridge?

If so, I would some day have to pay for my mistake. That much was certain.

I knew it. All I failed to realize was that the day would come so soon.

83

My son and I were paying another visit to the nicest place in Berlin for a child to die in, or so it was said.

'Really? The helicopter?' I said, jerking my chin at the open cardboard box I was carrying down the long corridor. 'Have you thought about it carefully? After all, it's a Captain Jack chopper with power-boost.'

Julian nodded eagerly as he dragged the bulging Ikea carrier bag over the lino.

I'd offered to help him more than once, but he insisted on towing the heavy bag through the hospital unaided. Typical of the 'I can manage by myself' fantasies to which all youngsters sooner or later succumb, usually between their 'Don't leave me alone' and 'Give me some space' phases.

All I could do without injuring his pride was walk a bit slower.

'I don't need the chopper any more,' Julian said firmly. He started coughing. It sounded at first as if he'd briefly choked on something, but the coughing grew harsher.

'You okay?' I put the box down.

I had noticed his flushed cheeks when I picked him up

at home, but he'd toted the heavy bag out into the garden all by himself, so I'd put his sweaty hands and damp curls down to physical exertion.

'Have you still got that cold?' I asked anxiously.

'I'm fine now, Dad.' He fended off my hand when I tried to feel his forehead. Then he coughed some more, but it really didn't sound too bad.

'Did Mum take you to the doctor?'

This is a hospital. Maybe we ought to have you checked over while we're here.

Julian shook his head.

'No, just...' He broke off, and I felt a surge of anger.

'Just what?'

He turned away, looking sheepish, then took hold of the bag handles again.

'One moment,' I said. 'Don't tell me the two of you paid another visit to that guru?'

He nodded hesitantly, as if confessing to some misdemeanour, even though it wasn't his fault. It was his mother who was straying down ever more esoteric paths. She would sooner have taken our son to a Indian spiritual teacher than an ENT consultant.

A long time ago, when I was falling in love with Nicci, her eccentricities had amused me. I even found it entertaining when she tried to infer my future from the lines in my palm or disclosed that she'd been a Greek slave girl in a previous existence. As the years went by, however, her harmless fads developed into the *idées fixes* that had undoubtedly contributed to my separation from her, mentally at first, then physically. At least that's what I like to tell myself; it absolves me of sole responsibility for the failure of our marriage.

'What did that charla— I mean, what did the guru say?' I asked, catching him up. It was an effort not to sound aggressive. Julian would have thought I was angry with *him,* and it really wasn't his fault that his mother didn't believe in traditional medicine or the theory of evolution.

'He said my chakras aren't properly charged with energy.'

'Your chakras?' The blood rose in my cheeks.

'Of course,' I harangued Nicci in my head, *'his chakras – why didn't I think of that myself? That's probably also the reason why our son broke his wrist two years ago while skateboarding.'* That time, she had asked the surgeon, in all seriousness, if hypnosis couldn't be substituted for the anaesthetic.

'You should drink something,' I said to change the subject, indicating the soft-drinks machine. 'What would you like?'

'A Coca-Cola,' he said promptly.

Okay, a Coca-Cola.

Nicci would tear a strip off me, that was for sure. My 'still-wife' (not yet ex-wife) shopped at eco-stores and organic supermarkets exclusively and on principle; her shopping list would never have featured a fizzy drink laced with caffeine and chemicals.

Yes, but there isn't any fennel tea here, I thought, patting my jacket in search of my wallet and its little pocket for coins.

I gave a sudden start at the unexpected sound of a young but world-weary voice behind me.

'Well, if it isn't the Zorbachs. What a nice surprise!'

I vaguely remembered the blonde nurse from our visit the year before. She had appeared from nowhere and was now standing in the hospital corridor with a brightly painted tea trolley.

'Hello, Monika,' said Julian, who had evidently recognized her too. She gave him a practised 'young patients are my buddies' smile. Then she caught sight of our burdens.

'Wow, what a lot of toys you've brought this year.'

I nodded – absently, because I still hadn't found my wallet.

Please, no! All my IDs and credit cards. Even the key card without which I can't get into the newsroom.

I remembered having it yesterday at the newsroom drinks dispenser. I could have sworn I'd put it back in my breast pocket, but now it was gone.

'Yes, more and more every year,' I muttered, annoyed with myself for sounding guilty. Although it may at first sight have seemed typical behaviour by the father in a broken marriage, the fact was, I'd always enjoyed buying Julian presents. A hand-crafted wooden tractor would, of course, have been more educationally worthwhile than the fluorescent water pistol the nurse was extracting from the Ikea bag. But 'educational' was an argument inflicted on me by my own parents, who had refused to see why I needed a Walkman or a BMX just because all my friends listened to the former and rode around on the latter. Call me shallow, but having experienced it, I wanted to spare my son an outsider's fate. That didn't mean I bought him any old rubbish just so he could 'belong'. But I wasn't going to send him empty-handed into the Darwinian fight for survival that raged daily in every school playground.

Meanwhile, Monika had unearthed a Spiderman doll. 'I think it's really admirable of you,' she said, smiling at my son, 'agreeing to part with all these lovely things.'

'No problem.' Julian grinned back at her. 'I like doing it.'

He was telling the truth. Although it had been my idea to clear out his room once a year before his birthday, when reinforcements would arrive, he'd adopted it at once.

'We'll make room and do some good!' he said, repeating my own words, and promptly set to work.

That was how our 'Sunshine Day', as we called it, came into being. The day on which father and son set off for the children's hospice, laden with discarded toys, and doled them out to its little patients.

'Tim'll like that, I'm sure,' the nurse said with a smile as she replaced the Spiderman doll with the other toys. Then she said goodbye and walked on. Looking after her, I was dismayed to find that I'd only just managed to restrain my tears.

Julian looked at me. 'Everything okay?' he asked. He was used to his father becoming a crybaby as soon as he entered Sunshine Ward on the second floor. Julian had never cried there, probably because death seemed so remote and unimaginable to him. To me, on the other hand, a ward devoted to gravely ill children was an almost unbearable environment. One might have assumed that a man who had shot someone would be rather hard-boiled, especially as I'd had to earn a living as a crime reporter since my retirement from the force. I had now been working for the city's biggest and most bloodthirsty paper for four years, following a period of recovery and retraining. In fact I'd made something of a journalistic name for myself by reporting on some of the most gruesome and violent crimes ever committed in Germany. But the more I wrote about some of the western world's worst murders, the less prepared I was to accept death. Least of all when it was the death of innocent children suffering from leukaemia or heart disease. Or Undine's Curse.

'The little boy whose life you saved was called Tim, wasn't he?'

I nodded and gave up looking for my wallet. With luck it would be lying on the passenger seat of my Volvo, but I'd probably lost it somewhere.

'Absolutely, but the one in here isn't him. He's got the same name, that's all.'

The Tim whose kidnapper I'd shot used to send me a Christmas card every year. The kind of card parents compel you to write: inscribed in squiggly handwriting with words no child would ever use. The kind you stick to the door of the fridge and ignore until it falls off of its own accord. Nevertheless, Tim's cards were a sign of life that proved he was leading a semi-normal existence at home with his parents in spite of his serious illness, not spending his final hours vegetating in a children's hospice.

Julian gave me a wide-eyed look. 'Mum says you've not been the same since that time on the bridge.'

That time on the bridge.

Words can sometimes define a whole universe. 'I love you' or 'We're a family', for example – a combination of innocuous letters that lend your life meaning. 'That time on the bridge' definitely came into this category. If it hadn't been so sad, one could have laughed at the fact that we behaved like the characters in a *Harry Potter* novel and spoke of 'You-Know-Who' instead of calling a spade a spade. Angélique, the mentally deranged woman whose life I'd taken, was my personal Lord Voldemort.

'Julian, you go on ahead to the recreation room. That's where the children will be waiting for us.' I knelt down so we were at eye level. 'I'm just going to nip out and see if I left my wallet in the car, okay?'

He nodded silently.

I watched him until he disappeared round the corner and all I could hear was the squeak of his trainers on the lino and the slithery sound of the heavy carrier bag being towed along.

Then I turned and made my way out of the hospital. I never went back.

82

The Volvo was parked beneath a huge horse-chestnut tree in the gloom of the winter morning, so I inserted the ignition key and turned on the reading light over the passenger seat. I looked everywhere: in the footwell, on the rear seats, under a stack of old newspapers. There were few things I hated more than driving with bulging pockets. As a rule, therefore, I tossed my keys, mobile phone and wallet on to the passenger seat before getting in behind the wheel. A ritual I seemed to have neglected this time, because I could find nothing there apart from a ballpoint pen and half a packet of chewing gum. No sign of my wallet.

After taking another look under the seats I opened the glove compartment, although I felt sure I'd never kept anything in there except the scanner I used to monitor police radio traffic. In my early days as a crime reporter it gave me a pang whenever I heard the voices of my former colleagues. Now I was used to not belonging any more. Besides, my boss, Thea Bergdorf, had only given me the job because of my inside knowledge. It had been made clear to me that that eavesdropping on the police, whenever I was on the move, was an unwritten clause of my contract. Especially on days like today, when we were expecting the worst. I had fixed the scanner so it came on automatically as soon as I turned the ignition key, which was why the thing was hissing away in the glove compartment and flashing like a Christmas tree.

I was just about to abandon my search and rejoin Julian when I heard a voice that banished all thought of my missing wallet.

'... Westen, Kühler Weg, corner of Alte Allee...'

I stared at the glove compartment, then turned up the volume.

'I repeat. One-zero-seven in Kühler Weg. Mobile units at the scene.'

My eyes strayed to the dashboard clock.

Damn it. Not again.

One-zero-seven. Official radio code for the discovery of a dead body.

81

(44 HOURS 38 MINUTES TO THE DEADLINE)

TOBY TRAUNSTEIN (AGE 9)

Dark. Black. No, not black. That's the wrong word.

It wasn't like the paintwork on Dad's new car. Nor like the blotchy darkness you see in front of your eyes when you shut them suddenly. Nor was it like the greyish gloom he remembered from the night-time nature ramble they'd gone on with Frau Quandt. This was different. Denser, somehow. Creepier. As if he were submerged in a barrel of oil.

Toby opened his eyes again.

Nothing.

The darkness around him was impenetrable. Nothing like the forest that surrounded the summer camp their class had gone to last summer. There was no moonlight or torchlight like there had been when they were combing the forest path for clues on that paperchase through the Grunewald. No smell of soil, vegetation or wild boar dung, and no Lea clutching his hand like a crybaby and starting at every rustle and crackle. There were no noises in here that would have scared his twin sister. In here – wherever 'here' was – there was... *nothing.*

Nothing apart from his boundless fear of being paralysed. For although he realized that darkness was insubstantial (just as he knew from Herr Hartmann, his art teacher, that black was merely an absence of light, not a colour), it seemed to be holding him in a vice-like grip.

He still didn't know whether he was standing up or lying down. He might even be upside down. That would explain the pressure inside his head and why he was feeling so dizzy. Or possibly *frazzled,* as his father used to say when he came home after work and told Mum to run him a bath.

He had never ventured to ask the precise meaning of *frazzled*. Dad didn't like his kids asking too many questions. Toby had learnt that lesson while on holiday in Italy two years ago, when he'd dared to wonder aloud over supper whether Dad's translation of *caldo* as 'cold' was really correct. Although Daddy had told him to stop his everlasting questions and the look on Mummy's face should have warned him not to cast doubt on his father's knowledge of Italian, he hadn't been able to resist pointing out that every tap in the hotel must be defective because only hot water came out of the ones marked *caldo*. Daddy's hand had shot out. He'd stopped asking too many questions after that slap in the restaurant. Now he didn't know exactly what *frazzled* meant, he had no idea why he couldn't move and he was feeling so sick. His feet and his head seemed to be imprisoned in a vice and he couldn't feel his arms any more. *No, wrong.* He could feel them as far as his shoulders. Maybe even a little lower down, where he'd suddenly developed the awful tingling sensation he got when his best friend Kevin gave him a Chinese burn. Kevin the big-head, who had really been christened Kornelius, but who threatened to thump anyone who addressed him by that 'poncey name'.

Kevin, Kornelius, Cacky Pants...

Everything below the elbow, or what normally lay or dangled to his left and his right – in other words, his forearms, wrists and hands *(Shit, where are my hands?)* – all these had disappeared.

He tried to scream but his mouth and throat were too dry. All he produced was a pathetic croak.

Why aren't I covered with blood if my hands have been cut off? Amputated, or whatever it's called.

A stale smell infiltrated Toby's nostrils. Sweetish like rancid butter but a lot less strong. It was a while before he grasped that the darkness must be enclosed by walls that were reflecting his bad breath back into his face. It was even longer before, to his infinite relief, he rediscovered his hands. They were behind his back.

I'm tied up. No, wrong. I'm wedged in.

His mind started to race.

I'm lying on my arms, that's for sure.

Feverishly, he tried to recall what he'd been doing just before he came here, wherever 'here' was, but his memory seemed to have been sluiced away by a tide of pain. The last thing he remembered was playing that silly game of computer tennis in the living room, the one where you had to jump around in front of the TV set and Lea always won. Then Mum had put them to bed. And now he was here. Here in this *nothingness*.

Toby swallowed hard, and all at once he felt even more scared than before. So scared that he didn't even notice the sharp smelling rivulet trickling from between his legs. Fear of being buried alive was now doing what the constraints of his invisible prison had failed to do completely: it was paralysing him.

He swallowed again, reflecting that the darkness was like a living creature which could hold you tight and tasted like metal when you gulped it down.

He felt as queasy as he had after that long car journey, when he'd insisted on reading and Dad got mad because they'd had to stop. He was holding his breath so as not to be sick when suddenly...

What the...?

His roaming tongue had encountered a foreign body.

What on earth is it?

The thing was clinging to the roof of his mouth. Like a potato crisp, but its surface was harder and smoother.

And colder.

He ran his tongue over the object, feeling the saliva accumulate. Instinctively breathing through his nose, he suppressed his urge to swallow until the foreign object detached itself from the roof of his mouth and came away on his tongue.

And then it dawned on him. Even though he couldn't recall *how* he had got here, *who* had kidnapped him and *why* he was being held captive – even though he hadn't the least idea *what* it was, this dark nothingness that hemmed him in – he had at least solved *one* mystery.

A coin.

Before confining Toby Traunstein in the darkest place imaginable, someone had inserted a coin in his mouth.

80

(44 HOURS 31 MINUTES TO THE DEADLINE)

ALEXANDER ZORBACH

'You insensitive, irresponsible, self-centred shit!'

'You've forgotten *stupid* and *objectionable*.'

I sounded calm. Far calmer than I usually did when arguing with my still-wife. At our last meeting we had finally agreed to get divorced. Now Nicci repeated the sentence she had hurled in my face that night: 'I sometimes wonder how I ever got together with you.'

Good question.

To be frank, I was utterly unable to fathom what women saw in me. Nicci and I had first met in the lecture room of the psychology faculty, a room full of men who were taller, better-looking and certainly more charming than I. Yet she had plumped for me. It couldn't have been my outward appearance. I hate seeing myself in photos. Out of two hundred snaps there'll be at most one of which I'm not ashamed. It will be a blurred or ill-exposed picture that doesn't show up my steadily developing double chin. People used to say I reminded them of Nicolas Cage because of my doleful expression; now, all I have in common with him is thinning hair. I've put on a kilo a year since my thirtieth birthday, even though I avoid junk food and go jogging twice a week. Nicci put her finger on it at the start of our relationship when she called me a 'collector's item' of no obvious value. Like an old banger: elderly enough to qualify for a scrappage scheme but too endearing, in spite of its quirks, to trade in for a new model. In that respect, of course, she had since changed her mind.

'What kind of father abandons his ten-year-old son in a hospice for the dying?' she demanded angrily.

I didn't even trouble to explain that Julian had been very understanding when I called him from the car and asked him to distribute the presents on his own because an emergency had arisen. I had to get to a crime scene, and I could hardly take a ten-year-old boy along.

'And what kind of mother takes her son to see a witch doctor when he's got bronchitis?' I retorted.

Damn it, what wouldn't I give for a cigarette at this moment...

Instinctively, I felt for the nicotine patch on my right arm. I was holding the phone wedged between my chin and my neck.

'That's a low blow, Alex,' Nicci said after a short pause. 'You didn't even leave Julian enough money for a cab.'

'Because I've lost my wallet someplace. Shit happens, for God's sake.'

'In your world, Alex,' she replied, 'in your world disasters follow one another in quick succession. It's those bad vibes of yours.'

'Please don't start that again!'

My hands were trembling. I tried to calm down by wrapping them more tightly around the steering wheel. My nerves had got even worse since I'd tried to give up smoking.

In spite of that itchy plaster on my triceps.

'It's your negative energy,' she said, sounding almost compassionate. 'You positively attract evil.'

'I only write about it. I report the facts. There's a psychopath on the loose who destroys families in such an atrocious way, even the scandal sheet I work for doesn't dare print all the details.'

He plays the oldest children's game in the world – hide-and-seek – and he plays it until an entire family comes to grief. He plays it until death.

My eyes strayed to the old newspaper lying on the passenger seat. I had written the headline myself:

THE EYE COLLECTOR STRIKES AGAIN!
CHILD NO. 3 FOUND DEAD

Like my former occupation as a police negotiator, my job at the paper had often taxed my powers of endurance to the limit. But the case of the Eye Collector had lent a new dimension to the word horror. He killed the mothers of the children he kidnapped and then gave the fathers a few hours to find their offspring before they asphyxiated in a hideaway to which he'd conveyed them. Throw in the fact that the psychopath removed the left eye from each little corpse, and you had a case which truly transcended the bounds of what was conceivable.

Nicci continued to pontificate. 'Negative thoughts find expression in reality,' she said. 'Positive thinking breeds positive experiences.'

'Positive thinking? Are you completely off your trolley? The Eye Collector has already struck three times.' *Six dead: three women, two little girls, one boy.* 'You think the madman will stop if I pull over on to the hard shoulder and meditate for a bit? No, better still, maybe I'll simply place an order with the Universe, like it says in that book on your bedside table.' I was talking myself into a rage. 'Or I'll call one of those astrology hotlines you waste a fortune on. Maybe the housewife at the other end take a quick look at her tea leaves and see where the Eye Collector is hiding?'

A click signalled an incoming call. I removed the mobile from my ear and checked the display.

'Don't hang up,' I told Nicci, and gratefully put her on hold.

79

'Hello, Alex. It's me, your favourite trainee.'

Frank Lahmann.

If he'd caught me at a better moment I'd have said, 'Favourite trainee? You mean you've quit?' But I wasn't in the mood for banter, so I left it at a curt 'Hello.'

'I hate to disturb your slumbers, Alex, but Thea wants to know if you'll be attending the midday conference.'

Most of my colleagues on the paper had problems with Frank's bumptious manner. Personally, I was fond of the twenty-one-year-old rookie, perhaps because we shared the same wavelength spanning the generation gap between us. Most of the young staff in our editorial offices were there for the wrong reasons. They thought it was cool to work in the media and hoped one day to be in the public eye as much as the stories they worked on. Frank was different. Journalism was a vocation to him, not a job, and he would probably have stuck with it even if the paper had cut his salary. Considering the amount of voluntary overtime he put in, his current hourly rate was on a par with that of a Somalian field-hand.

Once upon a time, when I was reading a novel and

came across the words 'You remind me of myself at your age', I would roll my eyes and dismiss them as sentimental rubbish. A month ago, however, when I found my trainee's sleeping bag in the copy room, I caught myself thinking just that. Frank reminded me of myself as a trainee policeman: utterly obsessed, pathologically hard-working, and – on occasion – thoroughly disrespectful to my mentor.

'I'm to tell you'd better come up with a few facts that haven't been gathering dust on our competitors' websites. Otherwise – and I quote the she-dragon's actual words – "I'll have his guts for garters."'

Frank sounded even more wound-up than usual, probably because of all the cups of coffee he was bound to have already poured down his throat.

The editorial conference.

I groaned softly. 'Please tell our esteemed editor I won't be able to make it today.'

Yet again...

He chuckled. 'Well, it's your funeral, but woe betide you if Thea takes it out on me and sends me to cover the Angling Club's annual press conference or some such crap.'

'She can forget that. I need you today.'

Frank let loose a nervous cough. At that moment he was presumably peering over his computer screen at the editor's glassed-in office and looking conspiratorial.

'So what do you want me to do, Mr President?' he asked in a low voice.

'Go to my desk. In one of the drawers – the bottom

left, I think – you'll find fifty euros and a credit card with a rubber band round them.'

All I heard for a while was a hiss of static and the noises typical of an open-plan newsroom.

'Who are you trying to impress? There are only twenty euros and a green Amex. It's not even gold.'

'I need you to bring them to me, pronto. I've lost my wallet and I'm nearly out of petrol.'

'Your wallet, eh? What a bugger.'

I heard an office chair creak and had a vision of Frank sitting down at my desk in his standard telephone pose: mobile clamped between chin and collarbone, both elbows on the desk and hands clasped behind his shaven head.

'Did it at least contain a photo of a child?'

Of Julian?

'My wallet, you mean? No.' I was faintly puzzled.

'That's bad. Very bad.'

He cleared his throat, always a prelude to a monologue on his part. The driver of the minibus just ahead of me switched lanes for no good reason, distracting me, and I missed the chance to nip Frank's lecture in the bud.

'According to a study undertaken by the University of Hertfordshire, lost wallets and purses tend to be handed in to the police if there's something personal in them. Snaps of little children, wives or puppies, for example.'

'Very interesting,' I said, but he didn't appear to notice the sarcasm in my tone.

'They dropped no less than 240 wallets to see how many of them were—'

'Frank, that's enough, okay? I really don't have time for this crap.' The tone of my voice got through to him. 'Grab the money and get going.'

I told him the address. 'And hurry,' I said. 'I think it's starting again.'

The line suddenly went dead. I was afraid I'd driven into a dead zone. Then I heard a faint rustle at the other end of the line.

'The Eye Collector?' said Frank.

'Yes.'

'Shit,' he whispered. He was still too young and too new to the game to greet the news in a blasé or hard-boiled manner. That was another thing I liked about him. He knew when the time for schoolboy levity was over.

It was a year since I'd fished Frank out of a shoal of job applicants. I did so despite opposition from Thea, who would have preferred to engage some cute dolly bird from the German School of Journalism in Munich, not a 'tenderfoot', to quote her reaction to his photograph. 'He looks like a youngster on a cereal packet. No one'll take him seriously.'

But Frank Lahmann had been the only applicant to stake his claim with a story rather than a CV. His report on the serious neglect of patients with Alzheimer's in private nursing homes ended up on page four of our paper. Furthermore, he was an absolutely ace researcher. Even if he did insist on taking every opportunity to air the useless knowledge he gleaned from news agencies, libraries and the Internet, regardless of how appropriate it may be.

'See you in fifteen minutes,' I said, and switched back to Nicci, who – to my surprise – was still on the line.

'Look, I'm sorry you're having to collect Julian,' I said, trying to sound friendly. The rain had grown heavier again, the temperature was just above freezing, and a driver in a hat was crawling along ahead of me. 'I promise it won't happen again, but I've really got to go and do my job now.'

Nicci sighed. She, too, seemed to have calmed down a little in the interim. 'Oh, Alex, what's happened to you? You could write about so many things. Love and happiness, for example, or people whose selfless thoughts and actions change the world.'

I was driving past some allotments. The asphalt ran out and the road ended in a potholed forest track. I had often played tennis near here in the old days, so I was familiar with the area. It wasn't the direct route to Kühler Weg, but in cases like this it could be an advantage not to blunder in through the front door.

'But that incident...'

The incident on the bridge.

'... it destroyed something inside you. You were acquitted on all counts, but not by the court in your own head, am I right? We went over it again and again: you acted in good faith. You were right to do as you did. There was even an amateur video that corroborated your evidence.'

I silently shook my head.

'But instead of accepting it as a stroke of fate and changing your life, you go on chasing after criminals. Not with a gun, maybe, but with a dictaphone and a ball-point. You're still dredging the depths.' Nicci's voice shook. 'Why? Tell me! What fascinates you so much about death that you neglect your own child, your family – even yourself?'

My trembling hands tightened on the steering wheel.

'Is it because you want to punish yourself? Do you seek out evil because you think you're an evil person?'

I held my breath and said nothing, just stared through the windscreen and thought hard. When I finally tried to answer, I found that the woman who used to believe that only death would us part had hung up.

To judge by the hoof prints, the track had dwindled to a path used by riders only. On my left was a succession of small allotments; on my right were the Borussia tennis courts. Ignoring the sign that denied access to motor vehicles of all kinds, I coaxed the jolting Volvo slowly round a bend.

The worst of it is, I thought as I spotted the flashing lights of the convoy of patrol cars that was blocking the access to Kühler Weg some 200 metres away... *the worst of it is, there's a smidgen of truth in Nicci's cockeyed view of the world.*

I reversed the Volvo and parked it alongside the muddy wire-mesh fence that separated the track from the deserted tennis courts.

There were reasons why I'd spent so many years with Nicci despite our differences – despite our everlasting arguments over how to bring up children and plan our future together. Although we'd been living apart for the last six months, she was, of course, still closer to me than any other adult on this planet.

I got out, opened the boot, and took out my crime-scene kit.

She sees through me, I thought as I put on the protective clothing designed to prevent me from contaminating a crime scene: a snow white plastic coverall and a pair of pale green plastic overshoes, which I pulled on over my old, worn Timberland boots.

Evil does attract me.

Irresistibly.

And I don't know why.

I shut the boot and peered along the track leading to the crime scene. Then I turned and disappeared into the trees.

78

(44 HOURS 6 MINUTES TO THE DEADLINE)

PHILIPP STOYA
(DETECTIVE SUPERINTENDENT, HOMICIDE)

Stoya could hear the dead woman's screams as he looked into her eyes. He sensed the mute reproach, of which the lecturer on forensic medicine had always warned his students at police college. Even if you succeeded in detaching yourself sufficiently from the horror that occasionally overwhelms the most hardened detective at the sight of a corpse – even if you tried to tell yourself you were looking at a piece of evidence, not an individual, when confronted by a body violated, abused, robbed of life by human hand and abandoned like garbage to insects, the elements and marauding animals – you couldn't fail to hear the admonitory cries hurled by corpses at those who discovered them. The bodies screamed with their eyes.

Philipp Stoya was tempted to turn away and put his fingers in his ears because the scream was louder than usual today.

Lucia Traunstein was barefoot and wearing only a flimsy

dressing gown with no bra or panties beneath it. A young woman, she was lying where her husband had found her outside their urban villa that morning: on the lawn not far from the garden shed. Although her legs were splayed, revealing an almost completely clean-shaven crotch, a sex crime could probably be dismissed from consideration.

The missing twins, Toby and Lea, and the stopwatch in Lucia's hand told another story.

A story told in the Eye Collector's demented language, thought Stoya.

The post-war era's most horrific series of murders had begun three months earlier, when Peter Strahl, a forty-two-year-old bricklayer, arrived home after spending the preceding few weeks on a large-scale construction site in Frankfurt. His marriage had suffered for years from his regular absences, and so, having been away on the job even longer than usual, he had come bearing some little peace offerings in the shape of flowers for his wife and a plastic doll for his daughter Karla. He never got to present them with those gifts. He found his wife lying dead in the hallway with a broken neck, clutching something in her hand. It proved to be a stopwatch; a standard model widely sold all over Germany.

When forensics detached the dead woman's fingers from this timer, it set the digital display in motion, the figures counting down to zero.

A bomb was initially suspected, so all twelve flats in the high-rise building were promptly evacuated. The cruel truth of the matter, however, was that the countdown related to Karla. The little girl had disappeared without trace. Neither the police nor her frantic father succeeded in finding the hiding place to which her psychopath abductor had taken her – a hiding place in which she was murdered when his forty-five-hour deadline ran out. This was the inescapable conclusion to be drawn from the pathologist's findings. The location where little Karla was found, a field on the outskirts of Marienfelde, was definitely not the murder scene because there was no water in the vicinity. It was assumed by the public that the Eye Collector asphyxiated his victims in his hideaway. Although this was essentially correct, one important pathologist's finding was suppressed for tactical reasons: the children were *drowned*. Traces of chemicals were found in the foam that builds up in the bronchial tubes when drowning people instinctively inhale water. Since these were present in all the kids he killed, it was assumed that the Eye Collector had taken the children to the same place. Analysis of the water, and of impurities on his victims' skin, indicated that they were not drowned in free-flowing water, but this did little to narrow down the search for his hideaway. Any house with an indoor swimming pool would have fitted the bill.

Even a fucking bathtub would do, thought Stoya.

Only one thing was certain: neither Karla, nor the two children who were murdered a few weeks later, Melanie and Robert, had been killed outdoors. *Nor had their left eyes been removed where they were found...*

'I'll kill the swine,' Stoya heard a voice behind him

growl as he knelt, motionless, beside the body. Not even death had succeeded in depriving Lucia of the well-toned, diet-conscious sex appeal often found in women whose husbands are considerably older, uglier and – last but far from least – wealthier than them. As the owner of Berlin's biggest dry-cleaning chain, Thomas Traunstein could definitely have afforded more than one house and more than one woman like Lucia.

'I'll kill him, I swear!'

The detective leaning over Stoya's shoulder could scarcely stand up in the tent that forensics had erected over the body a few minutes earlier. Nearly two metres tall, Mike Scholokowsky was the kind of friend you called when you were moving house and needed someone to carry a refrigerator up five flights of stairs.

'Or her,' Stoya murmured softly. His knee joints creaked as he slowly straightened up, staring intently at the dead woman.

'Huh?'

'You said *him,* Scholle. It could be *her.* We still don't know the perp's sex.'

None of the victims had been particularly big or strong, so they couldn't have offered serious resistance. The absence of any signs of a struggle suggested that the murderer had taken advantage of the element of surprise. Whoever was responsible for the death of Lucia Traunstein and the abduction of Toby and Lea might be either male or female, maybe even one of a team. Professor Adrian Hohlfort, the profiler who was working with the police on these cases, had already told them as much. But not, alas, anything more than that.

Scholle sniffed and kneaded his double chin, staring at the woman whose head was lolling sideways at a grotesque 90-degree angle. Her neck was obviously broken, another pointer to the Eye Collector's modus operandi.

The victim's wide-open eyes were staring past the two detectives at the wall of the tent.

No, not staring. Screaming.

'Fuck it, who cares?' Scholle literally spat the words into the cold air. 'I'll take down the Eye Collector even if he turns out to be goddamned nun.'

Stoya nodded. As head of homicide he should have insisted his subordinate be more objective. Instead, all he said was, 'And I'll help you.'

I can't take it any more either. I've had it up to here. This time they must win the Eye Collector's perverse game of hide-and-seek and catch him before his ultimatum expires and another jogger stumbles over yet another child's corpse.

A child's corpse with its left eye removed by a psycho. God, what a morning.

Looking at Scholle, who was angry enough to have torn the tent to shreds, Stoya had to concede, not for the first time, that he was impelled by motives that differed from his colleague's.

Scholle wanted vengeance. All Stoya aspired to was a better life. Damn it all, he'd been hunting down antisocial scum for over twenty years, and his reward at the age of forty was a face like a rotting apple. Blotchy skin, wrinkled pouches under his eyes and a bald patch on the back of his head. That was the price you paid for unrelenting stress and lack of sleep. None of this would be a problem if the job had at least generated the sort of bank balance that inclined most women to overlook outward appearances, but no such luck. Stoya was a confirmed bachelor, and most of the criminals he hunted earned more in an hour than he did in a month.

Scholle wants vengeance. I want a cushy number.

Yes, damn it. Unlike the rest of them, Stoya wasn't too squeamish to admit it. He was sick of grubbing around in shit with both hands. His ultimate aim was a more political job within the force, a spokesperson with fixed hours of work, better pay, and a big desk behind which to flatten his backside.

Let the others kneel beside women's naked corpses in the rain.

At the moment, however, he was light years from his objective, and if he failed to produce some results in double-quick time he'd be lucky to escape putting on a uniform again. Different motives or not, at least he and Scholle were pursuing the same goal.

'We've got to find this nutter.'

Stoya's cold, wet fingers felt for the little plastic bag in his trouser pocket. As soon as the pathologist arrived – Philippe had already informed him by phone of the special nature of the corpse – he would go inside the house, where a psychologist was ministering to the husband, and shut himself up in the bathroom. He hoped there was enough of the stuff left to keep him awake for the next forty-five hours...

What the devil...?

Stoya heard the change in his surroundings before he saw it. It was the sound of rain falling not on turf but on a hard surface just outside the tent. On plastic. More precisely, on the kind of white coverall worn by forensics.

'Shit! What's *that* arsehole doing here?' said Scholle. His impotent rage had found a lightning conductor at last. The reporter staring at them within earshot had long been a thorn in his former colleagues' sides. Alexander Zorbach had sneaked into the garden from the Grunewald and was now standing beside the fence with a man who was a head shorter and much younger.

Fritz, Frank or Franz. Stoya vaguely remembered being introduced to Zorbach's sidekick at a press conference.

'Piss off,' Scholle bellowed, reaching for his mobile, but Stoya laid a soothing hand on his shoulder.

'Stay here. I'll handle this.'

77

Stoya pulled the hood of his anorak over his head and stepped out into the pouring rain. Despite his mounting annoyance, he was glad of this brief opportunity to leave behind the pitiful sight in the tent.

'What do you want?' he demanded when he was facing Zorbach over the garden fence. The crime reporter's young sidekick remained hovering in the background. 'What the hell are you doing here?'

He didn't shake hands, nor did he go through the garden gate or seek shelter beneath a tree.

'Am I the first?' Zorbach asked. At least he sounded more surprised than triumphant. As long as Stoya had known him, Zorbach had never been interested in hogging the limelight. Facts were his sole concern. Unlike many of his fellow newshounds he never signed his well-researched stories with his full name, just two anonymous initials. This was irrelevant by now, however, as everyone knew who was hiding behind the letters 'A. Z.'.

Stoya thrust his wet hands into his trouser pockets.

'Yes, you're the first, and I'm wondering how you managed it.'

Zorbach gave a wry laugh. His hair was soaking and his hands were red with the cold, but it didn't seem to bother him.

'Oh, come on now, Philipp. How long have we known each other? I'm sure you wouldn't want me to tell you I dropped in by chance.'

'In forensics overshoes and a coverall? Like hell!'

Stoya wagged his head. 'By chance' was the crime reporter's traditional excuse, because it was an offence to eavesdrop on police radio traffic.

'No, Alex, I won't let it pass this time. I want the truth, and don't give me any crap about your powers of intuition.'

Zorbach was a phenomenon. Even in the days when he and Stoya were working together, the sensitivity of his 'nose' had sometimes seemed uncanny. Although he had never completed his university degree in psychology, he had been one of the best negotiators in the police force. His powers of perception and his talent for detecting the tiniest nuances in the emotional behaviour of others were legendary. A shame they had eventually proved his undoing on the bridge.

'I don't understand what you mean,' said Zorbach, wiping the moisture off his eyebrows. 'You know I've been working on this case from the outset. Nothing I write is detrimental to you. On the contrary, I do my best to be helpful. I thought we had an understanding.'

Stoya nodded. The faux-fur trim on his hood shed some fat raindrops. Although Zorbach had officially left the police force, a very productive symbiosis still existed between them. They held get-togethers at irregular intervals even now, seven years after the incident – unofficial conferences at which Zorbach often raised the all-important point that helped to further Stoya's investigations. In return, and for old time's sake, he received preferential treatment and was entrusted with vital information somewhat earlier than his competitors.

Today, however, Stoya's former colleague had overstepped the mark.

'Stop playing games and tell me the truth, Alex. How do you come to be here?'

'You know that perfectly well.'

'Tell me.'

Zorbach sighed. 'I was listening to your radio traffic, damn it.'

'Don't piss me about.'

'What's wrong with you?'

Stoya gripped his arm. 'That's what *I'm* asking *you*!'

Zorbach turned pale. The corner of his mouth twitched and he made a half-hearted attempt to free himself. 'Don't talk crap, man. You reported a 107.'

Stoya vehemently shook his head. 'For one thing, we don't use that code any more. For another, a departmental order was issued after the last discovery: anything to do with the Eye Collector is to be communicated via secure channels only. The press is making mincemeat of us as it is, thanks to your reports. You honestly think we'd broadcast such sensitive information to every radio ham within range?'

Thunder rumbled in the distance. The sky was growing even darker.

'No shit?' Zorbach said incredulously. He ran his fingers through his wet hair.

'No, no fucking radio traffic. We didn't broadcast a thing.' Stoya stared at him with a mixture of suspicion and anger. 'Now drop it, Alex, and tell me the truth: How the devil did you know we'd found a body here?'

76

(13 HOURS 57 MINUTES TO THE DEADLINE)

ALEXANDER ZORBACH

'It's getting worse,' I said, looking round the consulting room. 'I've started hearing voices now.'

As I had on my very first visit, I wondered where it all went, the money cascading into the clinic from its numerous private patients. The psychiatric institute made a shabby enough impression from the outside. Inside, it was even more in need of renovation. On my previous visits I had seen my doctor in three different consulting rooms. They had differed only in size and the location of the many discoloured watermarks streaking the walls from ceiling to scuffed linoleum floor.

'I didn't spend as long at university as you, Dr Roth. I never got to post-traumatic disorders, that's why I'm asking you now: Could there be some connection…?'

… *With the fact that I shot a woman seven years ago?*

The consultant eyed me intently from behind his desk and said nothing. Dr Martin Roth was a talented listener, a characteristic that had predestined him to be a psychiatrist. To my surprise he smiled faintly. I couldn't recall him ever doing so before during our sessions together, and it struck me that he'd chosen to trial this innovation at a thoroughly inappropriate juncture.

While I was sitting there, nervously crossing my legs and itching for a cigarette, his smile grew broader. It made him look even younger than he did already. At our first meeting I'd mistaken him for a student, not the expert whose treatment of the celebrated psychiatrist Viktor Larenz had hit the headlines in my paper a few years earlier.

I had underestimated him like many people before me, but one hardly expected a leading authority in the field of complex personality disorders to look so youthful. Roth's skin was smooth, almost rosy, and the whites of his eyes were brighter than the new T-shirt he wore under his sports coat. All that betrayed his true age was a receding hairline.

'For a start,' he said eventually, removing a slim folder from the perspex filing tray beside him, 'calm down. There's no cause for concern.'

No cause for concern? 'Yesterday I heard some non-existent voices on a non-existent police radio frequency, and you say I've no need to worry?'

He nodded and opened the folder. 'All right, let's review your medical history. You underwent treatment after the incident on the bridge. You were suffering from severe perceptual disorders at the time.'

My nightmares had spilled over into my life.

That was the best description I could give. I smelt, heard,

and ultimately *saw* things that had previously haunted me in my dreams. Not always the woman and baby on the bridge. Two weeks after the tragedy, for instance, I dreamt that shafts of lightning kept hitting the ground just beside me at one-second intervals. I ran for my life, lacerating my bare feet on the broken glass and rusty cans that lined my route. Noticing far too late that the lightning had driven me on to a rubbish dump with a shiny gold tree protruding from its midst, I instinctively sought shelter beneath its branches.

I knew that trees could attract lightning and felt sure I'd been lured into a trap. The realization that I might be struck dead at any moment made me burst into tears. As I clutched the tree with trembling fingers, a horrible thing happened: the bark turned soft and acquired a gelatinous texture. My fingers felt sticky. When I saw that maggots were squirming, not only over my hands but over my entire body, I started to scream. And when it dawned on me that the tree and the whole rubbish dump were one big confection of beetles, maggots and worms, I yelled myself awake.

But the foul miasma of the dump continued to pervade my bedroom after I woke up. I dashed to the window and threw it open, but still I couldn't breathe properly. What came flooding into the room was not fresh air but another disgusting stench from outside. And although it was a sunny, cloudless Sunday morning, a shaft of lightning struck the tree outside the window, which exploded into myriads of maggots. They formed a convulsively writhing column that flowed across the lawn towards our house.

And then, just as the maggots were climbing the outside wall on their way to me, someone caught hold of me from behind and dragged me away from the window.

My cries had woken Nicci and put the fear of God into her. I took a full hour to calm down, she told me later.

'You were immediately put on medication,' said Dr Roth, turning over another page in my medical record. 'Antipsychotics were administered and your condition improved. The symptoms disappeared altogether after a good two years.'

'Only to recur yesterday.'

'No.'

Dr Roth looked up from the file with the same unaccustomed smile on his lips.

'No?' I said, surprised.

'Look, I naturally can't venture a definite diagnosis, given the brief time we've known each other, nor would I dispute the visions you say you've had. It's just that I strongly doubt that you're still suffering from schizophrenia.'

'Why?'

'I don't want to commit myself prematurely. Please give me until tomorrow. By then I'll have the full results of your blood test and I'll know if they confirm my suspicions.'

I nodded without knowing what to make of this. Any other patient would surely have welcomed Roth's preliminary finding. I was only too eager to believe there was innocuous explanation for my symptoms. But if I wasn't suffering from some perceptual disorder, it would mean...

... that the voices were real. If so, the Eye Collector and I are connected in some way...

My right ear rang at the thought, almost as if someone had applied a tuning fork to my head. I smiled with an effort and got up to give Dr Roth's hand a parting shake, but I was finding it hard to concentrate. I had already left the consulting room and was about to turn back and ask him for a prescription for some sleeping pills – I'd hardly slept a wink in the last few nights – when the mobile phone in my trouser pocket vibrated.

Call me! said the text message, and the ringing in my ear grew louder.

Quick. Before it's too late.

In hindsight, I guess it was then that my race with death began.

75

'What's up?'

Frank had answered after the first ring. He sounded even more agitated than I felt.

'I'm worried.'

Worried? I couldn't remember a single occasion on which Frank had referred to his personal feelings. He usually went to great lengths to distract attention from his true emotional state by being flippant. He had, for example, christened his article on the maltreatment of old folk in nursing homes 'the geriatrics' charter'. But I could read between the lines and sense his underlying anger and despair, especially in the passage about an old woman with dementia and cancer of the breast who had been denied painkillers on grounds of expense. Frank had quoted a remark made by a cynical nurse who was doing his national service at the squalid nursing home in question: *'Who's she going to complain to? Her children visit her once a week, but she doesn't make sense when they do.'* Although he never admitted as much, I knew he was privately exultant when the all of the staff were replaced after the publication of his report.

'Where are you?' he asked quickly.

'Researching,' I said, emerging from the clinic's revolving doors. So far, only Nicci knew of my health problems, and I wanted it to stay that way. 'What on earth has happened?'

'I'm sure you're aware that ninety per cent of all miscarriages of justice are down to defective circumstantial evidence.'

'Just for once, spare me a lecture and come to the point. What's all this about?'

'Your wallet.'

Damn it. I clutched my head. Thanks to all the excitement, I'd completely forgotten to cancel my credit cards.

'Have the police been in touch?' I asked, looking up at the overcast November sky. The temperature had taken a noticeable dive during my appointment with Roth, but at least the rain had stopped.

'They came here to the office when they couldn't reach you on your mobile or at home.'

So that was why Stoya had persisted in calling me while I was on my way to Dr Roth. I'd meant to call him back after my session with the psychiatrist.

'Don't say my credit accounts have been drained!'

'Worse than that.'

Worse? What more can anyone do to the owner of a lost wallet once they've fleeced him?

'Oh hell, maybe I shouldn't tell you this over the phone.'

I scanned the hospital car park for my car. The place was considerably fuller now that lunchtime was approaching.

'Are you drunk, or something?'

'I only overheard it by chance when I passed Thea's office on my way to get a coffee.'

Thea? What could the police have been discussing with my editor?

'Stop beating about the bush, Frank, and tell me what the trouble is.'

'Well, unless I misheard, they've found your wallet with everything still in it. Even the ready cash.'

Some idiot had parked his four-wheel drive so close to my Volvo, I would have to climb in on the passenger side to avoid damaging its paintwork.

'But that's good news,' I said.

'Is it hell! They discovered your bloody wallet near the crime scene. Somewhere in the garden.'

Near the crime scene?

That was impossible. All at once the phone call seemed totally unreal. I couldn't— no, I didn't *want* to believe what my trainee had just told me.

'What garden?' I asked, although there could be only one answer.

'The one where they found the kids' mother,' Frank said in a low voice. 'The Eye Collector's fourth—'

I cut him off before he could complete his sentence.

74

I eventually squeezed in on the driver's side. Why should I show any consideration to someone inconsiderate enough to crowd me with his massive car? He might at least have retracted his wing mirror, which was the size of a tennis racket.

I had to force myself to observe the speed limit in the hospital grounds, but I put my foot down as soon as I emerged from the exit and sped off along Potsdamer Strasse.

Think. You've got to think.

I have never been noted for my circumspect and level-headed behaviour. Only a few months earlier I'd crossed swords with one of our paper's biggest advertisers, a food manufacturer. He offered me money not to publish some revolting photographs, taken with a concealed camera, of a slaughterhouse he owned. One of them showed a cow being winched out of an overloaded lorry dangling by one dislocated foreleg. I got him to pay me the 50,000 euros in cash. Then I put the picture on page one, as I'd always intended, and donated the hush money to an animal charity. Our paper lost one of its best customers; I got an award from the Press Club and a roasting from Thea.

But my present predicament differed from my problems in the past, most of which had been caused by my own impetuosity, in one important respect: I didn't know what I'd done to unleash the avalanche that was threatening to descend on me.

So the police had turned up at the newspaper office. A logical reaction, on the face of it. It wasn't just a Hollywood cliché that criminals tend to emulate a dog returning to its vomit. Whenever I hear that some guy has been spotted at a murder scene although its location is known only to the police, I start doing some research into him.

Then there was the wallet. I had searched all my pockets at the hospital hours before. It couldn't possibly have fallen out of my trouser pocket at the Traunstein villa, especially as I was wearing the white forensics coverall designed to prevent a crime scene from being contaminated by so much as a single fibre from my clothing. Stoya had seen me in this. At best, he might assume that I'd deliberately dropped the wallet there for some reason, but the worst assumption, which made me a suspect, was far more likely.

My brain bore an increasing resemblance to a bag of popcorn in a microwave. Countless thoughts were bouncing around in my head and bursting before I could catch hold of them. Sooner or later I would turn myself in for questioning by the police, but first I had to sort out my ideas. I needed to calm down and discuss things with someone I trusted.

I tried to call Charlie. She didn't answer her mobile, which was par for the course, and she'd never given me another number – any more than she'd told me her real name.

She normally called me back as soon as she got a chance, but today I lacked the patience to wait until her husband was out of the way. So I tried again, and again I got the anonymous mailbox message.

Where are you, damn it?

I hadn't spoken to Charlie for days.

Our affair, if you could call it that, had begun on the day when Nicci told me she wanted a divorce. The circumstances of our first meeting were not only absurd but embarrassing.

I could blame it all on the level of alcohol in my blood, which had exceeded a critical limit within only a few hours of the final breakdown of my marriage. My desire to take revenge on all the faithless women in this world probably also played a role. In retrospect, though, I think it was mainly a wish to punish myself that made me enter that place.

While getting undressed in the tiled anteroom and locking up my clothes in a locker, I tried to persuade myself that tonight marked the beginning of a new Zorbach era: a phase of existence during which I would never fall in love again, merely have sex. As soon as I made my way into the bar area, however, I realized I was making an utter fool of myself.

Although this was my first visit to a swingers' club, I

felt as if I'd been there a hundred times before. Everything looked just the way I imagined: brothel-red lighting, furniture that wouldn't have looked out of place in a pizzeria, and walls adorned with surprisingly innocent pictures of nudes. A sign directed patrons to the sauna, the S&M cellar and the jacuzzi. Immediately beside it was a notice reading: *Fuck and the world fucks with you.*

Above the bar that occupied the centre of the room was a small television screen positioned so that users of the 'playing field' to the right of the counter could watch a porn film while disporting themselves. The latex-covered mattresses were deserted on my first visit, but several couples and single men were seated at the bar. Nearly all were wearing flip-flops and towels around their middles.

I was surprised to note that most of them didn't look half as bad as I'd expected. One young couple made a very attractive impression. So did the slim blonde who came and sat down beside me, her hair still wet from the shower. I later learned that Charlie had just had enjoyed a threesome with two men and was merely intending to have one for the road before going home to her unsuspecting husband. She saw at once that it was my first time, and she was just as quick to see through the lie I'd concocted in case I bumped into an acquaintance.

Although it was wholly irrational, I felt embarrassed to tell her the truth – probably because I didn't want such a pretty woman to think I *needed* to patronize a swingers' club.

She grinned. 'So you're here doing research for your paper. Sure, and I'm a health and safety inspector.'

Although my parents had schooled me early in the facts of life, I was having one hell of a job concentrating on our conversation. Stark naked, Charlie told me she still felt she didn't really 'belong' there, but she was a woman with sexual needs and it was ages since her husband had shown an interest in her. Then she took me on a tour of the premises, showed me the mirror-lined room in which several couples were partner-swapping, and conducted me to the screen behind which some naked men were masturbating as they watched two women making love.

We ourselves didn't have sex that night, any more than we did at our many subsequent meetings. The platonic relationship we maintained was almost schizophrenic in view of the location of our regular chats. But Charlie insisted on meeting me at the swingers' club, nowhere else, 'Because the people here are far more discreet.'

So we met there again and again, chatting with increasing familiarity and becoming intimate in the truest sense of the word. Although not in the way a swinger's club would have intended.

We talked for hours while the other patrons were copulating. Little by little I discovered that her husband's cunning intelligence had made him a considerable fortune. I found out how he had taken advantage of this windfall to play the uncouth vulgarian who regularly got paranoically drunk on the world's most expensive alcoholic beverages. He had changed soon after their marriage, becoming moodier and more aggressive, working himself up into jealous rages and constantly accusing her of cheating on him – even though he'd been the first and only man in her life until a year ago. He even questioned the paternity of their children and threatened to take them away from her if she considered divorcing him. Finally, when he hit her once too often and called her a whore, she resolved to live up to his abusive description and visited the club, Hothouse, for the first time.

It was an act of pure desperation, so she was all the more surprised to discover that she liked this new, permissive environment – an attitude that I had so far failed to develop. And the more often we met, the more I sensed that our conversations would soon be insufficient, which led to a new problem. There came a time when I could no longer ignore the burning sensation in my gut when Charlie was at the club without me. The thing I'd wanted to avoid at all costs happened: I became jealous. Before long, if I wasn't careful, I would be falling in love.

'Please try again later,' said the computerized voice of Charlie's mailbox when I pressed the redial button a third time.

Angrily, I tossed my mobile on to the passenger seat.

Just when I really need you for once, I thought, and concentrated on the road.

Our many peculiar assignations had turned me into something of a confidant of Charlie's – I was a psychologist who sporadically broke off his therapy sessions so that his patient could amuse herself on the 'playing field' with some sexual partner who had taken her fancy. Meantime, he would nurse a gin and tonic at the bar.

I listened to you for hours. I waited for you.

Today I was the one who needed some advice from her, but I quickly dismissed the idea of driving to the *Hothouse* to see if she was there.

Damned if I was going to do that.

It wouldn't be the first time I'd had to cope on my own. All I needed was a place to relax and clear my head. A place where no one would find me for as long as I didn't want to be found.

In short, I had to take refuge where I'd last gone to ground two years ago, after trying to kill my mother.

73

(11 HOURS 51 MINUTES TO THE DEADLINE)

The first snow began to fall an hour-and-a-half later. A little too soon, in other words. If it had held off for another few minutes, my Volvo's tyre tracks wouldn't have shown up so clearly on the forest track. However, I doubted whether anyone had tailed me out to Nikolskoë. The wooded, hilly area between Berlin and Potsdam was popular with day-trippers but, fortunately for me, not in winter, as the Pfaueninsel ferry didn't operate and both restaurants were shut.

I had previously made a detour to my flat and stocked up with canned ravioli and mineral water. My emergency bag, which was now in the boot, also contained a change of underwear, my spare mobile with a prepaid card not registered in my name (I occasionally used it when phoning informants whose lines might be tapped by the police), and my laptop.

How did my wallet land up at the crime scene? For that matter, how did I come to be there myself?

I tried to put off considering the questions to which I

needed answers until I'd reached my hideaway. I didn't succeed, of course.

I was as incapable of ignoring them as I was the flashing light on the answerphone in my flat. Stoya had left several agitated messages requesting me to present myself at police headquarters in person, which made it seem probable that no warrant had yet been issued for my arrest.

A brief call to my wrathful editor proved equally unenlightening.

'Where the devil are you?' were Thea's opening words. She sounded even more caustic than usual.

'Tell Stoya I'll look in on him when I'm back in Berlin.' Before she replied I heard her slam the door between her glassed-in sanctum and the open-plan newsroom, the better to be able to yell at me.

'Get your arse back here at once, my friend. This isn't just about you. The paper's reputation is at stake. You know what people will think if there's even a sniff of a suspicion that some connection exists between our star reporter and the Eye Collector?'

No wonder his stories are always so well researched. He manufactures the facts himself.

Of course I knew. That was why it was so important for me not to venture into the lion's den unprepared. I knew from personal experience what would happen once the police closed in on a suspect, especially an ex-detective whose propensity for violence was on record. Despite my attempts at anonymity, I was now a high-profile suspect, because the media, first and foremost the paper that subsequently employed me, had acclaimed me as a hero following the incident on the bridge. I'd found the attention as intolerable as the many hours of questioning to which I'd been subjected by the board of inquiry and the district attorney. And now it was making my life even more problematic.

I parked the car beside a notice board that designated the area a nature reserve and got out.

Pure chance was responsible for my mother's discovery of the track leading eastwards from the notice board. Having originally intended to go for a walk to Nikolskoë Church, she had felt nauseous whilst driving and pulled up in a hurry. As she recovered from her migraine, she took a closer look at her surroundings. That was when she spotted the abandoned track through the woods. Barely wider than a small car and not marked on any map, its mouth was blocked by a big fallen tree trunk.

There are many beautiful places near water in Berlin – places where you can forget you're in a city with millions of inhabitants. The only trouble is, such spots are never secluded. The lovelier the lakeshore, the more popular it is with trippers. That day, when my mother followed the track to a tiny, almost untouched stretch of shoreline, she knew she had discovered a rarity, a hidden oasis in the midst of a metropolis. Upon finding the spot, her headache abruptly subsided, and it may have been this that convinced her to keep the hideaway to herself and tell no one but me about it. At the time, we still didn't know that it wasn't migraines she suffered from, but polycythaemia, an incurable disease that thickens the blood and occludes the circulation.

The first time she took me there I found that the tree trunk could be rolled aside with little difficulty. Far more obstructive were the luxuriant bramble bushes, encroaching on either side of the track, whose thorns needed treating with respect.

Now I found myself here again many years later. I got out of the car, leaving the headlights on, to see if I could make out anything in the gathering dusk. Myriads of snowflakes were whirling in the dull yellow beams, lending the scene a touch of magic. I surveyed my surroundings carefully.

There was no living creature in sight apart from a wild boar rooting around in the undergrowth some twenty metres away. Even the city's omnipresent hum of traffic had faded as suddenly as if someone had simply killed the soundtrack.

Okay, get going.

I threw my weight against the wet tree trunk, which detached itself from the ground with a sucking sound, enabling me to roll it aside with ease.

Having satisfied myself that I was still unobserved, I got back into the Volvo and drove it at a walking pace a little way into the woods. Thorns scratched the paintwork like fingernails on a blackboard and clods of dislodged snow fell from a tree, landing on my windscreen. I turned on the wipers. After a few metres I got out to cover my tracks. I rolled the tree trunk back into position and restored the look of the bushes my car had bent aside. I felt sure the secret entrance would escape notice, especially as no one had any reason to look around at this spot because the notice board indicated that the scenic walks, restaurant, church and graveyard were another good kilometre further on. Anyone who stopped here would do so purely by chance, as my mother had.

Back in the car once more, I drove on slowly. After rounding a tight bend in the track I pulled up, got out, and removed my licence plates with a Swiss Army knife. This made my battered Volvo look like a wreck abandoned in the wilds by some irresponsible violator of the environment. A forester would doubtless notify the authorities, but they were unlikely to turn out in this lousy weather. Besides, I didn't intend to spend the whole winter here. All I needed was a few days' peace and quiet.

I stowed the licence plates in the boot, took out my emergency bag, and set off along the path. It grew steadily narrower, zigzagging gently downhill, and I had to be careful not to lose my footing. My boots kept slipping on the icy tree roots that made the final stretch resemble a flight of steps. Fortunately, I had remembered to bring a torch, so I was able to see protruding stones and avoid wet fir branches before they lashed me in the face. The path seemed longer than it had on my last visit, but that was probably because of the heavy bag on my shoulder. When I finally stopped and looked at my watch, It was only 6.42 p.m. Getting down to the lake had taken me only a few minutes.

Here it is.

Whenever I reached the lakeshore, I realized how much mental ballast I was toting around.

My hideaway.

The place where I had managed to put the tragedy far enough behind me to lead the relatively normal life I led today. Even in heavy snow and two degrees below freezing, I immediately felt secure.

Nicci would probably have attributed my sudden sense of well-being to magical forces or pagan energy fields, but my own explanation was far more prosaic. Here in this secluded bay, nothing bad had ever happened to me. On the contrary, this was where I had spent some of the happiest times of my life, alone with myself and accountable to no one.

That was why I came here whenever I felt that life was escaping from my grasp. The first time I realised I could use the lake as a bolthole, during my time with the police, I bought an old houseboat and berthed it here.

The beam of my torch picked out the small, box-shaped wooden tub a few metres away. It lay in a narrow inlet densely overgrown with willows whose trailing branches formed a kind of natural port invisible from the open water.

'Back again,' I said, putting my things down. It was an old, established ritual initiated by my mother. She had always uttered those words in the days when she was still fit enough to come with me.

Back again...

Though only a murmured greeting, it seemed to reverberate across the water. The lake would soon freeze over, making it even more improbable that anyone would stray near here.

Here to this place I share with no one. My refuge, whose location is known to no one, not even my family.

It was, of course, absurdly puerile for a grown man to consider a secret refuge romantic. As a child I had constructed 'caves' beneath my bunk bed, using pillows and blankets, and imagined myself to be the only person in the world. I had dreamed of remote islands, of tree-houses high in the branches of mighty oaks. This secluded bay probably reminded me of all the hideaways that had existed only in my boyhood imagination. If I was absolutely honest, my secretiveness about this place had taken on a life of its own.

For a long time I found it plain embarrassing to admit to friends that I would sooner spend the weekend in the wilds, alone with my thoughts, than join them amidst the chanting ranks at football matches in the Olympic Stadium. Later on I simply found it reassuring to have a secret place in which no one would come looking for me if I took a day off work. The first time I felt a burning desire to share my secret was when I met Nicci. I was still in the initial phase of being in love, that period when you miss your partner even though you're sleeping next to them. I promised her a romantic excursion on which I would take her to 'my bay' blindfolded. The houseboat would be torchlit the first time she set eyes on it.

But the plan came to nothing. My Volkswagen Beetle gave up the ghost halfway there and conked out in the middle of an intersection. Just like that, for absolutely no reason, as the call-out mechanic later confirmed with a shrug. He couldn't find anything wrong, and the old bus, which had never let me down before, sprang to life as soon as he turned the ignition key. Call me an idiot, call me superstitious, but maybe I wasn't as immune to Nicci's zany ideas as I always claimed. In any event, I interpreted it as an omen.

It wasn't to be. I wasn't meant to bring anyone here.

I drew in a deep breath of cold air and played the beam of my torch over the mottled timber superstructure.

It was ages since I'd done any maintenance on the boat, and I was afraid it would take me a while to get the generator going. If it didn't, I could cope. I could make do with candles and the butane cooker. Warmth wasn't a concern as the old wood-burning stove in the houseboat's saloon was reliable. And the chemical toilet required no power.

I was just about to pick up my things when my state of mind changed abruptly. My sense of peace and contentment vanished in an instant. I approached the houseboat tensely, nervously. My nervousness gave way to a fear that became more intense with every step I took. At first I thought the fear irrational because I couldn't identify its source. But then I saw it.

A glimmer of light.

My reason for suddenly wanting to turn and run. *Away from my hiding place. From this place known to no one.*

No one but the person inside the houseboat, who had just lit a cigarette.

72

For the first article I wrote as a crime reporter, I interviewed an elderly couple whose flat had been burgled. The worst thing about it, they told me, was not the theft of articles of value – not even the loss of irreplaceable things like family photographs, holiday souvenirs and diaries. What really horrified them was the revulsion they would feel whenever they entered their own home from now on.

'By rummaging in our drawers, by laying hands on our underwear – just by breathing the air within our own four walls – those swine violated our privacy.'

The seventy-two-year-old husband did the talking while his wife held his hand and kept nodding in confirmation of every word he uttered.

'We weren't robbed, we were raped.'

At the time I'd thought their reaction grossly exaggerated. Now, as I tried to set foot on the foredeck without a sound, I understood what the old folk had been trying to convey.

Whoever was waiting for me in the houseboat's dark interior had destroyed the sense of security that had always greeted me there.

I unfolded the longest blade in my Swiss Army knife and tiptoed down the steps to the main deck. If the worst came to the worst my torch would provide an additional means of defence.

The stout planks creaked as I set foot on the last step leading to the deckhouse I'd once spent several weeks converting into my living room.

If the burglar was still inside the main cabin, I had cut off his only escape route – unless, of course, he jumped into the lake through one of the big lattice windows. There was nowhere to hide.

My houseboat was no bigger than a spacious garage. In addition to a little galley and an even smaller toilet, it was divided into two adjoining compartments. I was standing outside the larger of the two, which one had to cross in order to reach the bedroom in the bow. The front door, which I had never kept locked over the years, had a transom window set into it at head height. Cautiously, I peered through it.

Discounting the red dot hovering like a glow-worm in the left-hand corner, the room was in complete darkness. The houseboat was so darkened by the trees and bushes growing around its natural hiding place, I could scarcely see the door handle.

Holding my breath and listening to the thud of my heartbeat, I braced myself for a physical confrontation. When I felt sufficiently ready I flung the door open, burst into the living quarters, and shouted 'Hands up!' at the top of my voice.

Simultaneously, I turned on my torch and shone it on the sofa immediately beneath the window on the lake side.

I'd been prepared for anything: a tramp who had made himself at home in the cold weather; even for Stoya, who had somehow managed to locate my hideaway before I could reach it.

For anything.

But not this.

71

'Good God, are you crazy or something?'

A young woman I'd never seen before had made herself at home on the sofa in total darkness.

'First I nearly break my neck getting here, and now you scare me half to death.'

I raised my right arm and shone the torch straight at her face. To my surprise she neither blinked nor shaded her eyes with her hand. The stranger, whom I guessed to be in her late twenties, continued to sit there, gazing stolidly in my direction.

'Who the hell are you?' I demanded. I could have followed that up with two more questions: *What are you doing here? How did you find this place?*

Her low, rather husky voice went with the cigarette and a fairly masculine posture. She was sitting there with her legs crossed, left ankle on right knee.

'You tell me it's a matter or life or death, and then you keep me waiting for a good hour...'

She tapped the big watch on her wrist. For some reason the glass was hinged open and her fingers were resting on the exposed hands.

'... and now you appear to be drunk.'

Utterly bewildered, I removed the beam of my torch from her face and played it over the rest of her.

She was wearing tight jeans, slashed at the knees, and black paratrooper's boots. Instead of a winter jacket she had put on several multicoloured sweaters over each other. As far as I could tell in the dim light, her clothing might have been unusual but it wasn't dishevelled.

'Do we know each other?' I asked hesitantly.

'No.' She paused for a moment. 'That's why I'm here.'

An unpleasant thought occurred to me: Was I dealing with a madwoman? The Wannsee Home wasn't far away, nor was the Wald Clinic for psychosomatic disorders.

That's all I need.

How on earth could I get rid of a mentally sick woman without drawing attention to myself?

They're probably out looking for her already.

'Look, I've no idea who you are, so please leave at...'

I broke off in mid sentence and instinctively took a step backwards.

Jesus, what was that?

'Everything okay?' she said.

No, it damn well wasn't. I'd just glimpsed some movement beside the sofa. Clearly, this mysterious woman hadn't sneaked aboard my boat unaccompanied.

'What the hell are you doing here?' I demanded. The very thought of being confronted by a second intruder had set my pulse racing again.

'What are you blathering about?' she retorted, sounding as if she doubted my sanity. '*You* called *me*.'

'I did?'

The absurdity of her statement took the edge off my fear. She herself was looking somewhat disconcerted.

'You *are* Alexander Zorbach, the journalist?'

I nodded, but she repeated the question with a touch of irritation, presumably because she couldn't see me nod in the gloom.

'Yes, I am. But I didn't call you.'

No one could have. No one knows about this place. No one except...

She sighed and brushed a strand of hair off her forehead.

'So who gave me the directions to this arsehole of the world?'

No one except my mother, but she has spent years on a life-support machine.

I opened my mouth without knowing what I was going to say. The situation seemed so inexplicable. But before I could utter a word, the first of a whole raft of questions answered itself.

I suddenly realized who else had sneaked aboard with this woman. Or rather, *what* else.

The beam of my torch wandered downwards and lit up something on the floor beside the sofa: a handle attached to a leather harness, itself attached to a dog. *A Labrador or a Golden Retriever.* I wasn't sure which, but I realized something else. Something that seemed impossible.

I went right up to the sofa and shone my torch straight in the woman's eyes.

Bloody hell...

There could be no doubt. It all fitted: the hinged watch glass, the dog in the harness, her reference to having fallen over on the way here.

What's going on here?

I'd hit on an answer, only to find it even more incomprehensible. How had this nameless woman had made her way to my houseboat?

I only knew that she would never blink however long I shone the torch in her clouded eyes.

The woman who had discovered my hideaway was blind.

70

The wind had freshened and waves were slapping the hull at irregular intervals. The snow had been falling silently when I had reached the houseboat. At the time there had been no sign of an approaching storm, but now the planks beneath my feet were beginning to pitch and toss.

'I'd better go,' said my mysterious guest. I was lighting the old-fashioned paraffin lamp I always took care to fill and leave on the window sill before I left the boat.

'No, not so fast.'

I deposited the lamp on the coffee table in front of the blind woman. Its flickering, sulphurous yellow light transformed the whole room into a chiaroscuro, a shadow play.

Closer inspection caused me to revise my original estimate of the stranger's age. She was twenty-five at most, probably younger. I looked down at her boots, which were very dirty. Their sides were adorned with coloured transfers of naked Japanese girls. This suited her, because her taut skin, high forehead and wide-set eyes lent her face a subtly Eurasian look. The most noticeable feature of her appearance, however, was a multitude of dyed red dreadlocks.

My father would probably have described her as a punk. My mother, though doubtless less judgemental, would have been secretly worried that such a pretty girl might be ruining her hair by dyeing it.

'I'll be glad when you've gone,' I said. 'But first you must answer some questions.'

'Like?'

Who phoned you? Who told you how to get here? What did you think you'd gain by visiting me here?

'Let's start with your name.'

'Alina.'

She felt in the black rucksack between her long legs. 'My name is Alina Gregoriev, and I've had more than enough aggro for one day.'

Her breath was visible now. I hadn't been aware until then how cold it was on board. I would have to get the wood stove going as soon as I was alone.

'What do you want from me?' I asked.

'I'll say it again for the record, Mister Reporter: *You* talked me into this wild-goose chase.'

She mimed a telephone with her hand and imitated an imaginary caller: 'Take the bus to Nikolskoer Weg. Stay on that side of the road and walk to the next entrance on the right.'

This is impossible, I thought as she continued to give an exact description of the route I myself had followed earlier.

'After a while you'll reach a turn-off. Keep going until you come to a fallen tree, blah blah blah...'

Quite impossible...

'It wasn't me,' I said, struggling to retain my composure.

Who knows about this place except me?

Who would want to play a practical joke on me and a blind girl?

I hesitated, eyeing the figure on the sofa with renewed mistrust. 'Surely you can *hear* I'm not the person who called you.'

'Why?'

'Well, because you're—'

'Because I'm *blind*? she said with a wry smile. 'I'd have expected an investigative journalist to be rather better informed.' She shook her head, acting as if she was disappointed. 'It's a stupid misconception that *all* blind people can hear better. Sure, we concentrate better because we're not being distracted by visual stimuli, and our other senses often compensate for our inability to see. But that doesn't automatically make bats of us, and besides, every blind person is different.'

She grasped the handle on her dog's harness and stood up.

'For instance, I only have good spatial hearing. I can tell from the echo of my voice that there'd be room for a beer crate between my head and the ceiling. I also know I'd bump into a wooden partition after taking four steps or so.'

You do sound a bit batty, I thought, but I said nothing.

'But my voice recognition is poor,' she went on. 'I have

enough of a problem when someone greets me in the street by simply saying "Hi there" or "It's me." It often takes me a while to identify people by their voices. That even applies to close friends and patients I've treated for years.'

'Patients?' I said, mystified, as I watched her pulling at the longish object in her hands, which turned out to be a telescopic cane.

'I'm a physiotherapist.'

She felt for the feet of the coffee table with her cane. 'I recognize people better by their bodies than their voices.' She gave the handle a gentle tug. 'Come on, TomTom, let's go.'

TomTom? I thought briefly, somewhat distracted by the quirky sense of humour that had prompted her to name her guide dog after a satnav system.

The dog reacted at once.

'Hey, stop, not so fast,' I said as she started to make her way past me. 'I'm not letting you leave till you tell me why you came. This man who called you...'

...who pretends to be Alexander Zorbach and somehow knows the location of my hideaway...

'...he may have lured you here, but that doesn't explain why you let him talk you into it.'

Let alone in your condition, I thought.

'What did you hope to gain by coming to see me?'

Alina came to a halt. Her tone was weary, as if she'd told me the same thing a hundred times.

'I thought it my duty to come, so I didn't have to blame myself later. At least I have left no stone unturned, and since I'm familiar with your articles, Herr Zorbach, I honestly believed you'd phoned because you were interested in my evidence.'

'What evidence?'

Her face was in shadow, so I couldn't read her expression. In any case, I wasn't sure of the extent to which blind people's faces register their emotions.

'Yesterday I went to the police and told them all I know, but the idiots didn't take me seriously. I had to make my statement to some fool who didn't even have an office of his own.'

'What was it about?'

She sighed. 'I'm a physio, as I already said. Most of my patients are regulars, but yesterday a stranger turned up at my practice without an appointment. He complained of severe pain in the lumbar region.'

'And?' I said with mounting impatience.

'So I started to give him a massage, but I didn't get far. I had to break off the treatment.'

'Why?'

A wave made the whole houseboat shudder. I glanced at the window facing the lake, but total darkness prevailed outside.

'For the same reason we're talking together now. I suddenly realized who he was.'

'Well, who was he?' My stomach tensed even before I heard her reply.

'The person you've written about so often in the last few weeks.'

She paused for a moment. The cold around me seemed to intensify.

'I'm pretty sure the man I treated yesterday was the Eye Collector.'

69

Dry birchwood logs were crackling loudly in the stove. I'd quickly put a match to them after persuading Alina to stay.

'Just another ten minutes' were all she'd granted me. Then she would have to catch the bus back to the city centre, which only went once an hour. I still hadn't decided whether to offer to drive her home in the Volvo. I simply didn't know what to make of her and the whole situation.

I closed the little stove's soot-stained window. Together with the paraffin lamp, the flickering firelight was now generating the warm glow I had always enjoyed during my periodic retreats here.

To work. Or to sort out my thoughts...

But this time I failed to experience the snug sensation with which I usually sat down at the little desk beneath the window on the landward side. I was feeling even edgier than I did during the minutes preceding copy deadline, when I still had to type my last few lines and was battling simultaneously with the clock and the nicotine withdrawal symptoms that regularly assailed me now that Thea had banned smoking in the newsroom.

'Coffee?' I asked, going to the galley at the far end of the room. It was little more than a miniature worktop with a gas ring, two fitted cupboards and a sink.

'Black,' came the terse reply. Alina seemed far calmer than I, although just as many questions must have been whirling around in her head. After all, she was on her own in the wilds with a total stranger.

And she was blind!

I lit the butane gas ring.

'You say you recognized the Eye Collector?' I said as I looked in the cupboards for some instant coffee. I tried to rid my voice of any derisive undertone, but it wasn't easy. 'Does that mean you aren't completely blind?'

I had known, ever since my mother lost her sight after a stroke, that it was a widespread misapprehension that all blind people live in darkness. In Germany they are officially classified as blind if they can detect less than two per cent of what a sighted person sees. Two per cent can mean a great deal to those affected, but I wasn't sure how even this minimal residue of sight had enabled Alina to *see* the Eye Collector.

Four women, three children – seven dead in only six months. And there wasn't even a photofit picture of the serial murderer!

She shook her head.

'What about silhouettes, shadows and so on?' I asked.

'No. No silhouettes, colours, flashes of light or anything like that. In my case everything has gone. That's to say...'

She hesitated. 'Everything except my sensitivity to light and darkness. At least I've retained that.'

Retained...

So she hadn't been blind from birth.

The water in the kettle started to boil. I spooned some instant coffee into a mug.

'Just now, when you shone a light in my eyes, I sensed it. It's as though the light is filtered through a very thick curtain. I can't make out anything behind it, but I can sense a change.'

She smiled.

'It's a great help to me in everyday life. For instance, I can distinguish between times of day. That's why I always ask for a window seat on a plane. Most flight attendants can't understand why – in fact one tried to transfer me, but I told him to get lost. There's nothing lovelier than the intensity of light reflected by clouds, don't you think?'

I said yes, although I had to admit I hadn't looked out of the window at all on my last flight. I'd spent the fifty minute journey to Munich preparing for an interview.

I carried the mug over to the coffee table and deposited it beside the ashtray, then sat down in an old leather armchair at right angles to the sofa.

'So how did you recognize the Eye Collector?'

How, when all you can see is a shadow on the retina?

She smiled. 'That's the one-million euro question, isn't it?'

I said nothing. After conducting hundreds of interviews

I had developed an instinct that told me when to let someone run on and when an question was appropriate.

'Well, let's see how much longer you listen to me if I give you the answer right away. The policeman yesterday treated me like a lunatic. He wouldn't even let me speak to the detective in charge.' She chewed her lower lip. 'I can't blame him, to be honest. I can hardly believe it myself.'

'Believe what?'

She sighed audibly and clasped her hands behind her head, staring up at the ceiling with sightless eyes.

'It's so unfair. Shit, I didn't want this.'

'What?'

She didn't answer.

'What didn't you want?' I persisted after a while.

'Ever since I was three – ever since the accident that robbed me of my sight – I've fought not to be treated like a disabled person.'

She heaved another sigh.

'We were living in the States at the time. In California, where my father was employed on large-scale construction sites. He was a stiff-necked German civil engineer who had married an even stiffer-necked American woman of Russian extraction. My parents refused to send me to a special school just because I couldn't see any more. It took them six months to obtain permission to send me to Hillwood Elementary with my sighted friends.'

She gave a low laugh. I threaded my fingers together to prevent myself from drumming impatiently on the arm of my chair. It was a while before I realized how nonsensical it was to fear that she might notice my burning impatience.

'I inherited a tendency to go hell-for-leather from them,' she went on with a sweeping gesture that embraced the whole houseboat. It was presumably meant to imply that she would scarcely be here if she didn't keep plunging into reckless adventures.

'I'm what psychologists call a blind extremist. I taught myself to ride a bicycle early on. I go walking with a dog and without a cane as often as I can, and last year I went skiing. Hell, I keep falling flat on my face, just so people don't treat me like a leper. And now this shit happens.'

She folded her hands on her lap and screwed up her eyelids.

'This is nothing to do with me being blind, okay? Once upon a time I used to try to confide in people. My parents, my grandmother, my brother. But no one ever believed me. My friends thought I was pulling their leg. My mother got very worried and sent me to a child psychologist. I lied to him – told him I'd invented the whole thing just to make myself look important. Hell, it's enough of a stigma being blind. I didn't want people thinking I was crazy as well. I never mentioned it to another soul from then on.'

I prompted her despite myself. 'Mentioned what?'

'I've kept quiet about it for nearly twenty years, right? What's more, I'd have kept my trap shut for all eternity if it hadn't been for those poor children.'

We were once more at a point where a question would have stemmed her flow of words rather than encouraged it.

'I've got a gift.'

I held my breath and forced myself not to interrupt.

'I know how screwy that sounds. I don't believe in the occult myself, but it's a fact.'

What sort of gift? I wondered.

'I can see into the past'

'You *what*?!'

So much for my self-control. Furious with myself for having opened my mouth, I thought I'd broken the spell and expected her to clam up, but she only gave a resigned smile.

'These are the times when I'd really like to have my eyesight back, just to be able to see the expressions like the one that is doubtless on your face. I bet you're looking at me as if I were an extraterrestrial.'

'I'm not,' I lied, slowly shaking my head, and urged her to go on.

'As a physio, I've specialized in shiatsu.'

Shiatsu?

I vaguely remembered Nicci's thirty-fifth birthday present to me: a shiatsu session. I had looked forward to powerful hands massaging me with fragrant oils and creams and kneading the tension out of my neck to the accompaniment of soft chill-out music. Instead, I'd been spreadeagled on the hard floor of an Asian joint practice. A bony old Chinese woman proceeded to contort my extremities into such absurd positions and apply such extreme pressure to certain parts of my anatomy that my eyes watered. Her vigorous pressure-point massage involved the use not only of her fingers but of her entire body, in other words, her knees, elbows and fists – even her chin. It had left me feeling stressed rather than relaxed, and I wound up convinced that I'd narrowly escaped paraplegia.

'It happens very rarely, and I still haven't discovered who or what triggers it. The fact is, though, physical contact with some people enables me to see into their past.'

Aha...

This time I had my voice under control. It sounded entirely neutral when I said, 'And it happened again yesterday?'

Alina nodded. 'I was supposed to massage this man, but I had to stop. I'd barely touched him when I was transfixed by a sort of shaft of lightning. It was dazzlingly bright – brighter than my few memories of images from the time before my accident.'

She cleared her throat.

'Then the flash faded and I saw what he'd done to the child, who was already unconscious. And to the woman.'

She raised her head, and I had the unreal sensation that she was looking through me.

'Jesus, I saw him break her neck.'

68

'You *saw* him?'

The stove was giving out a cosy warmth. To my bewilderment, I found myself wishing for a return of the biting cold that had greeted me when I first came aboard. I was too hot and my throat felt sore. To make matters worse, the slight ache in my left temple heralded a migraine.

Alina nodded. 'I wasn't born blind, as I said. If I had been, I would have no conception of light, colour and shapes. There wouldn't be any images in my dreams, either. They would just be made up of sounds, smells and – of course – tactile sensations.'

I was surprised to note that I'd never given any thought to how the blind dream. I realized that people who had never seen anything must live in a world quite different from my own. If I shut my eyes and listened to the wind and waves and the sound of branches lashing the outside of the houseboat, the darkness didn't prevent me from having as vivid an idea of the wind, waves and woods as I did of the old leather armchair in which I was sitting. My brain substituted memories for the images it could not perceive; memories of a reality which a person blind from birth naturally lacked and could never acquire.

I turned away from Alina and focused my gaze on some snowflakes melting on the window pane. I wondered how one could describe snow to a blind man who had no conception of the word 'white'.

'But there used to be a time when I could see,' she said, jolting me out of my reverie. 'Mind you, it's twenty years ago and my memories are fading. Memories of my brother's face or the view from our kitchen window when it was raining. I can hardly remember the look of rain or the puddles I liked to jump in.'

She paused briefly, feeling for the untouched mug of coffee on the table between us. It was a moment before she grasped the handle and conveyed the mug to her lips. She rested it against her chin and went on talking without taking a sip.

'The one image that's ineradicably etched into my brain is that of my parents. Theirs are the only faces I'll probably never forget, and for that I'm both grateful and resentful.'

'Resentful?'

'In my dreams and visions,' Alina replied with a faraway expression, 'people all look the same and they all have my parents' features. That's a real drag, believe me, because my dreams tend to be nightmares. The scenes I witness are so frightful, most normal people would need the services of a psychotherapist.'

She took a big sip of coffee at last and sighed faintly.

'It's bad enough to dream of a man putting a bag over a woman's head and watching her suffocate with her eyes bulging from their sockets as she gasps for breath but only inhales a mouthful of plastic...' She swallowed hard. 'What's really bad is when the woman has your mother's eyes and mouth. She pleads for mercy – desperately, but the murderer will never remove the noose he's tightened around her neck because he's a pathological sadist. A sadist who looks exactly like the father who used to take me to kindergarten in the mornings and tell me bedtime stories at night.'

I felt a lump in my throat and coughed. 'But it wasn't a dream that brought you here?' I asked cautiously.

'No.' She replaced the mug on the table. 'I don't know what to call it. A vision, maybe. Or a flashback.'

A flashback?

'How do you know the term?'

'This may surprise you, Herr Zorbach, but I own a television set. I even turn it on, although there's less and less point. I used to be able to follow a plot quite well from the dialogue, but now all I hear for the first ten minutes is music and noises. I think movies are becoming more and more visual. Can that be so?'

Possibly. I'd never given any thought to that either.

'That's why I often invite John over. John is an old friend from the States who's been living in Berlin for the past four years, like me. He's gay, worse luck, so there's nothing doing in the bed line, but at least he can see. He always describes what's happening, so I know from him that movies sometimes perform a backflip. The colours change and everything goes slower, and sometimes you're just shown a brief glimpse of the past. A flashback, in other words. Am I right?'

I grunted affirmatively.

'I've had first-hand experience of flashbacks like that.'

I raised my eyebrows. 'You take drugs?'

'Not often.' She pointed to her eyes. 'Some blind people go to psychoanalysts, but most try to cope on their own. I usually take my mind off things with men, but once, when not even that did the trick, I resorted to an old and proven psychedelic drug.'

I laughed and told her I knew what she was implying, having written an article on the history of LSD some months before. Although the hallucinogen had been marketed for psychiatric purposes in the middle of the previous century, it wasn't until the 1970s that its dangers were recognized and further research was banned.

'I know what you're thinking,' she said with a smile. '"No wonder the woman sees ghosts if she blows her mind." But I've given up the hard stuff and I haven't even smoked a joint for weeks. All the same, I know what I'm talking about. Yesterday, when I was treating the Eye Collector, I had a flashback.' She tapped her forehead. 'I was inside him. Inside his head, and I saw what he did.'

I leant forward, debating what to do next. My instincts advised me to terminate the conversation at this point, but the little that Alina had said had aroused more than just my journalistic curiosity.

I had often interviewed disturbed people in the course of my career as a reporter. Hardly surprising, since I specialized in unsolved crimes of violence. I had spoken with psychologically broken victims, with demented sex offenders who insisted they were innocent and told me to listen to the voices in their heads. I had even interviewed a ten-year-old hospital patient who claimed to have been a serial murderer in a previous existence. To his lawyer's consternation, the boy actually seemed to demonstrate the veracity of his story by directing the police to the remains of people who had been murdered exactly as he'd described. Nicci was disappointed when we discovered that no supernatural agency had been at work, and I felt sure that Alina's fanciful assertions could be logically accounted for.

Just as there had to be some explanation of how I'd heard voices on the police radio frequency, how my wallet had been found at the crime scene, and why someone purporting to be me had lured this blind girl to my houseboat.

The most probable answer to the last question was that she was either lying or suffering from some form of mental illness.

Schizophrenia, for example?

'When you treated the Eye Collector, Alina,' I said, persisting with this most mysterious interview, 'what exactly did you see?'

67

'I had a bad feeling from the start. The man had got in touch anonymously via the contact form on my website. He called himself Tim.'

Tim? My stomach muscles tensed as they always did when I heard that name.

My involuntary 'Oh, no...' was taken the wrong way.

'Does it surprise you that blind people use the Internet?' Alina smiled indulgently. 'There are systems that read the pages aloud if they're correctly programmed. Besides, my computer has a display that converts text into Braille.'

'Go on about your patient,' I said.

About the Eye Collector.

'He barely uttered a word when he turned up,' said Alina. She took a new packet of cigarettes from her rucksack, which was once more at her feet. Her dog seemed to share my interest in watching her deftly break the seal, shake a cigarette out of the packet, and light it.

'He only whispered – said his vocal cords were inflamed and he wasn't allowed to speak. But his major problem was his back. Apparently, he'd hurt it lifting something.'

I had an involuntary mental picture of a man's shadowy figure burdened with an inert body.

A wisp of tobacco smoke drifted past my nose, reminding me of the useless nicotine patch on my arm. At that moment I would only too willingly have exchanged it for a real cigarette.

'I went to the bathroom to wash my hands. When I returned I stubbed my bare toe on a heavy urn with a pot plant in it.'

Alina took a hefty drag at her cigarette. Something about her body language puzzled me, but I couldn't put my finger on it.

'I was beside myself with pain,' she went on. 'Disoriented, too, because my sense of direction had never let me down before, not in my own place. I can find my way around blind, so to speak.' She smiled. 'In retrospect, I wonder if he'd moved it as a test.'

If so, the killer must be totally paranoid, I thought. No photofit picture of him existed and not a single witness had come forward. Why should the Eye Collector have played it safe with a blind woman, of all people, when even a sighted person couldn't identify him?

As if she'd heard me thinking aloud, Alina advanced another explanation.

'Mind you, people who don't know me too well can be careless. I've had to fire three cleaners because they didn't follow my instructions to the letter. For heaven's sake don't move anything, I tell them.'

She turned her head in my direction. It looked for one brief moment as if she was seeking eye contact.

'I didn't want to show any discomfort, so I gritted my teeth and carried on,' she said. 'Maybe I'd already sensed that there was something not quite kosher about the man and subconsciously wanted to get rid of him as soon as possible.'

She sighed and her eyelids resumed their restless fluttering. 'I begin my shiatsu treatment by kneeling behind the patient, who sits cross-legged in front of me on a futon. From that position I stimulate a meridian with my elbow, working downwards from the neck to the shoulders.'

I grunted reminiscently. I could still remember the procedure from painful personal experience.

'This form of massage is intended to dissolve neural blocks and enable vital energy to flow freely. A lot of people still laugh at the technique, although not many used to believe in acupuncture, and now it's available on medical insurance.'

So is root canal treatment, but I don't volunteer for it.

'Anyway, what normally happens next is that the patient is told to lie down on his back and the massage proper begins.'

'But it didn't come to that?'

'No, because I suddenly sensed something that has haunted me at irregular intervals throughout my life. Except that this time it was very much worse.'

'Go on.'

'I reckon someone who emerges into daylight after years in darkness must feel as I did. I exerted pressure on his shoulder, and all at once my eyes were seared by stroboscopic flashes – by an alternation of light and darkness. It was so dazzling at first, I saw less than I heard.'

'Which was what?'

'A woman's voice.'

'Could it have been your mother's?'

'No, I don't think so, although I wasn't really trying to identify the voices. I was far too horrified by the sensations that suddenly flooded over me.'

'What did the woman say?'

Alina deposited her cigarette in the ashtray and picked up the coffee mug instead. 'It was very odd. I think she was talking to her husband on the phone. I heard an electronic beep like the one my own phone makes when I turn the loudspeaker on. The woman laughed and said "Sorry to call you, but I'm very worried. I was playing hide-and-seek with our son, and the crazy thing is, I can't find him anywhere."'

'She laughed?' I asked, puzzled.

'Yes, but not in a happy way. It sounded nervous and forced, the way someone laughs when they're really close to tears.'

'How did her husband react?'

'He was absolutely panic-stricken. All he said was, "Oh my God, how could I have been so blind? It's too late."'

'It's too late?'

Alina nodded. 'And then he started shouting. "Don't go

down into the cellar whatever you do," he yelled in a frantic, trembling voice. "You hear me? Don't go down into the cellar!"' She sipped her coffee. 'That was when the flashes of light subsided and I was able to make out the first, vague outlines of my surroundings. The best way to describe what I saw is that it was like looking at an overexposed photo.'

I was wondering how she'd hit on such an analogy when she answered the question unasked.

'I once heard a medium describe his visions like that in a TV documentary, and somehow I grasped what he meant.'

A birchwood log exploded behind the stove's glass window. Alina fell silent for quite a while, running her fingers nervously through her hair.

'The man on the phone shouted "Don't go down into the cellar."?' I prompted her.

'That's what he said.'

'What happened then?'

'Then the woman turned towards me and I found myself looking into my mother's eyes.'

'She turned towards you?' I repeated, feeling bewildered.

'Yes, it always happens like that. I don't know why, but when I'm in physical contact with certain people – people who are highly charged with energy – I seem to *enter* them. It's as if I'm exploring some dark secret in their soul.'

She had moved her head a little while speaking and

appeared to be looking out of the window facing the lake. I followed her blank gaze into the darkness.

'So you saw your vision through the eyes of the...?' I hesitated, momentarily unable to believe I'd meant to ask such a crazy question.

She took advantage of the pause to complete my sentence. 'Yes,' she said, turning to face me again. '*I* was the Eye Collector. All that happened after that, I saw through *his* eyes.'

At that moment a sizeable wave struck the houseboat's hull. The spoon in her coffee mug rattled and the paraffin lamp flickered in a sudden draught. A gust of wind had found its way through cracks in the window surround.

'What happened then?' I asked when the gust had subsided.

Alina now spoke faster, as if eager to get something off her chest.

'I saw I was standing behind a wooden door. It wasn't quite shut, and I'd been peering through the crack into the room where the woman was phoning.'

'What did she do then?'

'What her husband had told her not to.'

Don't go down into the cellar.

'"You're scaring me, darling," she said, and took a step towards the door I was standing behind. Then a nightmarish thing happened.'

Alina's eyes were shut, but I could see them rolling around beneath her eyelids. TomTom raised his head and pricked his ears as if infected by his owner's inner turmoil.

'I leapt out from behind the door and wound a length of flex around her neck. She went rigid with fright.' Her voice had gone husky. She sniffed before whispering softly, 'And then I broke her neck.'

Involuntarily, I held my breath. Alina, too, sounded breathless.

'There was a sound like an eggshell being crushed. She died instantly.'

66

'What did you do with the body?' I asked, kneading my temples. My headache was still bearable, but I would have to take something soon or it would pass the critical point and put me out of action for hours.

'I hauled her outside by the flex. It all happened so quickly, somebody seemed to have pressed a fast-forward button in my head. But that's typical of my waking dreams.'

'Where did you take her?' I asked impatiently.

'I towed her across the living room to a terrace door and from there into the garden. It was very much colder out there. Snow crunched beneath my feet. I left her lying near the garden fence, a little way from a small shed.'

'Just like that?'

'No, not just like that.' Alina drained her coffee. 'First, I put something in her hand.'

'What?'

'A stopwatch.'

Of course.

My patience had been tried for long enough – I couldn't restrain myself any longer. Everything she'd told me so far could have been gleaned from reports in today's newspapers.

Even some of my own earlier articles would have been sufficient. It was no secret that the murdered woman had phoned her husband shortly before her death. This had emerged from a check on her line and had been splashed on the morning news, providing grist to the headline-writer's mill: 'A LAST FAREWELL?' Although no details of the conversation had been published, Alina could have figured it out. The stopwatch story had also long since stopped being a secret. The forensics officer who examined the first victim had been afraid he'd triggered the timer on a bomb by moving her. It turned out that the stopwatch had been rigged so that activated at a moment when the Eye Collector assumed his victim would be discovered – not a very accurate method for someone to adopt who had hitherto left no clues apart from a few clothing fibres. The lethal countdown had not started until four hours after the discovery of the second corpse, and the stopwatch had been ticking in the dead woman's hand for forty minutes after the police had mounted guard over the third of the crime scenes.

'Let me guess,' I said, making no attempt to disguise my sarcasm. 'The countdown had been set at forty-five hours precisely!'

To my surprise. Alina shook her head vigorously. 'No.'

'No?'

I stared at her cigarette, which was smouldering away in the ashtray.

The Eye Collector's deadline is common knowledge.

It was in all the newspapers. I'd been the first to write about it six weeks ago, after Stoya tipped me off.

Alina clicked her tongue and TomTom looked up. 'I know what you're thinking, but you're mistaken. The papers, the radio, the Internet – they all got it wrong. The deadline was forty-five hours seven minutes.'

She put her empty coffee mug down and got up off the sofa. 'Forty-five hours and seven minutes precisely. And now, it's time I was going.'

65

(10 HOURS 47 MINUTES TO THE DEADLINE)

'Where the devil are you?' Stoya barked in my ear. I had absolutely no intention of revealing my whereabouts until I'd grasped what kind of game I was involved in.

I was calling him from the deck of my houseboat for privacy's sake, having talked Alina into another mug of coffee by promising to drive her home. It was so dark outside, I couldn't even see the surface of the lake beneath me.

'I can't tell you that,' I began, but Stoya cut me short.

'Well, *I* can. *I* know exactly where you are, my friend: up to your neck in doodoo. What's more, you'll be in it over your head if you don't come down to headquarters right away. It's time you answered a couple of questions.'

What were you doing at the crime scene?

Why did we find your wallet there?

'Okay,' I said. 'I promise I'll drop in before long, but first I'd like some info from you.'

Stoya gave an incredulous laugh. 'Christ, man! Scholle suggested putting the squeeze on you at our last meeting. You're lucky we know each other so well or I'd have marched into the public prosecutor's office by now. If you're trying to pull some kind of newshound's stunt on me, forget it.'

I shivered. I'd lost all sense of time and had no idea how long I'd been talking to the mysterious girl. The temperature outside had definitely taken a dive since my arrival. The skin of my face felt taut, almost sunburnt, and it hurt even to breathe.

'Take it easy,' I said. 'Just tell me whether a blind girl named Alina Gregoriev turned up at headquarters yesterday, claiming to know something about the Eye Collector.'

'A blind girl?' Stoya said after a moment. The wind had dropped a little, so I was able to hear him better. 'Goddammit, Alex, ever since you hacks turned the Eye Collector into a cult figure like Hannibal Lecter, I've had all the nutters in Berlin knocking on my door. The tales they tell are worth a euro a word, if that. Only last night we had a visit from a social worker who claimed his late wife had opened the front door to him when he came home from work.'

A snow-laden gust of wind blew straight into my face. 'So did this girl come to the station?' I asked hesitantly.

'Could have.'

I wiped the melting snowflakes off my forehead. 'Okay, then tell me one more thing...'

'That makes two questions.'

'The ultimatum.'

'What about it?' he said impatiently.

'Is it possible you held out on me?'

All I could hear for a moment were the wind-lashed

trees and the sound of waves lapping against the hull. Then Stoya said grimly, 'What are you getting at?'

My stomach muscles tensed as they had yesterday, when I heard the 107 on the radio. It was standard police procedure to withhold or doctor relevant information about a crime so as to expose false confessions and sort out copycats.

But that shouldn't be the case here, because if the blind girl was right on this point, it would mean that...

'Seven minutes,' I said. The hand that was holding the phone to my ear began to tremble. 'The deadline was set at forty-five hours seven minutes.'

And if the children's father doesn't discover where they're hidden by then, they die.

Stoya realized he'd given himself away when he took too long to reply, so he didn't bother to lie to me. 'How did you know that?' he asked bluntly.

I shut my eyes.

It can't be true. Dear God, tell me it isn't true.

'Now listen carefully.' My former colleague's voice seemed to come from far away. 'First you appear like magic at the crime scene, then we find your wallet there, and now you're in possession of a piece of information not even known to my closest associates.'

I didn't make it up. She told me. Alina, the blind witness who can see into the past.

Stoya's final words made me shiver harder than ever. 'The moment you said that, you became our chief suspect. I suppose you realize that?'

64

(10 HOURS 44 MINUTES TO THE DEADLINE)

ALEXANDER ZORBACH

I was almost surprised to find Alina still there when I finished my conversation with Stoya and went back inside, although it would have been impossible for her to sneak past me unnoticed and go ashore.

Out into the cold, stormy darkness.

But her disappearance would have been only one more link in the chain of inexplicable things that had happened to me in the last few hours.

How did she know about the extra seven minutes?

Alina was still seated on the sofa, patting her dog, when I re-entered the warm, stuffy living area. TomTom was clearly enjoying himself. He'd stretched out on his side with all four legs extended to give his mistress easier access to his chest and tummy.

'Can we go?' she asked without looking up. I realized that it was little things which sighted people find so off-putting about talking with the blind.

We say almost more with our bodies than our mouths. Looks, gestures, movements – even a faint twitch of the lips – can express a kaleidoscope of emotions that are sometimes emphasized but often contradicted by what we say. This applies above all to posture. Under normal circumstances it is considered impolite not to look someone in the eye when speaking to them, and although I knew Alina was blind I felt slighted when she only presented her profile. Then it struck me that she was, logically enough, turning one ear in my direction.

'TomTom needs feeding and my own stomach thinks my throat's cut, so it'd be good to get home soon.'

'I've only one more question,' I told her, though I really didn't know where to start.

How did you know about the ultimatum? No one can see into the past, so why did you think up this crazy story? And why drag me into it?

Alina threw back her head and laughed. 'For someone who treated me like a burglar to start with, you seem very appreciative of my company.'

I laughed back. 'Journalistic interest, that's all,' I said, trying to sound casual.

She raised her eyebrows, and I suddenly knew what had previously disturbed me about her varying facial expressions and her posture a moment ago.

It was the fact that she communicated with expressions and gestures at all. To the best of my knowledge, registering joy and sorrow – even throwing up your arms after winning a race – were instinctive modes of behaviour. But what of the gradations in between? What of loathing, regret, disgust, or Alina's look of nervous impatience at this moment? I knew a blind greengrocer in Kreuzkölln who had once asked me to tip him off if he looked surly. Most of the time he was merely concentrating, he said, not angry at all. Ever since that conversation I had assumed that facial expressions were the result of a learning process in which you copied other people, but Alina had so many non-verbal modes of expression that this couldn't be true.

Unless the Eye Collector isn't all she's lying about...

'Can't we discuss your questions on the way?' she asked. I shook my head although I'd have been happy to accept her suggestion. I, too, wanted to get away as soon as possible. The possibility that Stoya had traced my call was extremely remote. I'd only been on his wanted list for a couple of minutes, after all, but Alina's arrival on the scene had destroyed my sense of security. The only problem was, I still had too little information on which to base my next move.

'It's tricky outside at present,' I said truthfully. 'There are big branches coming down every two minutes. I'd wait until the storm subsides a little.'

She stopped fondling her dog. 'All right, what do you want to know?'

How did you really know about this boat?

What's your connection with the Eye Collector?

Are you genuinely blind?

'Let's go on from where you left off,' I said, as much to sort out my own thoughts as for any other reason.

Go on from the murder. From the point where you

broke the woman's neck and dragged her corpse into the garden. 'What happened next?'

'After I put the stopwatch in her hand, you mean?'

A shadow seemed to flit across her face. She kept her eyes tight shut. Her lips were also compressed, which lent her face a tense expression.

'I went over to the tool shed,' she said slowly, as if she found it hard to unearth a long-buried recollection from the depths of her memory. 'It was made of timber, not metal. I knew that because I got a splinter in my finger when I slid the bolt open. Besides, there was a smell of resin when I went inside.'

She paused for a moment, nervously plucking at her left thumb with the fingers of her right hand.

'There was something on the floor. It looked like a bundle of rags, but it was another body. Smaller and lighter than that of the woman lying dead on the lawn. It was a little boy.'

'Was he still alive?'

'I think so. He smelt like my brother Ivan. I can scarcely remember Ivan's face, but I'll never forget the smell of sweets and grimy knees that filled my nostrils when we had a bath together. I always smell it when I dream of little boys.'

Or when you kidnap one.

'Can you describe his face?'

'No. I told you: the only faces I really remember are those of my parents.'

I apologized for the interruption and asked her to go on.

'I carried the boy to a car parked on the edge of the woods beyond the garden fence. I think it was early morning, shortly after sunrise. Suddenly everything went dark again and I thought the vision was over. Then two red lights came on in the boot of the car. I laid the boy down inside.'

'What about the girl?'

'What girl?' She looked genuinely surprised. 'I don't know anything about that.'

'Come on,' I said. 'The Eye Collector has kidnapped some twins for the first time. The papers are full of it.'

'I can't read newspapers, in case you hadn't noticed.'

'There's radio and television.'

'And the Internet. Thanks for the tip.'

'Then you must have gathered that the police are looking for *two* missing children, Toby and Lea. They're twins.'

'But I didn't, okay?'

TomTom raised his head, alerted by the indignation in his mistress's voice.

'Yesterday I went straight to the police, who questioned me in the same shitty tone of voice you're using now. They thought I was a crackpot, I grasped that at once. I was so furious when I got home, the rest of the world could get stuffed as far as I was concerned. So I settled down in front of the goggle-box with a bottle of wine and blotted out reality with some old Edgar Wallace movies until I got so sozzled I fell asleep. Today I was woken up by some lunatic who made a date with me out here in the wilds.' She snorted angrily. 'And I, being a silly cow, actually made my way here, only to be shat on a second time.'

The paraffin lamp flickered, reminding me that it was high time I attended to the generator, or I and my weird visitor would soon be sitting in the dark.

'And you expect me to believe all this?' I said.

Alina gripped the handle of her dog's harness and stood up. 'What the hell, you think I'm lying anyway. But ask yourself this: If I'd really made the story up, would it have sounded so poorly rehearsed?'

She was right. Crazy though it sounded, the very fact that she'd known nothing about the kidnapped girl endorsed her credibility. No one seeking to make herself look important by concocting false testimony would have been careless enough to overlook the second victim.

Unless that, too, was part of a plan I failed to comprehend.

'I can only say what I saw,' she said, shouldering her rucksack.

I also got to my feet – rather too abruptly, because I felt dizzy all of a sudden. My migraine had now reached the stage at which only prescription drugs would deal with it. Fortunately, there was a half-used pack of Maxalt somewhere amid the clutter on the Volvo's passenger seat.

'Wait,' I said, massaging the nape of my neck. This time Alina dispensed with her cane and relied entirely on the dog, which gently tried to tow her past me. I gestured to her to stop. She couldn't see, of course, so I caught hold of her by the sleeve of her sweater.

'What?' was all she said, and turned her head in my direction. We were close for the first time and I caught a whiff of the discreet scent she was wearing. It was light and less tangy than I'd have expected.

'Why waste time on me if you don't believe me anyway?'

It was a fair question, and I tried to answer it at length. I told her that I'd often interviewed people whom I didn't at first believe, but who had changed my mind. Checking a source was never a waste of time, I said, especially in the case of a story as exceptional as hers.

Suddenly, however, everything went blurry before my eyes. They felt as if they'd been staring at a flickering screen for hours on end. I was also feeling nauseous, so I limited myself to asking the one question that could definitely enable me to verify the truth of Alina's statements: 'Where did you take the boy?'

63

(10 HOURS 40 MINUTES TO THE DEADLINE)

TOBY TRAUNSTEIN

The walls of his prison were... *soft?*

Toby kneaded his hands together to make sure his sense of touch wasn't deceiving him. This was more than likely because his senses were currently monopolized by something else: *thirst*. He had no idea how long he'd been unconscious, but it must have been hours. Possibly days. The last time he'd woken up with such a sore throat had been New Year's Day, after he'd made a pig of himself on all those stupid crisps. But it hadn't hurt half as much as this.

And my arms hadn't exploded either.

He didn't know what had woken him, his unbearable thirst or the throbbing pain in his arms. They felt as if he'd been lying on them for a whole week.

Rolling over on his side in the cramped darkness, relieving his hands of the weight of his body, took a laborious eternity *(longer than one of old Hertel's maths lessons)*. The blood came coursing back into his numb limbs and he started to scratch the places that smarted most: his upper arms, the crook of his elbow and his wrists. His wrists, especially, felt the way they had when he was looking for his football in the garden next door and reached into that lousy clump of stinging nettles.

'You should only slap them, not scratch,' he remembered his mother saying. *Honestly, Mummy, that didn't even work with a mosquito bite. This itches so much, I feel like ripping the skin off my bones.*

He made a claw of his right hand, applied it to his left wrist at pulse level, and drew a deep breath.

Only slap, don't scratch.

Stuff it. He dug his fingernails deep into his flesh and groaned with relief when the itching abated a little. It even took his mind off his thirst, if only for a few seconds. He'd scarcely stopped scratching when the flames flared up again and the throbbing, smarting sensation maddened him even more than the impenetrable darkness surrounding him.

'Hello?' he called, and winced at the sound of his own voice.

Sniffly and tearful.

He didn't want to cry. It would be shaming enough if his friends discovered he'd peed his pants when they let him out of here. In the next ten minutes or so at latest, when Jens and Kevin lost interest in their practical joke. Because that's what it was, you bet. A stupid, rotten, lousy practical joke!

What else would it be, you little piddle-pants? Stop blubbing.

Kevin was always boasting about the knockout drops they sold in the chemist's shop his parents owned. He must have tried some out on him to pay him back.

Just because I hid his pants in the girls' changing room after swimming. But at least that was funny. Not like this...

Toby tried to stretch. His elbows dug into the walls of his prison. It surprised him again that they yielded under pressure. Had the idiots stuck him in a tent?

No, it was too cramped for that. Besides, the surface wasn't smooth. It didn't feel like rubber or canvas. It was much rougher, more like coarse carpeting or wallpaper, or...

Or a sack?

Toby started sobbing again. He couldn't help thinking of the horror video Jens had showed them during break at school. His parents were filthy rich. *(Dad always says their windscreen replacement business makes so much money, they could wipe their arses on banknotes if they ran out of toilet paper.)* That was why Jens was the first boy in his class with the latest iPhone. The kind you could use to view internet videos at a moment's notice.

They'd all met up behind the gym the very first day, and Jens had proudly showed them the clip where a naked girl was stuffed into a sack by a gang of youths. She tried to defend herself, lashing out with her arms and legs, but they got her into it in the end and tied the neck securely. Toby had joined in the others' laughter at first, because it really did look as if a dozen snakes were rampaging around inside the sack. But he'd felt sick when the youth with the cigarette in his mouth laughingly emptied a can of petrol over the squirming sack. He'd turned away and walked back to the playground. On his own.

They're probably doing the same to me. Because I was too chicken to watch.

'Okay, you win,' he called into the darkness. He pictured Kevin and Jens clutching their mouths so he couldn't hear them giggling.

'Come on, let me out.'

No answer.

Desperately, he rammed both fists against the material at head height, feeling the sweat run down his face. He was panting even harder than he would have done after running the 400 metres, although he hadn't exerted himself half as much as that in the last few minutes.

There's nothing much anyone can *do in here. Except feel scared.*

Toby sniffed and drew several deep breaths. His fingers still tingled as if they were thawing out after a snowball fight. He ran them over the yielding walls around him.

They weren't damp and there was no smell of petrol, thank God, so they'd left out that bit of the video.

So far.

All at once his fingers encountered something cold: a small metal object was hanging from the side of his cloth prison, roughly on a level with his tummy button. It was the size of the Zippo lighter that his father always topped up at weekends.

Hey, it even felt like a Zippo.

But it definitely wasn't one, because that sort of lighter had a hinged top you could open and a flint wheel you could turn.

And it certainly wouldn't be hanging from a cloth ceiling in the dark.

Toby held his breath so as not to be distracted by the sound of his own hoarse breathing. Then, when he felt the top of the foreign object and came across a tiny U-shaped shackle, he knew what he was holding in his hand.

It's a padlock. A little bronze padlock like the one I use to chain up my bike.

He coughed with excitement. He still wasn't sure what the discovery signified, but at least it *was* a discovery. Something that might help to get him out of here.

Is this a test, then? Are you guys testing me?

He shook the padlock impatiently, but nothing happened whichever way he tugged at it.

Brute force is useless! He heard his mother's voice again, and this time he took her advice. He explored the object cautiously with his fingers. When he ran them over the bottom of the thing, his certainty suddenly evaporated. Was it a padlock? Hell, where was the keyhole?

The pussy, as Kevin called the slit you stuck keys in.

There was kind of slit, but it was far too straight and smooth. Just a groove his fingernail fitted into, like the groove in the head of a screw.

Okay, concentrate. It doesn't matter if there's no keyhole, you don't have a key anyway. A screw is much better. Maybe it'll only need turning, and then...

He coughed, wondering if he'd forgotten to breathe again. For some reason, he seemed to drawing less and less air into his lungs.

...and then that will let the light in and I can tear off this lousy sack, or whatever it is, and breathe properly again. But how? How can I get the screw out?

He inserted his thumbnail in the groove on the underside and tried to turn it, but all that happened at the fourth attempt was that he tore the nail and made his thumb bleed.

Shit, I need a screwdriver. Or a knife.

He laughed hysterically.

Oh sure, Jens and Kevin have put a knife in with you, so you can cut your way out.

He coughed again. It suddenly occurred to him why he was sweating so much, why his throat was burning and he was growing more and more exhausted.

I'm running out of air in here. Shit! I'll suffocate if I don't find something hard soon – something I can fit into that lousy groove. Just a minute...

He shut his eyes and tried to breathe steadily.

Something hard.

His fingers started to tingle again as he remembered the coin in his mouth. The one he'd spat out into the darkness in disgust a good hour ago.

62

(10 HOURS 19 MINUTES TO THE DEADLINE)

ALEXANDER ZORBACH

'I don't know where I took the boy,' Alina said. She had taken my arm and let me lead her up the steps and across the narrow gangway to the shore. The wind had subsided a little.

How thin she is, was my first thought as we made our way into the trees. I could feel her ribs in spite of the thick sweaters she was wearing, and my thumb and forefinger would have encircled her wrist twice over. We paused for a moment so that I could adjust the focus of my torch, and the beam strayed across her jeans. I spotted a dirt-encrusted tear below the knee that had escaped my notice in the dimness of the boat. She had obviously done it on the way there.

'If I knew where the boy was hidden, I certainly wouldn't have been stupid enough to come traipsing out here,' she said as I strove to walk alongside. The path was so narrow, it was almost impossible. 'I could have shown the police I'm not a nutter.'

The further we got from the lakeshore, the denser the

Grunewald became. The wind scarcely penetrated the trees, but the snow that became dislodged from their branches concealed the dangerously icy stretches of path ahead of us. I nearly fell over twice, and once I failed to prevent Alina from stumbling when a fir branch caught her in the face because my torch had picked it out too late. I marvelled yet again at the willpower that had prompted her to plunge blindly into such an adventure, trained guide dog or no. TomTom was walking slowly and deliberately up the path, undistracted by snapping branches or other sounds. The area was noted for the numerous wild boar that roamed the woods in search of winter food, but even if we'd flushed a tusker or other wild animal, the retriever wouldn't have been put off the scent for an instant; he would have guided us safely back to my Volvo.

'It's like a movie,' said Alina, having removed my hand from her arm and got into the car without my assistance. I started the engine. As I was backing up I saw her take a handkerchief from her rucksack. She turned and threw the backpack on to the rear seat beside TomTom. Then she mopped her damp face and did her best to dry her hair, which was wet with snow.

Like a movie?

She was obviously waiting for me to comment, so I obliged her while reversing at a walking pace. Only another few metres and I would have to get out again in any case, to roll aside the tree trunk that blocked my secret entrance.

'What are you talking about?'

'My flashbacks. That's how I imagine a feature film.

Except that I can't simply fast-forward or rewind the video in my head.'

'So? How *do* you recall your memories?'

'I don't.'

We had reached the bramble thicket that marked the boundary between the track and the entrance to Nikolskoer Weg, so I braked to a halt.

'I don't understand,' I said. 'Just now you gave me a detailed account of what the Eye Collector did before he put the boy in the boot.'

She nodded and hugged her chest, shivering. In this temperature the car would take another five minutes to warm up.

'I've no idea why I can always remember the first few minutes of my visions so clearly. After that the film seems to fray. The images become blurred and whole sequences go missing. Strangely enough, though, the gaps sometimes close and I can recall other sequences days later. But I don't know how. It happens all by itself. I can't recall missing the missing scenes by an act of the will. See what I mean?'

No, I don't. Right now I don't understand a thing. I don't know what you're doing here, nor do I understand how I've suddenly become chief suspect in one of the most horrific murders of all time.

Instead of replying I got out of the car again and vented my anger on the tree trunk, which I thrust aside in one go.

Damnation! I'd meant to go to ground here in order

to put some distance between me and the crazy situation into which – for some inexplicable reason – I had stumbled. *And now I'm even further up the creek than before.*

I wiped my grimy hands on my jeans and got back in the car, which now smelt of cigarette smoke and wet dog.

I felt like gripping Alina by the shoulders and shaking the truth out of her. *Who sent you here? What do you really want from me?*

But that, an inner voice told me, would be the least likely way of disentangling the Gordian knot of questions in my head.

And besides, there must be something in her story. Stoya confirmed the deadline, after all.

I swallowed a Maxalt from the pack I'd taken from the passenger seat. Then I drove back along Nikolskoer Weg. My hideaway was blown in any case, so I didn't trouble to cover my tracks this time.

'Once more from the beginning,' I said when we reached the main road. 'Your visions are like movies, and this one broke off at the instant you put the boy in the boot.'

'No.'

'No?'

I turned my head. Alina's had closed her eyes again and was looking utterly serene. She might have been asleep.

'Not entirely. For instance, I have a distinct recollection of the radio coming on when I got into the car and turned on the ignition.' She chewed her lower lip. 'The Cure were singing *Boys Don't Cry*. I checked the rear-view mirror to see if I'd picked up a scratch or a bump, but all I saw was my father's laughing face. He was beating time to the tune on the steering wheel.' She gulped. 'I always see my father when some arsehole is hurting someone. God, how I hate that!'

Nothing could be heard for a while but the sound of the diesel engine as we drove along the deserted avenue, heading for Zehlendorf. There must have been a severe weather warning which the Berliners were taking seriously for once. We stopped at a red light.

'What happened after that?' I asked.

'No idea. That's when the movie gets patchy. I remember driving uphill for a bit. We rounded several bends. Then the car pulled up and I got out.'

'What did you do then?'

'Nothing. I just stood there and watched.'

I drove on. 'You watched?'

'Yes. All at once I was holding something heavy, a pair of binoculars or something. Anyway, the whole scene looked blurred to begin with. Then I suddenly made out what was happening down below.'

'What was it?' I could hardly believe I was seriously asking a blind woman that question.

Alina turned briefly to TomTom, who had started panting, and fondled the fur on the back of his curly head. 'I saw a car come racing along the road and skid to a halt in the driveway of the house I'd just left. A man jumped out. He tripped and fell over on the snow-covered gravel – for a moment he crawled along on all fours. Briefly hidden from view by a tree, he reappeared just in front of the tool shed. I saw his lips mouth a cry as he threw back his head and sank to his knees, weeping, beside his wife's dead body.'

She shut her eyes, but not quickly enough to prevent a tear from escaping. A small four-wheel drive was ahead of us. Seen in the red glow of its brake lights, the tear resembled a drop of blood.

'He kept hitting his head with both fists. Again and again. I couldn't hear what he was shouting, he was much too far away. But then...'

'What?'

'Then he suddenly made contact with me.'

'How?'

We were approaching the Drei Linden intersection. I decided to keep straight on.

'He stood up and looked in my direction.'

'Just a moment.' I massaged the back of my neck with one hand. 'He knew where you were?'

'Yes. I had the unreal feeling that we were accomplices, and it gave me a shock. I was a very long way from him, though, and when I lowered the binoculars I couldn't even see him as a tiny speck.'

'But *he* saw you?'

'That was the impression I got.'

The dull ache in my head was getting worse. The migraine remedy wasn't having the slightest effect.

Could there be some connection between the Eye Collector and Traunstein, the father of the kidnapped children?

We passed the Avus turn-off to Charlottenburg. I checked the rear-view mirror. All clear behind me, so I braked hard and sped back along Potsdamer Chaussee as fast as the Volvo could manage.

'What are you doing?' asked Alina, who had noticed our sudden change of direction.

'Making a short detour,' I replied. I signalled right and turned off on to the city expressway.

Perhaps the Eye Collector isn't playing his sick game of hide-and-seek solo.

There was only one way for me to find out.

61

(10 HOURS TO THE DEADLINE)

PHILIPP STOYA
(DETECTIVE SUPERINTENDENT, HOMICIDE)

'According to Hollywood, serial murderers are exceptionally intelligent, never of Afro-American descent, and only very rarely female.'

Seated in his chrome-plated wheelchair, Professor Adrian Hohlfort looked quite unlike his TV self. He wasn't smiling, his grey hair wasn't neatly parted, and he wasn't wearing the black necktie that he'd worn on every one of his talk show appearances to date. He hadn't even shaved, either, presumably because no member of tonight's audience was expected to buy his book after the show. *The Serial Murderer and I* had now been on the bestseller list for seventy-one weeks.

'They only kill members of their own ethnic group and are a largely American phenomenon. All these findings are said to be based on scientific FBI research, and they're all total crap.'

Stoya fired a warning glance at Scholle, who was seated beside him at the conference table, vainly trying to stifle a yawn. Unlike his associate, who considered profiling hocus-pocus, Stoya had faith in the abilities of the sixty-year-old expert, who had personally interviewed numerous serial murderers in the course of his career.

Many more than Zorbach.

Privately, he found the paraplegic psychologist extremely unlikeable, but his professional expertise was beyond dispute. Although their meetings in the last few weeks had not as yet proved productive, Hohlfort had often been helpful to the police in the past. Now that they had a definite suspect at last, they wanted to hear his expert opinion.

'Professor, you told us last time that we ought to look for a run-of-the-mill kind of individual. Someone who's rather retiring and not in the public eye.'

'That's right. Forget Hannibal Lecter, he's a novelist's invention. Lecter has about as much in common with reality as I do with an Olympic hurdler.'

Hohlfort gave the rims of his wheelchair a gentle slap and grinned at his little joke. No one else did.

'Serial murderers are the losers of our society. We're looking, not for an outstanding anti-hero, but for someone at odds with himself and his lot in life. A niche personality, as I term him. Outwardly quite normal and rather inconspicuous, but inwardly a mass of imponderables.'

Stoya made a meaningless note on the pad in front of him. 'Could he be a journalist?'

Hohlfort shrugged. 'Serial murderers pursue a wide variety of occupations. They can be petrol pump attendants, bus drivers or lawyers, supermarket shelf-stackers or civil servants.'

He glanced derisively at Stoya's colleague.

'They can even work for the police.'

Scholle groaned and turned to his partner. 'Come on, Philipp, we're wasting our time here. Grandpa's pearls of wisdom are about as precise as my horoscope.'

If the professor was stung by these disrespectful words, he didn't show it. He rested his elbows on the arms of his wheelchair and spread his hands with an air of unconcern.

'I'm not here to do your work for you, gentlemen. You're the investigators, not I.' He gave Stoya a look which conveyed that even the best profiler could do nothing if the police failed to find the hiding place in which the Eye Collector had held and murdered the kidnapped children.

'Nor have I come armed with a computer that'll spit out the perpetrator's profile at the touch of a button once you've fed it with information,' Hohlfort added. 'I can only provide you with another piece of the jigsaw. It's your job to insert it in the right place.'

Stoya frowned at Scholle and asked the professor to go on. Hohlfort needed no second bidding. If there was one thing he liked, it was sharing his inexhaustible store of knowledge with other people. Provided they didn't dispute it.

'To return to your question about the murderer's occupation...' Hohlfort stared at an invisible point on the room's bare ceiling and assumed a meditative expression. 'All I can tell you is this: the Eye Collector enjoys planning and may have some professional connection with projects that have firm deadlines. He's used to completing things within a given time.'

Stoya couldn't help thinking of the coffee mug on Zorbach's desk in the newspaper office. It bore the words: *Creative people have no working hours, only deadlines.*

'And he has at least a rudimentary grasp of medicine.'

Stoya nodded reluctantly. The eyes had not been professionally removed, but nor had the operation been botched, and just enough anaesthetic had been administered so that it lasted until the ultimatums expired. At least that's what they thought, given the absence of any external marks of violence indicating that the children had been unconscious when they were drowned. Stoya sometimes tried to console himself with that thought, but he never succeeded.

'In any event,' Hohlfort continued to pontificate, 'the perpetrator has left the planning and victim selection phase far behind him, or he wouldn't proceed in such a smooth and practised manner. We can also assume that years ago he attracted significant attention to himself in some way.'

By shooting a woman on a bridge, for instance?

'I've a question for you: What provides the trigger?' Stoya asked during one of the professor's few pauses for breath. 'Could the Eye Collector be working out some trauma by doing what he does?'

Hohlfort nodded vigorously. 'I would even lay odds he has a medical record. He has never left us any usable fingerprints or traces of DNA, unfortunately. Since we can't enlist the help of those, we must adopt the classical method of narrowing the field. And that begins with the vital question of motive.'

The professor smiled his TV smile for the first time and raised his hands in mock surrender. 'And here I leave the terra firma of science behind and venture on to the quick-sand of speculation.'

Scholle seemed to construe this as the final whistle and started to heave his bulk erect, but Stoya indicated to him to be patient for a little longer. He was eager to get out of there himself, not least because the stuff he'd snorted ten hours ago was losing its effect and he badly needed another kick. But that would have to wait.

First I must make sure we're really heading in the right direction.

Unlike Scholle, who was already convinced of Zorbach's guilt, Stoya found it inconceivable that a former colleague could have committed the most loathsome series of murders he'd ever encountered in the course of his career. Nevertheless, Zorbach had turned up at the latest crime scene before its location was widely known, his wallet had been found there even though it couldn't have fallen out of his coveralls, and he had displayed accurate inside knowledge. That made him their hottest candidate to date. That he knew the precise deadline on the one hand but not the modus operandi – drowning – on the other, Scholle dismissed as 'a psychopath's behaviour, incomprehensible to anyone of sound mind'.

Stoya thought this simplistic, but he naturally backed

the hunt for Zorbach, which was already in full swing. His home was being searched at this moment and a call had been put out for his Volvo. It was only a matter of time before he was found. Time which Stoya had to use in order to prepare himself to question his former colleague.

'So please speculate,' he told the professor, glancing at his watch.

Less than ten hours left...

'Exactly what does the Eye Collector want his murders to achieve?'

60

(9 HOURS 41 MINUTES TO THE DEADLINE)

ALEXANDER ZORBACH

Nothing about the sleepy residential district on the outskirts of the Grunewald betrayed that a brutal murder had been committed there only hours before. It was as if the fresh snow had not only covered the roofs, roads and gardens but obliterated even the memory of the horrific crime. If I hadn't known better, I would have thought this the safest place in the world. A district where parents gave their children names that wouldn't have looked out of place in an Ikea catalogue: Tombte, Sören, Noemi, Lars-Alvin, Finn. Where the kids' times for watching TV were strictly limited and they were expected back from piano lessons, not the football pitch. Where their elders leant on garden fences to discuss the best lawn feeds and excoriate the neighbour who had once more allowed his dog to foul the footpath without clearing up the mess, in spite of the ubiquitous blue boxes full of poop bags installed by the local council. Where last year's biggest scandal occurred when old Herr Becker turned up for the annual street party with an Asian girl decades younger than himself. *And now this!*

I drove at a walking pace, peering in at the illuminated windows. Some of them already displayed Christmas decorations: home-made paper chains, a wooden crèche, strings of single-colour fairy lights. None of the gaudy or garish stuff you found in less affluent districts. No flashing Father Christmases on the roofs or halogen reindeer in front of the garages. The decorations in this district were discreet.

And boring, in my opinion.

'We'll meet in Kühler Weg,' I said into my mobile.

'The crime scene, you mean?' Frank didn't sound exactly overjoyed to be playing the errand boy again.

'Exactly.'

'What do you want this time?'

'Your car.'

'Please don't tell me you're serious.' Frank gave a forced laugh. 'You're on the run, right?'

'No, just being careful.'

'Okay, don't tell me anything, but I'm not stupid. I know why Thea and the rest of the top brass are in a huddle in the conference room at this moment. The police are after you, and they don't know whether to sweep the story under the carpet or splash it on page one.'

Zorbach suspected of murder. How close did our star reporter really get to the Eye Collector?

I could already see the headlines and guessed that Thea was planning to jump in with both feet, whereas the moneybags were assessing the potential damages if I sued the paper for defamation.

Provided I managed to prove my innocence.

'No wonder Big Momma Thea made me swear to tip her off at once if you called me.'

'Don't do that.'

'No worries, I'm on your side. I won't breathe a word, but I'm not lending you my car just because your own has become too hot.'

His remark reminded me that I'd been idiotic enough to forget to replace my licence plates. Up till now I'd been blessed with more luck than judgement. If I wanted to make the most of the time that remained before the police picked me up, I would have to be a bit smarter. And that included getting hold of a car that wasn't on the wanted list.

'Why don't you just turn yourself in?' Frank asked. 'I mean, if you haven't done anything, nothing can happen to you.'

The problem is, I can't explain how I came to be at the crime scene, how my wallet got there, and how I knew about the exact deadline.

'Let me ask *you* a question: What would you do if you were suddenly approached by a woman who claims she witnessed the Eye Collector's most recent murder?'

'No shit?'

I omitted to tell him that my witness was a blind medium who had spent the last few minutes sitting beside me with her head propped against the car window. She seemed to have found her excursion to the houseboat more strenuous than she cared to admit.

'Man, that would be the story of the century.'

And how. You've no idea...

'So bring me your car.'

Frank sighed. 'Look, it's not really mine – it's my granny's Toyota. She'll kill me if you leave a single scratch on her beloved bus.'

'Don't worry, Frank, I'll be careful. See you in ten minutes.' I had reached the end of the street and hung up.

'We're there,' I told Alina. I parked the Volvo with two wheels on the pavement.

We were just outside the suburban house in whose garden Thomas Traunstein had found the dead body of his wife Lucia, fourteen years his junior. A pebble-dashed building with brickwork cornerstones and a double garage, it was the only home on the street in total darkness. Even the illuminated house number had been turned off.

Alina stretched and yawned. She extricated her watch from underneath the sleeves of her numerous sweaters and opened the glass lid over the dial.

'What are we doing here?' she asked sleepily.

'Finding out if you've been here before.'

I opened the driver's door, flooding the car with a gust of icy air. TomTom sat up on the back seat and started panting.

'You mean you want to find out if this place really is the one I told you I saw in my vision?'

Yes. Why don't we take this lunacy at face value? I want to know if a blind witness 'saw' a murder committed here.

I got out. My eyes began to water as I faced into the wind and looked along the street to where it petered out into the woodland path that I had driven up when I first came here.

The path to the Teufelsberg.

Recalling Alina's description, I asked her how long it took her to get to the top of the hill.

'I remember driving uphill for a bit. We rounded several bends...'

'No idea,' she said. 'Do *you* have a sense of time when you dream?'

No, but I don't kidnap little children either.

I raised my head and peered into the grey-black sky, trying to gauge the direction in which the Teufelsberg lay. The hill was a mound of debris overgrown with grass and trees. It was composed of rubble from buildings destroyed during air raids and house-to-house fighting in the Second World War. The place now served as a convenient recreation area for the inhabitants of Berlin, who went walking there, flew kites, or sped down the slopes on sledges in the snow. I wondered if the Traunsteins' garden was visible from the summit in daylight. I couldn't tell in the darkness, but I suspected it was too far away, even for someone with binoculars.

What else did you expect, you idiot? I asked myself, turning to face the house. *Did you really think there was something in this blind girl's nonsense?*

I leant against the car and debated my next move. The front garden was enclosed by a low fence. I could easily have vaulted it in my better days, and it wouldn't have presented a major obstacle even now.

'I don't mean to moan,' Alina said behind me, 'but it's almost nine o'clock and I'm still not home. TomTom's hungry and he needs to go walkies.' She laughed. 'That makes two of us.'

Her grin left me in no doubt as to what she was alluding to.

'Wait here,' I told her. 'I won't be long.'

'Where are you going?' I heard her call, but I'd already crossed the road and was walking past the garage and into the trees. After a few metres I turned left on to a narrow path, worn by walkers and cyclists, which ran parallel to the fence at the rear of the property. Another ten paces, and I came to a halt.

This was where I had stood yesterday in the pouring rain, only a stone's throw from the garden shed whose flat roof was now covered by a thick layer of snow.

The spot where Lucia Traunstein's body had been lying on the lawn was still enclosed by crime-scene tape and protected from the elements by the tent, which forensics had yet to remove. I was too far from the shed to see if the door had been sealed with tape, but I felt sure it had.

'It was made of timber, not metal. I sensed that because I got a splinter in my finger when I slid the bolt open. Besides, there was a smell of resin when I went inside.'

I screwed up my eyes, but it was too dark to tell whether Alina's description of the Traunsteins' garden shed was accurate.

Right...

I shook the fence, which was of green painted metal. The posts were embedded in concrete to prevent wild boar from digging their way in, and the top curved outwards, which made scaling it more difficult, but not impossible. I was just about to haul myself up when I heard something rattle nearby. It happened again when I released the fence. I turned to the right and shook it again to make sure.

No doubt about it. I made my way along the fence, and then I saw it: the garden gate wasn't locked. Or rather, it had been, but someone had failed to close it properly when turning the key, so the tongue of the lock hadn't engaged.

How can that be? This is a crime scene.

It should never have been left so easily accessible, even if forensics had completed their work.

Mystified, I pushed the gate open with my foot and looked at the ground.

The footprints leading across the lawn to the rear of the shed might have been left by various people. By the father, who had dashed into the woods to look for his children, or by a policeman or forensics officer who had come to check that the garden fence was secure and failed to do so. There must surely be an innocuous explanation even for the very fresh footprints in the snow, which led in only one direction.

Unless they belonged to whoever it was who had just turned on a torch on the ground floor of the house some twenty metres away.

59

No timber. Only metal and plastic had been used in the construction of the shed, but it did have a sliding bolt on the door. I was wondering briefly what it meant, if anything, that Alina's vision accorded with reality in this respect at least, when I was once more distracted by a light flickering inside the big terrace window.

So as not to be mistaken for a burglar myself, I walked straight up to the house without taking any precautions. To a neighbour who happens to glance out of his window, a man slinking along bent double looks very much more conspicuous than one who strides across a lawn as if he owns it.

It wasn't until I reached the window that I hugged the wall and peered through a crack in the curtains. I corrected my initial suspicion at once. No torch. No burglar. The sporadically flickering light I'd seen from the shed came from a projector attached to the living room's wood-panelled ceiling. There was no light source other than the film on the screen over the fireplace.

I couldn't even make out whether anyone was watching it from one of the two U-shaped sofas.

Watching what, exactly?

I screwed up my eyes, but the screen remained grey. Moments earlier it had been showing an ill-exposed black-and-white home movie: unsteady shots of what, with a little imagination, had appeared to be a spacious bathroom equipped with two washbasins, a loo, a bidet, and a shower cubicle. Then someone, either intentionally or inadvertently, had draped something over the camera lens – probably a towel, I guessed – with the result that Traunstein's living room was plunged in gloom again.

I was debating what to do next when I heard someone giggle. Although muffled by the window, which was shut, the sound was loud enough to seem wholly inappropriate. Laughter didn't belong in the living room of a man whose wife had just been murdered – a man who had only a few hours left in which to recover his kidnapped children alive.

The projector's beam brightened once more and the invisible cameraman no longer limited himself to shooting inanimate bathroom objects. The towel had disappeared and the new camera angle showed a corner bath in which a woman was seated, her back turned whilst she pinned up her hair.

Before I could tell what made me feel so uneasy about this, a man's naked buttocks came into shot, almost filling the screen. The giggling, which had sounded faintly frivolous until now, took on a suggestive note when the man stepped up to the bath and proceeded to massage the woman's shoulders. His slightly stooping posture indicated that her shoulders were not the only parts of her anatomy he was kneading.

I felt suddenly dirty, a voyeur who had invaded a stranger's privacy and was on the verge of crossing a threshold that would make it impossible for him to regain his decency.

I'd felt as shabby as this once before, just before I married Nicci. She was having to put in a vast amount of overtime, and I'd developed an irrational fear that she might be having an affair with someone. Her mobile, which she always left overnight on the shoe locker in our hallway, found its way into my hand. I don't know what eventually deterred me from looking through her text messages. Today, years later, I was glad I hadn't done so, even though I'd never been able to shake off the faint suspicion that she might have been cheating on me. I had retained my decency, and that was more important to me.

I felt doubly uncomfortable now, as I peered through that living-room window and caught the owner of the house watching a home-made porn film. Although I still hadn't sighted Traunstein himself, I felt sure that the overflowing ashtray and half-empty bottle of bourbon on the coffee table beside the leather armchair were his.

I went right up to the terrace door and stood there irresolutely. I hesitated just as I had when I was on the point of opening Nicci's mobile and checking her text messages. But tonight, I knew, I would go a stage further.

Maybe I'm only here because of a blind girl's demons, I thought as I put out my hand. *Maybe Alina is just a screwball and Traunstein has nothing to do with his children's disappearance.*

In the firm expectation that the door would be locked, I turned the cold brass handle.

But the fact remains, something here stinks.

Then, when the door yielded and swung silently inwards, I added an even feebler excuse for my curiosity: *And I'd be a poor journalist if I didn't get to the bottom of it.*

58

I recognized Thomas Traunstein the instant he turned towards me. He was still wearing the pale-brown double-breasted suit he'd worn at yesterday's press conference, when he made a public appeal for help in finding his children. But it looked as if he'd slept in it in the meantime. Crumpled and stained in several places, it looked thoroughly incongruous on the owner of Berlin's biggest dry-cleaning chain.

But not as incongruous as this whole scenario.

Traunstein hadn't heard me come in at first. It wasn't until I cleared my throat and called his name that he made a rather clumsy attempt to heave himself out of a deep armchair.

Without success. Half a bottle of bourbon had completely sapped his energy.

'W-what're you doing here?' he mumbled when I was standing in front of him. His bleary eyes displayed the dull-witted aggression typical of a drunk who is only looking for an excuse to start a punch-up.

'I could ask you the same thing,' I retorted, glancing at the screen. The images were growing more and more explicit. The woman in the bath had turned round, her head level with the man's hips and both her hands clutching his buttocks. Watching porn in the privacy of your own home certainly wasn't prohibited. Not even when you'd been a widower for only a day and a half and you knew that your offspring were in the clutches of a madman.

It isn't prohibited, but that doesn't make it right.

'Don't you have anything better to do?' I asked him.

He ran his fingers through his tousled hair and stared at me uncomprehendingly. I couldn't tell whether he was puzzled by my question or simply wondering who the hell had suddenly invaded his living room.

'What do you want?' he asked after a longish pause. I had been looking around for some indication of where the kitchen was. If I was going to get the man back on his feet, I would need to brew him some coffee.

'We need to talk,' I said curtly.

'What about?' Traunstein barked. He blinked wearily, making no attempt to wipe the dribble off his chin.

'About whether you may know something that could lead us to the man who murdered your wife.'

Whether she called you just before her death. Whether you actually warned her not to go down into the cellar.

'Lucia was a whore!' he yelled hoarsely. 'A filthy whore!'

I started as if his hate-filled words had slapped my face.

'All she did was screw around.' He reached for a remote control on the coffee table and, with an accuracy remarkable for a man in his condition, zapped the volume control.

The moaning left no doubt as to what the couple in the corner bath were up to.

'My house,' Traunstein said thickly. 'This is my house. My bathroom. My wife.' He laughed hysterically. 'Even my fucking camera. But that wanker there...' – he gestured derisively at the screen, which was once more occupied entirely by the man's hairy hind quarters – '... isn't me.'

'Look,' I said soothingly, 'your marital problems don't concern me...'

The truth is, nothing here concerns me. I'm merely chasing around after a blind girl's visions.

'... But shouldn't you be helping to look for your children?'

'For Lea? For Toby? The hell with them!'

I thought I'd misheard at first, but he repeated the last words and actually spat on the floor.

'Those lousy brats aren't mine!'

Traunstein dropped the remote control but finally managed to haul himself to his feet. Standing there unsteadily with one hand on the back of the armchair, he looked me in the eye. I felt he was on the brink of a nervous breakdown.

'They aren't mine, understand?'

No, I didn't. To be honest, I didn't understand a thing right then. The truth was to hit me all the harder only moments later – roughly at the same time as Traunstein, too, began to catch on. He stared at me intently.

Some disturbing thought was slowly but surely surfacing

in his drink-fuddled mind. His features tensed, as did the rest of his hitherto limp physique.

'I know who you are, damn it! I found your wallet today – I saw your ID.'

I nodded. Not in agreement but because pieces of the jigsaw were slowly fitting together in my head too.

I now knew why the woman's giggle had disturbed me so much when I heard it outside on the terrace. Why Traunstein's personality seemed so familiar although I'd never met him in the flesh. Not that that was necessary. I'd heard so many descriptive anecdotes about him, I'd stored a very detailed picture of him in my mind. It was not only negative but corresponded to the real thing in every detail. Even his crude vocabulary was familiar to me.

'Lucia was a filthy whore. Those lousy brats aren't mine.'

'Shit, you're that newshound! You already shot one woman, and now you've done for my wife as well!'

Traunstein was now standing so close to me, I could smell his foul breath. It reeked of Jim Beam and tobacco.

'It was you. You did it!'

I shrank back and caught sight of the screen, driving the last nail into a coffin of terrible certainty.

Her picture hadn't yet been published, perhaps because photos of her kidnapped children were more attention-grabbing and news editors wanted to save shots of her corpse for a day when there was no fresh information about the Eye Collector to print. Or perhaps I'd simply failed to see her picture because I'd disappeared from the scene for the last few hours.

I've been far too intent on myself.

The woman had got out of the bath. Her pinned-up hair had come loose again and was cascading over her breasts. When she laughed at the camera, recognition smote me like a fist and expelled every last vestige of joy from my soul.

Dear God, please don't let it be true, I thought, simultaneously realizing why she hadn't answered my calls. We would never again meet in that seedy club, never again pursue our intimate conversations.

And never fall in love.

I felt like weeping and yelling at the same time, but nothing I did would make any difference.

Charlie was dead.

And I would very soon join her, if I copped a bullet from the gun her husband was pointing at me.

57

(9 HOURS 17 MINUTES TO THE DEADLINE)

PHILIPP STOYA
(DETECTIVE SUPERINTENDENT, HOMICIDE)

Hohlfort was in his element. He had reassumed his benign, talk-show smile and seemed, in spite of his disability, to be a thoroughly happy man. Happy to acquaint two humble policemen with his theories on motive and modus operandi. Stoya wondered if he himself would some day find the time and leisure to parlay his professional experiences into a book. Nowadays every idiot wrote his memoirs, signed autographs at book festivals and presented his mug to the camera. Why shouldn't he be granted an opportunity to boost his income, not to mention his public image, as soon as he left this shit behind him?

'We may safely assume that there was some key event in the murderer's formative phase – a traumatic experience, probably. Killers have often been bullied, maltreated or abused in childhood.'

'Oh, sure,' Scholle said derisively, 'the Eye Collector is the real victim. That's every criminal's stock excuse!'

He had risen to turn the heating down a little. It was

almost impossible to maintain an even temperature in the windowless interview room at police headquarters. In summer you shivered because of the air conditioning, which had been installed as an afterthought, and in winter the overheated room gave you a headache.

'You're right. Nearly every violent criminal hails from a dysfunctional background, so that assumption isn't much of a help to us.' Hohlfort picked up his briefcase, which he'd deposited beside his wheelchair, and put it on his lap. Deftly opening it, he removed a bulky folder. This he placed on the table in front of them. 'Fortunately, however, these mutilations provide us with some important clues.'

He opened the folder with a flourish and turned it so that Stoya and Scholle could see the horrific photographs of the murder victims.

As if I could ever forget those little bodies and their empty eye sockets, thought Stoya, stung by the professor's histrionic gesture.

'Clues?' he said impatiently. 'Can you be more specific?'

'Every criminal has an objective. It may be incomprehensible to a normal person, but it exists nonetheless. And, in the Eye Collector's case, it's patently obvious.'

'Of course it is,' Scholle snapped, pointing to the folder. 'He's a sadistic paedophile. He gets his rocks off by torturing little kids.'

'Wrong. What suggests against that theory is the absence of any other traces of abuse on his victims.' Hohlfort gave a schoolmasterly shake of the head. 'And a sex crime wouldn't account of the removal of the left eye, would it?'

Although the question was directed at Scholle, who was clearly the professor's target, it was Stoya who replied.

'Killers who cover their victims' eyes are usually performing a symbolic act and trying to undo what they've done. Unable to endure the sight of their handiwork, they shut their victims' eyes in lieu of their own.'

'But then the Eye Collector would have excised *both* eyes,' Hohlfort countered. He picked up a photograph of the first victim, little Karla Strahl, and held it so the two detectives could see it. Suppressing an urge to look away, Stoya stared instead at the elderly profiler's permatanned face.

'So he collects trophies?' said Scholle.

Hohlfort gave a thin-lipped smile. 'Trophies, mementoes, rewards – those are the first thing a profiler in a cheap thriller thinks of whenever some portion of a victim's anatomy is missing.' He shook his head vigorously. 'No, I think we've been misled by the Eye Collector sobriquet. He isn't a collector.'

'So what is he?'

'I would prefer to describe him as a transformer. He manufactures a physical condition. He changes the nature of children by transforming them into Cyclopes.'

'Huh?' Scholle had sat down again and was tilting his chair back.

'The mythical creatures whose most noticeable feature was their single eye.' Hohlfort's tongue shot out and moistened his upper lip, reminding Stoya of a lizard. 'Although I'm sure you're well acquainted with the ancient Greek myths,' he went on with a complacent smile in Scholle's direction, 'permit me to indulge in a brief digression.'

He returned the photo of murdered Karla to the folder, which he closed.

'The first and probably best-known Cyclopes were the offspring of Uranus and Gaea, who, as we all know, symbolizes Mother Earth. Gaea and Uranus, the sky god, produced three Cyclopes in all, but they were hated by their father. Uranus detested them so much...' – Hohlfort paused briefly to lend his ensuing words greater emphasis – '... that he hid them!'

'Where?' Stoya had momentarily wondered whether they ought to waste any more time on Hohlfort's effusions, but the crippled academic had now regained his full attention.

'Deep in the earth,' the professor said. 'He hid his children in Tartarus. That was the gods' name for a part of the underworld even deeper than Hades.'

Stoya's involuntary nod evoked a nod of agreement from Hohlfort. 'I see you recognize the analogies.'

'So what happened to the one-eyed children?' asked Scholle, who had briefly stopped tilting his chair.

'They were personally freed by Zeus, the most senior of all the Greek gods. The Cyclopes were so grateful for their release, they made Zeus a gift of thunder and lightning.'

'Your general knowledge is most impressive, professor, but—'

'Have your deliberations produced a theory we can

actually work with?' asked Stoya, completing the sentence before Scholle could end it on a considerably less courteous note.

Hohlfort gave another of his grins. He suddenly looked so filled with vitality, Stoya half expected him to leap out of his wheelchair.

'I would go so far as to state that I've developed more than just a theory. I can provide you with a very, very important lead.'

Hohlfort inserted another pregnant pause for effect. Nothing could be heard but the incessant gurgling of the decrepit central heating system. Then he cleared his throat and said, in an almost pastoral tone, 'The Eye Collector selects children who have been disowned by their fathers.'

'Why?' The two detectives spoke almost in unison.

Hohlfort's expression conveyed that it would be beneath his dignity to utter such a self-evident truth aloud, but he finally deigned to do so:

'Because, like the Cyclopes of Greek mythology, those children are the product of an illicit relationship.'

56

(9 HOURS 11 MINUTES TO THE DEADLINE)

ALEXANDER ZORBACH

'This is wrong,' Alina said dully. She was breathing fast and her eyes were fluttering restlessly beneath her closed eyelids. 'We shouldn't do it.'

'Don't worry,' I told her, hoping that she couldn't hear the desperation in my voice. 'This won't take long.' I tried to shepherd her into the room, but she indignantly pushed my hand away.

I understand, I thought, relieved that she couldn't see the tears in my eyes. *I don't want to go back in there either, but this isn't just professional any more. It's personal.*

Stunned by the fact of Charlie's death, I initially made no attempt to defend myself against her husband. I didn't know how the gun had suddenly appeared in his hand – nor, to be honest, had I any wish to speculate on that or the reason why he hadn't shot me.

You don't have to be a psychologist to guess what an unfortunate man intends to do with a loaded gun in the darkest, loneliest hour of his life. If Traunstein had meant to turn it on himself, alcohol had not only robbed him of the strength to do so but rendered him even less capable of shooting me. And so, while we stood confronting one another, paralysed by the shock of realization, the gun had slipped from his hand to the thickly carpeted floor. It was still lying beside the armchair.

'Why are we here?' asked Alina.

'For some answers.'

My fate seemed to be linked to that of the Eye Collector by an invisible rope that was tightening around me minute by minute. Although I could barely endure my grief for Charlie, whose real name I'd just been compelled to learn in the cruellest way, I couldn't simply leave. I needed certainty, which was why I'd gone back to the car and persuaded Alina to accompany me into Traunstein's house.

'I smell cigarette smoke, drink and sweat,' she said distastefully, one hand on the door handle, the other gripping my arm at the spot where I'd stuck the nicotine patch. 'You mean there's something else?'

Oh yes, there is.

I gently removed her hand from the door handle and led her into the living room, where the projector still supplied the only lighting. I had stopped the film so as not to see those unbearable images any longer. They reminded me that I had lost yet another important person in my life, this time for good.

I cleared my throat. Traunstein raised his head and began to whimper softly.

Alina froze. 'Who's that?' she demanded. When the

moans became louder she squeezed my hand tightly. 'What on earth's the matter with him?'

'He's fine,' I said.

'Why doesn't he speak?'

'I gagged him.'

With the handkerchief from his breast pocket, to be exact.

Detaching my hand from Alina's, I went over to the swivel chair in the middle of the room. I had lashed Traunstein to this with a length of extension cable – certainly not the smartest decision I'd made in my already screwed-up life. However, once Stoya learned of my relationship with one of the victims (no one would believe it was platonic in view of our habitual rendezvous), the tied-up widower would be the least of my problems.

I swung the chair round so Traunstein was facing in Alina's direction. He uttered a grunt.

'You gagged someone?' Alina said behind me. 'Are you mad?'

No. Dr Roth says I'm completely sane.

'I only did it to prevent Traunstein from raising the roof while I went to fetch you.'

I bent over him. Sweat was streaming down his face, but he looked considerably more together than he had a few minutes ago.

'Traunstein?' I heard Alina exclaim in the background. 'The father of the kidnapped children? Good God, are you giving him the third degree? I don't want to be part of this. Get me out of here at once.'

'Who said anything about the third degree?' I retorted. 'Listen,' I said to Traunstein, 'here's the deal: I'll remove the gag but you keep quiet, okay? I don't want to hear a peep out of you, just the answers to a few questions. Is that clear?'

Traunstein nodded and I tugged the handkerchief out of his mouth. He coughed and spluttered for a while before quietening down. Determined to discover, step by step, whether the last phone call had really followed the course Alina had described to me on the houseboat, I used the time to marshal my thoughts.

'Right,' I said. 'Did you phone your wife shortly before you came home yesterday?'

'She...' He broke off to cough and had to start again. '*She* called *me*,' he said breathlessly. His tongue seemed to be obeying him with great reluctance.

'Okay, she called you.'

So Alina's account checks to that extent.

'What did she say?'

What did the woman, with whom I almost fell in love with, say before she died?

'She...' – he gulped – '... she was hysterical. I could hardly understand a word.'

'Did she say something about a game of hide-and-seek?'

'Huh?' His face registered total incomprehension. He tried to answer, but it was only at the third attempt that he got out something resembling a coherent sentence. 'No, nothing like that. She just yelled on and on because the kids were missing.'

'What about you?' Alina asked in the background. I was surprised she'd intervened in the conversation and wondered if something had struck her about the man's voice.

'Yes,' I said, 'what did you say to that?'

Traunstein's head sagged forwards. He seemed about to doze off, but before I could grab him by the chin he straightened up with unexpected vigour.

'I told the bitch to cool it. It wasn't the first time the little tykes had run off.'

I drew several deep breaths. Taking hold of Traunstein's shoulders, I looked straight into his angry, bleary eyes. On the one hand, I was strongly tempted to slap his face for every abusive reference to Charlie he'd uttered; on the other, I felt a sneaking sympathy for him. It always took two people to destroy a relationship, and whatever his faults, he'd had to pay dearly for them.

'You didn't tell her not to go down into the cellar under any circumstances?'

'Oh my God, how could I have been so blind? It's too late. Don't go down into the cellar whatever you do.'

As I fired the question at Traunstein I watched to see if, and how, his expression changed. I had conducted hundreds of interrogations in my first life and as many interviews in my second, so I felt capable of interpreting the emotions beneath almost any facial expression. In Thomas Traunstein's case I could detect not the slightest sign of bewilderment or surprise as to how I could have got hold of this information. He reacted as he had before, in a confused and aggressive manner.

'The cellar? What cellar?'

Not that he knew it, but that question got to the heart of the matter. All the previous victims had been murdered in upstairs flats – locations in which forbidding someone to go down into the cellar would have made no sense. If there was a grain of truth in Alina's vision, it could only refer to Charlie's murder.

'I said nothing about any fucking cellar.'

Traunstein must have choked on his own spit. The ensuing paroxysm of coughing shook his whole body.

Okay, this is getting us nowhere. Time for Plan B.

I turned to Alina. 'I need you to do me a favour,' I whispered too softly for Traunstein to hear. Standing close beside her, I caught another whiff of her perfume. The hairs on her neck stood up as my warm breath fanned her ear. I glimpsed the beginnings of a tattoo beneath the collar of her rollneck sweater.

As if she'd sensed my gaze, she pulled up the collar before I could make out what the letters said. It had looked to me like 'Hate'.

'What sort of favour?' she asked.

I took hold of her hands and led her slowly round Traunstein's chair until she was standing immediately to his rear.

'You said you began with the man's shoulders.'

'Hey, what is this?' Traunstein jerked his head back in an attempt to see what was happening behind him.

'Yes,' said Alina, 'but—'

'Fucking hell, what are you playing at? Who is this bitch?' Traunstein tugged at his bonds.

'Then do it again,' I told her. *Prove to me that you were telling the truth. Look into the Eye Collector's past once more.*

I placed her hands on Traunstein's shoulders.

'Now tell me what you see.'

55

(8 HOURS 55 MINUTES TO THE DEADLINE)

PHILIPP STOYA (DETECTIVE SUPERINTENDENT, HOMICIDE)

The Eye Collector selects children who have been disowned by their fathers. Because, like the Cyclopes of Greek mythology, those children are the product of an illicit relationship...

Stoya repeated the professor's last few words in his head. He was beginning to share Scholle's dislike of the know-it-all profiler, whose statements were deliberately designed to provoke questions that would expose his listeners' ignorance. Stoya eventually obliged him.

'Meaning what, exactly?'

'Uranus was Gaea's son.'

'Hang on!' Scholle guffawed. 'You mean old Mother Earth had it off with her own son?'

'To whom she'd given birth by immaculate conception. Yes, the ancient Greeks weren't as squeamish as we are. For example, Zeus was intimate with his sister. These days, of course, such a relationship would be frowned on.'

Stoya shook his head thoughtfully. 'We've checked the victims' family backgrounds. There wasn't even a hint of incest.'

Hohlfort cocked a forefinger. 'When I spoke of an illicit relationship, I didn't mean it in a legal sense. The Eye Collector's point of view is all that matters. To him, even a bit on the side can be sufficient.'

'You mean...'

'I mean that the kidnapped children are probably not their fathers' biological offspring.' Hohlfort gripped his wheelchair's chromium-plated hand rims and began to propel himself gently back and forth. 'That's why the fathers hate them. That's why the Eye Collector kills the women who have betrayed their husbands so shamefully.'

Galvanized by what the professor had just said, Stoya stood up and nervously kneaded the nape of his neck. 'That would mean he's an avenger!'

'Precisely.' Hohlfort continued to glide back and forth, looking like a gleeful schoolboy. 'The murderer punishes errant mothers for their infidelity. He plays the part of Uranus by hiding the children he detests in the bowels of the earth. And that provides us with yet another clue to where we should look. He holds his victims captive in a bunker or cellar of some kind, not at ground level or above.'

'Oh, thanks a lot, that narrows it down dramatically,' said Scholle, who had also risen to his feet. His stomach bulged so far over his waistband, it was impossible to tell if he was wearing a belt.

'You can waste time making snide remarks, or you can check the victims' family backgrounds for hushed-up affairs and extramarital escapades. Maybe all these women had a fling with the Eye Collector himself and gave birth to children whom he hates as much as Uranus hated the Cyclopes.'

'And maybe I'll go to the john and scratch my arse,' Scholle said with a dismissive gesture. 'I'm getting sick of all this mystical, mythical mumbo-jumbo. I prefer hard evidence. After all, we've at last got a suspect who not only has inside knowledge of the latest crime but left his wallet at the scene.'

Hohlfort smiled his TV smile and glided over to the hatstand beside the door. 'You wanted to hear my theory, gentlemen. I'm sorry if you feel you've wasted your time.'

He was just about to take his cashmere scarf off the hook when the door burst open and a young secretary hurried in.

'Sorry to interrupt, sir,' she said breathlessly, blowing her blonde fringe off her forehead.

Stoya frowned. 'What is it?'

'Zorbach,' was all she said, puce in the face with excitement.

Stoya felt everything inside him tense up.

'Has he been found?'

'No.' She handed him her mobile. 'He's on the phone.'

54

(8 HOURS 52 MINUTES TO THE DEADLINE)

ALEXANDER ZORBACH

'At his place?'

'Yes.'

'Tied up?'

'With an extension lead.'

'Tell me you're kidding!'

Stoya's voice was trembling with anger. In the background I could hear the medley of noises typical of a busy police headquarters: phones ringing, a babble of voices, doors slamming, computer keyboards clicking. It sounded unusually loud – more like eleven in the morning than late at night – but all available staff must have been on duty. Metaphorically speaking, it was always five minutes to midnight when the Eye Collector had issued an ultimatum.

'There's a DVD in the player in his living room. You should take a look at it.'

'Don't tell me what to do!' Stoya bellowed into the receiver.

I lowered the phone and gestured to Frank to turn left at the next intersection.

After Alina and I had been waiting outside Traunstein's villa for what seemed an eternity, my trainee had turned up just as Stoya took my call, so we'd got into our new getaway car as quietly as possible and without a word of greeting.

'Where are you?' Stoya demanded, his voice still at parade-ground pitch.

'Wrong question. You'd do better to ask why Traunstein has been getting blotto instead of helping to look for his children. The DVD could provide you with a clue.'

By this time, however, I seriously doubted whether there was any connection between Traunstein and the Eye Collector – and not only because Alina's visions had come to nothing. The garden shed wasn't made of timber and the crime scene wasn't near enough to the Teufelsberg, so her knowledge of the odd ultimatum was probably just a fluke.

Stoya changed his tactics. 'Come down to headquarters,' he said in a lame attempt to win me over. 'I promise we'll give you a fair hearing.'

'You're just wasting time. Forget about me. You should question the dead woman's husband.'

I swallowed hard, feeling my eyes grow moist.

Oh Charlie...

'Listen Stoya,' I said. 'I'm still on your side, believe me. That's why I'm now going to tell you something potentially incriminating, okay? I'll tell you it in confidence, as a former colleague.'

To help me retain my composure I opened the passenger

window a crack and let the icy headwind blow into my face. 'Traunstein's wife had affairs. Lots of them.' Then, so softly that the wind and engine noises almost drowned my words, I added, 'I knew her well myself.'

'What is this, a joke? *You* had an affair with Lucia Traunstein?' Stoya sounded flabbergasted.

'No. At least, not in the way you mean.'

I saw out of the corner of my eye that I'd failed in my attempt not to be overheard. Frank glanced at me and raised his eyebrows.

'I'm only telling you this because I don't want your investigations to get sidetracked. The children's father may know where they are, understand? Traunstein has a motive, I don't. His wife had affairs with other men and he doesn't think the kids are his.'

'Tell me at once where you are!' Stoya's tone of voice had changed. The anger had receded into the background. Unless I was much mistaken, he sounded far more impersonal, as if I'd finally dispelled his doubts about my guilt.

'I'm on the move, but don't bother looking for my Volvo. It's in Kühler Weg. The keys are in it.'

I looked at Frank, who was just signalling right and threading his way into the Theodor Heuss Platz roundabout. My own car was at least ten years younger than our new getaway car but far less spick and span. The Toyota looked as if it had spent its life in Frank's granny's garage except for the occasional Sunday airing. Not a scratch on the dashboard, just 12,000 kilometres on the speedo, and floormats that had been vacuumed after every outing. The glove compartment was neatly adorned with platitudinous stickers:

Carpe diem

The early bird catches the worm

It's easy to foretell the future
when you shape it yourself

I treated Stoya to a final piece of advice: 'Give my car a going-over. You won't find anything that connects me to the Eye Collector.'

'I reckon I've already got enough on you to—' I heard him say before I cut him off. Then I turned to Frank.

'You mean you had it off with—?' he started to say, but I hurriedly interrupted him by jerking my head in Alina's direction.

'Thanks for coming so quickly,' I said.

Frank gave a nod that conveyed he'd understood. 'I had to wait for a suitable moment before I could sneak out of the newsroom,' he said. He managed to stifle a yawn, but he couldn't conceal his look of fatigue. Work-related lack of sleep had imprinted dark smudges under his eyes, and the rest of his appearance reminded me of my own reflection after a night on the juice. It had taken only a few months in a newspaper office to transform the wholesome youth into a typical Internet junkie: hair unwashed, cheeks unshaven and clothing sketchy (his shoes lacked laces and all he wore beneath his anorak was a faded Depeche Mode T-shirt), but incredibly focused on his work. I doubted if he had a girlfriend who would tolerate her partner coming home at half-past two in the morning – not to sleep, just to have a quick shower before embarking on the next of his research projects for me.

'By the way,' I said, turning round in my seat, 'allow me to introduce Alina Gregoriev, the witness I told you about. The character sitting beside her is TomTom, her tail-wagging satnav.'

'Pleased to meet you,' said Frank, glancing at the rear-view mirror. 'And I'm the idiot who's allowing his boss to paddle him up shit creek.'

'Welcome to the club,' said Alina.

I put my hands up. 'No need to panic, people. I haven't been arrested or convicted, I'm merely under suspicion. In this country, no suspect is under a legal obligation to turn himself in, so none of us is currently committing an offence.'

'What about the trespassing and torture you involved me in?'

'You tortured Traunstein?' Frank gasped incredulously.

I ignored the question. 'You touched him for a moment, Alina, that's all.'

She hesitated, thinking hard, then turned to face the window and slowly shook her head.

'Nothing?' I asked her again as I had at the villa, when she removed her hands from Traunstein's shoulders. 'You really saw nothing at all?'

'No.'

'No images? No light?'

I wondered if I'd seriously counted on getting a different answer to my question from this blind girl.

'I didn't recognize him,' she said.

'Hey, hello? Anyone?' Frank changed lanes and glanced at me. 'Can someone explain what's going on here?'

'But you can't say for sure that it *wasn't* him?' I persisted.

'I can't exclude *anyone* from being the killer,' Alina retorted angrily. 'And now, can you please stop asking these stupid questions? I mean, first you call me and ask me to meet you in the woods...'

'That wasn't me,' I cut in, 'it was...'

...someone who wants to pin something on me. But why? If the Eye Collector is really trying to make me his scapegoat, why should he complicate matters by sending me this blind kook?

'... and then,' she went on, 'after I've almost broken my neck getting there, you can't remember calling me and try to throw me off your houseboat – only to lure me into a house and make me maul the father of the kidnapped children. And all this even though you believe me about as much as the police did yesterday.'

'The police? One moment...' The car swerved dangerously to the right as Frank turned his head to look at her. I grabbed the wheel and kept us from straying out of our lane.

'I don't believe this,' he said, looking ahead again. He switched on the interior light and glanced in the rear-view mirror.

'What?' Alina and I asked almost simultaneously.

It had started to sleet again.

'I know who you are,' said Frank, turning on the windscreen wipers at minimum speed. The rubber blades squeaked like fingernails on a blackboard. 'I think we ran into each other.'

53

'Really?' Alina stretched. She had removed one of her three sweaters and tossed it carelessly on the seat beside her. Beneath her remaining rollnecks I caught another glimpse of the strange tattoo and wondered what could have prompted a blind girl to go in for body art.

'It was you that blundered into me at police headquarters yesterday, wasn't it?' he demanded.

'Frank?' I cleared my throat.

'You bumped into me and didn't even turn to look.'

He changed lanes.

'Frank!'

'Anyone would think you're blind.'

'Fraaank!'

'What is it?' he asked brusquely.

'She *is* blind!'

'You're kidding...' He looked round in a hurry.

'Really?'

We both nodded and Alina opened her eyes. Two polished marbles that looked as if the corneas had been replaced by frosted glass.

'I... I never noticed,' he stammered.

'Thanks,' Alina said drily.

I turned off the interior light. For a while nothing could be heard but the monotonous hum of the engine, the hiss of tyres on wet asphalt and a sporadic squeak from the windscreen wipers.

Frank tried again. 'I mean, now you come to mention it, I do remember your cane.'

We had left Ernst-Reuter-Platz behind and were driving along Strasse des 17. Juni.

'But man, you were so purposeful. I mistook you for some kind of Nordic walker when you brushed past me.'

'I was furious.'

'You looked it.'

'How do you do it, though?' he asked. 'Yesterday you went running down the steps at police headquarters and today you get into this car unaided.'

'I'm blind, not paraplegic.'

Frank turned as puce as if she'd slapped his face. 'Sorry, I didn't mean to offend you.'

'You didn't. No more than anyone else does, anyway.'

Alina seemed aware of the slightly acidic undertone in her voice, because it had gone the next time she spoke. 'Don't worry, I've had a lifetime's practice at taking the piss out of people. For instance, if I'm trying to pick up a guy in a club where the lights are really low, I make bets with my girlfriends on how long it'll take him to notice I'm blind.' She laughed.

Frank's curiosity seemed to have been aroused. 'Know something?' he said eagerly. 'I did my national service as an orderly in a nursing home, and a group of blind people used to turn up there every Saturday. Sorry to be so blunt, but compared to you they looked kind of...' – I guessed he was going to say 'dumb', but he corrected himself before I could clear my throat again – '... well, kind of *odd.* Some of them wagged their heads and others kept rubbing their eyes. And most of their faces were stiff – like masks. I mean, they were quite expressionless, like after a Botox injection. Whereas you...'

'What about me?' Alina rested her elbows on the back of our seats and leant forwards.

'The first time I spoke to you, you nodded and raised your eyebrows. Now you're smiling and running your fingers through your hair. Which looks pretty cool, by the way.'

'Thanks,' she said, smiling more broadly. 'I've practised them.'

'What?'

'Gestures and facial expressions. I think that's the problem when blind or partially sighted people are segregated too young. My parents fought tooth and nail to prevent me from being sent to a special school after the accident. Sure, I went to a summer camp for blind kids once a year, but the rest of the time I attended an ordinary school and horsed around in the playground with my sighted friends. There were differences, of course. I had my own computer for making notes in class, and I had to cycle between two girlfriends so I could get my bearings from the sounds they made, but I *did* ride a bike.

Although I fell over more often than the others, my classmates soon got used to the sight of the little lunatic who bumped into the climbing frame in the playground but didn't let it get her down and scrambled to her feet right away.'

She sank back against the seat. With its brown loose covers and the emergency loo roll on the parcel shelf, the car could only have belonged to an old age pensioner. I would have bet a year's salary on what I would find in the glove compartment if I looked: a scrupulously maintained service record together with all the right documents and the phone numbers to call in the event of a crash or breakdown. Me, I didn't even have a regulation warning triangle in my boot.

'I don't know what it's like here in Germany, but in the States there are a lot of institutions where the blind are more or less left to themselves. If sighted kids get bored they start picking their noses, pulling faces, chucking building bricks at each other – things like that – but there's usually someone around to tell them off. When blind kids are among themselves, nobody notices if they act strangely. Often, even their supervisors are blind too. Or uninterested.'

She fondled TomTom's head. The guide dog was dozing. Like a soldier in combat, he was clearly used to grabbing some sleep whenever he could.

'By the time rubbing your eyes and rocking to and fro have become second nature, they're very hard habits to get out of. Most normal folk assume that this "hospitalism", this institutional behaviour, is part of a blind person's clinical condition and don't dare say anything. They'd find it even more embarrassing than telling a person they've got some snot dangling from their nose.'

She laughed loudly. TomTom raised his big head in surprise.

'Right from the start I was lucky enough to have the help of a good friend at nursery school. John always corrected me if I behaved oddly – if I looked sour when I was simply concentrating, or if I unconsciously rolled my eyes and made people nervous. He was my reflection, so to speak.'

I instinctively looked in the rear-view mirror and Frank glanced over his shoulder.

'He taught me gestures and facial expressions – showed me all the tricky conversational tactics.'

Alina leant forwards again. She made a moue and ran her tongue lasciviously over her lower lip, then fluttered her eyelids coquettishly with her head on one side, looking demure.

Frank, who had been watching this sample of her acting technique out of the corner of his eye, couldn't help laughing.

'It was John who taught me how to flirt.'

And lie?

The longer I spent with this girl, who was exceptional in almost every way, the more of an enigma she seemed. On the one hand, she talked rationally and gave me fascinating insights into the world of darkness in which she lived and of which I knew next to nothing; on the other, she claimed to have supernatural powers even Nicci would have been staggered by. I came to the conclusion that she was either deranged or a consummate actress.

Or both.

When I look back on those minutes in the car today, in the knowledge of all that happened later, I have to laugh at my cluelessness. But it's more of a death rattle than a laugh. The sort of hacking sound someone makes on the verge of spitting up blood.

I have to laugh because I seriously believed myself to be the master of my fate. I thought my instructions to Frank were determining our route, which ultimately led, not to Alina's Prenzlberg flat, but straight to death's door.

I was exhausted and confused, admittedly, but I thought I still had a firm grip on the reins. In reality, the Eye Collector had taken them over long ago.

It would be only a few hours before I made that agonizing discovery for myself.

52

(8 HOURS 39 MINUTES TO THE DEADLINE)

Frank spent the rest of the drive firing countless questions at Alina and me in turn. He eventually prevailed on me to give him a brief résumé of the events of the last few hours, starting with our rendezvous on the houseboat (whose exact location I concealed from him, along with my appointment with Dr Roth). I told him about the ultimatum's additional seven minutes and our fruitless incursion into Thomas Traunstein's villa.

His response to Alina's bizarre testimony turned out to be far less sceptical than mine.

'You mean you believe her?' I asked uneasily. Now that all the details she'd supplied apart from the length of the ultimatum had gone up in smoke, all I wanted was to keep my promise and take Alina home as soon as possible. Having had my fill of inexplicable phenomena for the time being, I had no wish to go chasing after any more figments of her imagination.

Frank avoided a direct answer. 'The idea of employing mediums to solve cases goes back a long way,' he said.

We had reached Brunnenstrasse and were heading for Weinberg Park.

'Leipzig's one-time police chief, Detective Superintendent Engelbrecht, carried out a paranormal experiment with a telepathically gifted person back in 1919,' Frank went on. We pulled up at the entrance, set between two brightly-lit but deserted art galleries. One of them exhibited a saddleless bicycle suspended above a flickering electric bulb, the other an old valve TV set painted pink and displaying a snowy test card. The art, if that's what they were meant to be, left me at even more of a loss than Frank's verbal diarrhoea.

'And in 1921 there even existed a Viennese institute devoted to forensic telepathic research, though only for a few months.'

'How do you know all this?' asked Alina.

'He needs a spam filter in his head,' I explained. 'He remembers every word he reads. Saves me taking a note-book when I research a story with him.'

I yawned and stretched. I wanted to get rid of Frank and Alina and head for Radow as soon as possible.

To see Nicci.

I looked at the clock on the dashboard.

And Julian.

Ten p.m.

Two hours to my son's birthday.

Even though I hadn't bought Julian a present, the least I could do was wish him a happy birthday before I surrendered myself to Stoya's tender mercies.

'The first case that really made waves in Germany was that of Minna Schmidt, the Frankfurt "dreamer", in 1921.' Frank, who showed no signs of drying up, seemed to have acquired an interested audience in Alina. Although TomTom kept thrusting his muzzle into her hand, she made no move to get out of the car.

'After two mayors of Heidelberg were murdered in quick succession, she dreamt the exact location of their bodies.'

'Coincidence.' I yawned.

'Possibly, but there are plenty of documented cases in which clairvoyants have assisted the police.' He looked at me, flushed with enthusiasm for his subject. 'Even you must have heard of one of them. The Hanns-Martin Schleyer case. You know, the captain of industry who was murdered by the Red Army Faction.'

'What of it?'

'Do you remember how *Bunte* splashed it in 1977?'

'Thanks, I'm not that old.'

'"*Clairvoyant Saw Schleyer's Hideaway*".' He grinned triumphantly. 'That was the headline. *Stern* got in on the act too, and *Spiegel* even carried an interview with Gérard Croiset, the Dutch psychic. It's on record that he was consulted by special investigators, a police psychologist, and an officer from the German armed forces, during the second week of the search for Schleyer.'

'The armed forces too?'

'They have a department for psychological defence.'

TomTom whimpered and Alina gave his head a soothing pat. The poor beast evidently needed to go again.

'The German CID were embarrassed that Croiset's involvement had become public. Two years later, however, the police psychologist confirmed that he had supplied definite clues to the high-rise building in which Schleyer had been kept hidden. According to the psychologist, his life would have been saved if the authorities had followed up Croiset's leads.'

'That's just a modern myth,' I objected.

'But not the only one. In the early 1990s alone, over a hundred so-called sensitives offered their services to the Bavarian authorities. Nationwide the figure must be much higher.' Frank turned to Alina. 'So you aren't an isolated case.'

'I don't know what I am,' she said, sounding very weary all of a sudden. 'Apart from tired.' A moment later, very quietly, she added, 'And thirsty.'

She opened her mouth as if to say something more but appeared to think better of it. Her face froze. Silently, in an almost apprehensive manner, she got out of the car.

'Something wrong?' I asked. I caught her up and repeated the question. Frank, who had also got out, was watching us intently over the top of the car. Alina seemed to have been struck by an idea and looked as if she was trying hard to banish it from her mind. She gestured to TomTom to keep still, then turned her rucksack round in order to unzip an outer pocket. I waited for a young couple to pass us, giggling and snuggling up beneath an umbrella. 'What did you think of just now?' I asked.

Just after you said you were thirsty.

'Yesterday. I stopped to drink something.'

Yesterday. After the murder!

I froze.

'I was going to tell you that earlier, but you turned off to Traunstein's place.'

'Where was it? Where did you stop?'

'In some kind of entrance. I definitely hadn't driven far.'

'How do you know?' I asked. 'I thought you had no sense of time in your visions.'

'I was still feeling exhausted.'

After putting the child in the boot...

'And my back felt moist. I was sweating. I know the sensation – I get it when I've been jogging and slow down. I know how it feels when I take a longish rest. I was still wringing wet.'

She had been rummaging in the outside pocket the whole time. At last she seemed to find what she was looking for. There was a jingling sound. Then she produced a big bunch of keys. Each was attached to a ring of a different shape, some with little projections, others with notches in them. Having felt them all in turn, she selected a medium-sized security key.

'So you drove for less than five minutes?' I hazarded.

She nodded. 'More like three. I was very thirsty, as I told you.'

'What sort of entrance was it? The entrance to a fore-court? A block of flats?'

'No, no, I got it wrong. Driveway would be a better

description – the kind we had in California. Where you park your car in front of the garage.'

'So the driveway belonged to a house?'

'Yes.'

'A terrace house?'

She shook her head. 'Detached. It was small, though. I think it was a bungalow, but I'm not quite sure.'

I thought for a moment. 'What else can you remember? Any distinctive features? Modern, pre-war? Any special colour? Was it fenced off, did it have shutters? What about the roof?'

She shook her head again. Then she suddenly stopped short and screwed up her eyes. 'A basketball hoop,' she said.

'What?'

'In the driveway. But not above the garage doors in the usual away. A little to one side, screwed to a tree on the boundary between the driveway and the neighbouring property.'

'Okay, Alina. So you drove to a house with a basketball hoop in the driveway, somewhere in the same district as Traunstein's place.' I took a step towards her. We were within touching distance now. 'What did you do there?'

51

Alina was trembling. It might just have been the cold, but I wasn't sure.

'I went into the kitchen.'

So the front door was either unlocked or she had a key.

'And got yourself something to drink?'

'Yes, a Coca-Cola.' She passed a hand nervously over her face and tucked one of her corkscrew dreadlocks behind her ear.

'You know what the bottles look like?'

'White lettering on red. Any blind person would recognize a Coca-Cola if it was put in front of them.' She laughed and pulled TomTom a little closer to her.

'Anyway, it was a can. There were four of them in a side compartment in the fridge. I helped myself to one.'

'And then?'

She shrugged. 'Nothing. That's all I can remember.'

My eyes strayed to Frank, who had been listening to her spellbound. I took advantage of the break to tell him to get back to the office in double-quick time.

'Oh please!' he groaned. 'Not now. It's just getting exciting.'

'Sorry, kid, but all hell must have broken loose there, and people will smell a rat if they can't contact my favourite trainee just when the police are looking for me.' I gave his bony shoulder a farewell pat. 'But not a word to Bergdorf, and stay near the phone in case I need your help again.'

Frank put his hand to an imaginary peaked cap, army fashion, and plodded off after saying goodbye to Alina.

I looked at my watch and proceeded to do some mental arithmetic. According to the police press release, the Traunstein children had been kidnapped early in the morning. Charlie's husband hadn't discovered her body in the garden until later, around nine a.m., or just before the stopwatch set itself going automatically at exactly nine-twenty. The Eye Collector would certainly have left the scene well before that, but I was unable to work out when the psychopath had made his pit stop.

If he ever did.

Frank had set off for the taxi rank on the next corner. I watched him go, shaking my head. The very fact that I was running another check on a blind girl's visions made me doubt my own sanity.

After taking a few steps Frank turned, shook some snowflakes out of his hair, and pulled the hood of his anorak over his head.

That was the crucial moment.

If he hadn't done that, the lunacy might have ended at that point. I would have gone to see my son before surrendering to Stoya and the subsequent course of my life would have been different. But the instant when my trainee paused outside the art gallery's window changed everything.

Everything. What I did next. My destiny.

My life itself.

As if in a trance I set off after Frank. Without turning round again, he had already reached the next intersection.

'Well, this is where I live,' I heard Alina say. She evidently thought I was still beside the car, whereas I was already standing on the spot where Frank had pulled up his hood.

Right in front of the gallery's display window.

Alina, waiting outside her block of flats, was preparing to insert the key in the front door.

'What did you say?' I said absently. I took another step towards the window, now so close to it that my breath filmed the glass. Visible in semi-profile on the television screen that had been showing a test card was an unshaven, dark-haired man waving jerkily at an invisible camera inside the gallery. I was looking at *myself*!

'I said I'm home. I'm also thirsty,' Alina replied. She smiled faintly when I turned to her. With her ramrod straight stance and her eyes shut, she looked like a girl waiting for a farewell kiss from her boyfriend. I turned away and stared straight into my own face.

It was no illusion.

The picture on the screen had momentarily changed when the young couple walked past the gallery, but I hadn't registered that until just now, when Frank turned round.

The 'installation' was filming passers-by!

'Well, mister ace reporter, how about it? Coming in for a drink?' Alina asked with a touch of impatience.

I massaged the back of my neck, surprised to find that my headache had gone until I remembered the Maxalt I'd taken. Logically, the angle from which I could see myself on the TV screen indicated that the camera must be located somewhere above me and at an angle. Sure enough, I spotted the flashing LED on the gallery ceiling and over to my left.

I sidestepped once, then again, until I was out of the camera's range. Only two seconds later the screen was again filled with snow.

'Well, thanks for the chat,' said Alina, but I continued to ignore her.

Instead, I confirmed my suspicion by testing the motion sensor a second time. I moved to the right once more, and once more the screen reacted.

'Exactly what time did the Eye Collector visit you yesterday?' I asked eagerly, but this time it was Alina who didn't answer.

When I looked at the entrance to the flats, she and TomTom had disappeared inside.

50

(8 HOURS 25 MINUTES TO THE DEADLINE)

ALINA GREGORIEV

Home again. The smell of her flat was the first reassuring sensation she'd sensed in hours.

It was a familiar blend from various rooms. The hours-old aroma of breakfast coffee lingered in the air together with that of her expensive perfume and the cheap, vinegar-based cleanser her home help swore by. Today was Thursday, and so, during her absence, the woman had overlaid the dusty odour of the books in the living room with the scent of fresh laundry.

Alina drew several deep breaths and smiled.

She hadn't smoked for once.

'Come here, doggy. You'll get something to eat right away.'

She removed TomTom's harness and knelt down to unzip her boots. She wondered as she did so if the Others always paused on entering their homes and drew several deep breaths before they removed their coats.

The Others.

She had always, throughout her life, tried to avoid being

given special treatment, not only at kindergarten but in school and especially at college. Her desire to be a normal member of society was so extreme that she'd once applied to be a lollipop lady, or, in American parlance, 'school-crossing guard' – a curiosity that had even found its way into the local news section of a Californian newspaper. The school principal had naturally rejected her request, but she was at least permitted to assist her sighted best friend. Alina was still convinced that she could have managed by herself. She could tell whether a vehicle was approaching and – more importantly – whether it was accelerating or pulling up. Most of *the Others* found that inconceivable.

The Others, who grab your arm uninvited and shepherd you across the street when mobility training has taught you how to get by without assistance.

The Others, who think that the blind recognize people by running their hands over their faces, a procedure only to be found in kitschy Hollywood movies.

The Others, of whom I'll never be one.

Alina put her rucksack down, then pulled off her red dredlock wig and deposited it on the chest of drawers in which she kept all her other wigs; her 'masks', as she called them.

A television documentary she'd chanced to see many years ago (no blind person speaks of 'listening' to TV) had made clear to Alina the extent to which hairstyles send out signals and characterize people. When asked to describe the perpetrators of crimes they'd witnessed, people tended to remember their hair, and the more noticeable this was, the better they recalled it. Psychologists ascribed this to the fact that one's eye is drawn first to a person's face and hair – hence nicknames such as 'Curly' or 'Carrot Top'.

Alina had been nineteen when she first shaved her head and startled her friends by wearing a long, dark pageboy wig. Now the possessor of some fifty different 'masks', she could transform herself, according to mood, into a peroxide blonde bimbo, a raven-haired dominatrix, or a rustic innocent in braids.

And today I felt like manga punk, she thought as she made her way along the passage and peeled off her sweaters one by one. Her maisonette comprised the fifth and sixth floors of the old apartment block and was accessible by lift. Earlier on, when she hadn't felt so sure of herself, she would use the lift to get to her consulting room on the fifth floor, but now she generally went down the narrow spiral staircase.

Alina pulled the T-shirt over her head and made her way to the bathroom, stripped to the waist. As in the homes of most blind people, everything – tables, chairs, vases – had its own allotted place, and the cleaner had strict instructions not to move anything. She also had to vacuum up every crumb. Alina liked to walk around barefoot but hated the idea of treading on anything – or in it.

It's been a fiasco, the whole thing, she thought. Not because nobody believed her. Nor because she'd turned down several patients just to go on this wild-goose chase.

But because I couldn't help the child.

The faint ticking of the old grandfather clock indicated that she'd reached the balustrade overlooking her practice's reception area.

Or children.

She wondered why she'd seen only *one* child and tried to suppress the thought that the girl might no longer be alive.

It wasn't the first time her visions hadn't been a hundred per cent accurate. Nor the first time she'd begun to doubt her gift.

Her flashbacks normally spanned a few seconds only. They were short sequences in which she saw accidents or blood-soaked bedclothes, saw her father strangling someone or her mother stirring rat poison into baby food. These distressing visions beset her sporadically, although they didn't happen every time she touched someone. That was why she guessed they occurred only when she came into physical contact with people who carried a heavy charge of negative energy. Like the classmate who hit on her at a college shindig and slapped her face when she refused to go to bed with him. He didn't let up until she told him to stop raping his sister. She informed the police at once of her suspicion but wasn't believed until the young man's body was found. He had hanged himself, but not before violating his sibling one last time.

The passage opened out and her surroundings became somewhat brighter. She paused and turned to face the wall, as she always did, running her fingers over the smooth surface that reflected the light she always left on in the bathroom across the way.

Day and night.

Most of her visitors were surprised by her apartment's light-flooded rooms and numerous mirrors, just as they wondered why her living room contained a huge photographic blow-up, two metres square, of an abandoned gold-mining town. An ex-boyfriend had given her such a graphic description of Michael von Hassel's sepia masterpiece that she could taste the dust in the dilapidated saloon on her tongue. She could also *hear* the picture whenever visitors stood in front of it, lost in admiration of the technique with which the artist had created such a breathtaking work.

As for the mirrors, Alina liked the cold, smooth feel of them under her fingertips. She also liked their reflective properties, which proved her sensitivity to light and shade: a residue of what still linked her to *the Others'* world since the explosion. Besides, she quite often entertained sighted visitors.

Slipping off her jeans, panties and socks, Alina stood naked in front of the wall mirror. A faint draught played around her ankles, and she felt herself getting gooseflesh. She put a hand to her close-shaven head and ran her forefinger over the decorative labyrinth the hairdresser had incised into the stubble at her request. Then she slid her hand down the back of her neck and fingered her tattoo, going right up to the mirror in the vain hope of discerning at least the outlines of her figure just once, for a fraction of a second, so as to compare it with the mental picture her sense of touch painted day after day.

She knew that her breasts were too small for most men's taste, but they were firm and needed no bra. Her nipples seemed to compensate for this inadequacy because all her lovers to date, both male and female, had spent an eternity stroking, squeezing or sucking them. Luckily, they were her most erogenous zone apart from her feet.

Her hand slid down to her stomach, stroked her pierced navel and strayed to her hips.

'If you were a car,' John had quipped on one occasion, 'you'd be a 1968 Mustang.' She often walked around the flat naked, simply because she felt happier without any clothes on and didn't have to put on an act with John. 'Angular and compact but timelessly elegant.'

Alina had no idea what a Mustang looked like but found this a delightful compliment, especially as her father had always driven a Ford.

Oh John...

Too bad he was away on holiday with his boyfriend. And, to make matters worse, on a backpacking tour of Vietnam, where she couldn't just call him and sob down the phone. She debated what time it was in New York, where Ivan lived, and wondered how he would react to an unexpected call from his big sister. They hadn't managed to keep in touch after she left the States for Germany. Although they undoubtedly loved one another and their annual birthday and Christmas cards came from the heart, they didn't do anything else to keep in contact.

Not a sound basis for sharing a horrific experience like mine.

Alina turned to face the bathroom. She had chosen the strongest halogen lights in the DIY superstore. John always moaned about her 'Gestapo dazzlers' whenever he stayed over at her flat, but for her they generated no more than a faint recollection of light. They did, however, help her to get her bearings when making up her face in the bathroom mirror. Her best girlfriend had shown her how to do this, but she would never get the hang of the confounded eyeliner, not in a hundred years.

She stooped to pick up her discarded clothes and went into the bathroom. While her bath was running she used a gadget that recognised colour to check whether she'd put on a white or coloured T-shirt that morning. 'White,' said a high-pitched electronic voice. The little device, which fired a beam of light at articles of clothing and identified their colour by the light's reflection, was one of the world's finest inventions apart from the Internet. At least for blind people who cared whether their nice white blouse had acquired a greenish tinge because they'd once more washed their whites and coloureds together.

Having identified the colour of her socks and panties in the same way and dropped them into the appropriate laundry basket beside the loo, Alina went out into the passage again and shut the bathroom door behind her. She could only faintly hear the water gushing into the free-standing enamel bathtub as she set off for the kitchen, where she planned to put two handfuls of dried food in TomTom's bowl.

But she never got that far. Another two steps, and her foot encountered something warm.

Something soft.

She smiled. 'Well?' she said, giving the retriever a gentle nudge with her toe. But TomTom didn't budge. Instead, his body tensed even more.

'What's the matter with you?'

She took a step to the right, meaning to walk past him, but he blocked the move.

'Aren't you hungry?'

She bent down and tried to pat him, but he didn't lick her hand in the usual way.

'What is it?'

He's rigid, concentrating hard. He refuses to be distracted because...

She shivered suddenly.

TomTom had been trained – at a cost of 20,000 euros – to prevent his owner from having accidents. From unprotected obstacles, potholes, open manholes.

But there's nothing like that on the way to my kitchen.

'Come on, let me pass,' she said, trying to thrust him aside. But TomTom did something unique in her experience.

He started to growl.

The ominous sound mingled with the monotonous murmur of the bathwater, creating an almost hypnotic atmosphere.

What the devil's going on? Alina felt her body stiffen like the dog's. She had suddenly noticed what TomTom had clearly sensed some time earlier: the familiar smell of her flat had undergone a change. It had taken on a masculine note.

Cinnamon. Cloves. Alcohol.

A man's strong aftershave.

'Hello?' she called, her voice puncturing the murmuring sounds. She almost vomited with terror when she felt his breath on her ear.

'Stop playing,' he said in a low voice.

The man, who had appeared from nowhere, laid his hand on her bare shoulder. Almost tenderly, which made it infinitely worse. At the same time, she felt a cold, metallic object prod her cheek.

Alina swung round and lashed out impotently. She drew a deep breath in preparation for the cry that slowly took shape in her throat and emerged as a guttural roar. She aimed a second blow at thin air, turned anticlockwise, and lost her balance, knocking a vase off a chest of drawers. The heavy lead glass vessel landed on her foot and forced another cry from her lungs.

The unbearable pain coincided with something else: her eyes were flooded with light.

Bright as a flash of lightning. Like an overexposed photo...

Then she fell to the floor.

And into the depths of another vision.

ALINA GREGORIEV (VISION)

The room is dark and the sick woman isn't alone. Someone can be heard breathing in a bed nearby. At least one other person in the room is dying like her.

Dying.

Without a doubt.

The smell of disinfectant is no match for the perfume of death, the stench of rancid breath, suppurating bedsores and watery excreta.

'Here I am again,' she hears herself whisper in a man's voice.

Quickly, breathlessly. Hoarsely.

The woman, who has her mother's eyes but is unknown to her, doesn't answer. How can she, when there's a transparent mask over her face?

The device resembles a shadow Alina can't interpret, probably because it's unfamiliar to her. Because she never saw one as a three year old or can't remember doing so.

Something in the room is beeping, like a digital alarm clock left to its own devices.

A door behind her creaks open and the room grows lighter. Someone claps their hands. 'How nice of you to look in again,' says a woman's resonant voice. A shadowy figure flits over to the other bed behind her.

A rustling sound. A current of air created by the raising and lowering of bedclothes. Pillows are plumped. Someone moans.

Alina reaches for the hand on the bed; grey, papery skin on a starched white sheet.

The sick woman's chest slowly rises and falls. There are times when her heart seems to debate whether or not to go on beating.

Leaning forward, she brushes a strand of hair off the old woman's forehead and kisses her.

Gives her arm a final squeeze before she goes.

And then, at about the same moment as the siren goes off in the distance, she turns to the bedside table and straightens a small, rectangular object.

A photo frame.

The picture in it shows neither father nor mother, so it can only be of a child. A boy or a girl. The shadowy form in the photo is impossible to identify. She can only make out the eyes. Or rather, the eye. The other is invisible.

Or not there at all.

She turns and looks at the open door. The siren grows louder. At the same time, the world around her darkens...

The flashes of light turn back into black specks, and

the black specks combine to form a shroud of all-embracing darkness...

... in which Alina recovers consciousness, roused by the burglar alarm of the art gallery six floors below. And by someone hammering on her front door.

48

(8 HOURS 17 MINUTES TO THE DEADLINE)

ALEXANDER ZORBACH

She opened the door in the nick of time. Another moment, and the bulky thing would have slipped through my bleeding fingers. I had climbed the stairs, misjudging not only my physical condition but the weight of the machine I'd stolen from the gallery.

Alina let me in without a word, trembling all over.

I put the HD-DVD recorder down. 'What's happened?' she asked dully. I might have asked her the same thing.

As if it weren't enough that she was facing me stark naked and making no move to cover herself, she had suddenly lost all her hair as well. That was accounted for by the wig on the chest of drawers beside the door. But far more disconcerting was the fear that I sensed in every fibre of her body. She was breathing fast, with her arms hanging limp at her sides and her hands trembling uncontrollably. For one who attached such importance to expression, her face now resembled a rigid mask. She had been weeping. Big fat tears had rolled down her cheeks, streaking them with eye shadow and accentuating her doll-like appearance.

I reached for her instinctively, but she retreated a step.

'Don't touch me,' she whispered, fending me off with both hands.

'What's the matter?' I asked.

'He was here.'

'Who?'

'Who the hell do you think?!' she yelled, and I felt almost glad she was capable of such an outburst. Blazing anger was preferable to fear. 'The swine had his knife with him. The knife he uses to...' She left the rest unsaid. It wasn't necessary.

I ran my eyes over her naked body to see if the Eye Collector had injured her anywhere, but all I saw was the rather too thin but undeniably shapely figure of a young woman whom I would, under other circumstances, have found sexually attractive. Correction: whom I found sexually attractive even under present circumstances, though I swiftly suppressed the thought.

'Where did he go?' I demanded, setting off along the passage. The confounded burglar alarm died away at last.

'Don't bother,' Alina called after me. 'He's gone.' She folded her arms over her breasts with one hand covering the strange tattoo on her neck. In the gloomy passage it looked like a big birthmark.

'How do you know?'

'Because TomTom has stopped reacting.' I looked down the passage to the door of what I assumed, from the sound of running water, to be the bathroom. The dog was lying outside it in a sphinx-like pose. His tail thumped the floor in welcome.

'He can't scent danger any more. Besides, the balcony door is open, I can tell by the draught. I think he must have gone down the fire escape.'

I approached the bathroom door. Clouds of steam were drifting out into the passage. I peered through the haze.

Nothing.

Nothing of note except an old-fashioned enamel bathtub on the point of overflowing.

I turned off the tap and and nearly scalded my hand extracting the bath plug. As I went out I caught sight of some make-up articles on the shelf in front of the brightly lit bathroom cabinet. This surprised me, but now wasn't the time to dwell on it.

'What did he want?' I asked.

'To persuade us to stop.'

Alina briefly described what had given her such a shock minutes earlier. '"Stop playing," he told me. He could only have meant his sick game of hide-and-seek.' She broke off. 'And you? Why have you come back?'

'I need your TV set.'

She presented her right ear to me, a gesture that assured me of her full attention.

'What for?'

I told her about the camera in the art gallery. 'It films anyone who passes the door of this building,' I concluded.

'So?'

'It's hooked up to a DVD recorder.' I pointed along the

passage to where I'd left it – stupidly, since she couldn't see me. 'A gadget like that can store up to 172 hours of pictures, probably more.'

'Shit, don't tell me *you* set off the alarm down there.'

'Amazing what you can do with a loose cobblestone.' I tried to inject a smile into my voice. 'Come on, it'll only be a matter of minutes before the police put two and two together and ring your doorbell.'

She shook her head and drew a deep breath. A little more of her physical tension seemed to leave her. Although she probably wouldn't have admitted it, even to herself, I sensed that she found my presence reassuring.

'I must be nuts,' she said, but she set off towards her TV.

I followed her once I had hurried back to the chest of drawers and retrieved the heavy HD-DVD recorder. The cut I'd sustained when smashing the gallery window had stopped bleeding.

Our route through the flat, which was surprisingly brightly light, led past the bathroom and into a living room with an open kitchen adjoining it. I noticed only now that the flat was a duplex.

Swiftly and unerringly avoiding a downwards-leading spiral staircase, Alina opened a door on the far side of the living room. TomTom had trotted after us but hunkered down beside the living-room sofa.

'Aren't you going to put something on?' I asked when we were standing in what was readily identifiable as her bedroom. I was once again surprised by all the mirrors, one of them even on the ceiling.

'Why?' she demanded, calmly walking over to the big television set facing the bed.

'You're naked,' I said. *And I'm only human,* I added in my head.

'The central heating's on,' she replied tersely.

She bent down to remove the plug of her DVD player. I didn't know where to look for a moment, not wanting to feel like a voyeur. Piercings and tattoos didn't grab me as a rule, and shorn heads, even if shaved into a labyrinthine pattern, weren't high on my scale of what I considered attractive.

Although Charlie had once tried to explain to me how close sex was to pain, I'd never been able to comprehend this SM fetish idea. Well, perhaps she'd been right. Perhaps sexual desire really could interact, not only with pain but with death itself. That was the only way I could account for my urge, at this of all moments, to touch Alina's bare flesh, when my senses should have been entirely focused on the thought of escaping from a serial killer.

And from the police!

In any event, it wasn't common sense but my sad recollection of Charlie that reminded me of what I had to concentrate on next.

Alina got to her feet again and surrendered the television set to me. It took me only a few seconds to hook up the HD-DVD recorder.

'Did you really have to smash the gallery window? The artists who own the place are really nice people.'

She handed me the remote control and I switched the AV feed on the television.

'I had no option. I'd called Stoya and invited him to watch a video on which the Eye Collector may be visible.'

'And?'

I sighed. 'He refused to waste his time on my diversionary tactics.'

I looked up at Alina, who was now perched on the edge of the bed. She was so slim, there wasn't a sign of a crease in her tummy even though she wasn't sitting up particularly straight.

'So I'll have to check it myself. When did the man turn up here?'

'Just after three.'

'And when did you get rid of him?'

'A few minutes later.'

'He left, just like that?'

'Yes. That surprised me too. He must have noticed something. I was scared stiff when the vision suddenly broke off. I said something about a migraine and asked him to leave, which he promptly did. Rather odd, don't you think? He didn't even ask for his money back.'

I set the hard-disk recorder's timer at 3.10 p.m., hoping that this would be neither too far after the event nor so far in advance that I would waste time viewing useless footage.

3.10 p.m. yesterday? I thought. *I was in the paper's underground car park. I had just made myself comfortable on the back seat of my Volvo, intending to take a nap, but I'd had so little sleep in the previous few days, I slept until the five-o'clock conference.*

It took me only a few minutes to find the relevant place. The recorder didn't operate during fallow periods, luckily, so it only stored what the camera actually shot. Although I still couldn't fathom what the installation had to do with art, I made a mental note to compensate the gallery owners for the damage as soon as I was in a position to do so.

If I ever was.

I stared in disbelief at the picture before my eyes and forgot to blink. It wasn't until Alina spoke to me that I realized I must have been sitting there like a stuffed dummy, gazing at the screen for a considerable time.

'Well?' she asked. 'What can you see?'

Shit. It can't be true.

My mouth went dry as I cast about for a plausible reply.

'See anything?'

'Yes,' I said hoarsely, but I didn't want to betray the truth. 'No... I mean... I'm not sure,' I stammered helplessly. That was a lie. Of course I'd seen *something*, but I couldn't possibly tell Alina what it was, not right now. I welcomed her blindness for the first time. It meant she couldn't see what I could: that the fellow in the green parka and the down-at-heel Timberland boots – the one whose figure the HD-DVD recorder was currently projecting on the television screen – bore a strong resemblance to someone well known to me.

Someone *very* well known to me.

Myself.

47

It was a while before I recovered my composure. Before the blood stopped roaring in my ears and the sensation returned to my fingers.

'I can't see his face,' I said, which was true. The man, who had my slightly stooped way of walking and was imitating my mode of dress, had pulled the hood of the parka over his head.

Something I would never do. Not even in the rain!

I tried to freeze-frame another picture by zapping back and forth, but the view didn't improve. It was quite impossible to tell whether the man's height and build were similar to mine because he was too far away from the display window.

But he's wearing my parka. My jeans. My boots.

A fist seemed to clench inside my stomach. The sight of the vague figure on the screen had triggered a disturbing déjà-vu.

'No idea who he is,' I said, feeling like I was lying under oath at court.

'But it proves he was here,' said Alina. She was either feeling cold after all or had changed her mind for some other reason. Whatever the truth, she was now standing in front of an open wardrobe and removing various articles of clothing with slow, deliberate movements.

'No, it only proves that *someone* left your building around the time in question.'

I pressed the 'Play' button in the hope that the unknown man would make a mistake and inadvertently turn to face the camera. Not a bit of it. Probably because of the sleet blowing into his face, he walked on with his head down, eyes fixed on the pavement. But then, just before he disappeared from the camera's field of view, it happened.

The collision.

Perhaps because he looked neither right nor left, he failed to see the guitar case lying at an angle to his line of advance. He must have trodden in it, because some coins cascaded on to the pavement and a scrawny, emaciated young man made his furious appearance on the screen.

'Your patient is having words with a beggar,' I told Alina.

'This beggar – what does he look like?' she asked.

'Medium height. Dark, straggly hair but not too much of it, and he's holding a guitar.'

'I know the man.'

I turned to her. 'Who is he?'

'A busker. Plays here every other day. I always give him something, though I've never heard anyone sing more off-key.'

'Do you own a printer?' I asked, momentarily forgetting what a stupid question that was.

'No, and my set-up doesn't include a PlayStation either.'

We couldn't help smiling, either of us. At least Alina saw the funny side. I took out my mobile and quickly reinserted the battery but left the phone in flight mode so it couldn't log on to a network and betray my position to Stoya.

Always assuming the cops hadn't located me long ago.

Then I photographed the television screen. After three attempts I had a passable, flicker-free photo of the street musician and one of my unknown doppelgänger.

'Ready?' I heard Alina ask behind me. I turned round to find her fully clothed. She was wearing jeans with leather patches and a red-and-brown checked lumberjack shirt knotted over her midriff. In keeping with her new look, her feet were shod in down-at-heel cowboy boots that looked a size too big.

'Oh no, I'm not dragging you any deeper into this business,' I said, still rather confused by her abrupt transformation. The left-wing hipster had turned into Annie Oakley.

'Don't talk bullshit. You think I'm staying here by myself?'

She made her way out of the bedroom and back down the long passage to the front door with such speed and assurance, I had trouble keeping up with her.

'Here, TomTom, we've got to go out again,' she called. Ignoring my objections, she opened the chest of drawers and deftly identified several wigs by touch. It took her only a moment to decide on a blonde bob with a graduated fringe.

Then, having put on TomTom's harness with a few practised movements, she took a fur-lined cord jacket from a hook, went to the door, and opened it. The fact that she kept her eyes shut throughout these procedures made her look like a sleepwalker.

'This is crazy,' I said, more to myself than to her.

'Maybe.' She donned the jacket and turned up the collar. 'But if we hang around here much longer the police will appear.' She went out on to the landing and the glaring, sensor-operated ceiling lights came on. 'And then I won't be able to take you to that busker you saw just now.'

46

(7 HOURS 31 MINUTES TO THE DEADLINE)

ALEXANDER ZORBACH

Some witless PR consultant must once have convinced Paris Hilton of the necessity always to stand sideways-on to the camera with her chin pointing bosomwards and a spuriously coquettish grin on her face. The elderly barkeep, who had been warily eyeing us ever since we entered his deserted establishment, was standing behind the counter in a similar pose: leaning on his right elbow with his chin on his chest and his head in semi-profile. His rimless glasses had slipped down his nose, accentuating his look of condescension.

'Hi, Paris,' I said. Even I realized that I'd tried to break the ice with better quips in my time. The guy didn't bat an eyelid, and I doubted he'd ever heard of the hotel heiress.

Alina, who evidently knew her way around the gloomy dump, felt for a stool and sat down. Still hoping to break the ice, I was about to boost the bar's turnover by ordering some drinks when he got in first.

'Know why this world is going to the dogs?'

That intro's no better than mine, I thought, but I refrained from saying so. I knew from experience that you never interrupted a barman you wanted some information from, no matter what bullshit he talked.

'Fashion,' he said with a portentous nod, his rheumy eyes straying to Alina's cowpoke jeans. 'Goddamned fashion, that's what's ruining us.'

There was a longish silence. 'Uh-huh,' I said dutifully, but it was as I'd feared: the man had far from finished his lecture.

'What does it mean when things go out of fashion? Something that still works gets thrown away just because it's got a little scratch on it.'

He slapped the counter with the flat of his hand.

'This counter here is sixty years old. It's stood up to a lot of things in its time. Glasses, bottles – it's even fractured the odd skull.' He chuckled reminiscently. 'Yes, people have done plenty on this counter. Danced, fought, slept, fucked...'

Out of the corner of my eye I saw Alina smile faintly.

'So it isn't the finest bar counter in Berlin, but it's okay. It's good for another sixty years, like the rest of this stuff.'

He made a sweeping gesture, familiar to me from those scenes in movies where a father tells his son 'All this will be yours one day.' In this case, 'all' comprised of some grimy curtains, several ochre-coloured wooden chairs with worn upholstery, a decrepit pinball machine, and an assortment of booze that probably wouldn't have fetched more than 2,000 euros.

'Nothing in here is broken, so why should I replace it?'

Perhaps because you wouldn't be your only customer at this hour?, I thought, but I could tell where he was going.

'"Lounge bar furniture" – that's what some limp-wristed interior decorator advised me to invest in. "Club sofas" that customers can "chill" on. That's the "in" thing, apparently.'

I couldn't remember when I'd last seen a look of such revulsion on anyone's face.

'What the hell's so good about a bar where you trip over people's legs?'

I shrugged, trying to sneak a glance at my watch. The bar was only two streets away from the gallery.

'We use up our raw materials, suck the planet dry like leeches, chuck away things that are still in perfect working order. My dumb fuck of a nephew bought three new mobile phones last year alone. And for what?'

'Fashion,' I said, thankful that he'd let me speak at last. I was now on the same wavelength. Genuinely so, as a matter of fact. I'd had my ear bent by dumber bar room philosophers, so it was a pleasant change.

'Okay, what are you having?' he asked, finally treating us to a nicotine-stained smile.

'Two G and Ts,' I said. 'And we'd like a word with this guy here.'

I held out my mobile. The barkeep stared at it in surprise, then adjusted his reading glasses.

'This mobile's over four years old,' I lied, nipping any criticism in the bud.

'And it still takes perfect pictures,' he said with an approving nod.

I smiled. 'Do you recognize the man?'

'Linus? Sure.'

Linus? I glanced at Alina, glad to have followed her suggestion. 'Know where I can find him?'

The elderly barkeep's smile widened. 'In there.'

He jerked his head at a door in the far corner of the murky bar. A door with two crossed pool cues over it.

'Okay if I have a word with him?'

'If you must, but I'm afraid you're too late.'

'Too late?' I looked at the barkeep enquiringly. He wasn't smiling any more.

'Go on in, but don't say I didn't warn you.'

45

(7 HOURS 26 MINUTES TO THE DEADLINE)

TOBY TRAUNSTEIN (AGED 9)

They had once bet which of them could stay underwater longest. It was just after the school trip to the public baths, when they should really have been taking a shower. Kevin had bet his entire Panini album on the result.

Toby's throat was parched. He swallowed hard, then greedily sucked in some air from the darkness around him. It was getting harder and harder to inhale. He was reminded of drinking a thick milkshake through a straw. Breathing had become as difficult as that.

Kevin's Panini album had been at stake!

His own was nowhere near complete.

So they'd made this bet.

Me, Jens and Kevin.

Although...

He really should have put it the other way round. Kevin, Jens, and me.

Or Jens first.

Only donkeys put themselves first, he thought as he reinserted the coin in the head of the screw.

He'd been told that by Frau Quandt, their German teacher, who had read the story about the thirsty shipwrecked sailor with them. The guy who kept biting his tongue to produce spit.

Toby clamped his teeth together even harder.

Crap idea. It doesn't work.

He coughed despite himself and the coin slipped out again.

Effing screw. Effing darkness. Effing Frau Quandt.

Still no spit. His tongue hurt more, but that was all. It was really sore and it felt like a strip of leather. And his head was buzzing the way it had when he stayed underwater too long, just to win that stupid album.

Which he hadn't won, any more than he'd managed to open this padlock.

Four turns, he'd counted. Maybe even five. Then the coin with which he'd been unscrewing the screw in the lock had slipped through his fingers and he'd fallen asleep while looking for it. Now he didn't know how long he'd slept for in this everlasting darkness. If his head wasn't aching so much, he wouldn't have known he'd woken up at all.

He replaced the coin in the groove and managed another half-turn.

Shit, why am I sweating so much the coin keeps slipping through my fingers, whereas my mouth is as dry as...

Yes, as dry as what? He felt empty all of a sudden. His head was buzzing and he was too tired to think of a suitable word.

As the bottom of a bird cage, he wanted to say, but it didn't make sense.

Toby flinched when he heard a hysterical laugh. Then he realized that he was the one giggling.

He licked the sweat off his upper lip and knew it was a mistake. Like in the story of the shipwrecked sailor who drank sea water and only felt thirstier. He had wondered at the time why the man on the raft hadn't drunk his own blood.

But that was probably as dumb an idea as fiddling with this padlock.

He would never get out of here. Never be able to open the thing he was inside.

Whatever that is.

He would suffocate and sweat to death at the same time.

Hee-hee!

Toby giggled. *Sweat to death... Can you actually do that?*

Click!

He froze.

Click!

A creaking sound, then a last, somewhat fainter click.

He propped himself on his elbows and braced his head against the yielding surface above him. He had once more lost the coin that had served him as a screwdriver, but that was immaterial now. He couldn't stop laughing.

His laughter grew louder by the second and culminated in a loud cry of triumph.

Done it!

First he'd heard it; now he could feel it. The padlock had sprung open and was hanging by its shackle alone. Although his fingers were trembling, they didn't slip off the padlock when he detached it. He felt for the eye through which the shackle had passed and found there were *two* of them. *Two* wafer-thin slabs of metal with holes in the ends.

Everything went very quickly after that.

Toby grasped that they were the pull tabs of a zip fastener that ran lengthwise above him. Because the zip had been hidden beneath a strip of material, he had mistaken the projection for an unimportant seam. In reality, it was...

...the way out?

He held his breath and mobilized the last reserves of energy in his scrawny body.

Then, with sweaty fingers, he tried to pull the tabs apart.

No problem.

This is great, he told himself, pulling the tabs ever further apart. The zip's sliders glided along as smoothly as skates across an ice rink.

He was about to utter another cry of triumph when he felt the plastic film overhead. His spirits sank as quickly as they had revived.

Good news, bad news. Easy come, easy go.

He had opened the zip but not the rubbery sheath into which he had evidently been sealed. The thing that had almost exhausted his air supply.

He dug his forefinger into the film and felt it give way without tearing. It stretched but didn't break, like chewing gum when you tried to scratch it off the sole of your shoe.

His eyes filled with tears. He sobbed and cried for his mother.

Not for Dad, the old fart. But Mum. I wish Mum was here.

With a strength born of despair he grabbed hold of the two flaps of material above him...

It's a bag! I'm sealed up in a plastic bag.

...and yanked them in opposite directions.

Once, twice. The third time he uttered a yell that drowned the faint tearing sound.

Bloody hell, I've done it!

The film had parted. Quite suddenly. He couldn't see or feel it, but he could smell it. The air smelt...

...different.

He thought he was yelling, but the throaty, whistling sounds he made were intakes of breath.

He propped himself on his elbows. His head was in the open now. He could sit up straight.

Avidly, he drew in great gulps of air. Although still thin, it was considerably richer in oxygen than the interior of his previous place of confinement.

Once his initial euphoria had subsided, however, he felt even more wretched than he had done minutes earlier.

Where am I now?

He crawled on all fours out of the container in which he'd been imprisoned.

He was out of his original prison.

And now?

He tried to stand up, but he was so weak he managed to stay on his feet for a second or two only. Then his knees buckled.

While falling, all he could tell about his new surroundings was that he still couldn't see a thing.

Not a thing.

It was just as dark in there, wherever 'there' was, as it had been before.

Total darkness. There's no difference.

Apart, perhaps, from the fact that his new prison had a bit more headroom, because he'd been able to stand erect.

And the walls aren't soft any more, he thought. Then his head hit the floor.

44

(7 HOURS 24 TO THE DEADLINE)

ALEXANDER ZORBACH

He's dead.

That was my first thought. My second was why the barkeep, who had accompanied us into the windowless back room, should be smiling so benevolently when a body was decomposing on his pool table.

The man we were looking for lay sprawled across the green baize with his head hanging limply over the rail nearest to us, between the end and centre. His eyes were wide open and a thread of reddish spittle was oozing from his mouth. The spreading pool of blood beneath his chest did not look too fresh.

'What smells so bad in here?' Alina asked in disgust, one hand over her mouth and nose.

'I, I don't know exactly, but I think...'

'He's really had it, hasn't he?' the barkeep said with a contented laugh. I retreated a step and trod on his foot. While wondering if we'd left any fingerprints in the bar and whether the police would be able to nail me for this murder as well, I activated my mobile.

'Don't touch anything,' I told Alina as I keyed in the SIM code.

I was about to call the police when the phone nearly jumped out of my hand. The vibration alarm signalled several messages and a new call that was just coming in.

'Hello? Alex?'

Damn it. Nicci!

This wasn't, of course, an appropriate time for a conversation with my wife, but I'd inadvertently pressed the wrong key and now she was on the line.

'At last. Thank goodness, I've been trying to reach you for hours.'

She sounded anxious. Filled with foreboding, I suddenly felt lousier than the barroom décor.

'It's Julian. He's not too well.'

Oh no...

For a moment everything and everyone were secondary. Alina, TomTom, the barkeep – not even a corpse counts for anything when your own flesh and blood is in trouble. The signal was very weak. I could only hear snatches of what Nicci was saying, so I left the back room without a word to the others.

'What's the matter with him?' I asked when my mobile's display showed four bars again.

'He's coughing. I'm afraid it's getting worse.'

My stomach twisted itself into a knot.

'Is he running a temperature?'

'Yes, I think so.'

Meaning what? Since when does a thermometer register vague hunches instead of degrees Celsius?

I suppressed an acid remark. After all, I should have been there for our son's birthday, not spending my time with a blind girl, a dead body and a crazy barman.

'The last time I took his temperature it was 38.9 degrees,' she said.

I felt relieved. 'That's only borderline,' I said. A bit higher than it should be, but far from a high fever.

Nicci surprised me by asking a sensible question. 'Should I call the doctor?'

I heard Alina say something in the room next door. The barkeep gave another laugh.

'Yes, do that,' I told her. I thought she was being over-anxious, to be honest. Still, better safe than sorry. 'But please don't go private. They always send some quack who tries acupuncture first.'

I was relaxing a little. Julian didn't sound too bad and his mother hadn't – for once – called in a faith healer.

'What have you got against acupuncture?' Nicci demanded.

'Nothing.' I snapped. 'It just isn't my first choice when it comes to treating the sick.'

Nicci seemed deaf to the anger in my voice. The corpse we'd just discovered in the adjoining room surfaced in my mind once more.

'Oh, Zorro,' she said, using a pet name I hadn't heard her use for ages, 'what's your problem?' She sighed. 'Why do you always sound so bitter when we talk together?'

What's my problem? Furiously, I switched the phone from one ear to the other. *You want to know what my problem is? Okay, I'll tell you.*

'I'm feeling rather annoyed, darling. That's because I'm hunting a sicko who seems to be trying to pin his serial murders on me, and the only person who can exonerate me is a blind girl who claims she can see into the past. *That's* my problem.'

Quite apart from the rotting corpse in the poolroom next door.

I looked in that direction. The barman hadn't moved, so he couldn't have got at Alina in the meantime.

'A blind girl?'

I shut my eyes. How could I have been stupid enough to broach such a subject? I might as well have handed Nicci an invitation to a séance. Now that her interest had been aroused, she would bombard me with questions ad infinitum.

'She's a medium, right?'

'Forget what I said.'

I went to the bar room entrance and put the chain on the door to prevent any potential customers from bursting in on this madhouse.

'Listen to me, Zorro. This is very important, you hear?'

'Darling, I really can't talk now!'

I heard a pool cue fall to the floor, then Alina murmuring something. Meanwhile, Nicci was saying, 'I know you don't believe in these things – things we can't explain – and that's your privilege, but—'

'I've really got to...'

I glanced at the poolroom. The barkeep had disappeared from view.

'You must stay away from her.'

'What? Why?'

I couldn't hear a word after that, neither from Alina nor from the barman. Instead, a protracted, heavy snoring sound came drifting out into the taproom.

'I've told you a thousand times,' Nicci was saying, but her voice had melted into the background like the ominous film music that accompanies the hero to his doom.

Except that I'm not an actor.

'You attract evil like a magnet. You only wrote about it before, but now it's all around you...'

True. It's with me here and now...

'... and it'll destroy you, Alex. I don't know this blind girl, but I can sense she's involving you in something you'll never be able to escape from, understand?'

'Yes,' I said. For one thing because she'd unwittingly put her finger on the truth. I really did feel like someone sinking ever deeper into quicksand the more he struggled. For another, because I had to cut this conversation short.

'Keep away from all forms of negative energy, Alex. Don't provoke evil or it'll destroy you. Come home – come home for Julian's birthday!'

So saying, Nicci hung up and left me alone with the madhouse otherwise known as my life.

With Alina, TomTom and the barkeep.

And the corpse, which gave me a wave as I went back into the poolroom.

43

'Woshuwon'?'

The dead man, who had until recently been sprawled across the baize in a welter of blood with his neck broken, was now sitting on the edge of the pool table, dribbling. He was also engaged in other activities which murder victims normally can't manage. Breathing, for example. And speaking, albeit in a language I didn't understand.

'Karnaguy'avakip?'

My eyes strayed to Alina, who had pulled up a chair and was sitting not far from the pool table. TomTom, lying at her feet, yawned. Linus did likewise a few moments later.

'I thought he was...' I broke off and rubbed my eyes. My headache had suddenly returned with a vengeance. There was a rectangular, lace-curtained lampshade over the pool table, and although the bulbs inside didn't generate much more light than a few candles, they had dazzled me when I made the mistake of looking straight at them.

'I thought he was dead,' I said, completing my sentence with an effort. Multicoloured UFOs danced before my eyes as I looked at the barkeep.

'Dead? Nonsense, Linus always sleeps with his eyes open. It isn't his only trick, as I'm sure you've noticed.'

I nodded, brushing the baize with my hand as I made my way round the table. It was dawning on me that I'd completely misinterpreted the scene in my agitation. The 'bloodstain' was an old one – either the result of an overturned beer glass or possibly bodily fluid of some kind. It definitely wasn't the squalid street musician's lifeblood, because he was unscathed, and his bloodstained spittle stemmed from a serious but far from fatal gum infection. As for the unremitting stench of a corpse, that appeared to be his natural body odour. A blend of excrement, urine, sweat and grime, it was testimony to life on the Berlin streets.

'Phosiapatikil',' Linus proclaimed with a portentous air when I was standing directly in front of him.

Looking into his emaciated face and trying to establish eye contact with him, I was reminded of why so many people are mistakenly pronounced dead. Only two months earlier I'd written a piece about a woman who had leapt off the autopsy table in a leading Berlin hospital. Linus's eyes were as lifeless as Alina's.

'What happened to him?' I asked.

'I already told your girlfriend,' the barkeep replied, but he clearly relished an audience and seemed only too willing to repeat himself. 'Linus used to be a star performer. He played with various bands in big venues – even at the old Wembley Stadium in England, so he says.'

Linus gave the sort of approving nod a person gives

when talking about the good old days, when all was still well with the world.

'They say his manager took him for a ride – paid him in drugs instead of cash. The poor devil wound up not only broke but completely bananas. He swallowed one pill too many or shot up once too often and just collapsed after a gig. He's been talking a lingo of his own ever since.'

'Woshuwon', eh?' said Linus, seemingly in confirmation.

'Anyway, he did a spell in a loony bin somewhere in the Grunewald, but he came out goofier than he went in, believe me.'

I went up to Linus, who was still perched on the edge of the pool table but swaying precariously.

'Can you hear me?' I asked.

He shrugged.

Okay, here goes. The most he can do is spit in my face.

I risked it and showed him the photo on my mobile. It was the shot of his encounter with the unknown man.

'Do you remember this guy?' I asked. Linus's shoulder-shrugging became more violent. Sudden fury carved deep furrows in his brow and he started to pluck at his few remaining strands of hair.

'Wankabumpami!' he said. He repeated the meaningless word several times in succession.

'Any idea what that means?' Alina asked the barman.

'None.' He laughed. 'I don't speak Druggy.'

'Wankakikmigit!' said Linus, who was far less amused.

If my eyes hadn't deceived me, he'd just pulled out a long hair and stuffed it into his mouth.

'He's talking about his guitar case, isn't he?' I said.

'Could be. If anyone can translate his gibberish it's the girl who goes around with him.' The barkeep's's gaze strayed to Alina, then lingered on the dog. 'But she's got a screw loose too, if you know what I mean. Calls herself Yasmin Schiller and was in the same loony bin, but on the staff. She often sits at the bar and goes on about their plans to form a band together – things like that. Anyway, Yasmin told me Linus mixes up different words in the wrong order. His head's like a cocktail shaker, she says.'

He gave another laugh.

Linus's eyes glazed over. I wondered if he still grasped we were talking about him.

'For instance, he often says "Eetmaishiwanka." Must have something to do with wankers.'

'Of whom there are plenty in his life, no doubt,' Alina put in.

Linus turned to her. 'Wankakikmigit!' he said again. It sounded as if he were requesting confirmation of his statement, but only TomTom was paying much attention to him. The retriever gazed intently at the busker with his tongue lolling out.

'What did you show him just now?' The barkeep had removed his glasses, which were dangling from the corner of his mouth. He was so close I could smell his bad breath. 'Can I see?'

I handed over the phone, remembering too late that the

man in the picture bore a strong resemblance to me. However, the barkeep took a cursory glance at the miniature screen and didn't seem to notice.

'The guy with Linus is a professional conman,' I said, quickly concocting an innocuous story. 'That picture of him bumping into Linus was caught by a CCTV camera yesterday. We thought Linus might be able to give us some more pointers.'

'And who would you be?'

Suddenly alert, the barkeep's eyes darted from me to Alina and back. I produced my press pass from the hip pocket of my jeans. 'We're writing a story about the man.'

He guffawed loudly, then pointed to Alina. 'Oh, sure, and the blind girl's your photographer, right?'

Unable to think of an appropriate retort in time, I felt caught out. The barkeep seemed unworried.

'I couldn't care less who you are. Just as long as that bastard in the picture isn't a pal of yours.'

'No way.' Alina and I spoke almost simultaneously.

I put my press pass away and took the phone back. It was moist from the barkeep's fingers.

'All right,' he said. 'I'll tell you something about that shit in the picture.'

'You know him?'

The Eye Collector?

'No. But yesterday afternoon, around four, Yasmin came in here. She was hopping mad – cussing and swearing about some arsehole who'd had a spat with Linus. The guy had kicked his guitar case.'

Wankakikmigit.

I looked at Alina, who had gone down on one knee and was patting TomTom. She nodded to convey that she was thinking the same as me.

The time and place both fit. It was the man on the tape.

'Linus's takings were scattered across the pavement – a whole day's worth, I reckon. An hour later he came in and spent it all on booze.' The barkeep nodded at Linus. 'With obvious results.'

'This girl Yasmin,' I said, 'where can I find her?'

'Do I look like an effing social secretary? I don't keep my customers' appointments diaries. Sometimes she drops in every day, sometimes not for two or three weeks.'

Terrific.

I'd just decided that we'd wasted far too much time barking up the wrong tree when there was a loud smack.

Everyone in the room gave a start. Everyone but Linus.

'Wankaparkatikki!' He gave the edge of the pool table another slap with the flat of his hand.

'Yes, yes, I know,' said the barkeep, turning to go. 'Come on, Linus, I'll stand you a coffee. There may even be some sausages left in the kitchen.'

He clearly considered the conversation at an end. Telling Alina to stay put, I followed him into the taproom and barred his path before he reached the counter.

'What did Linus say just then?'

The old man stared at my hand, which was gripping his shoulder, then looked me in the eye. He didn't speak until I'd let go of him.

'Linus is still furious with the guy, but not because he kicked his guitar case, nor because he had to spend half an hour looking for his coins in the gutter.'

'So why?'

'Because he'd left his car in a disabled parking space.'

Wankaparkatikki...

I massaged my neck, applying pressure to a migraine spot immediately beside the cervical vertebrae – a trick a neurologist had shown me once.

That took some working out.

'Linus is a good guy, really. His brains may be scrambled but his heart's in the right place.'

'Tikkikosta!'

I turned at the sound of Linus's voice. He was standing in the poolroom doorway, grinning with his fist raised. Alina came into view behind him.

'Tikkikostapulenti!'

'Yes, you're happy about that, aren't you? The wanker's in for a nice, fat parking fine.' The barkeep formed an O with his thumb and forefinger and made an obscene gesture.

'A fine?' I said, feeling more and more of a dork at having to get a mentally deranged busker's gibberish translated by a no less peculiar barkeep. Then I suddenly grasped, without his help, what Linus had just said.

Tikkikostapulenti!

The Eye Collector had been given a ticket.

A ticket that could identify him.

THE EYE COLLECTOR'S FIRST LETTER
EMAILED VIA AN ANONYMOUS ACCOUNT

To: Thea Bergdorf <thea@bergdorf-privat.com>
Subject: The truth...

Dear purblind Frau Bergdorf,

This email is probably as futile as the frantic efforts of my youthful guests to escape from their allotted hiding place before their time finally runs out.

I shall inevitably fail in my attempt to wash off the bucket of pigswill your paper empties over me daily. That is as certain as the fact that this email will pass through dozens of hands in the next few hours. Tremulous hands like yours, as jittery as those of the IT technicians who will wind up looking somewhere in Rwanda if they try to trace the account from which I'm sending this. Other hands will be calmer and more professional: those of the psychologists and philologists who will dissect every phrase, every word in this sentence – indeed, even the colon. But please don't show this letter to Professor Adrian Hohlfort, whom I think is more likely to be recruited into our national football team than successfully track me down. That so-called 'super profiler', to quote his job description in the rag you claim to be a newspaper, would even fail to spot that the very first sentence of this email contains a clue. I spoke of children in the *plural* but only *one* hiding place – a one-fits-all solution, so to speak. That hiding place has so far remained as far from discovery by the police as my prick from Madonna's pussy (to descend to the level of your brain-dead journalists). So save yourself the 500 euros an hour Professor Wheelchair would charge for telling you that, by addressing myself to the media in the manner of serial killers like Zodiac, I'm displaying megalomania. I've no wish to pour scorn on my pursuers. I need no publicity.

On the contrary, I want you to stop writing rubbish about me. Take my sobriquet, for a start. Like a starving mongrel, you've merely fallen on the most obvious piece of meat I've thrown you: the missing eyes. Shame on you and those incompetents in homicide for being so easily deceived! One simple trick, and I've been stereotyped as a demented sex maniac. Trophies are of no interest to me. I'm not a *collector,* I'm a *player.* And I play fair. As soon as I've settled on the participants in my game, marked out the field of play and – metaphorically speaking – blown the whistle, I abide by the rules. Mother, child, deadline, hiding place – I lay down the ground rules that I observe throughout every phase of the game. I guarantee every player a fair chance of bringing the game of hide-and-seek to an end. I lay no false trails, even if my pursuers come too close, nor do I prolong a game no matter how exciting it gets. I'm not impartial, I admit. I do intervene now and then, but always for the benefit of my opponents. You would never understand that without my help. And that's why I'm writing you this email. As a rejoinder to all the lies you've been spreading about me.

I'm not a lunatic, not a monster or psychopath. I'm carrying out a plan, and my game has a purpose. If you had undergone what I've been through, you would agree. You might not approve of my actions, but you would at least be capable of understanding them.

I bet you're shaking your head at this moment. 'What a sicko,' you're thinking, but secretly you're working out your revised advertising rates for the edition with this email splashed across page one. But what if I cite you a motive that puts my actions in a different light? Well, are you still shaking your head, with its lousy hairdo? I bet you aren't.

You'd like to believe me, wouldn't you? You'd like to believe that I'm not just any old sexually motivated psychopath, and that there's a comprehensible plan underlying all I do.

For that, dear purblind Frau Bergdorf, would *really* be a story. You're itching to know my reasons for reviving the oldest children's game in the world: hide-and-seek!

All right, go on. Submit this email to all the incompetents mentioned above and await my next communication. I'll write you again as soon as I find the time. Don't worry, I won't keep you waiting long.

Not even seven hours. Plus the half day I'll need to dispose of the bodies.

42

(6 HOURS 39 MINUTES TO THE DEADLINE)

ALEXANDER ZORBACH

The symptoms got worse the moment we pulled up at some road works, our first red light after a longish succession of greens.

Fortunately, before smashing the gallery window I had the presence of mind to park the old Toyota in a side street, around the corner from Alina's block of flats. If I'd left it double-parked outside, the car would have been towed away long ago or confiscated by the police, who would inevitably have established a connection between the vandalized art gallery and myself. After all, I had personally informed Stoya that I would have to pursue my own enquiries if he continued to disregard my evidence. *Evidence seen by the eyes of a blind girl.*

I had to admit that my own eyes weren't too good at present. They were watering so much that the red lights looked fluorescent and beads of cold sweat were breaking out on my forehead. Much as I hoped my steadily worsening state was the first sign of a cold, I was afraid it stemmed from something quite different.

I called Frank. 'How long will you need?' I asked him.

'To check a parking ticket? In the middle of the night?'

I glanced at the dashboard clock and swore beneath my breath. *Eleven-fifty.* Only ten minutes to the birthday of my son, who would probably celebrate it with some strange doctor instead of his Dad.

'What do *you* think?' Frank went on. 'It's the kind of info you can only get from contacts, and mine is asleep at this hour.'

Mine isn't, worse luck. Stoya has just put me on the Wanted list and is working flat out to catch me.

'Okay, Frank, I'll give Stoya another call and try to convince him.'

'No, don't do that.'

'Why not?'

'Because I may already have what you're after.'

The lights turned green, dazzling me for a moment. Someone behind me honked his horn. I opened my eyes again, but it was a while before the gauze obscuring my vision lifted and I could see the road ahead.

'How come?' I asked.

How could Frank have traced the owner of a vehicle when he didn't even know its licence number?

'Research,' was his laconic reply. Appropriately enough, I could hear the familiar background music of several phones ringing in the open-plan newsroom.

'If there's one thing I'm good at, it's digging up info. Trust me.' He lowered his voice. 'The question is, though, how far can you trust the female Stevie Wonder beside you.'

I glanced at the rear-view mirror. Alina had got into the back with TomTom as if I were her chauffeur, but right now the distance between us suited me fine.

'Meaning what?' I asked in a low voice.

We were driving along a broad avenue, whose name escaped me, in the direction of the urban expressway. Although I still had no definite destination in mind, something told me it was better to remain on the move. Instinctively, no doubt, I was taking a route that led to my houseboat.

'Correct me if I'm wrong, but didn't she say something along these lines: that we should look for a detached house with a driveway, and that the Eye Collector parked immediately outside it after the murder?'

'Right.' Alina's last vision, which she'd described to me in Frank's presence, had completely slipped my mind.

'All right. Let's assume, just for fun, that our psychopath really did drive to a house after the murder – for a celebratory drink, maybe. If so, the likelihood is that he was using the same car that attracted the parking ticket one day later, right?'

'A few too many hypotheses for my taste, but I can see what you're getting at.'

Find the house and we find the owner – providing there's some degree of correspondence between reality and Alina's surreal fantasies.

'Okay, so far so good. I also assumed that the killer

would stick strictly to the speed limit so as not to attract attention. Then, taking my cue from what Alina said, I based my calculations on a window of four minutes maximum. Starting out from the Teufelsberg, the Eye Collector couldn't have left a traffic-calming zone in that time. The neighbourhood is full of schools and kinder-gartens, playing fields and sports complexes.'

'Fine, so you've narrowed down the relevant area to several square kilometres.'

'To within a radius of five point six kilometres, to be precise, but most of it is agricultural land or woods.'

I heard a computer keyboard clicking away beneath Frank's fingers.

'There are also a number of allotments and recreation areas, et cetera. The relevant streets and roads can't add up to more than the length of a marathon.'

I laughed. 'Which you've run, of course.'

'Correct.'

I braked sharply. A pedestrian anxious to catch a bus on the other side of the street had darted out in front of me. Alina grumbled at my driving. TomTom had almost slid off the back seat despite her efforts to prevent him from doing so.

'You're pulling my leg,' I said after taking a moment to recover from the shock.

Frank chuckled. 'Never heard of Google Earth?'

Of course.

I put on speed again and turned the windscreen wipers up a notch, but all they did was smear the glass. Snow was falling in coin-sized flakes, but it wasn't wet enough to loosen the winter grime. As a result, I could hardly see a thing.

Very appropriate.

I felt as if the same worn, old windscreen wipers were working away inside my head.

The more I strove for clarity, the more indistinct the picture before my eyes. The peculiar hallucinations that had led me to consult Dr Roth didn't help. Even though he believed they weren't psychopathological, they impaired my ability to concentrate. I had failed to think of the simplest research tools at my disposal.

Google Earth, for example.

'Using the satellite map you can find a lost front-door key on your lawn if you zoom in close enough.' Frank was saying eagerly. He laughed at his own exaggeration. 'But it gets better. In the office we've got—

'Street View. Exactly.'

For a considerable time now, Google had sent vehicles equipped with special cameras driving along the streets of selected cities so as to give users a 3D view of them all. Far from every city had been covered and hordes of lawyers were grappling with the data protection problems posed by this project, but it was already installed on any iPhone and my newspaper had access to an extensive test programme. This was what Frank was using to look for a house that matched Alina's description.

'Every street in Berlin, every damned nook and cranny,' he said euphorically, and I heard more keyboard noises.

'I can view them as if I'm driving along them in person.'

'It's bound to take hours, though.'

'Not if you're lucky like us. The residential district in question consists mainly of blocks of flats or middle-class terraces. The Traunstein villa is one of the rare exceptions.'

'So how many?' I demanded eagerly. 'How many detached houses have you counted?'

Glancing at the dashboard, I saw I was exceeding the speed limit by more than 30 kph.

'Twenty-seven, but only nine of them are bungalows with a driveway like the one your new girlfriend described...'

He paused like someone preparing to deliver the punchline of a long story.

'... and only two of those driveways are equipped with a goddamned basketball hoop!'

41

Although the bungalow was probably the lowest building on the entire estate, it was visible from a long way off.

The road, a cobbled cul de sac, was so out of the way that one of the lamp posts still bore an election poster. Some party activist had forgotten to remove the photo of a pinstriped politico grinning inanely. Ever since September, visitors to the street had been greeted by the meaningless slogan 'Our Future is Strength'.

I wondered if there was a law that compelled even the ugliest and most undistinguished politician to have his photo mounted on cardboard, and if there was a single person on our planet whose voting intentions had been swayed by an election poster. I debated the possibility of launching a readers' opinion poll once all this was over.

If I'm still in a position to.

We had left the car around the corner rather than park immediately outside the address Frank had given me. My certainty that we were wasting our time grew stronger the nearer we got to the bungalow.

'I don't think this is the house you described,' I said to Alina, who was waiting for TomTom to mark a tree.

'Why not?'

'It's too conspicuous.' I screwed up my eyes, watching my breath condense right in front of my face.

For all that, acting conspicuously could often be the best form of camouflage. Not long ago a semi-detached house in a Berlin suburb had been completely emptied in broad daylight by thieves who had simply driven up in a furniture van. Nobody thinks of a robbery when he sees a furniture remover with a plasma TV under his arm.

And nobody thinks of an empty eye socket when he's confronted by Father Christmas.

Alina told TomTom to sit and shuffled from foot to foot, shivering.

'Describe the place,' she said.

Describe it? I conducted a brief survey.

How was I to describe *this* to a blind girl? It certainly compelled me to revise my preconception that people celebrated Christmas more discreetly in this residential area.

The one-storey building looked as if it belonged to an affluent ten-year-old orphan who had squandered his inheritance in a store that specialized in Christmas decorations. A string of blue halogen lights ran along the eaves and picked out the drainpipes, up one of which a life-size Santa was attempting to climb in the direction of the chimney. He was dressed in white, the original outfit dating from the time before some advertising genius employed by Coca-Cola took it into his head to colour Father Christmas red.

But that was the only discreet feature of the decorations. The whole of the front garden was given over to reindeer, illuminated snowmen and the Three Wise Men from the East. Only Jesus and his crib were missing. Though they may have been obscured by the stack of logs beside the double garage, whose doors had been sprayed with artificial snow, like the shutters and the garden gate. Then there was...

... the basketball hoop!

It was even where Alina had said: beside the garage and not above the doors.

'Let me put it conservatively,' I said. 'Whoever lives here must be his electricity supplier's prize customer.'

Alina seemed to have stored her few visual memories better than a sighted child, perhaps because no new impressions had superimposed themselves on the old images she'd retained from her third year of life. In any event, she still had a vivid recollection of Christmas in California, so I didn't find it hard to give her a rough idea of the illuminations, which would have induced a migraine in anyone who looked at them for long. I could well understand why all the neighbours had copied the bungalow's owner and closed their shutters.

'You mentioned the basketball hoop and a Coca-Cola, but you didn't say anything about reindeer and Father Christmas.'

Alina shrugged. 'I can't remember anything like that.'

I took a step towards the hoop. The green ring was reflecting the pre-Christmas illuminations. It made a curiously new impression, as if it had been only just been put up.

'Well, what now?' I heard Alina ask behind me. Fine snowflakes landing on her wig glittered in the reflected glow.

Telling her to wait in the driveway, I tried to open the gate that gave access to the path between the garage and the house, which evidently led to the main entrance facing the garden. Unsurprisingly, it was locked. I would normally have rung the bell, but there was neither a nameplate nor a bell, so I reached through the bars and turned the knob until the gate sprang open. Having assured Alina that I wouldn't be long, I made my way round the back of the house.

The massive wood-panelled door looked as if it might be reinforced with steel on the inside. As usual in a residential area like this, a CCTV mounted on a buttress projected downwards like a bird of prey poised to swoop on its quarry. On the door, roughly at chest height, was a long, illuminated display panel.

It looked just like the ones in the windows of lottery agencies or cheap amusement arcades, except that the red electronic letters gliding across the LED display from right to left weren't advertising a jackpot. As I strained my eyes to read them, they spelt out the words of a familiar Christmas song:

Jingle bells, jingle bells,
jingle all the way

I went up to the door and looked in vain for a bell. All the external shutters at the rear of the bungalow had also been lowered.

Oh, what fun it is to ride
in a one-horse open sleigh

Being very close now, I made the mistake of looking straight at the ribbon of text. The luminous letters seemed to sear my hypersensitive eyes like branding irons.

Dashing through the snow
in a one-horse open sleigh,
o'er the graves we go,
laughing all the way

I quickly averted my eyes from the illuminated display and wielded the heavy bronze door-knocker.

Nothing. Not a rustle, nor a shuffling footstep, nor any sound indicative of someone's willingness to answer the door.

Perhaps the occupants are asleep, I thought, convinced in any case that I was standing outside the wrong house. *If* there was a right one.

Jingle bells, jingle bells, jingle all the way... I started to hum the words in my head. Incredible how the anodyne melody had bored its way into my brain so swiftly, just because of the words on the illuminated display.

Dashing through the snow in a one-horse open sleigh, o'er the...

I stopped short. The bells in my head abruptly fell silent. What had I just been humming? Over the *graves* we go?

Wondering how on earth I'd hit on such a morbid

variant, I looked at the display again. The relevant lines reappeared:

> *Dashing through the snow*
> *in a one-horse open sleigh,*
> *o'er the fields we go...*

Hm, all quite normal.

I could have sworn I'd seen the altered wording for one brief moment, but there was no sign of it now.

My weary, watering eyes must have played a trick on me. No wonder, considering I'd hardly slept at all in the last few days, spent my waking hours hunting a madman, and wound up on the run myself.

> *Laughing all the way.*
> *Bells on bobtail ring*

Wondering whether to knock again, I was just about to resume humming along when the words before my eyes changed once more. This time there was no room for doubt.

> *The key's beneath the pot.*
> *Use it and you've had your lot.*

I let out a yell and staggered backwards – and yelled even louder when I bumped into the figure hovering in the darkness behind me.

40

'Did you see that?'

I was stupid enough to address that question to Alina. Unlike me, she was highly amused by my terrified squawk.

'To be honest,' she retorted, 'I'm wondering which of us has a pair of eyes in their head.'

'I'm sorry, but...' I hesitated, not knowing how to explain what had just happened to me. Especially as the display was once more reeling off the traditional innocuous lyric and I couldn't have explain what I'd just seen, even to a sighted person.

'Why didn't you stay out front?' I asked in a whisper, looking at TomTom. She had let him off the lead, but he was hugging her side and licking some snow off his paws.

She smiled defiantly. 'I didn't feel like spending another half-hour in the cold, waiting for his lordship to involve me in some more third degree.'

'I didn't give Traunstein the third degree...'

At that moment I caught sight of an overturned flower-pot. It was lying on the lawn not far from Alina. Kneeling down, I detached it from the half-frozen ground with a faint sound like someone smacking their lips. Several small beetles, their night's repose disturbed, scuttled off into the darkness. Then I spotted the black, faux leather wallet. It contained a single key.

The key's beneath the pot.
Use it and...

'What is it?'

Slowly, feeling half-dazed, I brushed past Alina on my way back to the door.

She caught me by the sleeve and insisted on being told what had happened, so I did my best to explain. If she doubted what I'd seen, she didn't show it. On the contrary, my story of the warning on the display seemed to fill her with a spirit of adventure.

'I'm coming with you,' she said when she heard me insert the key in the lock.

Just to see if it fits. Sure, Zorbach. And now? What are you going to do now you've unlocked it?

'No, you stay here and send for help if I'm not out in five minutes,' I said, well aware that Alina wasn't the kind of person to take orders from a man like me. A blind girl who'd learnt to ride a bike wasn't afraid of spooky houses.

There was a click and the door swung open, seemingly by itself.

Use it and...

'Hello?' I called into the darkness ahead of me.

Nothing. Just a dense, dark, impenetrable hush.

... you've had your lot...

'All right,' I thought, reactivating my mobile so as to be able to summon help if necessary. Then, with Alina and TomTom at my heels, I went inside.

It's only a harmless bungalow, as imagined by a blind girl. What could happen to me in there that's so terrible?

39

(6 HOURS 20 MINUTES TO THE DEADLINE)

TOBY TRAUNSTEIN

He didn't know how long he'd been asleep. He wasn't even sure he *had* been asleep, for when he woke up in the dark he felt sleepier than ever before.

Air was his first thought, because he felt he was suffocating. Then he hit his elbow on something hard. Wood.

Not soft any more was his second thought. The walls of his prison were no longer soft and yielding. He thought he must be lying in a coffin.

Groping around on the floor, his hands came into contact with the material that had enclosed him until recently. It felt like the surface of his waterproof jacket, or like his jeans that time the Advent candle dripped wax on them. Thin, elastic material with a zip running round the sides. Just a minute, was it a...

... *a case?* Yes, of course. They'd zipped him up in a black case with wheels like the one Dad always took with him on business trips. Except that it was much bigger – capacious enough to hold a boy's body.

But where am I now? First I was in that shitty trolley case...

Okay, it's a game. Jens and Kevin shut me up, but they also gave me something to escape with.

The coin.

Although he somehow couldn't imagine his friends putting a coin in his mouth, he didn't want to think of an alternative. Better to be at the mercy of his pals than a stranger.

Okay, the coin was for the zip fastener. What else is here?

Maybe a key or a lighter. Or a mobile phone.

Yes, a phone would be great.

He would call the police or Mum. Or even Dad, if he had to, but Dad never answered because he was far too busy, and...

Just a minute. Daddy once got angry with Lea and me because he thought we'd pinched his mobile. He went on and on at us until Mummy found it in his case and handed it to him.

In the outside pocket of his case!

Of course. Those cases have pockets... Maybe...?

Toby pulled the case towards him and felt for the external zip fasteners, opening one after the other. He eventually found something in a small, narrow side pocket.

A screwdriver?

Incredulously, he ran his fingers along it from the wooden handle and steel shaft to the blunt end. Then he started crying.

How the hell can I call Mummy with a broken screwdriver?

This time the tears that sprang to his eyes were tears of rage. He was unwise enough to clench his fist and punch the wooden wall of his prison. It sounded hollow. The pain made him cry all the more.

Fuck you, Kevin and Jens! What have you shut me up in?

Toby blew on his knuckles the way Mummy always did when he came home bruised after playing. He was involuntarily reminded of his seventh birthday, when his grandfather had given him the silliest present ever: an ugly, pot-bellied wooden doll you could unscrew into two halves. He'd asked the old man if it wasn't meant for Lea.

Oh Lea, why aren't you here with me now? And what am I supposed to do with a screwdriver that's lost its tip?

'You have to let the dolls out!' He could hear his grandfather's quavering voice in his head. And then he remembered what the stupid present was called: a babushka. Grandpa had said something about Russia and told him that babushkas were a big hit there because each doll could be unscrewed to reveal another one inside it.

Oh God, I'm inside a babushka!

Every place of confinement he escaped from would prove to be inside another. First a trolley case, then a wooden box.

What'll come next?

Probably an even bigger box, but just as dark and airless.

Toby coughed. He felt he was losing his balance and

crouched down. All he'd done by escaping into the box was buy himself some time.

And a bit more air, but that's running out too.

The case had been wrapped in a plastic film he'd only just managed to tear. And now, after only a few breaths, his lungs were subject to the same pressure. Even though the dark box was still as impervious to light, he was starting to see stars.

He wondered for a moment if he ought really to exert himself and use up the air even faster, but he decided he had no choice.

Galvanized by a mixture of rage and desperation, he used the end of the broken screwdriver to stab one point in the side of the box again and again.

38

(6 HOURS 18 MINUTES TO THE DEADLINE)

ALEXANDER ZORBACH

At the age of nine, when I was old enough to cross Berlin by public transport on my own, I was given the job of taking Granny her lunch every Sunday. Granny didn't like coming to us because she had no love for my father – who, significantly enough, was her son – and she only liked me when I came bearing her favourite fare: Königsberg meatballs.

I think the only feature of our family home she really liked was the big television set in the living room, on which she watched *Little Lord Fauntleroy* every Christmas, only to fall asleep every time.

Whenever I think of Granny, I'm reminded of her open mouth and the rivulet of saliva that used to trickle down her double chin as the final credits were unfolding. I can't be sure, but I'm very much afraid she departed this world without ever seeing the end and must still, even in the hereafter, be excoriating the Earl of Dorincourt, whose miraculous change of heart she always missed.

My Sunday visits continued for only six months, after

which she fell over in her kitchen and had to go into a nursing home. However, those few encounters had been enough to crystallize my certainty that death isn't a living creature – not the Grim Reaper familiar to one from horror stories – but a smell.

A multifarious, omnipresent, ultra-pervasive smell dominated by the reek of a cheap toilet cleaner as inadequate to overpower the scent of excrement in the toilet as peppermint creams were to disguise the stale breath of an old woman with ill-fitting dentures. Whenever my grandmother opened the door to me, I was assailed by that 'death perfume', as I secretly called it: an amalgam of sweat, urine, advocaat and warmed-up leftovers mingled with the sweet-and-sour aroma of greasy hair and cold farts. I always pictured it in a bottle with a death's head on the label.

If that concentrate actually existed, I thought as my eyes became accustomed to the gloom, *someone had spilt a vast quantity of it inside this bungalow.*

'Pooh,' said Alina, 'this place needs airing badly.'

'Hello?' I called for at least the fourth time. 'Anyone at home?'

The fact that so little of the glare outside penetrated the venetian blinds made me feel unpleasantly claustrophobic. All there was to guide me was the faint light from the door, which was ajar. I felt for a switch on the wall, but nothing happened when I turned it on. I swore beneath my breath.

'What's that?' said Alina, who had made her way past

me and was groping her way round a table in the middle of the room. She could hardly be puzzled by the absence of light in there, so I guessed it must be the cold that surprised her.

'There's no power. Presumably that's why the heating isn't on.'

'I don't mean that.'

'What, then?'

'That hissing sound. Can't you hear it?'

I held my breath and cocked my head without knowing exactly what had caught Alina's attention and where it was coming from. I heard... *nothing*.

'It sounds like a spraycan,' she whispered.

TomTom had also pricked up his ears, which usually hung limp. With the dog close beside her, Alina was making for the far end of the room. The darkest end, in other words. I was amazed yet again by the self-assurance with which she advanced across unfamiliar terrain.

Perhaps we become more fearless if we can't see the dangers the world has in store for us, I thought. Perhaps that was the sole benefit of her disability. What we don't know doesn't worry us. Did that mean that what we can't see doesn't *exist*?

The living-room floor was covered with badly-laid parquet or laminate that creaked faintly beneath Alina's feet. Following her more by ear than by eye, I stumbled over something that was too low for a table and too heavy for a flower vase, possibly a work of art: a small sculpture or one of those ugly china dogs whose open mouths catch dust in the homes of the wealthy. Then, to my right, I saw a faint finger of light that showed me the way out of the living room and into an adjoining passage.

Heavens. My sense of direction was poor enough at the best of times – I was capable of going astray in a deserted car park. *And now this!*

The dim yellowish glow was coming from the far end of the passage, as I saw when I emerged from the black hole behind me. My pupils must have been the size of coins, so the night light plugged into the skirting board seemed to dazzle me like a halogen spotlight.

I couldn't help thinking of Charlie, and my stomach turned over again.

Charlie... Headstrong, sex-starved, big-hearted Charlie, murdered by the madman who had chosen me to be, willy-nilly, a participant in his game and the finder of her children. There had been a so-called 'darkroom' at our usual rendezvous, the Hothouse: an unlit room in which total strangers could copulate on latex mattresses. Anonymous sex with invisible partners was a form of self-gratification I'd never been attracted to, unlike Charlie. She had been so desperate, she wanted to sample all life had to offer.

I had once followed her into the darkroom, only to leave it as soon as I felt a stranger's hands on my body. I couldn't even tell their owner's sex, although total darkness never prevailed in there. As soon as someone drew aside the heavy baize curtain covering the doorway, a handful of weary photons descended on the entwined forms, producing as vague a memory of daylight as the night light plugged into the wall at Alina's feet.

She had already reached the end of the passage and was standing immediately outside a heavy metal fire door, which was slightly ajar. TomTom had planted himself directly in front of her with his shaggy body up against her legs, preventing her from going any further.

'Wait,' I said, catching her up. I quickly saw that the retriever had good reason to bar his mistress's path. Beyond the door, a steep flight of steps led down into the bungalow's cellar.

'Hear that?' Alina whispered, and I detected a trace of fear in her voice for the first time.

'Yes!'

I not only heard it, I could smell it as well. The rhythmical hiss of the spraycan had become louder, the 'death perfume' stronger.

'TomTom can sense danger,' Alina said. Superfluously. One didn't need an animal's sense of smell to know that something here was badly wrong.

No, you're mistaken. There can't be anything here. We're merely pursuing the hallucinations of a blind visionary.

I pulled the door open.

I was naturally familiar with movies in which some idiot ventures barefoot into a cellar instead of listening to the audience's advice and running a mile from the mad axeman who's lurking down there. It was, therefore, completely out of the question for me to set foot on those stone steps – even though I felt impelled to do so by professional curiosity, and even though Lea and Toby might be desperately waiting for us in the Eye Collector's hideaway only a few metres below.

TomTom's instincts were sound. We shouldn't court danger, I fully realized that. At least for the first few moments. At least until I heard those frightful, inhuman sounds that could only be coming from a creature that needed my help *at once,* not half an hour from now.

'Jesus, what's that?' Alina asked, sounding a trifle more apprehensive than before.

Somebody's dying down there, I thought. I opened my mobile and texted our location to Stoya.

It happened just after I'd sent the text and was about halfway down the flight of steps: a motion sensor activated an overhead light. Down here in the cellar, immediately below the living room, it was suddenly as bright as day.

More's the pity.

When my eyes had recovered from the dazzling glare, I looked down into the little chamber with the rough-hewn walls – its vaulted ceiling was reminiscent of a wine cellar – and started to tremble.

How dearly I yearned for the darkness I'd just left.

What wouldn't I have given to be spared the sight that met my eyes.

37

When light penetrates our cornea, passes through the pupil and finally hits the retina's sensitive photoreceptors, an image results, at least on a very small part of the retina: the macula lutea or 'yellow spot'. What really results is more than one image, because our optic muscles ensure that the eyes never remain still but scan an object for fractions of a second, building up an overall picture out of countless details. Thus, our brains process a flood of neural stimuli into visual patterns by comparing what is seen with what is already familiar to us. Strictly speaking, the eye is merely a tool or extension of our true organ of sight: the brain, which never permits us to see reality, only an interpretation of the same.

But the sight that bludgeoned its way into my skull in the bungalow's cellar was without precedent. My brain had no recollection of anything comparable with such a horrific spectacle. I had never seen anything so appalling.

The woman looked like an exhibit in an anatomical collection, the only difference being that her spatchcocked body was still alive. At first I assumed that the hissing ventilator beside the couch was solely responsible for the fact that her bisected chest continued to rise and fall. Sadly, though (I wished so ardently she were dead, God forgive me), the mouth beneath the mask with the laryngeal intubator was open and breathing heavily. Moreover, her eyes were rolling. I clutched my mouth.

This can't be true. It isn't real – it's just an optical illusion. We're merely acting on a blind girl's hallucinations...

I blinked, but I couldn't blot out the frightful images. Neither the couch, nor the ventilator, nor the...

... telephone? What on earth is a telephone doing on the instrument table beside this dying woman?

I could only infer the victim's sex from her long hair and breasts, whose nipples had already rotted away. She certainly wasn't a kidnapped girl of nine, but her age was impossible to guess, the more so since all her teeth and several fingers and toes were missing.

'What's going on down there?' Alina's voice broke in on my thoughts. She had evidently defied TomTom and was now standing where I had triggered the motion sensor, halfway down the steps. TomTom was waiting one step below her, panting and trembling with agitation.

'I can't tell you,' I said in a choking voice, at pains not to contaminate the crime scene by an unguarded movement.

I don't know what to do. God in heaven, this is more than I can endure.

The image of the woman who was no more than a living, breathing wound refused to disappear, even when I briefly shut my eyes.

She was done up in a way I'd never seen before. Her entire body was sheathed in transparent film like an outsize joint of meat in a freezer bag. The madman responsible for this perversion must have sucked out all the air, with the result that the plastic film clung tightly to the flesh beneath the shredded skin.

When the purpose of this dawned on me I started to retch.

Because of the neighbours. So that her animate corpse doesn't smell as much as it rots away.

She had been sealed up in transparent film like some kind of vacuum-packed foodstuff.

'Need any help?' asked Alina.

'No, I...'

Help? Yes, of course I need help.

I looked at my mobile and groaned.

Naturally not. We're in a cellar. No reception.

Worse still, the connection must have been severed in the entrance because my phone was displaying a text message in the outgoing mail. My attempt to send it had failed. Stoya didn't know where we were.

Swiftly, I turned my back on the scene of martyrdom in front of me and went back to the foot of the steps.

'We must get out of here and call—'

Bang!

'Alina?'

I almost bellowed her name, the unexpected noise had given me such a shock. She was now trembling as noticeably as TomTom.

'What was that?'

No, please not. Don't let it be that!

I had noticed the current of fresh air at the top of the steps, before I had started down.

Damn it!

We had left all the doors open on our route from the front door and along the passage to the cellar. The wind had got up since our arrival. It was still moderate, still not a winter gale, but strong enough to send a draught whistling through the house and...

'Shit!'

Hurrying up the steps past Alina and TomTom, I aimed a furious, despairing kick at the cellar door, which had just slammed shut.

I rattled the handle, then threw my weight against the door, but my shoulder was no match for the expanse of metal that barred our way out. The mobile in my hand displayed no reception bars, even up here, so I squeezed past Alina and the dog and went back down the steps.

'What are you going to do? Come on, tell me!'

I ignored Alina's impatient question and checked to see if the telephone on the instrument table was working.

Well I'll be... It's connected!

I hadn't seen such an ancient phone since the eighties. It still boasted a rotary dial.

Like Grandma's. Everything reminds me of Grandma, not just the smell of death.

Even the dialling lock was there, a relic of the days when long-distance calls still cost the earth and you automatically secured your telephone against uninvited callers before going away on holiday. The tiny lock permitted only two numbers to be dialled: the 1 and the 2.

But they're enough for me. I don't need more than two numbers to call the emergency services.

I inserted my forefinger in the finger plate.

1... 1... 2.

In some strange way, the dial's old-fashioned purr seemed to harmonize with the hiss of the ventilator beside me. I held my breath and strove with all my might to avoid looking at the living corpse on my right.

The phone rang.

Once. Twice.

The third time, darkness enveloped us.

36

(6 HOURS 11 MINUTES TO THE DEADLINE)

FRANK LAHMANN (TRAINEE JOURNALIST)

'Where is he?'

Thea Bergdorf must have snuck up behind him. He wondered how long she'd been watching him.

'I know you keep in touch with him, laddie, so don't mess me about!'

The editor-in-chief was now confronting Frank like a goalkeeper intent on defending his penalty area by any available means, physical violence included. She made a point of wearing tight-fitting, cream-coloured trouser suits that suited her about as well as a shrunk pinstripe suit would have suited a bouncer. She was quite frank about the fact that she set no store by outward appearances.

'I've got where I am *because* of my fat backside, not in spite of it,' she'd informed a dumbstruck business tycoon at her paper's New Year's party. 'If I were young, pretty and anorexic I'd waste too much of my time screwing the wrong men.' She obviously possessed a sense of humour, but Frank couldn't detect a trace of it in her current demeanour and the peremptory tone of voice.

'For the last time: Where is Zorbach at this moment?'

Frank uttered a weary groan and ran his fingers through his hair. 'He asked me not to tell anyone.'

'I'm his boss, in case you'd forgotten.'

'I know, but he's my mentor.'

'Oh, you think that embroils you in a conflict of interests, do you?' Thea's lips twisted in a sarcastic smile. 'Very well, I hereby release you from it. You're fired!' And she turned on her heel.

'What?!' Frank jumped up from Zorbach's chair and hurried after her. 'Why?'

She didn't even turn round. 'Because I can't tolerate subordinates withholding important information from me. I asked you to tell me at once if Zorbach called you. You ignored that and went on playing by your own rules. Well, tough.'

'But this makes no sense,' Frank exclaimed angrily. 'You certainly won't get any information out of me if you fire me.'

'Oh, you've no need to tell *me* a thing.' She finally came to a halt, but only to point to the reception area, whose automatic doors were just opening.

Two men walked into the newspaper office.

Thea gave Frank an evil smile. 'I'm sure the police will have more effective ways of extracting the truth from you.'

35

(6 HOURS 10 MINUTES TO THE DEADLINE)

ALEXANDER ZORBACH

'Hello, yes?' The amiable voice at the other end of the line was puzzling in itself, and the background noises sounded even less appropriate to an emergency call centre. The mélange of alcoholic laughter and discordant singing might have been emanating from a karaoke bar.

'Turn the music down,' the man called, as if to confirm that a boisterous party was in progress in the background. Someone actually seemed to have heard him, because the thudding disco bass abruptly lost some of its volume.

'Am I through to emergency?'

'Eh? Emergency? Oh sure, of course!' The man's laughter was as long and loud as his speech was slurred. He was quite clearly drunk – certainly not the kind of person you wanted to answer the phone when you dialled 112.

'Sorry, I wasn't expecting your call so soon.'

Expecting it?

'Are you taking the piss?' I yelled. 'I'm standing beside a woman in urgent need of medical assistance, and...' I broke off. Something had started to vibrate, and it wasn't the ventilator.

'Ah yes, the Murder Game. I get it. Just a minute.'

I heard a rustle of paper. The next moment, he sounded as if he was reading out a prepared text: '"I did warn you. You shouldn't have challenged me, but you insisted on joining in the game. Very well, listen carefully, here are the rules."'

'The rules? What rules?'

The vibration, which had intensified, was now superimposed on a sound that was vaguely reminiscent of a vacuum cleaner.

What's going on here? What the hell is happening to us?

'There are always rules in these shitty games, amigo.'

The man on the phone belched softly. 'Oops, sorry,' he said with a laugh.

'Who are you?' I shouted.

'Oh, fuck, sorry, I've screwed this up. But it was such short notice. Normally I get my instructions at least a week in advance. Just so happens we're throwing a party and I've already had a couple. That's why I didn't catch on at first, comprende?'

No, I don't. I don't understand why I'm having to bandy words with a tipsy imbecile when I dialled emergency on behalf of the decomposing woman with whom I and my blind companion are shut up in a dark cellar.

'What the hell are you talking about?'

'Okay, but you must promise not to tell anyone, right?

I used to do a lot of this stuff, that's why my number's still on the Internet, but these role-playing games get really boring after a while. I only agreed to spout this rubbish because the guy on the phone promised me a hundred euros.'

Role play? Oh God, the Eye Collector must have put a call through to a student who thought he could earn a few extra euros by passing on clues to the participants in an interactive manhunt.

Except that this is no game. Not, at least, for anyone but the Eye Collector himself.

'The man who gave you money to answer the phone when I dialled this number – what were his instructions?'

'Well, to read you this email.'

I coughed, suddenly beset by the unpleasant sensation that the air I was breathing had grown thinner.

'"You still have fifteen minutes' worth of oxygen,"' the man read out. The monotonous vacuum-cleaner noise had become an incessant hum. '"That's how long it will take for the pumps to suck the air out of the cellar. If you haven't come to solve the riddle on your own, it'll run out even sooner. But a game isn't a game unless the players have a chance of winning. You can turn off the pump and win!"'

He paused. Someone in the background uttered a raucous obscenity.

'Well, go on.'

'That's it.' He gave a sheepish laugh.

'What do you mean, that's it?'

How was I expected to turn off the pump that was transforming our prison into a vacuum chamber when I didn't even know where it was? I clasped my dry throat.

'Hey, amigo, don't tell him I screwed up, will you? Got to go now.'

The music had grown louder again. The man seemed to have moved to another room. He sounded as if he were standing in the middle of a dance floor.

'No, don't hang up!' I yelled above the background noises and the mechanical hum of the suction pump. 'There must be something else!'

'No, amigo, honestly there... Hey, just a minute.'

He broke off, and I clamped the old-fashioned receiver to my ear even harder.

'Hell, I almost missed it. The subject of the email, I mean.'

'What is it?' I asked as calmly as I could manage.

Stay calm. I forced myself to breathe slowly and deeply. *You still have plenty of time,* I tried to tell myself. *Even though Alina and TomTom are also using up oxygen and the cellar's capacity is only a few cubic metres, ten minutes is plenty long enough to work out a plan.*

'What's the subject, damn it?'

I heard a last rustle of paper at the other end of the line. Then the man said something that finally blew my mind.

'Just three words, amigo: "*Remember your mother!*"'

34

My mother died in our kitchen on the morning of May 20, shortly after some flour got up her nose while she was baking. Her best friend, Babsi, who happened to be visiting, yelled at the foreign on-call doctor to examine her nose.

'She held her nose!'

Babsi repeated this at least a dozen times. Not only when they lifted Mother on to the stretcher and slid her into the ambulance under the neighbours' wondering gaze, but also to the staff in the intensive care ward: *'Why on earth did she hold her nose?'*

Babsi thought it obvious that this was what had made the pressure build up in her brain and caused the aneurysm to burst. It wasn't until much later that a doctor with tired eyes and projecting teeth informed me that my mother couldn't have averted the bleed even if she'd sneezed into a handkerchief in the normal way.

'The cerebral haemorrhage probably occasioned the sneeze reflex. Either that, or it was purely coincidence that she got something up her nose just when the aneurysm burst. Anyhow, it wasn't that which caused the stroke.'

How comforting. So my mother wasn't hooked up to a battery of ultra-modern hospital equipment because she was too stupid to sneeze normally. Her time had come, that's all. Very reassuring.

Today, five-and-a-half years after the event, she was in the clinical ward of a private nursing home. Her room resembled a showroom for hi-tech aids to intensive care. The medically correct term for her condition was apallic syndrome or waking coma. Whenever I visited her I felt tempted to wrench off the clipboard at the foot of her bed, cross out the diagnosis, and substitute 'deceased'. Because that's what she was to me: *dead.*

My mother may still have experienced phases of waking and sleeping, and her organs hadn't stopped functioning thanks to an abundance of pills, infusions, tubes and instruments. The doctors and nurses may well have thought that this constituted living, but to me she had died in our kitchen on May 20 five-and-a-half years ago.

I also knew that she would think the same if her brain were still capable of entertaining a single, lucid idea.

'Promise me you'll never let it come to that!'

Her tone on the way back from the nursing home had been almost imploring. We'd paid Granny a visit – an even more harrowing occasion than usual. Granny had apparently chucked her turds around the dining room ('See what *I* can do!') and then tried to eat her own hair. By the time they let us in to see her she was in the seventh heaven, pharmaceutically speaking, and dribbling the way she used to when dozing in front of *Little Lord Fauntleroy.*

'Dear God, I don't want to end up like that,' my mother told me tearfully in the car. Then she extracted a far too ambitious promise from me never to leave her alone in a situation in which she had ceased to be in command of her senses.

'I'd sooner they turned off the machines.' Taking my hand, she gazed deep into my eyes and said it once more: 'Promise me, Alex. If I ever have an accident and can only get by with constant help like your Granny, I want you to do your utmost to see that I don't end up like her, you hear?'

I'd sooner they turned off the machines.

If only she'd signed a living will. If only my father had still been alive to take the decision in my place. If only I myself had had the courage to carry out her last wish.

I'd tried to once. I drove to the sanatorium firmly resolved to switch off the ventilator – and failed miserably. After the tragedy on the bridge I lacked the mental strength to take another person's life. And so it was my fault that my mother, once such a robust, vivacious, emancipated woman, who wouldn't even let a waiter help her into her coat, was dependent on the whims of the underpaid nursing staff without whose assistance she couldn't even empty her bowels in the right place.

She wouldn't have wanted that. She would rather have died, she'd made that absolutely clear to me, but I hadn't managed to kill her.

And the Eye Collector seemed to be aware of that.

Remember your mother.

He must know me well. He seemed to know that I'd spent a long time staring at the ventilator switch with which I could have ended all her sufferings and incurred a murder charge. He knew I was too weak. In shooting Angélique I'd used up all the courage I would have needed to kill another woman, even though death was her dearest wish.

The Eye Collector was confronting me with an insoluble problem.

A game isn't a game unless the players have a chance of winning...

He hadn't challenged me to find the suction pump. If I wanted to save my own life and Alina's, I must turn off quite another machine: the one within arm's reach of me, which was keeping the tormented woman alive.

You can turn off the pump and win...

The ventilator beside the unknown woman's bed!

I shouted into the phone, telling the student our location and begging him to send help. The words came tumbling out of my mouth as I tried to convince him that this was a deadly serious situation, not a game, but he merely laughed.

'Yes, yes, the guy told me you'd come out with something like that,' he said, and hung up.

I pressed the cradle, dialled 112 again and waited for a ringing tone. In vain.

I wasn't permitted another call.

The antiquated telephone had been disconnected.

33

(6 HOURS 4 MINUTES TO THE DEADLINE)

FRANK LAHMANN (TRAINEE JOURNALIST)

'That's bullshit,' said the detective sitting nearest to him. 'He's gone in search of a parking violator with a blind witness? You expect me to believe that?'

Frank was seated at the end of the massive glass-topped table whose edge was buried beneath the inspector's plump buttocks. He guessed that Thea was waiting for him outside the conference room and might even be listening at the door. She had been eager to sit in on the interview, but the other policeman had opposed the idea. Although thinner and more sensibly dressed, he looked just as shattered as his uncouth colleague. Flaky skin and red-rimmed eyes with dark circles round them – Frank was acquainted with those signs of fatigue in himself. They manifested themselves when you were working against the clock and sleep was a luxury you couldn't afford. Frank could even recognize the facial side effects of the remedies they took to cope with stress. The guy named Scholle drowned his lack of sleep in coffee and Red Bull. His dark-suited superior resorted to harder measures. His dilated pupils were as informative as the fact that he kept sniffing – like Kowalla, the cokehead from the paper's sports section.

'Why not just check the info?' said Frank. 'Maybe Zorbach's right. Maybe the guy with the parking ticket is the one you're looking for.'

He repeated the address in Brunnenstrasse where the man Zorbach thought was the Eye Collector had left his car in a disabled parking space.

'Check it out. What have you got to lose?'

'Time,' said the man who had introduced himself as Philipp Stoya. 'The deadline's approaching and I've no wish to set eyes on another child's corpse because I wasted time checking parking offenders.'

The corners of his mouth quivered as he tried to suppress a yawn. Hurriedly, he fished a handkerchief out of his trouser pocket just in time to sneeze into it several times. A thin trickle of blood dribbled from his right nostril. The chief investigator seemed to have noticed this, because he tersely excused himself and left the conference room.

That's great, Frank thought apprehensively, *leave me on my own with Rambo.*

Scholle smiled at him, nothing more. He simply sat perched on the edge of the table, jiggling his right foot as if bouncing a ball, and grinned. Broadly. Amiably. Unmaliciously. Like an old pal. Saying nothing.

Frank bowed his head and thought hard.

Should I give him the address?

Zorbach had asked him not to do so before he okayed it by phone, but he hadn't called in for the last ten minutes, nor had he answered the phone when Frank called him just before the detectives turned up. *The number you require is temporarily unavailable.*

'It wasn't Zorbach,' he said for at least the third time since the interview began. 'You're wasting more time chasing after my boss than you would if you checked that parking ticket.'

No response. Scholle's grin persisted.

Shit. Frank guessed what was to come. He knew the type. Although his colleagues on the paper regarded him as a greenhorn because of his youthful appearance and limited experience, he could spot the kind of men who were used to getting their way. He recognized them because they were so like his father. In his private life Scholle might be a good-natured family man who would barbecue you a nice, thick steak while his kids rode him piggyback. When confronted by a professional impasse, however, he wouldn't hesitate to use the whole of his considerable body weight to solve a case. That, no doubt, was why he only played second fiddle. Doubtless lacking in patience and sensitivity, he only knew of subtle interrogation techniques through rumour – unlike his coke-sniffing superior.

Frank had been a lifelong outsider until Zorbach gave him a job on the paper. Always on the sidelines, never in the thick of things, he was in the best possible position from which to observe people. Having developed a capacity for reading others' minds from childhood, he knew that, far from being an olive branch, Scholle's grin was a prelude to something very, very unpleasant.

He wasn't wrong, either.

In one fluid movement of which he would never have thought the overweight detective capable, Scholle had straightened up and imprisoned him in a necklock from behind. Frank felt as if the policeman had trapped a nerve. Then the pain shot down his spine to his loins.

'Okay, fun's over!' Scholle increased the pressure. 'Your pal lost his wallet at the scene of the crime. He even came back and worked Traunstein over.'

Frank's cervical vertebrae creaked. He flailed his arms about and tried to get to his feet, but his upper body might have been set in concrete.

'He knows more than he should and he's on the run.'

He's crazy.

'So don't tell me we're after the wrong man!'

The bastard's crazy – he'll kill me.

'Maybe I'll be subject to disciplinary proceedings. Maybe torture is prohibited in this country. But you know what?'

Scholle wrenched Frank's head back until his gaze was involuntarily focused on the big wall clock at the other end of the conference room.

'I couldn't care less when kids are involved. We're running out of time, and I'll deliver you to A and E before I let another child die because of an obstructive little wanker like you!'

Relieved to find that he could still breathe despite the pressure on his throat, Frank made another attempt to free himself. Then he froze. Didn't move a millimetre. Kept absolutely still. He knew, even without being told so by Scholle, that to turn his head so much as a few degrees would be appallingly painful.

'Know how I take notes in difficult cases?'

Frank didn't even dare nod. His pulses raced and sweat broke out all over his body.

You're a sadist! The words were on the tip of his tongue, but he couldn't afford to feed Scholle's fury. Didn't want the sharp object that had just been inserted in his ear to probe any deeper.

'With a pencil,' said Scholle. He chuckled. 'I always come equipped with a nice, long, freshly sharpened pencil.'

The detective's warm, moist breath on the back of Frank's sweaty neck made him shiver.

'Okay, okay, I'll tell you,' he groaned.

'Really?' The necklock remained as tight as ever. The pencil felt as unpleasant as a Q-Tip inserted too deeply into the auditory canal.

'I actually believe you're going to talk at last. But you know the difference between me and my colleague?'

Once again, Frank couldn't nod without risking a punctured eardrum.

'Stoya's at the end of his rope like me, but unlike me he isn't a hundred per cent convinced your boss is the bastard we're after. That's why, although he might get carried away and threaten you, he'd leave it at intimidation.'

Frank started to hyperventilate with fear.

'I, on the other hand, want to make sure you know what'll happen if you give me a load of bullshit,' said Scholle, and he gripped the pencil still tighter in readiness to ram it home.

32

(6 HOURS 2 MINUTES TO THE DEADLINE)

ALINA GREGORIEV

'I can't do it!'

'What can't you do? Please tell me what's going on!'

Alina had noticed the almost instant echo as soon as she entered the cellar. Her words reverberated as they bounced off the walls, so she knew that the chamber in which they were confined could not be large. Besides, she had bumped her head when descending the steps. That meant she was standing in a low, stone cellar in which the light had just gone out. The faint, misty glow she'd previously perceived thanks to the remains of her eyesight had disappeared. So had much of the oxygen they needed in order to breathe.

The air seemed to have grown steadily thinner since Zorbach had finished telephoning, and her lungs were subject to ever-increasing pressure.

'There's a sick woman in here,' she heard him say hoarsely. He sounded breathless and bewildered. 'If we want to get out I'll have to kill her.'

She had been breathing through her mouth ever since

entering the bungalow, but the cloying stench of corruption was the least of her problems. She was imprisoned in unfamiliar surroundings, could hear horrible noises and had breathing problems. On top of that, Zorbach seemed to have lost his mind.

'Stop! No, keep away!' he snapped when she bumped into him. Alina normally had a good sense of direction when on unfamiliar terrain. It didn't always manifest itself, but sometimes she could *feel* when something was in her way, for instance because the air pressure changed just before she collided with a bulky object. But down here, in these cold, noisy surroundings, this was impossible.

Too many distractions. They're overwhelming my senses.

The unpleasant hissing sounds, the hum of the suction pump, the panic in Zorbach's voice – no wonder she'd blundered into him, lost her balance, and clumsily groped for some means of support.

What was it?

The thing she was touching felt like a vacuum-packed joint of meat.

'What is this?' she demanded, but before she could continue to run her hands over the warm plastic film, Zorbach caught hold of her arms.

'No, don't touch her.'

Her?

'What are you talking about?'

'I told you there was a woman here,' he said angrily. 'One of his victims. That's all you need know, believe me.'

You could be right. Maybe I really don't need to know...

But she found out nonetheless. Not from Zorbach, who continued to hold her by the arms and said nothing, presumably wanting to protect her from the sight he'd been compelled to endure all this time.

She learned the truth when she pulled away and Zorbach could restrain her no longer. Her sense of touch conveyed the scene of torment better than words could have described it to her. Beneath the hot, thin film in front of her lay a festering wound. She could feel raw flesh, exposed muscles and sinews – even, in places, bare bones.

A horrible suspicion took shape in her mind: *necrotizing fasciitis...*

She knew of this rare bacterial disease whose victims literally rot away. Whoever was lying there must be in agony, like a neglected patient with sores all over her body. Alina had once treated a businessman who, having been infected with the bacillus while in hospital, had survived but needed physiotherapy in order to recover his full mobility. 'I burst like a ripe tomato,' he'd told her. 'To begin with, everything became inflamed and bloated. Then the skin broke open and my flesh started to putrefy. I had a high temperature and was shivering violently.' His life had been saved by numerous operations and a whole raft of antibiotics – measures that were bound to be too late to save this dying woman, even if she wasn't suffering from the disease.

Perhaps she wasn't even infected. Perhaps she's gangrenous only because she's immobilized inside this plastic film.

'Who is she?' Alina asked. She couldn't help coughing.

The air in the cellar was already heavily saturated with carbon dioxide.

'Search me. I only know the swine must have hooked up the power supply to the ventilator. If I turn it off the light will go on and the door will unlock itself.'

Zorbach sounded as if he was on the verge of panting like TomTom.

'But I can't do it. I couldn't even do it for my mother!'

Alina didn't know what he meant, but this was no time to quiz him about his family history.

'How much time do we have left?' she asked, gingerly feeling for the woman's arm.

'No idea. Five minutes. Maybe less.'

Her fingers encountered some cartilage, a patch of necrotic skin, and travelled cautiously upwards.

'Perhaps we'd be doing her a favour. Perhaps she'd ask us to put her out of her misery if she could still speak.'

Alina could hear Zorbach weeping. There were tears in her eyes too.

Perhaps... No, definitely, if the victim's condition was even half as terrible as her sense of touch conveyed.

But *perhaps* and *if* were insufficient to justify sacrificing an innocent woman for the sake of their own survival. She didn't know about Zorbach, but she knew that she herself would never summon up the strength to snuff out a human life.

Not, at least, while they still had some air left to breathe.

Some air.

Five minutes. Maybe less.

31

SPECIAL TASK FORCE

Fourteen minutes and forty-three seconds after Frank Lahmann caved in, the seven-strong mobile task force had left headquarters and was making for the address he'd given Scholle.

The briefing, which took another five minutes, was given by the task force commander while the police van was en route.

By the time the armed men had deployed outside the bungalow eleven minutes and thirteen seconds later, equipped with bulletproof vests and titanium helmets, three squad cars and two ambulances were already there.

While the two doctors on call were debating why both of them had been summoned to the scene, the occupants of the neighbouring houses were instructed to remain indoors.

At this juncture, the two detectives leading the Eye Collector team, Philipp Stoya and Mike Scholokowsky, drove up.

They had brought a thermal imaging camera to pinpoint

the location of the person or persons inside the house, but they left it in the boot of their car. The Christmas illuminations would have rendered it useless. The task force commander spent fifty seconds wondering whether to turn off the power but decided against it so as not to alert those inside the building that a raid was imminent. To minimize the potential dangers, it was planned to break down the front door and secure each of the bungalow's rooms in turn. The use of force proved unnecessary, however, because the door was open.

It took the police less than fourteen seconds to verify that the ground floor was deserted. That meant they had to gain access the cellar.

At 1.07 a.m. the massive fire door was forced and two men dashed down the cellar steps behind a defensive shield.

By this time, twenty-three minutes had elapsed since Frank Lahmann's disclosure of the suspect's whereabouts.

All these times were carefully entered in a log completed by the task force commander before he persuaded the police medical officer to send him on a week's sick leave. What the log did not record were the unbearable seconds during which the policemen had simply stood there, transfixed by the horrific sight that confronted them in the cellar – seconds that traumatized two of the hardest-nosed cops in Berlin because they'd never seen such 'fucking carnage' before (from a verbatim radio message in response to the question: 'What's going on down there?').

In the end, the doctors were grateful for each other's company. Neither of them was ashamed of his tears when it became clear to them that any medical assistance would be too late.

Blinder than blind is the fearful man
who tremulously hopes it isn't evil.
Defenceless and tired of fear,
he gives it a friendly reception,
hoping for the best
until it's too late.

Max Frisch,
'Biedermann and the Fire Raisers'

30

ALEXANDER ZORBACH

The mist drifted inland from the lake, creating a magical dreamworld. From the ground up, the reeds and trees and the legs of the hunters' hides looked as if they were swathed in silk. A dirty grey silk redolent of moss and wet bark, it left a thin film on the skin. Here on the outskirts of the city, few would have noticed this natural spectacle because of the cold and the lateness of the hour, for who goes roaming through the Grunewald at half-past one in the morning? The ground mist had largely evaporated in the neighbouring residential districts and was scarcely perceptible, but right beside the water, its point of departure, all was seemingly veiled in cloud. The swaths of vapour would not become clearly visible for a few hours yet, after sunrise. Till then the minuscule droplets of moisture were no more than a presentiment, a dark shadow beyond the grimy windows of the old houseboat in which I was standing, mobile in hand.

'I'm sorry, I know it's far too late but I'd really like a word with him.'

Nicci sighed. 'Oh Zorro, Julian stopped coughing half an hour ago. I'm so relieved he's asleep at last.'

'I understand,' I said sadly, amazed that she was remaining so calm although I'd dug her out of bed in the middle of the night. For all that, I felt sure she would have done the same in my position. Anyone who had just escaped certain death felt a need to commune with his family, regardless of its current state of dissolution.

I debated whether to ask her to go upstairs and see if Julian had been woken by the phone, but it proved to be unnecessary.

'Oh, damn!'

Nicci had lowered the phone, but I could hear her berating our son for padding downstairs in his bare feet.

'You'll catch your death.'

She was so scared of electro-smog, she wouldn't have a cordless phone in the house. I prayed to God she wouldn't send Julian upstairs again.

There was a rustling sound. A moment later I was speaking to the person I loved best in the world.

'Hi there, Jules. Happy birthday.'

'Thanks, Daddy.'

The sound of Julian's sleepy but happy voice was almost more than I could bear just then.

'Sorry I woke you. I only wanted to...'

He took advantage of my hesitation to break in eagerly.

'Mummy hung some things on the line today.'

My fingers tightened on the phone as I struggled with an urge to weep.

The line. It had once been my job to tie it to the banisters on the stairs leading to the first floor. Throughout the year, Nicci and I used to hoard little oddments we felt Julian would enjoy getting: a set of transfers for an album, a CD, a new pencil box, but also big presents like an iPod, or, last year, a PlayStation. Wrapped up separately and interspersed with fruit and sweets, these surprises were suspended from the 'birthday line' and Julian was allowed to open one a day from the first day in Advent onwards. The biggest on his birthday, the last one at Christmas.

'I'm coming home today, so I'll hang something on it too,' I promised.

'Really? You bought it for me?' It almost broke my heart, he sounded so enthusiastic.

His wants list this year had included a shockproof watch with a built-in radio. Needless to say, I hadn't found the time to buy one.

'When will I get it?'

'As soon as you've had a good night's sleep, pal.'

I shut my eyes before a tear could escape.

The older you get, the more your life is founded on unfulfilled promises. There is always, of course, a good reason why you can't accompany your son to the school play or attend a PTA meeting, or why, when on holiday, you send the rest of the family down to the beach and wait for an email in your hotel room. God must have thought that by giving people an awareness of their mortality he was creating a paradise on earth: a world filled with individuals who realize that their life must end and will therefore make the most of the little time allotted them. Most of the people I know are well aware that life affords them daily opportunities to squander their time on making money, whereas they only have one chance to celebrate their child's eleventh birthday. A chance I'd just missed.

'At seven o'clock?' he asked. That was the latest time for breakfast if he didn't want to be late for class, though I doubted if Nicci would let him go to school in his present condition.

'I'll be there,' I said, feeling that I genuinely meant it. 'Seven o'clock, word of honour. And please forgive me for not being there tonight, when you were feeling so poorly.'

He laughed. 'No problem. Mummy told me you're looking for the man who kidnaps children.'

Really? Did she now!

'It's okay. That's more important.'

Utterly disconcerted, I groped for words. Before I could ask what else Mummy had said about me, Julian started coughing. A moment later Nicci was on the phone again.

'I'd better get him back to bed.'

'Thank you.'

'What for? I'm his mother.'

'I mean, for what you told him. I know you don't like my job, and I'm quite sure it's partly responsible for the fact that the gulf between us is wider than the San Andreas Fault, but I'm really grateful to you for not letting it affect my relationship with Julian.'

Silence. For a while, all I could hear was leaves rustling outside the houseboat and logs crackling in the stove. Then Nicci sniffed.

'Oh Zorro, I'm so sorry.'

'That makes two of us,' I said. Then I added to my mountain of broken promises. 'I told Julian I'd look in at seven. What say we have breakfast together?'

'Okay.'

'Let's make it a real birthday breakfast, the way we used to. Remember how I carried Julian downstairs while he was still asleep and the first thing he saw when he woke up were the candles on his cake?'

She gave another sniff. I was loath to break the spell by blathering on, so I said goodbye.

'See you in the morning,' she said. Then, just before she hung up: 'You won't forget about Thursday, will you?'

Seven words. Seven knives that pricked the bubble of hope.

Thursday.

The divorce preliminaries.

'No,' I said, feeling like the pathetic fool I doubtless was. 'I'll be there. With my lawyer.'

29

(4 HOURS 8 MINUTES TO THE DEADLINE)

ALEXANDER ZORBACH

First I felt her hand on my shoulder. Then the breath on my neck that accompanied her words.

'May I ask you something?'

Alina was standing just behind me. So close, I couldn't have turned round without touching her. But I didn't want to do that at the moment. All I wanted was to stand beside the window and stare out into the darkness of the forest, which suited my present state of mind so well.

'That depends,' I replied, checking to see whether Nicci really had hung up. My mobile contained an anonymous prepaid SIM card, a crime reporter's basic equipment, but I suspected Stoya might be able to trace me all the same. I didn't care now, I decided. I had no idea what to do next in any case, and the thought of spending the next few nights on remand had lost much of its deterrent effect after what had happened to us.

'That business tonight...' Alina said softly.

The cellar.

'What... what *was* it?'

I didn't answer although I knew what she was getting at.

Alina had just come into contact with *evil* in the truest sense of the word. The Eye Collector had wrapped his mutilated victim in airtight plastic film and thereby caused her to putrefy while still alive. Then, in order to prolong the unknown woman's sufferings, he had deliberately kept death at bay by installing a catheter, together with other devices that kept her supplied with what she needed to survive including a ventilator.

I turned to Alina and looked at her. The fact that she had kept her eyes shut since our escape struck me as indicative. She wanted to cut herself off, to sever all visual connection with a world in which perverse psychopaths demanded human victims.

'Would you have brought yourself to do it?' she asked me after a while.

Do what, throw the switch? Turn off the ventilator so the light came on and the door opened again? Kill the woman so we could live?

'I don't know,' I answered truthfully.

The poor thing was past saving, of course, and I knew it. As with my mother, the intensive care machines had prolonged her death, not her life, yet I'd once more lacked the courage to kill someone, on the off chance of finding another solution.

On the smallest possibility!

Because I had never, at any point, felt sure of having solved the Eye Collector's riddle.

You can turn off the pump and win...

'Luckily, we didn't have to make that decision in the end,' I said. I removed Alina's hand from my shoulder and sat down on the sofa where I'd found her for the first time yesterday afternoon.

Sitting down beside me, she ran her slender fingers cautiously across the top of the table in front of her. I pushed the large mug of coffee – I'd brewed some before phoning – towards her. She raised her eyebrows but said nothing. Then she took a big drink. When she put the mug down her lips glistened in the light of the candle I'd lit as well as the stove as soon as we got there. Eventually she said, 'Yes, we made it anyway. Luckily.'

Alina had ignored my urgent admonitions in the cellar of the bungalow. She had run her hands over dying woman's arms, hands and fingers and come across the little box enclosing her index finger: a photoelectric pulse oximeter of the sort with which patients are fitted before surgery so that their oxygen saturation and heart rate can be monitored during the operation. Alina's reasoning had been as simple as it was logical. Turning off the ventilator couldn't guarantee the unfortunate woman's death on its own. Only the absence of a pulse would convince the Eye Collector that his victim was dead. And that permitted another solution: that one didn't have to turn off her life-support systems in order to set off the chain reaction which would, I hoped, liberate us.

It took me several tense seconds to tear the surprisingly tough plastic film encasing the woman's mutilated body and remove the pulse oximeter from her finger. When I finally succeeded, nothing happened.

Absolutely nothing.

The darkness persisted, the suction pump continued to hum. But then, just as I was about to hyperventilate, TomTom stopped whimpering and silence fell. Total silence.

A moment later the lock on the cellar door opened with a faint click and the ventilator resumed pumping air into the putrescent woman's lungs. She herself seemed quite unaware of what had been going on around her. I wasn't even sure whether the responses I'd noticed on entering the cellar were intentional or an uncontrolled reflex.

Taking Alina's hand, I hurried up the steps and out into the passage. The door slammed shut behind us before I could stop it, but I didn't linger. We raced back along the passage, through the living room and out into the open, where I filled my lungs with cold air untainted by the smell of death. I got through to emergency and gave them the address.

'Quick. Someone's dying here!'

We ran on across the unfenced back garden, which adjoined a narrow lane, and followed TomTom back to the place where we'd left the car. For a moment I'd been tempted simply to give up, to turn myself in and explain everything to Stoya.

But explain what? That a blind girl's visions had led me to the Eye Collector's torture chamber?

In the end it was Alina who had urged me on, shouted

at me not to waste time and drive off – to leave this scene of horror, the concentrate of all my future nightmares.

Hearing her cross her legs on the sofa beside me, I gave a start and opened my eyes. Exhaustion had almost sent me to sleep in the midst of my horrific memories.

'At times like these I curse my lot,' she said in a low voice. 'And I don't mean my blindness.'

She drank some more coffee. Her lower lip quivered. It persisted in doing so even when she bit it.

'I'm talking about my *gift*.' A tear crept from beneath from her right eyelid.

I took her hand. 'Back in the cellar,' I said softly, 'when you touched that dying woman, it happened again, didn't it?'

'No.' She raised her head. 'Worse than that.'

What could be worse than what we've just been through?

'I discovered something in that cellar.'

'About the Eye Collector?' I asked.

'No. About myself.'

Pulling off her wig, she shook her shaven head and tapped herself on the chest. 'I discovered something quite awful *about myself*!'

28

(3 HOURS 59 MINUTES TO THE DEADLINE)

PHILIPP STOYA
(DETECTIVE SUPERINTENDENT, HOMICIDE)

'Where is he?'

'I'm sorry. This time I really don't have a clue.'

Frank rubbed his right ear. He seemed relieved that Scholle wasn't present at this second interview, which was taking place at police headquarters. Stoya still wasn't sure what would have happened if, after visiting the toilet, he'd returned to the conference room a moment later. He had seen Scholle relax his grip on the budding journalist's neck and remove a longish object from his ear – all in double-quick time.

'Just been tickling him a bit for fun,' Scholle had assured him. But the hatred in his sidekick's eyes and the undisguised belligerence in his voice had told a different story.

He'd have rammed it home!

Stoya knew what Scholle was capable of when making no progress with a case. Yet he hadn't always been as ruthless. Divorce had changed him, transforming a good-natured cop into an unpredictable bloodhound. His marriage to the Russian dancer he'd met during a raid on a nightspot had been doomed from the start. Not for the first time, Scholle had mistaken pity for love – a side effect of his well-developed helper syndrome. He paid the brothel to release her, bought her a new wardrobe, and hoped to wean her off drugs if he married her and moved out into the countryside. His attempts at therapy ended the day he came home and found Natasha in their marital bed with a punter from the old days.

If the judge hadn't granted her the right to take their child away once a year, Scholle might still have been the good pal whose weekly session at the bowling alley mattered more to him than wrapping up a case.

He got there only a minute too late, having lingered at his desk and wondered if he really ought to let Natasha and Marcus fly off to Moscow for a holiday. True, the terms of the custody agreement were quite specific. He would be committing an offence if he drove to the airport and prevented Natasha from leaving the country with their son.

In the end his gut feeling triumphed. He sped off to Schönefeld, left his police car in a no-parking zone, and sprinted into the terminal. Too late. The Aeroflot machine was still standing on the tarmac but the doors had closed a minute earlier.

Scholle took six months' unpaid leave in order to scour the villages around Yaroslavl for his son, but without success. Natasha and Marcus never reappeared. The ground seemed to have swallowed them up.

When Scholle returned, empty-handed and broken-hearted, he swore he would never let things ride again; never hesitate, even for a minute, to break regulations if his gut feeling said otherwise.

'For the last time: Where is Alexander Zorbach hiding?'

'Even if you get out a pencil like your colleague...' Frank shrugged. 'I can't tell you.'

'Really?' said Stoya. 'How about these?' Opening a buff folder, he removed several enlarged photographs and spread them out on the table in front of Frank. 'You've nothing to say about these either, I suppose?'

The young man shut his eyes.

'Katharina Vanghal, nurse, a widow of fifty-seven,' Stoya went on. The crime scene photos looked like something out of an abattoir from hell. 'Neighbours describe her as extremely retiring. No men or women friends, not even a household pet. Discounting her well-known mania for lighting up her house like Coney Island at Christmas, she led a thoroughly boring and inconspicuous existence.' He paused briefly. 'Until the Eye Collector decided to transform her cellar into a vacuum-sealed coffin and torture her there for the last few days of her life.'

'Frightful.' Frank turned away.

'Yes, frightful's the word. He wrapped her up in plastic film. Because of its pressure and the fact that she couldn't move, she literally decomposed alive. To prevent her from dying too quickly, the madman sedated her, laid her down on a cooling mattress, and kept her hovering between life and death by means of artificial respiration. It's clear that he not only has medical knowledge but is an amateur technician as well. After all, we found he'd powered his torture chamber by installing a generator in the garden.' Stoya held up two fingers in an unintentional V-sign. 'One generator for two pumps with which to suck the air out of the cellar!'

'Zorbach's all thumbs, you know,' Frank retorted. He was looking tired and his lips were cracked. Stoya decided to apply a little more pressure before offering him a glass of water.

'He has a motive, though.'

'Come again?'

Stoya nodded casually. He might have been commenting on the weather. 'Until two years ago, Katharina Vanghal worked at the Park Sanatorium, where Zorbach's mother is a resident. She was a nurse there until she was summarily fired. According to her file, several of her bedridden patients were found to have developed fourth-degree decubitus ulcers, or bone-deep bedsores, because she hadn't turned them often enough.'

'So my boss revenged himself on his mother's ex-nurse?' Frank laughed. 'You don't believe that yourself.'

'No. I don't *want* to believe it, to be honest, but why are his prints all over that cellar if he has nothing to do with the affair?'

Frank sighed and cast his eyes up at the ceiling. 'Christ, how many more times? It was the blind girl. She led him there.'

'God Almighty!' Stoya slapped the table with the flat

of his hand. 'I've had enough of this mystical mumbo-jumbo. I want to know what—'

'Excuse me, sir.'

The superintendent swung round. He'd been shouting so loudly, he hadn't heard the uniformed policewoman knock.

'Yes?'

She handed him a folder.

'What's this?'

'The parking ticket we were told to check.'

'Well?'

The blonde's upper lip was trembling with nerves, but her voice was firm. 'The car is a green VW Passat, year of manufacture 1997.' Then she named the registered owner.

Stoya's ears started to buzz and his mouth went dry. Now it was his turn to need a drink badly. 'Say that again.'

'It's registered to a Katharina Vanghal.'

It can't be.

Stoya looked across the table at Frank Lahmann, whose expression at that moment was just as disconcerted.

This is impossible.

The tortured nurse's car really had been standing in a disabled parking place the previous afternoon, just as Zorbach had claimed the whole time.

'You see?' Frank said triumphantly when the police-woman had closed the door behind her. 'The Eye Collector went to the blind physiotherapist yesterday afternoon, just as I told you. He was caught on video as he left the building, a piece of information you've disregarded for far too long. No idea how the blind girl knows all these things, but I reckon it's time you started listening to her.'

'Oh, you do, do you?' Angrily, Stoya tossed the folder containing the parking ticket onto the table in front of him. 'You really think I should go chasing after a ghost?'

'A ghost?'

Stoya uttered a bark of laughter when he saw the surprise in Frank's eyes.

'I've run a check on her. Nobody took down a statement from an Alina Gregoriev yesterday. None of my men saw her. She was never here, get it?'

Frank had been listening with his mouth open.

'But that's not all. The computer knows nothing about her either. Alina Gregoriev isn't a registered resident of Berlin. There isn't a physiotherapist of that name anywhere in Germany, so don't give me any more shit about a blind medium who can see into a person's past by touching them. If Zorbach isn't the perpetrator, where does he get all his information?'

Stoya leant both forearms flat on the table and looked the trainee journalist in the eye. 'And don't say Alina Gregoriev. The woman doesn't *exist*!'

27

(3 HOURS 31 MINUTES TO THE DEADLINE)

ALEXANDER ZORBACH

I could sense it. Alina was in the process of withdrawing into herself. It was apparent from her body language: arms folded on chest, knees clamped tightly together, mouth turned down at the corners. In spite of her butch cowboy boots and patched jeans, she looked like a stubborn little girl as she rejected my advice to drink her coffee while it was still hot. Her face was expressionless.

What is it? What did you discover about yourself that was so awful?

She was visibly clamming up. At the same time, I felt sure she wanted to talk. She needed a safety valve. The question was, which would gain the upper hand: her desire to jettison mental ballast or her fear of self-exposure?

All my experience, both as a police negotiator and as a journalist, had taught me neither to pressure a person caught on the horns of an emotional dilemma nor to give them too long to think. It was a tightrope act.

My best results had come from steering the conversation

into supposedly safe channels by asking questions the interviewees could answer in their sleep. Questions they were bound to have been asked a hundred times before.

In Alina's case, only one question occurred to me: 'How did it happen?' I watched her hands, lips and eyes to see if I had got any physical reaction. 'Say if you don't want to talk about it, but it would really interest me to know how you lost your eyesight.'

She drew a deep breath, held it, and expelled it in one long exhalation. Then she sighed faintly.

'It was an accident.'

She opened her eyes and pointed to them. They looked like dull, polished marbles in the dim candlelight. Unzipping her cord jacket, she took out a packet of cigarettes and lit one from the candle.

'It happened twenty-two years ago. I was three at the time and wanted to build a sandcastle with my new girlfriend from the neighbourhood. We hadn't been living in California long – being a civil engineer, my father had spent most of his life globe-trotting from one big construction site to another. This time, however, Dad was employed on a huge hydroelectric dam project that would take years to complete, so we'd bought a house for the first time. A typical American clapboard house with a picket fence, driveway and garage.' She paused. 'That garage...' she said, as if to herself.

'What about it?'

She took a big drag at her cigarette and blew the smoke at the candle, which flickered. 'The previous owner had used it as a workshop. There was a trestle table, a workbench, tools hanging on the walls, and cans of paint everywhere. My father had intended to clear the place out as soon as possible. But I was too quick for him.'

She swallowed hard.

Now it gets serious. Now we're entering the red zone, the place where painful memories lie buried.

'To build our sandcastle we needed a mould for the turrets, so I went to get an old glass jar from the garage. I was a tidy little girl. Tidier than I am now, probably.' She gave a mirthless laugh. 'Anyhow, I ran some water into it to rinse it out. And that was a mistake.'

'Why?'

'Heaven knows what the previous owner of the house had used it for, but the jar contained some calcium carbide. Luckily there was a loud explosion, or my mother wouldn't have known so quickly that an accident had happened.'

Alina blinked as if a movie visible to her alone were unfolding behind her eyelids, which were now closed again.

'Calcium carbide and water produce acetylene, an unstable explosive gas. I might have died if the rescue helicopter hadn't turned up so promptly. As it was I only lost my eyesight.' She sketched some inverted commas in the air to accompany the 'only'. 'The corneas are damaged. Irreparably.'

'I'm sorry.'

'Shit happens,' she said tersely, stubbing out her cigarette.

'Too bad,' I said softly.

At the age of three, long before she'd had a chance to see all the wonders of this world. It's understandable she's bitter.

'Is that why you had that "hate" tattoo done?'

'Hate? What gives you that idea?' she asked in surprise. Then her lips curled in a faint smile. 'Hang on.'

She stood up, took off her jacket and undid the top three buttons of her blouse.

'Is this what you mean?'

She sat down again and presented her bare neck for my inspection. The font used was Runic in character, so the letters on her skin spelt the word 'Fate', not 'Hate'. They glistened like wet ink in the warm candle-light.

'It reads "fate",' I said.

'Depends which way you look at it,' she said with a smile.

Depends which way you look at it. Au revoir. Be seeing you.

Our language is full of visual turns of phrase, and I wondered if all blind people used them as naturally as Alina. She surprised me once more by turning her back on me. 'Look again!'

I didn't understand what she meant at first, but then, as I looked over her shoulder, it positively hit me in the eye.

'Why, it's an ambigram,' I said, though I wasn't sure if I'd used the correct term. The ambigrams familiar to me, like in the thriller *Angels and Demons,* were symmetrical pictures that could be inverted 180 degrees but still spelt the same word, the simplest example being the combination of letters 'WM'. Alina's tattoo was different, however. I had never before seen anything of the kind. If you stood the line of characters on its head they spelt an entirely new word with an entirely different meaning.

'Luck,' I whispered.

She nodded.

Fate or luck, I thought. *In real life, it just depends which way you look at it.*

'It's an asymmetrical ambigram, to be precise. You don't grasp its meaning at first sight, that's why I had it done. Our eyes aren't important. I'll carry the proof of that on my body forever.'

Her big, misty eyes seemed to be focused on my mouth. 'I don't think it matters what we see, only what we perceive. That's what I try to tell myself, at least, but you know what?' She blinked, but it was no use. The dam had broken and tears streamed down her cheeks. 'It just doesn't work!'

'Alina...'

I tried to take her hand, but she swiftly withdrew it and turned away.

'It doesn't matter how often I tell myself that I don't need my eyes,' she said in a muffled voice. She drew up her legs, planted her boots on the sofa, and rested her head on her knees like an airline passenger in readiness for a crash. 'That I don't need to see the world I live in...'

I tried again. I stroked her back, but she merely curled up even tighter and hunched her shoulders as if my caresses were blows. It was as if she wanted to present as small a target as possible.

'I can wear trendy gear, go in for make-up and tattoos and tell myself it makes my blindness a little less extreme.' Her body was shaking. 'But it doesn't work that way.'

'Let me help you.'

'Help me?' she cried. 'How? You've no conception of the world I live in. You close your eyes, everything goes dark, and you think, "Ah, so that's what it's like to be blind." But it isn't!'

'I realize that.'

'Like hell you do! Ever had someone grab your arm and propel you across the street against your will because they think a disabled person has to be helped? Ever been infuriated by dropped kerbs installed for the benefit of wheelchair users, with the result that my kind can't tell where the pavement ends and the road begins? Do people behave as if you aren't there and talk exclusively to the person you're with? The answer's no, am I right?'

She swallowed hard.

'You act as if you understand, Alex, but the fact is, you're clueless. Christ, I bet you've never even thought twice about the No. 5 Braille dot on your push-button phone. You touch the key daily because it's on *every* 5. Phone, pocket calculator, ATM, computer. You make physical contact with my world day after day but you never spare it a single thought, so don't tell me you understand me and my life.'

She sniffed and wiped the tears from her cheeks with her forearm, breathing heavily. The verbal thunderstorm had dispelled much of her tension. The next time she spoke her voice was subdued once more. She was far from through, though. I felt that the crux of what she had to tell me was still to come.

'Sometimes when I'm asleep at night, I dream I'm falling down a well. Down and down I go – my descent into the darkness never ends and the darkness becomes darker still. I stretch out my hands to touch the sides of the well, but there aren't any. They dissolve like my memories of the world before the accident.'

The silence that followed was broken by a log spitting in the stove.

'They disappear, understand? Everything goes. My memories of light, colours, shapes, faces, objects. The further I fall the more they fade. And you know what the worst of it is?'

It doesn't stop when you wake up.

'I shout myself awake and the falling sensation ceases,' she said, sounding infinitely weary all of a sudden. 'But only that. Everything else persists. I'm still imprisoned in that black hole, that nothingness. I sit up in bed, trembling, cursing the day I wanted to make a sandcastle and wondering if I still exist at all.' She turned her head as if trying to look at me. 'Does the outside world exist?'

I didn't know what to say, least of all in answer to her next question, which disconcerted me.

'Do *I* exist?' She grasped the hem of her lumberjack shirt and crumpled it like a sheet of paper. 'Do I, Alex?'

I hesitated, then took her hand and gently prised her fingers open.

'Of course you do.'

'Prove it to me. I want to believe it, so please show me.'

She put a hand to my face. Her fingers caressed my chin, traced the line of my lips, lingered briefly on my eyelids.

I experienced one of those rare moments in life when nothing matters but the present. I forgot about the baby on the bridge and my failed marriage. Even the face of Charlie, whose children I aimed to rescue from the Eye Collector's clutches, disappeared from my mind. Instead, I was pervaded by a sensation I'd almost forgotten.

I had last felt it when seeing Nicci for the first time. Not with my eyes or brain – Alina was mistaken if she believed that they were what perceived the truly important things in life. When you yearn to be so close to another human being you would happily exchange bodies with them, the intellect cuts out and the soul becomes the only sensory organ still in operation.

'Show me,' she repeated insistently. 'Show me I still exist.'

Then she put her lips to mine, and I was surprised to discover how much I'd been wanting her to do just that.

26

(2 HOURS 47 MINUTES TO THE DEADLINE)

FRANK LAHMANN (TRAINEE JOURNALIST)

'Shared hallucinations,' said a grumpy voice. It was issuing from the loudspeakers of a telephone located between them on the interview room's laminated brown table. Professor Hohlfort had been connected from his home in Dahlem. 'My guess is, you're suffering from an induced delusional disorder.'

'But Alina exists,' Frank protested. He looked at Stoya. 'I saw the blind girl with my own eyes.'

The phone crackled and the profiler's next words were preceded by a loud atmospheric hiss. 'Am I right in thinking, Herr Lahmann, that you've been working closely with the wanted man for months?'

'Yes.'

'You're stressed? You seldom get more than four hours' sleep a night?'

This time Frank merely nodded.

'Well, it has often been found that mentally healthy persons subjected to such pressure will take on their partner's hallucinations. This phenomenon usually occurs in persons forming part of a clearly defined pecking order – married couples of whom one is the dominant partner, for instance. However, another possible factor might be the professional dependence of a trainee on his mentor.'

'Are you telling me I'm bananas?'

'No, Frank. You've merely taken on the hallucinations of your father figure, for want of a better term. This is unusual but quite conceivable, given the exceptional strain to which you've both been subjected for the last few weeks. After all, you've been up against one of the most atrocious serial murderers of recent decades.'

Frank stared at the phone open-mouthed. Was the old fogey being serious?

'I'm not crazy and neither is my boss.'

'Well, his medical record says differently, doesn't it?'

Stoya confirmed Hohlfort's statement with a regretful shrug. 'Zorbach and I were colleagues, and there's little you don't know about someone when you've worked so closely with them for years on end. It's an open secret that Zorbach has been undergoing psychiatric treatment since that business with the Ondine baby. He isn't the first ex-cop whose name appears in Dr Roth's appointments diary, and he certainly won't be the last.'

Frank shook his head. 'I can't believe it.'

The phone emitted another hiss. 'Show him,' said Hohlfort.

Frank looked at Stoya enquiringly. The inspector opened a small laptop. Less than twenty seconds later, he angled it so that Frank could see what was on the screen.

'We found this on Zorbach's office computer.'

Frank raised his eyebrows and stared at the screen.

'An email?' he said.

To: a.zorbach@gmx.net
Subject: Eye Collector's motive

His eyes travelled from the email's header to its text.

'He sent it to himself,' he heard Stoya say. It sounded like a question.

'He often does that,' Frank said. 'It's his way of creating a backup. Other people store important material on a USB stick. Alex sends it to himself. The advantage is, he can access it on any computer in the world.'

'Interesting,' said Hohlfort, 'but can you explain the contents?'

Frank stared at the screen for a while, then shook his head.

To: a.zorbach@gmx.net
Subject: Eye Collector's motive

Why does everyone concentrate on the eyes alone? They're just a diversion. He's like a conjurer who sets off an explosion with his right hand so we fail to see the rabbit he's pulling out of the hat with his left. The families are far more important. He's merely carrying out a love test!

'Do you know what he means, Herr Lahmann? What is this love test?'

Stoya had stationed himself behind Frank and was casting a shadow over the screen.

'No, no idea. He never discussed it with me.'

Hohlfort's rasping voice issued from the loudspeakers. 'In that case, I think it's high time *we* discussed it with him.'

The inspector returned to his place and shut the laptop. 'Your boss's inside knowledge is hard to explain, you know that yourself. He had contact with both the mutilated nurse and the latest victim, Lucia Traunstein, whose mobile he called some hours after her murder. This may be proof of either his innocence or his mental instability. But now it appears he also knows the Eye Collector's motive. I've no idea what this goddamned love test means and I don't know how deeply involved he really is, but of one thing I'm absolutely certain: I must find him as soon as possible. No matter what.'

Stoya planted both palms on the table and looked down at Frank menacingly. Their faces were so close, Frank could see the droplets of blood that had lodged in the fine hairs in the detective's nostrils.

'I'll find him, Frank, and you're going to help me. Whether you like it or not.'

25

(2 HOURS 29 MINUTES TO THE DEADLINE)

ALEXANDER ZORBACH

Just as I felt she was on the point of losing control, she stopped. Just like that. Still astride me, she clasped her hands behind her head and froze.

I was taken aback. 'What is it?' I asked, removing my hand from under her shirt.

A moment ago I'd had the feeling I could read her thoughts, we were so tightly fused together, but all at once, although I was still inside her, she was miles away.

'I don't feel a thing,' she gasped.

I stared at her in bewilderment. She had cried out and sunk her teeth in my neck, seemingly overwhelmed by a tidal wave of desire.

'No kidding?' I said flippantly, trying to lessen the distance between us. I took hold of her hips and thrust my pelvis at her. She moaned and bit her knuckles.

'You really can't feel a thing?'

'Idiot. I don't mean that.'

In one swift movement she freed herself from my embrace and climbed off me.

'What, then?'

Her discarded jeans were lying in front of the sofa table. She felt for them with her foot.

'Absolutely nothing happens when I touch you. I only touched the Eye Collector's shoulders for a moment, but I can make love with you and... nothing.' She shook her head. 'I've had a lot of men. I know, of course, that physical contact isn't enough on its own. What puzzles me is why it only happens with arseholes who hurt me, not with someone like you. With you it's just nice.'

With you it's just nice... There are times when you don't need a lot of words to make a poem.

'I can't see into *your* past,' she said.

'That's a mercy for both of us, take it from me.'

Alina didn't laugh. She didn't even smile faintly. She simply continued to sit beside me with one leg in her jeans and the other on the sofa, sighing.

'Maybe I don't have enough negative energy inside me,' I hazarded. A few hours ago I would have advised her to seek psychiatric treatment for her delusions. Now that her visions had introduced us to the Eye Collector's underworld, my sceptical outlook on life had been shaken.

'No, it isn't that.' She finished buttoning her jeans and drew up both legs on to the sofa. 'Until today I also thought it had to do with negative energy in the people I touched. But that poor woman in the cellar was full of it, and I felt no more than your own fingertips did. That was when it dawned on me. Sometimes I get these feelings and sometimes I don't. I suddenly realized why.'

'Why?' I asked softly.

What did you discover about yourself in the cellar?

'It isn't just physical contact that enables me to see into some people's past.'

'So what is it?'

'Pain!'

I tried to withdraw my hand, but she hung on to it.

'I only remember when I'm hurt.'

And then the words came pouring out. 'I had my first vision when I was seven, just after a car had knocked me down. I only have to think of it and I can still smell the driver's breath. It stank of decaying food and cheap spirits when he hauled me to my feet. I tried to put my weight on my right leg and the vision transfixed me like a flash of lightning. I saw a reprise of the accident amidst the aura of pain.'

'You *saw* him knock you down?'

She nodded.

'From the driver's perspective, with his eyes. I saw him screw the cap back on the bottle he'd just taken a swig from at the last traffic lights. Then I saw a child walking along the street. I heard him curse loudly. Then came a cut. Next thing I saw, he was bending over the little girl, who was howling with pain in the roadway. Over me.'

'But earlier on, in the cellar?'

'I was agitated, frightened, scared to death, but it wasn't like that time when the man drove into me, or like just before I started to massage the Eye Collector, when I stubbed my toe.'

'You mean...'

'Yes.' She nodded. 'I have to be hurt.'

I stood up so abruptly that TomTom, who had been dozing beside us, gave a jump.

'I know it sounds incredible, Alex, but when that vase fell on my foot back at the flat it happened again. More details came back to me.'

'You can't be serious.' I looked around for my own jeans.

'I am.' She presented her ear to me as she always did when paying full attention to someone. 'Pain not only summons up new visions. If it's intense enough it can summon up old ones as well.'

I found my jeans on the floor and felt in the pockets for my mobile.

'What are you doing?' Alina asked.

'Calling the police. We're going to turn ourselves in.'

'What? No!'

'Yes!'

Enough of this. It's over.

'I'm putting an end to this nonsense right now.'

The mobile vibrated as soon as I turned it on.

Seven phone calls. One text message.

`There really is a parking ticket!` I read, and quickly opened the rest of Frank's message.

`The police have found the Eye Collector's car.`

My head swam when I read the address.

This makes no sense. Why should he do that?

The Eye Collector had left his car outside my mother's nursing home.

24

FRANK LAHMANN (TRAINEE JOURNALIST)

'You did the right thing.'

Stoya put his hand on Frank's shoulder and relieved him of the mobile he'd just used to send the text message. The young trainee started at his touch.

'Really?' he said. 'So why do I feel like a two-faced bastard?'

23

(62 MINUTES TO THE DEADLINE)

ALEXANDER ZORBACH

Something's wrong here.

I knew it the moment I entered the room.

Alina had remained behind with TomTom in the car, which was parked in a side street behind the sanatorium. It was hard enough for a sighted person to sneak into the ward unobserved. A couple complete with guide dog and white cane wouldn't have got past the reception desk.

'Hello, Mother,' I whispered, taking her hand. My uneasy feeling that something was wrong intensified. 'Here I am again.'

Something's different.

I'd been prepared for the worst throughout the drive, expecting to be greeted by the sight of a nurse making up my mother's empty bed. She would have turned round, casting her eyes up to heaven in annoyance because the hospital authorities had failed to inform me in good time and left the thankless job to her.

'... sorry to say your mother died during the night... It

wasn't entirely unexpected, though... A mercy, actually, from one point of view...'

But it wasn't like that. There was no empty bed, no nurse, and the gadgets that prevented my mother from dying had not been switched off.

Not yet.

They continued to hum and hiss their electronic hymn of praise to intensive care, a morbid symphony performed for an apathetic audience that had long ceased to register the sounds in its vicinity.

Everything's the same.

Almost.

I felt tempted to remove the breathing tube that distorted her face, but I had only to look into those pale green, watery eyes, which were staring up at the dim ceiling lights, to see that it really was my mother lying there in a waking coma. She twitched occasionally, but that was normal too. They were unconscious reflexes. After-images of the person she was, like the fading speck of light on the screen of an old-fashioned television set after it's been unplugged.

Everything's the same. Her occasional moans and the smell of the body lotion with which they rubbed her every day.

For all that, something here is wrong.

Just then my mobile buzzed. It informed me, yet again, that a diverted call had been made to my number. I listened to the message.

'It's the nicotine patch!' Dr Roth, the person whose

voice I had least expected to hear, sounded as if he had won the lottery.

I switched the phone from one ear to the other in the vague hope of enhancing my comprehension of what he had to tell me.

'The smoking cure you're taking contains varenicline, a substance very similar to laburnum, an extremely poisonous plant. In the States, the Federal Aviation Administration has already banned airline pilots from using it because, like laburnum, it can induce hallucinatory daydreams.'

I felt for the patch on my upper arm.

'So-called varenic dreams. We've found substantial traces of varenicline in your blood, Herr Zorbach. This may account for your nervous condition, and it wouldn't surprise me if you perceive colours, smells and light more intensely than normal.' Dr Roth chuckled. 'You aren't having any schizophrenic hallucinations. Simply remove the thing and you'll be fine.'

Will I? I crumpled the patch between my fingers and pressed the red button on my mobile.

I was far from fine. I couldn't get hold of Frank, the police wanted me for murder, and I'd been told to not worry about my perceptual disorders.

I looked at the window – it was still dark outside. My gaze travelled from the mottled grey lino on the floor to the battery of medical appliances around the bed. I didn't know what they were called, but their instruction manuals had to be as thick as phone directories. The bedside cabinet containing Mother's old diary caught my eye. It was the one I always read aloud from when I visited her. She herself would never again be able to open it and wallow in nostalgic memories such as the day we discovered the track to my subsequent hideaway in the Nikolskoë Forest. I was just about to see if the little, gold-blocked, leather-bound volume was still in the drawer when I spotted what had been disturbing me all the time.

The photograph.

What the...?

It hadn't been there the last time I visited her. The frame, yes. I had given it to her for Christmas many years ago, together with one of the few snaps of myself that even I liked. Taken by my father outside our front door, it showed a seven-year-old Alex doing up his shoelaces with an air of intense concentration. The photo had always put me in a melancholy frame of mind because it was a reminder of a time when being teased in the school playground on account of my cheap sneakers was my greatest cause for concern.

I picked it up.

The picture of me on the stone steps was still in the frame, but it wasn't as I remembered it. It was a close-up no longer.

I don't believe this!

I had shrunk to about half my original size. This meant that more of my surroundings were visible and I was...

...no longer alone?

My hands began to shake as I stared at the face of the

other boy who had suddenly materialized on the steps beside me and was watching me do up my shoes.

Who are you? I whispered to myself. *Who on earth are you?*

The boy's face seemed familiar, but he looked younger than me and wasn't recognizable as one of my friends at the time in question.

What are you doing in my picture?

I turned the frame over, opened the clips that held the cardboard backing in place, and removed the photo.

And how did you get on to my mother's bedside cabinet?

The boy had flaxen hair. His left eye was covered by a pink plaster of the kind young children are made to wear to cure a squint.

...his left eye...

My bewilderment grew when I discovered the note in pencil on the back:

Grünau, 21.7.(77)

I never got a chance to put the photo back. I was still pondering on the significance of the date – and the fact that I'd never been to Grünau as a child – when I was arrested.

THE EYE COLLECTOR'S SECOND LETTER
EMAILED VIA AN ANONYMOUS ACCOUNT

To: Thea Bergdorf <thea@bergdorf-privat.com>
Subject: ... and nothing but the truth!

Dear, purblind Frau Bergdorf,

I must, I'm afraid, continue to address you in this manner because you're still *blind* to the hidden 'pieces' in my game.

Your eyes will be opened by this second email, which I'm sending you even before the game is over. I hope you'll be grateful, although I'm assuming that you check your private account a great deal less regularly than your professional email address. If you did you'd long ago have discovered my first letter and passed it on to the authorities, or at least published it on your paper's website.

Well, as I'm sure you can imagine, my own commitments make it hard for me to keep up with everything at this hectic stage in the game. That being so, I'll come straight to the point: my motive, which I'm handing you on a plate simply so that you and the miserable lie machine you call a newspaper can inject a little moderation into your malicious campaign against me in the future. (Wow, I'm sure that was far too long a sentence for someone whose mindless rag normally confines itself to printing sentences in which no commas occur.)

All I do, I do in order to preserve the only true system of values in the world worth fighting for: the family.

Your paper, which (pardon me) is worth less than the shit on its pages after your readers have used it to line the bottom of their bird cages, condemns me – *me!* – for being a destroyer of families. The opposite is the case. Nothing is closer to my heart than the restoration of the orderly, protective relationships that my brother and I were not privileged to enjoy.

I think that my little brother suffered most from our father's lack of love, perhaps because his grave illness rendered him more sensitive than I was. The loss of his left eye at the age of five affected more than his eyesight. It was almost as if the cancer had eaten into his soul after the eye's surgical removal had failed to assuage its hunger.

Mentally more stable than my brother, I found it easier to accept our father's continual absences, which I sensed even when he wasn't – for once – away on a business trip or spending time with his friends.

There came the day when our mother, too, abandoned us – and I mean that in more than a metaphorical sense. Having stowed all her jewellery, cash and papers in the little sports bag she always took to the gym, she went off and never came back.

Father was furious. 'What am I supposed to do with you two brats?' he bellowed. He seemed less annoyed that Mother had skipped out than he was about the fact she'd neglected to take us with her.

My little brother couldn't understand at first. He scoured the house in search of our mother for hours on end. He searched the cellar, the attic, the summer house. He even got into the wardrobe, buried himself sobbing among her clothes, sniffed her perfume, and discovered that she'd taken her favourite blouse with her.

The salmon-coloured silk blouse had suited her. We, her children, had ceased to do so.

That night, when my brother raised the subject of the 'love test', I went along with it for the first time. Until then it had never been more than a wild idea, an unrealistic fantasy entertained by two sad and lonely children. The thing was, my brother had thought up a test that would prove whether or not our parents loved us. It was simple, really: one of us would have to die.

Hitherto we'd always spoken of drawing lots. The winner would check to see if Mother and Father really wept at the loser's funeral.

On the day our mother deserted us, however, I suggested another way of testing our father's love for us.

We would hide!

Not in our tree house or the shack beside the lake, but somewhere we'd never been before.

'If Daddy still loves us he'll come looking for us, and the sooner he finds us the more he loves us.'

It was a puerile method such as only a seven-year-old boy and his heartbroken little brother could have devised. But, childishly naive though it was, it displayed a logical simplicity that still fascinates me today, many years later.

We found a suitable hiding place the following night. Whoever had dumped the old chest freezer in the woods had at least taken the trouble to wash it out with hot water. Nothing – no smells or labels or scraps of food – gave any indication of what it had contained before we lay down inside it.

We were glad the capacious thing was so close to home. It had been left on the edge of a clearing, beside the path our father took when he went jogging every evening. No one could have failed to see it, so we weren't unduly worried when we found we couldn't open the freezer once we'd pulled the lid down over our heads.

At first we even made jokes about the broken screwdriver with the wooden handle which the previous owner must have left inside the chest, and which kept digging into my backside. Later, when the air became steadily thinner, it proved as little use to us as the coin in my trouser pocket.

The lid wouldn't budge because the chest freezer was so old it didn't yet have a magnetic seal, as modern safety regulations prescribe, but was equipped with a bolt that could only be opened from the outside.

Our love test had unintentionally become a test of life or death.

'Daddy will come soon,' I said.

I said it again and again. At first loudly and with conviction, but then, as I grew tired, ever more faintly. I said it just before I dozed off and immediately after waking up.

'Daddy will come soon.'

My little brother heard me say it when he wet himself, when he started crying, and when thirst woke him up again. I also repeated it while he was sleeping his way to extinction.

'Daddy will come soon. He loves us, so he'll come looking and find us.'

But that was a lie. Daddy didn't come.

Not for twenty-four hours. Not for thirty-six or forty hours.

We were eventually released by a forester.

After forty-five hours seven minutes.

By that time my brother had suffocated. I was told later that my father thought Mummy had changed her mind and come back to fetch us, so he blithely went drinking with friends instead of looking for us.

I still can't rid myself of the notion that he might have downed a cold beer at the precise moment when my brother, mad with thirst, ripped the plaster off his empty eye socket and started chewing it. Never a night goes by but I dream of gazing at that hole in the head of my lifeless brother, who was doomed to die simply because his father had failed the love test.

My grandparents, to whom the juvenile welfare department entrusted me when my physical condition improved, confessed how worried they had been that the dearth of oxygen in the chest freezer might have inflicted permanent damage on me. Grandpa, a village vet who continued to practise in old age, believed that contact with fellow creatures in need of help would do me good, so he took me with him to his surgery, allowed me to assist him, and initiated me by degrees into the secrets of veterinary medicine, which are still of use to me today. For instance, how to gauge the amount of ketamine to administer in relation to an animal's age, weight and condition so as to ensure that anaesthesia remains stable during an operation. How to fit the mask over a St Bernard's muzzle before you cut its stomach open. Or how to remove a cat's cancerous eye. Grandpa praised me for my skill and my eagerness to learn.

And, since my grandparents never discovered the remains of the stray village cats – neither those I buried alive nor the ones I stuffed into sacks before pouring petrol over them – they eventually stopped worrying about the sodden bedclothes in which I regularly woke up.

'It's no wonder, considering all that boy went through,' they kept telling themselves.

They were excellent foster parents.

Kind.

Elderly.

And unsuspecting.

22

(59 MINUTES TO THE DEADLINE)

ALEXANDER ZORBACH

They had waited until I disappeared into my mother's room and watched me for a while through the crack in the bathroom door, which was ajar, presumably to satisfy themselves that I was alone and unarmed. At last, when I was distracted by the photo and holding the frame in both hands, they made their move. Two uniformed policemen, the younger one with a moustache, the older less muscular but with surprise on his side, rushed out and grabbed me from behind.

They needn't have pinned me to the floor or plasticuffed my wrists; I'd intended to give myself up in any case.

Scholle was waiting in front of the lifts with a broad grin on his face. 'Oh sure,' he said sarcastically when they marched me up to him, 'of course you meant to turn yourself in.'

I wondered why the hospital corridor hadn't been cleared before my arrest. Although there were few people about at that early hour – only one scared nurse flitted past us – what would have happened if I'd really been the Eye

Collector? What if I'd resisted or taken hostages? Even more puzzling was the fact that these cops didn't look the kind you'd choose to employ to capture a violent criminal.

Scholle briefly checked my cuffs. Then he and I and the uniformed policemen got into a goods elevator.

'Minus one?' I said, when Scholle pressed the relevant button. 'Are you taking me out through the basement?'

The youngster with the moustache stared indifferently at the bare concrete lift shaft gliding past. The older man, who was casually chewing gum, looked straight through me. Only Scholle responded to my question.

'What would *you* do?' He glanced at his watch. 'The deadline's only fifty-nine minutes away, so tell me what you'd do in my place.'

Beads of sweat were trickling down his forehead. He wiped them off with the back of his hand, staring at me as if he meant to hypnotize me. 'What if it was your kid?'

We passed the first floor.

'Would you waste time taking a suspect back to headquarters and wait there for his antisocial brief to turn up while Julian was suffocating in some lousy hole?'

Julian? Did he know my son's name from my record, or had we sometime chatted about our children informally?

I tried to recall what I knew about Scholokowsky. He hadn't been with Homicide for long in my day. I'd never had a proper conversation with him, just a few chance encounters in the canteen and at the annual police party, but I naturally knew his history – everyone at headquarters did. The press usually made a meal of cases where foreign fathers robbed German wives of their joint offspring by whisking them off, especially when it was to countries with fundamentalist governments. Scholle's fate had provided a drastic demonstration that such cases didn't always involve the male sex or a particular religion.

'Christ, Zorbach, you shot a woman in the head to save a baby's life. What would you do if you were face to face with the Eye Collector?'

I realized to my surprise that I was seriously considering Scholle's rhetorical question. Looking into his piggy little eyes, I recognized the rage-driven conviction in them and nodded.

Little though we had in common, I understood what the man was trying to tell me. Scholle was an obsessive who had lost someone because he'd hesitated too long. He wasn't going to make the same mistake twice.

Not in my case.

The lift jolted and came to rest. It had reached its destination.

Minus one.

'That way,' Scholle told the two policemen. He shoved me, too, along the basement passage to the left, which was coldly illuminated by energy-saving bulbs.

'Once upon a time,' I said, 'I'd have done exactly the same as you – beaten the shit out of the Eye Collector until he revealed his hiding place – but everything changed after I killed that woman on the bridge.'

Twenty metres along the passage we came to a halt in front of a big brushed steel door.

'Is that so?' Scholle told the policemen to wait outside. 'Why?'

'Because I now know how it feels when you aren't sure you've got the right man.'

He laughed.

'You're making a mistake. I'm not the Eye Collector.'

He brushed some more sweat off his forehead and stared at me, narrowing his eyes. 'We'll see,' he said eventually.

Then, opening the door, he thrust me into the gloom.

21

(55 MINUTES TO THE DEADLINE)

TOBY TRAUNSTEIN

Babushka... It really was like being trapped inside one of those dolls. Toby had no idea what he'd exchanged for the wooden coffin, but at least breathable air had ceased to be a problem. For the first time for many, many hours he no longer felt as if his chest were straining beneath the weight of a crate of Coca-Cola. Stars were no longer dancing before his eyes, either, and he could keep his balance even when he stood up. Which he could, in his new, steel-walled surroundings.

True, the darkness was still as absolute and his head was throbbing even worse than it had in the trolley case. No wonder, after he'd driven the screwdriver into the side of the 'coffin' until splinters and then whole chunks of wood came away and the shaft eventually broke through. The tiny hole he'd made at first was only just big enough to admit his forefinger. Later, when he could insert his whole hand and forearm, he'd realized that he would have to start all over again, a little further to the right and higher up. That was bad luck, but it could have been worse. If his first hole had been only a few centimetres lower he wouldn't have been able to feel the bolt that held the lid of the crate in place. His fingers had touched the thing but were too far away to shift it.

So where am I now?

Toby felt a new wave of fear surge through him. He couldn't remember ever having been in a room whose walls were so cold and smooth.

A garbage truck, he thought, panic-stricken. *This is how I imagine the inside of a garbage truck.*

It didn't smell like one, luckily. More like a workshop. Or a boat.

Yes, that's it! It smells like the motorboat Daddy wanted to buy one time.

Lubricating oil and brackish water, that's what it smelt of. It was rocking gently, too.

Toby had searched the whole of the floor and walls. He'd even climbed back into the wooden crate, but he hadn't found anything he could use on the metal walls.

He had discovered a narrow crack on one side of the compartment, but he couldn't lever it any wider open with the screwdriver. The third time he tried the shaft came away from the wooden handle and hit the floor with a loud clunk. It was now lying, abandoned and useless, on the floor.

On the *swaying* floor.

At first he thought his sense of balance had gone again. He hadn't had anything to eat or drink for days, after all, so he was feeling faint and exhausted. It wouldn't have been surprising if the floor had seemed to sway beneath his feet. But there were also those sounds. Creaking sounds, like a rope being stretched to breaking point.

There... there it goes again!

Toby struggled with his fatigue, the incredibly heavy, leaden fatigue that had descended on him as suddenly as the darkness in which he'd woken up.

Fear, hunger, thirst, stress, exhaustion – he might have withstood them all for another half-hour, had he not lacked something he needed almost more than the air he'd managed to regain. And that was... hope.

He couldn't imagine ever getting out of there. Not unaided. He hadn't the strength even to get to his feet one last time. He'd heard somewhere that accident victims shouldn't go to sleep. They had to remain awake or die.

So I'd better stand up again. I've never fallen asleep on my feet, only lying down. I mustn't...

'Hey!'

His heart was pounding beneath his T-shirt, which was sodden with sweat.

What was that?

He staggered backwards and felt it touch his shoulder again.

I don't believe it! Where did that come from?

He must have missed it in the darkness.

A rope? Why would a rope be hanging from the top of this metal compartment?

Reaching up, he cautiously grasped it and slid his fingers

down the nylon rope until they were gripping the plastic handle on the end.

What now?

He hesitated, but only for a moment. Then he did what anyone would have done who is offered a helping hand in the dark. He gave it a tug.

Oh no, please not...

He quickly let go of the rope, but it was already too late.

I didn't mean to... please no...

The floor beneath his feet had started to sway again, but more violently than before.

20

(49 MINUTES TO THE DEADLINE)

ALEXANDER ZORBACH

Dusty white tiles, matt aluminium tables, extractor hoods over the worktops – I was momentarily afraid I'd wound up in the sanatorium's pathology lab.

Then I saw the crockery cupboards and the grimy pass-through dishwasher in the middle of the room and began to grasp where I was. Scholle had refrained from turning on the neon lights overhead, so our only source of illumination was a street light in the grounds outside whose meagre rays slanted down through the semi-basement windows. All I could make out in the gloom were vague shapes and shadows. I had the feeling I was part of a blurred black-and-white photograph.

'This used to be the hospital kitchen,' said Scholle. He indicated three massive cauldrons on his right, which would have looked more at home in a brewery. 'Nowadays they do their cooking in the new annexe. The basement is completely deserted, which means we won't be disturbed.'

A lump of plaster crunched beneath his leather soles as he went over to the island unit that occupied the right-hand third of the abandoned kitchen. Roughly the size of a small family car, it incorporated a stove equipped with four ceramic hobs, twin sinks, and a brown tiled worktop strewn with the kind of rubbish that inevitably collects in derelict buildings: a broken electrical adaptor, ripped-out lengths of electric cable, dirty cardboard plates, plastic bowls pressed into use as ashtrays, and a half-empty Coca-Cola bottle. Scholle swept the whole of the clutter to the floor with his elbow.

'Does Stoya know we're here?' I asked.

He laughed. 'Sure he does, not that he'll ever say so on the record. He's too chicken to want to ruin his career by making an illegal arrest. Unlike me, Stoya doesn't think it was you. He hasn't even called the DA.'

An illegal arrest?

'You mean you don't have a warrant?'

'Why do you think I've stationed Laurel and Hardy outside there instead of a couple of real pros? Those two owe me a favour.'

He produced a street map from his jacket pocket and spread it out on the ceramic hobs he'd just swept clear of rubbish.

'Stoya only wanted a chat with you, cop to ex-cop. He wanted to give you a last chance to explain your presence at two crime scenes and your intimate knowledge of the circumstances. Luckily, I managed to convince him I'm more likely to get the answers out of you in time.'

Of course. Stoya had probably told him – officially, in

front of witnesses – to bring me down to headquarters for an informal chat. Unofficially, he would have winked at him.

I took advantage of a moment when Scholle had turned his back to look around for the fire exit any industrial kitchen was bound to have, but he'd left the lights off for a reason. All I could make out were four small skylights I'd never get to before the fat detective hurled himself at me. Under normal circumstances he wouldn't have been a match for me. His knowledge of boxing, unlike mine, was limited to television films. Neither height nor bulk could compensate for years of training. Not so the plasticuffs around my wrists.

'Let me go, Scholle. It's not too late, even now.'

'Sure.' He glanced at his watch and sighed. 'Time's running out, so let's dispense with the small talk and make a deal: I'll tell you all I know and you tell me what I want to hear, okay?'

'You're making a big mistake, Scholle, I—'

'Okay, done, I'll kick off. We've found the car you used to transport the children. A patrol found it about ten minute's drive from here, in the car park of an abandoned recycling plant.'

He tapped the bottom right-hand third of the map.

'You've got the wrong man,' I said.

'The boot contained solid evidence. Hair, fibres, broken fingernails.'

'Maybe, but the car wasn't left there by me.'

He wasn't listening to me. 'Stoya's already on the spot.

Eight dog handlers are combing the area, but it's a helluva big industrial estate, as you can see.' His lower jaw pumped angrily up and down as he spoke. It was as if he had to chew over his words before spitting them out at me. 'Far too big for us to cover in the time that's left. That's why I'm relying on your cooperation.'

'Scholle, please...'

'Well, that's my end of the deal. Now it's your turn. Tell me where the kids are.'

'I don't know.'

'Where were you planning to drown them?'

Drown them?

'I'm just as keen to catch the swine as you are, I swear.'

He shook his head with the air of a father who's gradually losing patience with an obstinate child.

'Okay, have it your way,' he said as he folded up the street map. 'At least the power's still on down here.'

I heard a click followed by an electrostatic noise like an old-fashioned television set being switched on. Simultaneously, a red light on the front of the kitchen range lit up.

After that, several things happened in quick succession.

First I felt a gust of air. Then my neck was transfixed by a shaft of agony. I couldn't move my head for fear my spine would snap. Scholle's forearm had cut off my air supply so effectively, I couldn't utter a sound as he dragged me over to the cooking unit by brute force. The hobs were already glowing faintly.

Next, he kicked my legs from behind and I collapsed.

Just as my knees hit the flagstones, the kitchen was suddenly flooded with light.

At first I thought it was pain that had projected its dazzling glare on to my eyeballs. Then, as the flickering neon tubes on the ceiling attained their full luminescence, I grasped that someone must have turned the lights on.

Stoya? I thought, praying that Scholle's verdict on his boss had been mistaken.

But then I saw a pair of muddy boots appear in the kitchen doorway, and my last hope of escaping torture at his hands was dashed.

19

'I told you I didn't want to be...' Scholle relaxed his grip and laughed. 'Well, fancy that!' He sounded surprised.

He thrust me aside and left me gasping on the floor in front of the island unit.

'I was just getting myself a coffee upstairs in reception,' I heard one of the cops say, 'when I heard her ask the receptionist for Zorbach's mother.'

Damn it, Alina, you should have waited for me in the car.

'You told us about her, Inspector, so I thought you might like a word with her as well.'

It was a moment before I managed to raise my head. My crushed larynx was hurting so badly and it was as much as I could do to replenish my lungs with air, but I'd already recognized her scuffed old cowboy boots by the time she spat in Scholle's face.

'Take your hands of me, you wanker.'

Scholle thanked the man with a grin and dismissed him. He waited until the door had closed. Then, gripping Alina's arm, he wrested the walking cane from her grasp and thrust her roughly in my direction.

'Well, well, so the phantom does exist.'

The phantom?

I struggled into a sitting position. I would dearly have liked to massage my throat, but my hands were cuffed behind my back.

What the devil does he mean? Surprised a moment later when Scholle answered my question, I realized I must have uttered it out loud.

'Alina isn't your blind girlfriend's real name, Zorbach. Yes, that surprises you, doesn't it? She never left us a statement either.'

A false name? No sworn statement?

The ringing in my aching head was subsiding only gradually, so it was a while before the questions crystallized in my mind.

'Is this true?' I asked hoarsely.

Alina resembled a living corpse in the harsh glare. Her face was pale, her full lips looked bloodless, and her dull eyes might have been those of a discarded doll.

'You never went to the police?'

I couldn't help remembering all the things she'd confided to me since we first met on board the houseboat. Her visions of the Eye Collector's last crime, some of which had proved to be accurate: ... *forty-five hours seven minutes, the bungalow with the basketball hoop beside the garage*. Mingled with recollections that were definitely mistaken: ... *only one child. He didn't kidnap two*... Or nonsensical: ... *then the woman laughed and said, 'I've been playing hide-and-seek with our son... I can't find him anywhere... Oh God... Don't go down into the cellar whatever you do.'*

'Bullshit,' she snarled. 'Of course I went to the fucking police. They fobbed me off with some arsehole who probably didn't do his paperwork properly.' She tried in vain to break Scholle's hold on her arm. 'And since when is it illegal to work under a pseudonym? Shiatsu is an art, and Alina Grigoriev is my professional name. Jesus, if you're so bad at researching your facts it's no wonder you can't catch the Eye Collector.'

'Wait.'

Scholle gripped Alina's arm and dragged her over to cooking hobs, where he cuffed one of her wrists to a tap at the opposite end to me.

'A deadbeat ex-cop and a blind screwball,' he said, shaking his head. 'Some combination!'

'You're making a big mistake,' I said. A moment later I couldn't even whisper. Scholle had returned to my side of the unit and kicked me in the stomach as hard as he could. Before I could catch my breath I was lying with my chest and stomach pressed against the cold tiled worktop and my face – *for God's keep your head up!* – immediately above a glowing hob.

The last thing I saw before I thought I would be seared to death was Alina wiping her sweaty forehead on the sleeve of her jacket. Although she was standing less than two metres away, she might as well have been in another room altogether for all the difference it made. She could have reached across the hob with her free hand and still failed to touch me even with her fingertips. Besides, Scholle was no novice. He had ruled out any unpleasant surprises by kicking any of the rubbish on the floor that could have been used as a weapon or a missile – old buckets, spatulas, rolls of wire – out of our reach.

I've had it, I thought, wondering if I could endure the heat on my face for a second longer. It got worse.

'All right,' Scholle said tensely, 'I'll ask you one more time: Where have you hidden those children?'

The distance between my chin and the hob decreased. Scholle's great paw was forcing my head inexorably downwards.

'I don't know!' I gasped. With a hiss, a drop of sweat landed on the incandescent spirals just below my face. They came still closer. I had to shut my eyes before they dried up.

'Where have you hidden them?'

Oh God, I thought, *he's out of his mind and I can't do a thing about it.*

My cervical vertebrae creaked. I could sense my strength giving out. I wouldn't be able to brace my straining neck muscles for much longer. 'I don't know,' I gasped, not knowing whether Scholle could even hear me any more.

The heat burned like hellfire. My nose was now only a finger's breadth from the hob. I felt as if the hairs in my nostrils were melting.

'Stop it!' cried a woman's voice. Alina's, I assumed, though my powers of perception had shrunk to the minimum necessary for survival. I thought I also heard her say things like 'You're wasting your time' and 'You're torturing the wrong person', but I wasn't sure of anything at that moment – not when my lips were about to kiss a glowing hob and all the blood in my body was trying to flow into my head, which seemed to have swollen to twice its normal size. Everything was throbbing: my veins, my ears, my skin, which in my mind's eye was already peeling off my face.

With the strength that only despair can generate, I resisted the pressure on the back of my neck, opened my eyes one last time... and tried to cry out.

Oh God, no, I thought, puzzled by Scholle's shadow, which was looming ever larger. *Don't, please don't...*

I hoped – no, I prayed – that Alina wasn't as mad as I feared, but in vain. She made it clear how insane she was. 'You want some answers?' she shouted. 'It's *me* you need to hurt!'

Scholle just managed to whisper a horrified 'Shit!' before she brought her free hand down on a red-hot hob.

18

(39 MINUTES TO THE DEADLINE)

'What the hell was that?' asked the older of the two cops stationed outside the entrance to the abandoned hospital kitchen. He tongued his gum to the other side of his rhythmically chomping jaw.

His youthful colleague froze in mid movement. He'd been about to open the door to the room in which Alexander Zorbach had uttered such a loud, horrific cry.

'Nooooooo...'

'Do you think we should...'

'What?'

The woman started screaming too. Her voice sounded even louder and more pain-racked than the man's.

The moustachioed young cop turned pale.

'... take a look. I reckon we ought to take a look.'

'Listen, youngster, he wasn't too pleased when I took the blind girl in there – said he didn't want to be disturbed under any circumstances.'

Something cut the woman's scream in half. The piercing

higher frequencies died away at once. The darker, throatier sounds persisted awhile longer.

'Let me tell you something,' the older man said quietly but firmly. 'What did you think was going on in there? Man, there isn't another soul in this part of the building.'

They heard a thud, then Scholle swore at the top of his voice. The young policeman's hand strayed to the door handle again.

'Go in there now, lad, and it'll be a life-changing experience. It's up to you, but take it from me: whatever you decide, nothing will ever be the same again.'

Another dull thud, followed by groans. Then a sound like a sack being dragged across a stone floor.

'What if you see something you feel duty-bound to report?' the older man went on. 'If you do, you'll make an enemy for life and no one'll ever want you as a partner.'

The gum changed sides again.

'Take a leaf out of my book. If you want a break, go upstairs and get yourself a coffee from the machine.' He laughed. 'But don't come back with another blind girl.'

The youngster nervously clasped the nape of his close-cropped neck. 'If I don't report it, I don't think I'll be able to look myself in the face.'

'Report what?'

'Well, the shit that's going on in there.'

'What are you talking about?' The older man cupped his right ear. 'I can't hear anything.'

It was true.

The young cop held his breath and listened for the sounds that had ceased to be audible.

Silence reigned beyond the door.

Dead silence, he thought, feeling sick, as his fingers slowly released their grip on the door handle.

17

ALINA GRIGORIEV

'Sorry to call you, but I'm rather worried. I was playing hide-and-seek with our son, and the crazy thing is, I can't find him anywhere.'

Alina could still hear the woman's agitated voice, but only faintly, as if it were coming from far away. The pain that occupied the greater part of her consciousness and brought back memories was spreading out inside her like a stream of lava. For a short while she continued to alternate between the agonizing reality in which she smelt the cloying stench of seared flesh – *her own flesh* – and the dreamworld into which she was sinking ever deeper, in which the helpless husband and father gave his wife a last warning over the phone's loudspeaker: "*Oh my God, how could I have been so blind? It's too late. Don't go down into the cellar whatever you do.'*

She felt herself fall to the kitchen's flagstone floor. Then all that remained of the pain was the light blazing behind her eyes – the light in which she once more *saw* the last few seconds before the kidnap.

From a place of concealment behind the cellar door. With the Eye Collector's eyes!

'You hear me? Don't go down into the cellar!'

The last words the husband uttered before his wife's death faded. Then someone fast-forwarded the film in her head.

Once more she was forced to undergo the experience of inhabiting someone else's body, breaking the woman's neck and dragging her out into the garden, and transferring the child – *Only one of them? Where on earth has he hidden the other?* – from the garden shed to the boot of the car. She drove up the hill again and watched through binoculars as the husband arrived and collapsed on the lawn beside his murdered wife's body. Then the director of her nightmare inserted a jump cut and leapfrogged the sequence in which she drove to the bungalow and drank a Coca-Cola. Instead, he showed her an entirely new memory. And here the images no longer formed a homogeneous scene but were juxtaposed almost at random, like a hectic, jump-cut trailer.

A wheelchair. Leaning back against the headrest, a child's motionless face. The big, trainer-shod feet of a man who pushes the wheelchair first across some gravel and then up a ramp...

No, not a ramp. More of a...

... gangway. Yes, a ship's gangway.

She can make out the water beneath the wooden planks – it shimmers, black as ink. Surrounding her are a host of white flecks and dark shadows. They're surrogates for objects with which she wasn't familiar before she was blinded and cannot, therefore, *see* in her dreams.

The film fast-forwards again. Now she sees an eye. A brown eye, it blinks once and moves towards a mirror.

God, I'm seeing his eye. I'm seeing the murderer's eye, but not in a mirror...

No, through the magnifying lens of a spyhole in a door.

The eye disappears when it feels its lashes come into contact with the cold metal door...

... heavy and painted white, with a lever handle like the one on her old-fashioned American refrigerator, but very much bigger.

And then she looks inside. Into the hiding place. She sees the boy lying on the bare floor, knees drawn up in an embryonic position, sees him twitch and gag and clasp his throat. And she suddenly notices that she's holding a watch in her hand.

It must be a stopwatch of sorts, because it shows there are only a few seconds left.

Next, she feels her eyes fill with tears.

I'm weeping, she thinks, and corrects herself at once. *No, that's not me. I'm not weeping, the Eye Collector is.*

Then she hears herself scream, and this time the voice is her own, not another's. She bangs on the door and kicks it, but the bulkhead, behind which the last few seconds of the ultimatum are running out, has vanished.

She lashes out harder, screams louder, and, when she feels the pain flare up once more, opens her eyes.

The film breaks off. The images have disappeared.

Alina is back in the familiar, all-devouring dark void of her life.

16

(26 MINUTES TO THE DEADLINE)

ALEXANDER ZORBACH

'I'm on my way to you now,' I shouted into the mobile and flattened my foot. Beside me, Alina groaned aloud because she'd made another attempt to flex her fingers. The untreated skin on her palm looked as if it had been dipped in wax and was already forming blisters.

'Just a minute.' Stoya sounded utterly flummoxed. 'Zorbach? Is that you?'

Yes. That surprises you, doesn't it?

I glanced at the rear-view mirror. Frank was absently stroking TomTom's head. He looked as if he himself couldn't grasp what had just happened.

Him bursting through the rear entrance. Alina's self-mutilation. The fight. Our getaway.

So much had happened within the space of a few seconds, Frank's brain would surely take weeks to digest it all. He was still bitterly reproaching himself for having yielded to Stoya's pressure and sending me the text message that had lured me out of hiding. I couldn't hold it against him, though. Lying shit that he was, Stoya had promised him

I wouldn't be arrested, just questioned. No one could have foreseen how matters would escalate. Besides, Frank had just atoned for his mistake by rescuing us.

'Where's Scholle?' Stoya asked.

'It might be worth looking in the hospital's former kitchen.'

I refrained from elaborating. I could, of course, have told him that it had been a mistake to turn my sidekick loose, merely because he wasn't under suspicion. Frank might not be a criminal, but he was loyal. As soon as he'd gathered that Scholle was to pick me up, he took a cab to the Park Sanatorium. Having originally asked to be dropped at the main entrance, he told the cabby to pull up next to the Toyota they'd passed in a small side street. While paying the man he saw Alina, sans guide dog but cane in hand, making her way slowly along the pavement.

He called her name, but the wind carried his words away unheard, so he pulled the hood of his coat over his head and became one of the hospital's faceless visitors. When he got to reception he saw Alina being accosted by an elderly policeman, who walked off with her a moment later. He was surprised, firstly, when the man ushered her into the goods lift. And, secondly, when it descended into the basement.

The illuminated display read -1.

Frank took the stairs.

Construction work. No access, said a sign on the door of the semi-basement. By now, Frank's surprise had given way to a strong suspicion that something was amiss.

The door wasn't locked, presumably for safety reasons. Laurel and Hardy failed to notice him when he turned right and made his way into the big, abandoned kitchen through a rear entrance, which was also open.

I could have told my former colleague all this, together with the fact that Frank had appeared from nowhere just as Stoya's sadistic subordinate was trying to brand me on the face with an electric hob. The shadowy figure looming up behind me hadn't belonged to Scholle; it was Frank, who, armed with an iron bar he'd found on the floor, had taken the big cop by surprise. He hit Scholle at the precise moment when, horrified by Alina's self-mutilation, the fat detective had momentarily relaxed his grip on my head.

But there was no time to impart all this information. The ultimatum would expire in twenty-five minutes, and I didn't want to waste them on a description of how we'd escaped through the emergency exit and made a dash for the Toyota, in which we were now speeding along the urban expressway.

'Where are you?' asked Stoya, clearly at pains to sound as calm as possible.

'On the way to you, but that's immaterial. Just tell me whether you found the car near some water.'

'What car?'

'Don't play games – you're only wasting time. Yes or no. River, canal, lake – whatever. Is there any water in the vicinity?'

A moment's hesitation. Then, finally, a curt 'Yes.'

'Good. It's only a shot in the dark, and don't ask me where it came from, but...'

I can hardly believe it myself.

'... you must look for those kids somewhere afloat.'

'Afloat?'

'On board a ship or boat of some kind.'

That's if you're prepared to be guided by a screwball and believe in the accuracy of her most recent 'memories'.

'I feel sick,' Alina groaned softly beside me. I lowered the mobile for a moment, but she again declined my offer to drive her back to the hospital.

'Bloody hell, we don't have time to search every tub in the area,' I heard Stoya yell as I put the mobile to my ear once more. 'We've less than half an hour. If you throw me off the scent...'

'What scent?' I cut in. 'If the hideaway is on water, is it any wonder your dogs haven't barked yet?'

No reply. All I could hear was the hum of the traffic I was threading my way through. 'I can't guarantee I'm right,' I said in a further attempt to sway him. 'I'm not convinced myself, to be honest, but if you're groping in the dark anyway, where's the harm?'

The ensuing lull in the conversation was even longer than the first. After twenty seconds, which to me felt like twenty minutes, I heard Stoya come to a decision. It proved to be a mistake.

15

(19 MINUTES TO THE DEADLINE)

PHILIPP STOYA
(DETECTIVE SUPERINTENDENT, HOMICIDE)

Stoya surveyed the poorly-lit parking lot: an expanse of potholed asphalt, a warden's dilapidated hut with shattered windows, the barrier beside the entrance wrenched off its base. The whole place was strewn with discarded products of the affluent society.

The waste disposal company, which had gone bust years ago, was just one more proof, thought Stoya, that the German industry was going to the dogs. As you'd expect, a vehicle abandoned here would have remained unnoticed until bulldozers moved in to demolish the incineration plant, complete with its chimney.

Having previously declined to cooperate, chance was now eagerly working overtime.

Of all cars, it was nurse Katharina Vanghal's car on which some young hooligans had chosen to vent their fury after an abortive visit to a disco (the bouncers wouldn't let them in). They did so just as a bleary-eyed police patrol drove past. This meant that the car, which had meanwhile lost a window and both wing mirrors, became a matter of record. And this, in turn, meant that all the warning lights on the police computer lit up a few hours later, when Vanghal's car was sought in connection with the Eye Collector.

'How many potential hiding places?' Stoya had pulled in to the kerb and was questioning the commander of the special task force by radio.

Recalling what Zorbach had said to him a minute earlier – *'Yes or no. River, canal, lake-whichever. Is there any water in the vicinity?'* – he almost broke into hysterical laughter. *Goddammit, Zorbach,* he thought, *this is Köpenick, not the Sahara. There's more water here than dry land. That gives the Eye Collector only ten million places to drown his victims.*

The industrial estate they had been searching, hitherto without success, was situated beside a triangular stretch of open water at the confluence of the Dahme, the Spree and the Teltow Canal. Even the street names had liquid connotations. His present location was the Regattastrasse-Tauchersteig intersection.

Tauchersteig... The second name, roughly translated as 'Diver's Rise', struck him as a bad omen.

The radio in his hand crackled. 'There are masses of private moorings here,' the task force commander replied. 'Around a dozen cabin cruisers have been laid up here for the winter.'

'Forget the cabin cruisers.'

Zorbach had said something about a big compartment

with a massive steel door, and you didn't find those aboard a cabin cruiser.

'It would be something sizeable – a vessel in commercial use, probably.'

'That leaves only two possibilities.'

Stoya nodded. A coal barge and a container ship. Although very little moonlight was filtering through the overcast sky, the landing stage was bathed in a sulphurous yellow glow by several street lights, so Stoya could easily make them out from where he was.

Goods traffic on the Berlin waterways had greatly declined with the advent of winter, and even the two commercial vessels seemed to be out of operation. They were lying motionless on the opposite side of the Teltow Canal.

'The coal barge is nearer the landing stage,' the team leader said over the radio.

Stoya was still nodding. That was why he had returned to the parking lot, to gain some idea of how the Eye Collector might have transported the two unconscious children from there to his hideaway.

'In a wheelchair,' Zorbach had said. So the perpetrator must have had to do everything twice over: open the boot, ensconce his drugged victims in the wheelchair, trundle them unobserved to the landing stage on the other side of the road, and then...

Yes, and then what? Unless the Eye Collector had grown wings, there was only one possibility. He must have put them in a small boat of some kind and rowed them across to the far bank.

But why? Why hadn't he simply driven his car around to the other bank?

'Let's take the container ship,' he said, privately wondering whether he'd lost his marbles like Zorbach. The man had clearly flipped, but he seemed to be well-informed. First the ultimatum, then thc parking ticket, and last but not least the bungalow. He still couldn't believe that his former colleague was personally implicated, but he couldn't dismiss the possibility that Zorbach had access to inside information. Quite how, they didn't have time to find out now that Scholle had so obviously screwed things up. Hell, they didn't even have the time to run a careful check on the blind girl's hallucinations.

'Mind you,' said the task force commander, 'the coal barge can be reached more quickly from the landing stage.'

Stoya could hear the sound of an outboard motor in stereo, over the phone and from across the water. The rubber dinghy containing the commander, four of his men and a sniffer dog had set off for the far bank. They seemed to be obeying his instructions and making for the long-hulled vessel on which at least forty steel containers were stacked in three layers.

'The very fact that it's moored a bit further away makes it our first choice,' said Stoya.

The coal barge was readily visible from the busy waterway, whereas the container ship was partly obscured by it. There was nothing but a rubble-strewn wilderness beyond the landing stage – an ideal set-up for someone wanting to convey bulky objects aboard unobserved.

Besides, thought Stoya, *the coal barge looks too squat. Too squat to have a lower deck capacious enough to accommodate a hiding place like the one Zorbach described.*

But he kept that thought to himself. If he proved wrong he didn't want to be blamed for basing his decision, not on hard facts, but on the recommendations of a blind medium.

Not to mention those of the principal suspect!

'Wow,' said the task force commander, who was steadily nearing his destination. 'This tub is huge.'

'Exactly. And we certainly don't have time to raid them both.'

Stoya detached his sweaty fingers from the radio microphone and prayed he was doing the right thing.

14

(13 MINUTES TO THE DEADLINE)

TOBY TRAUNSTEIN

After PE one time, Kevin had – just for fun – released the strap that attached the heavy blue plastic safety mattress to the wall of the gym. Toby, busy doing up his shoes, had failed to react quickly enough and was buried beneath the monstrous great thing.

What pinned his skinny body to the floor more firmly even than the thick foam plastic mattress was paralysing fear. He couldn't get up because several chortling classmates leapt on top of it to prevent him from doing so. Convinced that he would suffocate within seconds, he'd screamed...

... like a girl. Jesus, how embarrassing...

... and burst into tears...

At least I didn't wet myself, though I nearly did...

And afterwards, when Herr Kerner had quelled the rumpus, he didn't speak to Kevin for a whole week.

Or was it Jens? Oh well, whoever it was...

Now, as he lay on the cold floor with his knees drawn up, staring into the darkness, he realized how absurd he'd been to be scared that time. The mattress hadn't touched the ground all around, so he'd had plenty of air to breathe. Now that he'd extricated himself from the wooden chest, oxygen was no longer a problem either. It seeped through the cracks in the metal compartment in which he was lying. The difference between now and that day in the gym, it dawned on him, was the absence of a Herr Kerner. There was no PE teacher around to put an end to the nonsense and haul the mattress off him. Then, his ordeal had been over within seconds; now, he'd been in total darkness for ever so long. Not a thing to eat or drink. His prison stank of shit and piss, but he'd ceased to notice that. He was drifting off...

... Did I bring my atlas? he wondered. *It's geography after PE, and I've forgotten my atlas...*

He heard something go bang immediately beneath the steel floor pressed against his ear. The floor had stopped swaying, which could be a good sign – in fact the whole compartment seemed to have stopped moving the way it had moved just after he pulled that confounded rope.

'The rope!' he groaned. 'Why on earth did I do that?' Then he slipped back into the feverish dreamworld in which his direst fear was to get a black mark in the class book.

Herr Pohl will give me another black mark if I turn up again without my atlas. That would make three, and Dad'll be really mad at me...

Another noise made him jump, but it sounded nicer than that bang just now. It was like a gentle whisper. Soft and soporific. Toby started to drift off again...

... because three black marks in the class book equal one detention...

But he was prevented from drifting off by a novel, quite genuine sensation. Suddenly it was everywhere – wherever in the darkness he propped himself up on his hands or stretched out his fingers and touched the floor: icy cold, invisible moisture!

Greedily, he opened his mouth and licked the wet floor like a dog.

Water at last.

The first few drops stung his raw throat like acid, it was so long since he'd drunk anything. Then things improved a little. Whatever the source of the water, it was seeping into his prison from below and rising higher every second. Although this made it easier for him to drink, he became too greedy.

He choked and started retching. When he vomited he thought his skull would explode into fragments and land in the slightly brackish water around him.

I've had it, he thought in despair, suddenly feeling too weak even to drink.

Only a couple of centimetres deep at first, the water rose steadily higher, chilling him to the bone and making him shiver violently.

That's it. I give up.

Swallowing, even opening his mouth, was taking superhuman effort. Standing up was out of the question, even lying there was tiring, and staying awake seemed impossible.

The best thing I can do is go back to sleep, he thought, half in the present and half in a merciful dreamworld.

Daddy can't get mad at me if I go to sleep, can he? I won't get a black mark in my sleep, will I?

He was lying on his side, curled up like an embryo with his left eye already submerged, when – somewhere outside the walls of his prison – someone called his name.

13

(10 MINUTES TO THE DEADLINE)

SPECIAL TASK FORCE
(ON BOARD THE CONTAINER SHIP)

'Toby?'

Within minutes of boarding the boxy, ungraceful-looking vessel, the men had grasped the futility of their task and started to bellow the children's names.

'Lea? Toby?'

In spite of the reinforcements that had joined them from the shore, they couldn't possibly break open and search each container in the time remaining. Besides, the dogs hadn't made a sound on the bridge or on the first of the lower decks, which reeked of diesel and lubricating oil. The only time they'd barked, and then only briefly, was outside a cabin in which the ship's captain, awakened by the sound of his door bursting open, had been scared to death when men in black combat gear and ski masks dashed in and dragged him out of his bunk.

A minute later three policemen stormed the internal cargo spaces while their colleagues on deck began the

Sisyphean task of breaking the seals on the locked containers.

'Toby? Lea?'

Their voices went echoing across the waters of the Teltow Canal. Several interested spectators had gathered on the bank: two joggers, a man out for a walk and a female dog-owner, all of whom were debating the significance of an ever-growing array of police vans, patrol cars and emergency vehicles in the early hours of the morning.

The cries of the men in the bowels of the ship rang out, unanswered, amid the steel plates and pipework and in the cable tiers below deck.

Growing more and more desperate, some of the policemen threw caution to the wind when opening bulkhead doors, dashing round corners, or shining their torches down passages that hadn't been secured beforehand.

Another seven minutes.

It simply can't be done, thought Stoya, who had also come aboard by now.

We were wrong, he told himself – just as the dogs in the engine room started barking.

12

(5 MINUTES TO THE DEADLINE)

ALEXANDER ZORBACH

'It's too late.' The flashing lights of the police cars looked somehow ominous. I knew, as I stared at them, that the operation hadn't a hope.

'What can you see?' Alina asked me. She had got out of the car accompanied by Frank and TomTom.

We had parked the Toyota at a safe distance from the police cordon, some 200 metres before the road became a bridge that spanned the Teltow Canal.

A bridge!

Again I was up against the clock, and again fate had directed me to a bridge.

Fate or luck? I thought, and Alina's tattoo took shape in my mind's eye.

I was just about to tell her that there were too few men to search the ships in time when my mobile rang. I expected it to be Stoya, but a glance at the display compounded my despair.

'Well, are you on your way?'

No form of greeting, no name, just a curt, reproachful question.

Nicci seemed to know the answer, because her voice dripped with scepticism.

No, damn it. I won't make it.

Not knowing what to say, I started blathering. The truth – that I was watching a bunch of policemen vainly attempting to save two children from death by drowning – was so unendurable, I didn't want to misuse it as an excuse.

'Honestly, Alex, you promised him. He's been awake for the past hour, terribly excited because you said you'd have breakfast with us at seven. Can you imagine how sad he'll be when he comes downstairs to find that his father has forgotten his birthday yet again?'

'I haven't forgotten it.'

'But you aren't here. There'll be no family breakfast and your present won't be on the line.'

I groaned and clutched my head in despair. Frank looked at me inquiringly.

His present! How could I have promised Julian a watch? A cruel, lethal contraption whose only purpose was to tick away the seconds separating us from death.

I looked at my own old-fashioned watch, a bequest from my father, and hoped that the expensive Swiss timepiece was malfunctioning for the first time ever; that the hands had revolved too fast for some reason. I blinked, suddenly aware that my brain had registered something in the vicinity – something I couldn't immediately interpret.

Closing my eyes, I tried to recall what had occurred to me just before fear crept deep into my pores. And then the penny dropped. I opened my eyes, tilted my head back, and there it was.

The street sign!

'He'll get his present,' I whispered into thc phone, and hung up.

'What is it?' asked Frank.

My fingers felt clammy and bloodless as I took off my watch. 'It isn't the make Julian wanted, but it's worth ten times as much.'

I held it out with a trembling hand.

'Oh no.' Frank shook his head. 'I'm not leaving you. Not now.'

'Please, as a personal favour. You know where I used to live. Take the thing to Nicci. Tell her to give it a clean and wrap it up. And tell her I'll make it up to the boy.'

'No.'

'Please, we're running out of time.'

Alina, who had been leaning against the car without moving, turned an ear in my direction. She looked as tense as I felt. It was as if she could sense the threat I'd just become aware of.

The threat inherent in the street sign.

'What if you need help?'

Frank looked me straight in the eye, and I could tell he knew. He might be young, but he was no fool and had proved it more than once. Frank could put two and two together. He guessed, of course, that I wouldn't send him away for no good reason.

'You'll help me most of all by taking my son his birthday present, okay?'

I saw him purse his lips to utter a final objection. Then he yielded. He got into the car, gave me a rueful, disappointed look, and drove off without saying goodbye.

My gaze returned to the street sign. According to the faded lettering we were in Grünauer Strasse. Not just anywhere in Grünauer Strasse, either, but immediately outside a dark, dilapidated warehouse.

Grünauer Strasse.

That was what my brain had registered even before my eyes took it in.

217 Grünauer Strasse.

The numerals on the back of the photo I'd found on my mother's bedside table weren't a date, but the number of a building.

21.7 Grünau.

And we were standing right outside it.

11

(3 MINUTES TO THE DEADLINE)

ALEXANDER ZORBACH

It wasn't very long since I'd made a trip to the Babelsberg film studio with Julian and looked at the set of a war film in production there. I still recalled how impressed we'd been by a mock-up of a bombed building. Dilapidated walls, shattered window panes, charred roof timbers through which remnants of masonry jutted skyward like splintered bones – all these features had been reproduced with convincing but spurious authenticity. However, that set was nothing compared to the scene that confronted me now.

Why is he doing this? Why is the Eye Collector giving me all these hints?

Standing in the outer yard of the derelict industrial estate at 217 Grünauer Strasse, I felt yet again that I was being led to perdition on an invisible leash.

He's playing a game with me, I told myself, trying to marshal my thoughts. *Hide-and-seek, the oldest children's game in the world, and I'm playing it according to his rules – following the leads he drops at my feet like the trail in a paperchase.*

'You've got to help me,' I told Alina.

Daybreak wasn't far off, but Berlin lay beneath heavy cloud cover, dampening sound like a bell jar over the city. If you looked up at the sky the moon seemed reminiscent of a torch under an eiderdown. The pre-dawn light barely penetrated the alleyways linking the various factory yards.

'I need a clue from you.'

Alina clenched her left hand and I saw her grimace with pain.

I need another memory!

I had informed Stoya as a matter of course of the new clue as a matter of course, but he'd made it quite clear that he wouldn't withdraw a single man, just to check on yet another figment of my imagination. Even if he'd sent a whole army right away, it wouldn't have been enough.

'The area is simply too big, Alina. There are at least four yards surrounded by ruined factories and warehouses. That's all I can make out from here.'

'I'm sorry, Alex.'

She opened her eyes but promptly shut them again, stung by an unpleasant gust of fine, icy drizzle.

'All I felt before was a ship. No factories or warehouses.'

You must be wrong. The photograph, the numerals – it can't be a coincidence.

Why were some of Alina's visions so consistent with reality and others so wide of the mark?

'Anyway, I can't see anything more because...'

'Because what?'

'Nothing,' she said dismissively, but I knew what she'd almost blurted out.

'Because the children are already dead.'

'What about TomTom?' I asked.

'He can't help either. Even if we had a sample of the children's scent, he isn't a sniffer dog.'

I know.

I also knew that the ultimatum had almost expired. Although I no longer possessed a watch, I could sense that there were only seconds left.

Think, Zorbach, think.

Dark, deserted buildings surrounded us on every side, each indistinguishable from the other. There were no lights on anywhere. Every gate and door gaped open, every entrance was choked with mounds of mysterious industrial waste. I could make out a lot of it, but I couldn't see a lead or pointer of any kind.

The Eye Collector wants to play. He lays down clear rules. Forty-five hours seven minutes...

The outer courtyard was so huge, the stack of HGV tyres in the middle resembled the remains of a toy truck. There were countless places the twins might be hidden. They could be immediately beneath our feet or behind that stack of empty cat-food tins against the wall over there.

'Where are you going?' I heard Alina call as I went back to the entrance that led to the street. I was obeying an urge to do *something* rather than following a definite plan when I opened my mobile and used the display's feeble glow to illuminate the board on which old firms' nameplates were mounted.

The uppermost and biggest bore the name *Köpenicker Textilfabrik*. The other enamel plaques had either been wrenched off or were so scratched and grimy, the lettering that had originally listed the individual departments was almost indecipherable: *Printing, Design, Administration, Sales...*

I rested my palm against the cold metal.

Think, Zorbach, think. He wants you to look for the children. It's a game, and a game isn't a game unless every player has a chance of winning. If he's giving you clues, it's only to level the odds.

Why should he lure you here?

To humiliate you? To see you fail at the very last minute?

Or perhaps he's left you another clue?

I stepped aside and shone the display on one of those obligatory notices forbidding unauthorized access to a prohibited area.

Another lead?

'Danger – No Entry,' I read aloud.

Most appropriate...

My eye lighted on a second warning just below the first:

'Cellar 77 completely flooded!'

I shouted so loudly, TomTom started barking in the yard.

Cellar 77!

Was that the answer? Was it another ploy?

I had a sudden, vivid recollection of the photo as I dashed back to Alina.

Grünau 21.7 (77)

From that point on, everything was terrifyingly straightforward.

10

(ONE MINUTE TO THE DEADLINE)

TOBIAS TRAUNSTEIN

He was swimming. Treading water. Dying.

Toby had never given any serious thought to death until the last couple of days. Why would he? He'd only just turned nine, after all. 'You've got your whole life ahead of you,' his grandfather used to say whenever they came to Sunday lunch.

Wrong, Grandpa, I've got nothing ahead of me any more. My head's already nudging the roof of this iron coffin. I've only got a tiny space left to breathe in, and even that is gradually filling up with water.

He wept and spat out the first few drops of water that had found their way into his mouth. Pouring in through every chink in the metal compartment, seeping up through the floor and in through the seams in the sides, the water had converged from all directions to form a reservoir whose surface had now reached the roof. A deep, dark, ice-cold reservoir in which Toby was on the verge of drowning.

I'll suffocate, he thought. It was like that time beneath

the gym mattress, but this was completely different. Although he'd wept then too, he'd known in his heart of hearts that Herr Kerner would come and rescue him. Except that this wasn't a gym and his father wasn't a PE teacher who would haul the mattress off him so he could breathe again. His father was...

... a write-off. Dad's never been there for me, so why should he show up now? Mum, more like.

Yes, Mum was bound to be looking for him. Like when he and Lea forgot the time while out tobogganing and Mum had come running through the woods to meet them, worried sick.

Toby, she'd kept calling. *Lea, Toby...*

He'd been half pleased and half ashamed. Although it had naturally saddened him that Mum had cried on his account, at least he knew how much she loved him.

Toby? Hello? Where are you, Toby? He seemed to have heard someone calling him earlier, before the water (*which isn't* caldo *in the least, but* molto freddo) finally woke him up. Could Mum be coming?

Yes, Mum. Not Dad. Stuff Dad and his lectures at the dinner table and his lousy Italian. Most of all, stuff his job, which always prevents him from playing with me in the garden. Dad won't come, but Mum...

His lips sucked in the last of the air between the surface and the metal roof. Then the water level rose another millimetre and his head became entirely submerged. He knew he was drowning, but he was still hopeful that Mum would find him soon.

9

(INSIDE THE FINAL MINUTE)

PHILIPP STOYA
(DETECTIVE SUPERINTENDENT, HOMICIDE, ON BOARD THE CONTAINER SHIP)

'What's behind there?' Stoya thumped the steel door with his fist.

'You mustn't open that,' said the ship's captain.

'Why not?'

'It's a bulkhead door. Open it and we'll be in trouble.'

Stoya gripped the rotary valve. He strained at it with all his might but failed to budge it so much as a millimetre.

'Hey, what are you doing? Didn't you hear what I said?' the captain protested loudly when Stoya asked the task force commander if he had any C4 explosive. 'I'll lose my job if you open it.'

'Why?'

'That's why we're stuck here. The old tub's leaking like a sieve.' The captain indicated the bulkhead door. 'That compartment's neck-deep in water. Your dogs were only barking at some water rats, take it from me.'

8

ALEXANDER ZORBACH

As a rule, we only question our mistakes, never our successes. If something goes well we take it as our God-given right. We grieve if we lose money or are ditched by those we love, but we wonder why they stay with us as seldom as we wonder how we passed an examination. In my opinion, however, we learn more from our mistakes than we do from our undeserved successes. Unless we question those, they lull us into a state of complacency and we can never repeat them.

I forgot my own maxim when the last minute of the ultimatum came.

The entrance to Building 77, which was in the second inner courtyard, could not be missed. Alina took the lead for the first time, because it was pitch-dark inside the former warehouse. The only eyes that might have seen anything were TomTom's.

And so we performed a kind of weird Polish dance in which I, with my hands resting on Alina's shoulders from behind, entered a stairwell redolent of lubricating oil and stagnant water. I prayed that my sense of time had deceived me, and that we still had a few minutes' grace, just as I also prayed to an invisible power that I had not become the plaything of a madman who was luring me into the void for his own malicious amusement.

In the end I had no more time, not even another second, in which to reflect on the insanity I was living through. It was my own eyes, not TomTom's, that spotted the first sign of life.

Red, glowing, circular.

A little button on the wall – the kind you look for when the light goes out on the stairs in a block of flats.

The LED was on, which proved that the building had power.

'Someone's been here.' I felt Alina's shoulder muscles tense beneath my hand as I said it.

What happened when I pressed the button resembled an explosion.

Light!

Here of all places, in Building 77, 217 Grünauer Strasse, someone had screwed in the fuses.

Or installed a generator. Like before, at the bungalow...

'What happened?' Alina asked. The sudden illumination had been so bright, even she must have detected the difference.

'We're in the entrance to an old warehouse,' I told her. 'Stairs on the right, goods lift on the left.'

And straight ahead...

'Where are you going?'

I can't recall if I answered Alina before or after I depressed the handle and wrenched the door open.

Perhaps I didn't say anything at all. All I can remember is my own cry of joy when the heavy, bulky door detached itself from the rubber seal with a sucking sound and I looked into the eyes that were gazing out at me.

From inside an old American refrigerator.

'Mum?' said the soft, childish voice that went with the eyes.

Behind me, Alina uttered a groan of relief. My eyes filled with tears.

Charlie's dead – murdered by the madman who shut you up in there.

'I'm not your Mum, but I'm here to help you.'

Her dark, fearful eyes regarded me in silence. I held out my hand, which was promptly grasped by her own little hands.

She was such a featherweight, I could easily lift her out of her prison with one arm.

Out of the Eye Collector's hiding place.

'All right,' I said, 'you're safe now.' I checked her pulse.

Weak but regular.

'But someone else needs *your* help now.'

She nodded shyly. She knew what I meant.

'Lea,' I said, trying to conceal the despair in my voice, 'have you any idea where your brother is?'

7

'In the lift?'

'Mmm.' Lea nodded timidly. 'Where's Mum?'

'Later, Lea.'

We'll both weep for Charlie later. First I must rescue your brother.

'I heard it going down,' she said.

I stroked her head, which was moist with sweat, and turned to look at the goods lift behind me.

Down? Please not, please don't let it have gone down into the cellar.

I had a vision of the notice in the entrance to the outer courtyard:

Danger – No Entry. Cellar of Warehouse 77 completely flooded.

From then on, everything seemed to speed up. First I tried to wrench the lift doors apart with my bare hands. Luckily, I didn't waste more than ten seconds on that fruitless endeavour. I recalled seeing an iron bar protruding from a mound of rubbish we'd climbed over on our way there, but there was a danger I would fail to find it quickly enough in the darkness outside.

I undid TomTom's harness and jammed the metal handle in the crack between the doors. The aluminium gave, but it was strong enough to enable me to widen the crack until I could insert my fingers, then my foot. Next, I wedged one knee and my shoulder in the gap. The doors were evidently programmed to open when obstructed, but I couldn't afford to indulge my sense of relief. Least of all when I looked down the lift shaft.

Oh no... I could see the top of the goods lift a couple of metres below me. Which meant that it really had descended into the cellar when the ultimatum expired.

Into the *flooded* cellar!

Wedging the doors open with the dog's harness, I jumped down the shaft and landed so awkwardly I nearly fell on my face.

Oh Jesus!

The top of the lift was awash.

One minute? Two minutes? How long could a child hold its breath underwater?

I soon spotted the source of the water. It was coming from the hatch some bright manufacturer had installed for technicians and emergencies, though he'd certainly never imagined a child would drown inside his lift.

Above me I could hear Alina summoning help on my mobile. I opened the hatch with ease.

Too late, I'm too late! I thought, although all things considered, everything had gone surprisingly smoothly until now.

Too smoothly!

Water was welling up through the hatch, black as Indian ink.

'Toby?' I called – nonsensically. I plunged my arm into the dark void below me and gasped when the water closed around it like an icy sleeve.

There's no point. It's all been in vain.

Feverishly, I racked my brains for some other way.

But there wasn't one. I had no choice.

So I hyperventilated briefly at the thought of what I was about to do. Then I sucked as much air as possible into my lungs and lowered myself into the icy water feet first.

6

There comes a point at which the intensity of cold is measured, not in degrees Fahrenheit or Celsius, but in pain. Immersing myself in the icy void, my skin was pierced by countless millions of the finest needles, and the further I sank the deeper they were driven into my body. The shock was so extreme, all I could think about for a moment was myself and my own survival. Then, before I finally touched down on the floor of the goods lift, I struck my shin on something hard.

Toby?

I stretched out my arms and opened my eyes in the hope of feeling or seeing the boy. No such luck.

What happens to someone when they're drowning? Do they drift to the surface? Do they sink? Or do they float halfway like a fish?

All my questions went unanswered and I could feel myself running out of air.

Even though you've only been underwater for a few seconds.

My God, I thought, *it's no use, not any more.*

I felt I would burst. My blood, the air remaining in my

lungs – everything seemed to be pressing against the confines of my body from within. And then came the most wonderful sensation ever, because at last...

... at last I'd touched something.

I sank to the floor by expelling a little air from my lungs and inwardly rejoiced because I hadn't been mistaken.

Hair, ears, a mouth – yes, yes, yes, it really is a face.

I grasped the boy's head and pulled him towards me, and for the first time for many, many hours my hopes outweighed my fears.

Perhaps it hasn't all been in vain. Perhaps we'll make it after all...

Get out of here!

All I wanted, now that I'd found Toby at last, was to escape. But with hope came a renewed feeling of exhaustion. I'd been deprived of sleep, threatened with torture and subjected to the worst ordeal I'd ever undergone in my life. And now the little energy I still possessed was being sapped by the temperature of the water surrounding me. I couldn't tell if the boy in my weary arms was still alive, but I could certainly feel my own pulse slowing.

Badumm, badumm, badumm...

The interval between my heartbeats was increasing.

We must get out of here. Out into the light and air.

I clasped Toby in a rather inefficient headlock and pushed off the floor of the lift with my feet.

5

Black. Dark. Nothing.

The light overhead – *damnation, was it ever up there?* – had gone out so suddenly, I almost let go of the boy in shock. The water had become an opaque, oily film. I no longer knew where to make for.

Where the devil is the light? Where's the hatch?

Up, down, left, right. Those words had lost their meaning. I was completely disoriented.

My panic had reached the *ne plus ultra* of intensity. That may have been the reason for my sudden calm. My tension subsided as if a critical threshold had been crossed, releasing a safety valve.

Or is that what it's like when you're drowning? I myself had written an article on the subject. It had transpired from interviews with survivors of drowning that, although the moment when the water pours into your lungs is frightening in the extreme, your fear gives way to a feeling of intoxication.

I would soon experience that for myself, I knew. I wouldn't be able to resist the temptation to open my mouth and draw a deep, deep breath.

That sweet, irresistible sensation. Like an addiction, a lethal drug to which one willingly surrenders.

Just as I felt my hands begin to lose their grip on the boy's body, my leg caught in the rope.

A rope? Where in God's name did a rope suddenly appear from?

I tugged at it with my free hand and was surprised when it didn't give. I was past thinking clearly in any case, so it didn't occur to me to wonder if it was attached to the floor or the ceiling, even though this might spell the crucial difference between life and death. Why? Because that dictated the direction in which I ought to haul myself. Myself and Toby Traunstein, whose body seemed to be growing heavier and more inanimate by the second.

I kicked out like a diver, except that I was wearing heavy boots, not flippers, and they were weighing me down.

Really down?

One-handed, I hauled myself gradually up the rope.

Up? Or down?

Am I hauling myself in the wrong direction? To my death?

I opened my eyes. I didn't expect to see anything down there in the inky darkness, but my head felt as if it would burst and it was an absurd reflex rather than a conscious decision, almost as if I were trying to equalize the pressure through my eyes or filter oxygen out of the brackish water. I was all the more surprised when I actually saw something.

Light!

Yes, up there at the end of the rope I saw a faint ray of light.

The weirdos were right all along, was my last thought before the rope slipped through my fingers. *This is how it ends. We fight our way through a cold, dark void, but when it's all over we see a light at the end of the tunnel.*

I smiled and breathed in. Deeply.

4

(55 MINUTES AFTER THE DEADLINE)

ALINA GREGORIEV

'Can you please tell me what's going on?' Alina asked. The man who was dressing her hand had neither introduced himself nor said anything at all.

'Sorry, not authorized to,' he replied. His surprisingly high-pitched voice sounded far too reedy for his body.

All she had felt so far was the paramedic's hand on hers, but that was generally sufficient to enable a blind person to gauge a person's body weight. When wanting to form an initial impression of a someone's stature, Alina grasped their wrist for a moment. At present, though, nothing could have mattered less to her than the physical appearance of the overweight man who was preventing her from leaving the ambulance.

'Relax, I'm not done with you yet.'

She yielded to the pressure of his hands as he forced her back on the stretcher.

'To hell with me, what about the others?'

What about Zorbach and the boy?

Alina didn't know whether to be angry or grateful to be spared the sight of Stoya's men when they finally hurried to her aid in Building 77. The pictures in her head, her memories of those terrible minutes beside the goods lift, consisted almost entirely of sounds and smells.

She had heard the lift doors close again, heard the aluminium handle Zorbach had jammed between them slip out with a loud, grating sound and fall to the floor. Her residual sight told her that the light had gone out. Lea, suppressing her sobs like the brave little girl she was, confirmed this. Meanwhile, down in the lift shaft, Zorbach had been utterly helpless – trapped without tools or light in a place which Alina could picture only through the medium of omnipresent smells: stagnant water and mildewed masonry, refuse and excrement.

Had she known that Toby's prison had long been flooded, her fears for the two would have intensified beyond all measure. She asked Lea to press the light switch again – not that this did Zorbach any good. Although it was once more light on the landing, it couldn't penetrate the lift shaft from which her cries were eliciting no response. She couldn't do what Zorbach had done earlier. The handle of TomTom's harness was bent out of shape and she wasn't strong enough to prise the lift doors apart on her own. Neither TomTom nor Lea nor her blistered left hand had been a great help to her, so all she could do was wait and comfort Lea, who was trembling with exhaustion, by burying her face in the little girl's hair.

Although Alina had lost all sense of time, she felt sure the men had arrived on the scene far too late.

Four policemen. Many minutes too late.

They came dashing into the building almost simultaneously, their boots clattering on the stairs. The thunder of boots died away abruptly when they saw Lea. Their orders had been to arrest Zorbach, but the sight of the kidnapped girl *alive* in Alina's arms changed everything.

That was when they started to believe me, Alina reflected, but she derived no satisfaction from the thought.

'Are they still here?' she asked the paramedic, who was still dressing her hand.

Or have they been taken away?

Feeling a slight movement, she guessed that the man had nodded his head.

Or shaken it.

'Damn it all, stop treating me like a child who's not allowed to know anything! I heard what they said!'

'It's a waste of time – they were dead meat by the time I fished them out,' said the policeman who'd been smoking a cigarette and discussing the operation with a colleague outside the ambulance half an hour ago. *'There'd be more point in giving my daughter's teddy bear the kiss of life.'*

Alina had felt like jumping out of the ambulance and slapping the man's face. *'How can you talk like that, you arsehole?'* she'd wanted to shout. *'You got the doors open and let some light in. You jumped down the shaft and shone your torch on the water and hauled them up by the rope they'd got entangled in – yes, but you showed up too damned late!'*

'Have you ever had to deal with a victim of drowning?' she asked the paramedic, who was taping her dressing into place. She just managed to hold her tears at bay.

He grunted an affirmative.

Either he'd been instructed not to speak to her or he was still too dismayed by what had happened.

'How long do you...' Alina swallowed hard. 'I mean, how soon do you give up trying to resuscitate someone after a swimming accident?'

He clearly felt he was on safer ground. 'It depends. We once got a man back after twenty minutes, but that was exceptional.'

'And what would be normal?'

Alina fingered the dressing on her left hand.

'A minute or two.'

A minute or two?

It had taken at least two minutes for Zorbach to gain access to the lift shaft. Heaven alone knew how long Toby had been underwater by then.

Under stressful conditions, minutes flash past like shooting stars – so fast, you barely notice them. But perhaps this had been more like a session in a dentist's chair. Perhaps the seconds had only felt like hours. Perhaps less time had elapsed than she feared.

Alina felt sick. The survival of two people had become a straightforward arithmetical problem, the adding together of periods of time whose combined total would spell certain death. *Zorbach had taken two minutes to get into the lift, spent two minutes submerged in icy water, and been hauled out after another two minutes...*

That was too long. Too long for the little boy, for Alex, and – it had suddenly dawned on her – for herself as well. Alex Zorbach had something in common with her eyesight. She hadn't grasped its vital importance until she lost it.

He shouldn't have given away his watch, she told herself, unable to suppress the thought although she knew how childish it was.

He gave away his time...

Weeping now, she failed to hear the paramedic get to his feet. He cleared his throat in an embarrassed way.

'Did you know that the world record for holding one's breath stands at seventeen minutes four seconds?'

The sudden onset of emotion was so overwhelming, Alina thought she would suffocate.

'It was set by David Blaine, the professional magician and stunt man. Mind you, he did breathe pure oxygen for twenty-three minutes beforehand.'

Big tears welled up in her sightless eyes. The whole world had been transformed from one moment to the next. The poles swapped places, Germany ceased to be in Europe, Berlin was on another planet, and Alina herself, a human being no longer, had become pure energy.

'Still, nearly three minutes without any training isn't too bad, is it?'

Positive energy.

She sprang to her feet. Her one remaining wish was to fall into the arms of the owner of that hoarse voice, who was standing just outside the rear doors of the ambulance.

'You're alive?' she said, smiling happily through her tears.

'Yes, but be thankful you can't see what a wreck I look.'

Zorbach joined in her laughter. She felt the ambulance lurch as he started to climb aboard.

'And Toby?'

Leaning against the edge of the stretcher on which she'd just been lying, she sensed that Zorbach had stopped short.

No, please, no.

She buried her face in her hands.

'He must have been submerged for five minutes or more.' She wondered why Zorbach was imparting this frightful information with such composure. His tone was calm, almost contented. 'They almost lost him twice, but it seems he's a tough little bugger. His heart is beating again. He's still on the critical list and he'll have to spend some time in an artificial coma, but the doctors are hopeful he'll pull through.'

From that moment on, nothing could stop her. Stretching out her arms and throwing caution to the winds, she made for the ambulance's open double doors and the top of the folding steps on which she guessed Zorbach was standing. She laughed aloud, euphorically convinced that he would catch her if she fell.

Alex is alive. Both the children are safe.

All would now be well, she felt sure. Nothing else could go wrong.

Seldom had anyone been so mistaken.

3

(7.27 A.M., ONE HOUR AFTER THE DEADLINE)

ALEXANDER ZORBACH

There are very few times when we succeed in living for the moment alone – times when there is no past or future, only here and now.

In my own life I can definitely remember only two such occasions. One I experienced when holding new-born Julian in my arms for the first time. The second occurred when, weak at the knees and swathed in a warm blanket, I waited for Alina to embrace me on the steps of an ambulance.

It was my moment of greatest elation and uttermost exhaustion. Only a minute earlier I'd had to fight my way past worried doctors loath to remove my oxygen mask after successfully reviving me. I'd also had to sidestep Stoya, who would have liked to debrief me the moment they detected my heartbeat.

My bronchial tubes were still full of water and I needed careful medical supervision like Toby, who had been deprived of oxygen for very much longer. At that moment of boundless jubilation, however, my health mattered as little to me as the innumerable questions that still needed answering as soon as we could come to rest.

Why had Alina never envisioned more than one child? Why did she think it had died in its hiding place if Toby was still alive?

I had often wondered too, in the last few hours, why her mysterious 'memories' were partly accurate – the strangely specific deadline, the description of the bungalow – but had almost led us astray at the crucial moment:

'All I felt before was a ship. No factories or warehouses.'

Even the question of why the Eye Collector had chosen to involve me, of all people, in his game by sending Alina to see me, directing me to the dying woman in the cellar, and placing the photo on my mother's bedside table – even that no longer mattered. Now that we'd snatched his victims from him in the nick of time, I didn't even want to know the Eye Collector's identity. There was no past or future at this moment. Only the present.

A present in which Alina made a blunder that changed everything.

As she hurried towards me, her foot caught in one of the struts supporting the stretcher. She tripped and made an instinctive attempt to save herself, but she couldn't, of course, see the grab handle mounted on the wall beside the medicine cabinet. Her hand slid helplessly downwards, pulling a defibrillator to the floor, and was brought up short by a metal rack.

The smile left her face and tears of pain sprang to her eyes.

'Your hand!' I cried, as though that could help, and knelt down beside her.

Your left hand – the one you burnt!

She'd put all her weight on it, and the edge of the rack must have dug into her flesh through the dressing.

'I'm all right,' she said through gritted teeth, her forehead filmed with sweat. 'No problem.' The pain seemed to persist as I folded her in my arms – clung to her like a drowning man and never wanted to let her go again. 'I'm all right,' I heard her say again. She started to repeat it but failed. I wouldn't have believed her in any case, for the tighter I held her the greater her resistance. It was as if the blood in her veins had stopped flowing – as if I were holding a marble statue in my arms, not a living creature.

'I felt something!' she said in a low voice.

No!

I shut my eyes.

'It isn't just physical contact... I only remember when I'm hurt...'

I shrank away from her, my legs trembling.

'What is it?'

'Your telephone!'

I looked up at the clothes hook on which the paramedic had hung Alina's cord jacket.

The buzzing grew steadily louder.

'What about it?' I asked, getting to my feet.

'Don't answer it,' Alina sobbed. She buried her face in her hands. 'Please don't answer it.'

2

Cynics contend that dying begins at birth. Like every extreme proposition, this drastic statement contains a germ of truth. Everyone reaches a point at which life ends and dying begins; an infinitesimally small but logical, measurable moment at which we cross an invisible boundary that marks the watershed of our existence. Behind it lies all we once regarded as the future; ahead of us lies only death. Where most people are concerned, that watershed is located somewhere in the last quarter of their lifeline. Others, for instance those afflicted by some terminal illness, may be only halfway along it when they get there. Scarcely anyone crosses the watershed knowingly. Very few people can say when the vital phase of their life ends and dying begins. But I am one of them. I can tell you precisely.

I started dying in that ambulance, the moment I put the mobile to my ear and heard my wife's nervous laugh.

"Sorry to call you, but I'm rather worried. I was playing hide-and-seek with our son, and the crazy thing is, I can't find him anywhere.'

Crash!

A door seemed to slam in the innermost depths of my soul, cutting me off from all I had ever lived for.

Oh God, I thought, and said the words out loud.

'Oh God!'

Everything around me started to spin as I blundered out of the ambulance in a daze.

'How could I have been so blind?'

All those unresolved questions. All those potential answers. In a terrible, horrific way, everything now made sense.

'It's too late,' I sobbed into the phone, paralysed by the realization that we'd been looking in the wrong direction all the time. Backwards, into the past.

Alina couldn't see into the past and had never been able to do so. None of what she'd told me had happened.

Not yet.

Outside the ambulance I tripped and fell headlong, face down in wet gravel and gasping for breath. I felt sick when I grasped the true significance of what had just dawned on me.

It's still going to happen, all of it.

The true horror still lay ahead. Alina had never looked into the past, always into the future!

'Don't go down into the cellar, you hear?' I yelled into the phone, scrambling to my feet.

Where's the way out? Where's my car?

'Don't go down into the cellar!' I repeated.

Insane though it seemed, if my direst imaginings proved correct I would have to stick to Alina's version of the Eye

Collector's script – with one exception. If Nicci was to survive, I must persuade her to heed my warning at all costs.

'Don't go down into the cellar!'

I stumbled, my knees buckling, but I couldn't give up. I had to resist the inevitable – the thing I'd failed to see although it had been staring me in the face all the time. Even when Nicci spoke the last words she ever uttered: 'You're scaring me, darling.'

Then I heard the sounds of a struggle.

A man hiding behind the cellar door. He attacks her, breaks her neck, drags her out into the garden...

The sounds matched the scenario Alina had described.

I started yelling when I remembered that there was a wooden shed in Nicci's garden.

1

ALEXANDER ZORBACH

Later (very much later), in the few brief moments when my cocktail of antidepressants and sedatives permitted me to think coherently, I wondered how I could have laboured under such a fatal misapprehension for so long.

Alina had never discussed her gift in detail with anyone before. Had she done so under less chaotic circumstances, she might have realized far sooner that no feature of her visions proved beyond doubt that she was remembering *the past*. In the case of her earliest vision – the accident with the inebriated driver – she thought she saw herself lying on the asphalt, but why should she have been the last girl the drunk ran over? And what of the fellow student she accused of raping his sister? That case was actually on record! He committed incest at least once more before taking his own life, so it was probably that future rape Alina saw, not one he'd already committed.

Blind... We were so blind...

The drive from Grünauer Strasse to Nicci's house would

normally have taken fifteen minutes. I did it in ten, but I got there an eternity too late.

'And then I broke her neck. There was a sound like an eggshell being crushed. She died instantly.'

Like a cheap stereo effect, the words Alina had uttered yesterday resonated in each of my ears in turn. I thumped myself on the head and turned up the radio as loud as it would go, but nothing could erase the memory of our first conversation on the houseboat.

'What did you do with the body?'

'I towed her outside by the flex... across the living room to a terrace door and from there into the garden... I left her lying near the garden fence, a little way from a small shed.'

I prayed once more to a God I no longer believed in, imploring him to prove me a fool – *no one can see into the future, it's impossible* – when, a few seconds later, I drove along the street in which I'd spent twelve years of my life with Nicci.

Had the road ahead of me parted and engulfed the car, I would have reacted more calmly – indeed, I would have welcomed being spared what lay ahead.

'What happened next?' I heard myself ask.

'After I put the stopwatch in her hand, you mean?'

I floored the accelerator and raced towards the house at the end of the street.

'I went over to the tool shed... It was made of timber, not metal... There was something on the floor. It looked like a bundle of rags, but it was another body. Smaller

and lighter than that of the woman lying dead on the lawn. It was a little boy.'

Julian!

'Was he still alive?'

A flock of crows took wing as I parked the Toyota in the driveway.

Please not, dear God, please not. Don't let today be the day when I pay for my mistake on the bridge.

I jumped out of the car, bit my hand to prevent myself from crying out, and lost my balance. It was colder on the outskirts of the city, so the snow took longer to melt. I slipped on the smooth driveway, and the moment I hit the ground something inside me broke beyond repair.

I crawled along on all fours, then got to my feet and ran into the garden past the big lime tree from which I'd meant to hang a swing. 'Nicci!' I called at the top of my voice, throwing back my head.

Nicci!

I called her name over and over, louder and louder, but her eyes were unblinking and her lips would never open again.

At that moment I wanted to be as dead as she was. I hated myself for still being alive – hated myself for having lived a life that was one big mistake. It had cost my wife her life and my son would now pay dearly...

Good God, Julian!

I looked over at the shed. The bolt had been drawn and the door was wide open.

'I carried the boy to a car parked on the edge of the

woods beyond the garden fence. I think it was early morning, shortly after sunrise. Suddenly everything went dark again and I thought the vision was over. Then two red lights came on in the boot of the car. I laid the boy down inside.'

I hit my head with the heel of my hand as if to rid it of the bitter truth.

'I remember driving uphill for a bit. We rounded several bends. Then the car pulled up and I got out.'

'What happened after that?'

'Nothing. I just stood there and watched.'

'You watched?'

'Yes. All at once I was holding something heavy.'

Once, long ago, when Julian was a baby and being a good father was all I could conceive of, I had sat with him at this very spot. Here, where my agony of mind was rending me apart.

I had cradled his sleeping head against my chest – gently, to prevent him from slipping sideways. Almost the way I was holding Nicci's lifeless body now.

What dreams we'd had, what plans had once held our little family together, and how quickly I'd succeeded in destroying them all.

I removed the stopwatch from Nicci's cold fingers and stood up.

We had meant to grow old together, here at the foot of the Rudower Dörferblick, a hill on the outskirts of Berlin, eighty-six metres high and composed of rubble from the ruins of the war-torn German capital. On sunny days it presented a panoramic view of three villages: Bohnsdorf, Schönefeld and Wassmannsdorf. And, of course, of our own house and garden.

I looked down at the body of my murdered wife, then up at the summit of the grassy hill at the foot of which all our hopes had first come into flower and then been blighted forever.

I wasn't sure if the tears in my eyes were deceiving me, or if I could really make out the figure of a man whose binoculars were reflecting the cold winter sunlight.

THE EYE COLLECTOR'S LAST LETTER, SENT BY EMAIL VIA AN ANONYMOUS ACCOUNT

To: Thea Bergdorf <thea@bergdorf-privat.com>
Subject: Final words...

Dear Frau Bergdorf,

This email will, I think, be the last you receive from me for a long time. I trust you'll note that I've addressed you more respectfully than in my previous letters, though I doubt if your paper will accord me the same respect.

Despite the twins' release, you probably continue to regard me as a monster deserving of his nickname. It would, however, be mistaken of you to believe that the scene I witnessed through my binoculars left me completely unmoved. I was deeply saddened when I saw Zorbach go to pieces from my vantage point on the hill.

It wrung my heart to see someone I liked so much in such a state – emotionally shattered and looking years older, as if drained of vital energy the instant he took his dead wife in his arms.

Alexander Zorbach was my mentor, the father I never had. He was my role model, and not only in the workplace, where I strove to emulate his enthusiasm and sense of humour. I even tried to resemble him in outward appearance by secretly purchasing the sort of clothes he favoured – clothes in which I was filmed by the gallery's camera when leaving Alina's block of flats.

I went to such lengths, just to be close to him, and now he's ruined everything. Why on earth did he keep his eyes so firmly shut? Didn't he *want* to see my innumerable clues, intended to point out the dangers of the game? Intended to warn him not to rush into it without thinking. I wanted to play it, admittedly, but not with him. He had no business taking part in this particular round.

I'm open to reproach, I'm sure, but not for having run the game unfairly. I wrote this to you already, and now you have the proof: I stick to the rules I've laid down, and if I do change them, it's always for the benefit of my countless opponents.

In Zorbach's case I left it up to him, long before the first round began, whether or not to take the field at all.

The voices on the police radio frequency were produced by a little jamming device I built with the aid of a few components obtainable in any well-stocked electronics mart. Then there was his wallet, which I purloined in the newspaper office and planted at the scene of the crime. It was up to him to interpret the signs. Were they an invitation to bring the Eye Collector to book in order to clear himself of suspicion? Or a warning to attend to what really matters in this life: the family?

Zorbach came to a decision. He put his work before the welfare of his child and set out to hunt me down. He was like all the other fathers whose children I've hidden so far. Fathers who had a choice throughout their lives between earning money and whoring around or taking good care of their own flesh and blood. Fathers as self-centred and uncaring as my own, who went boozing with his pals when he might have rescued us from the chest freezer. His selfishness cost my little brother his life and me my sanity – or so, at least, a psychiatrist's analysis would have it. It is of course noticeable – I freely admit this – that I always reproduce my own and my brother's attendant circumstances: a mother who needed removing from the field of play at the outset; a father who neglected his offspring; a hiding place in which the air lasted for forty-five hours seven minutes; and a corpse with its left eye missing like my brother's.

I spent a long time working out how to guarantee a precise deadline, because it would violate the rules of the game if a participant suffocated before my ultimatum expired. It would be equally unfair if one child had more time available than another. My brother had only forty-five hours seven minutes' worth of air, and there was no way he could have obtained any more. I would have preferred to use a chest freezer myself, but it's almost impossible, alas, to calculate exactly how long a person will survive in an airtight container. Someone who hyperventilates in a panic will use up air more quickly than someone asleep, and I myself am living proof that two people can survive for different periods of time on the same amount of oxygen. Consequently, the only way I could see of creating almost identical conditions was to extract the air from the hiding place at a time determined by myself. Consider that my attempts to pump the air out of the cellar in the nurse's bungalow were not overly successful. Anyway, I doubt if Zorbach and Alina would have asphyxiated down there because I hadn't managed to create a really airtight seal. So I opted for another way of depriving my hideaway of oxygen: I flooded it.

You're playing a sick, horrific game, I hear you say. *A fair game,* is my response. Even the victims have a genuine chance, as you can see in the case of little Toby.

He didn't *have* to toil away for hours on end. He wouldn't have died before the ultimatum expired even if he'd remained inside the trolley case and failed to escape from the wooden chest; he would simply have gone to sleep. Nor did I leave him those implements in order to derive a perverse pleasure from his futile exertions. The coin and the screwdriver weren't burial gifts; because I'd changed the scenario, they were genuine aids to escape instead of the useless implements available to my brother and I. Unfortunately, Toby allowed himself to be unduly alarmed when the lift suddenly descended a few metres, just because he'd tugged at the rope. Had he kept a clear head and hauled himself up it, he might have managed to open the hatch through which Zorbach climbed.

Toby missed his chance. A little later – after forty-five hours seven minutes precisely – the lift descended into the cellar. This proves yet again how magnanimous I am: I didn't add in the time a healthy person can survive underwater.

'What about Lea? Why wasn't she in the lift too?' If you ask me that, it shows you haven't understood a thing. I'm not interested in wiping out an entire family. *I* survived the love test as a boy, so one child was also permitted to survive this time around. The oxygen in Lea's refrigerator wouldn't have run out for ages. She was more likely to die of thirst in there.

I play fair no matter which way you look at it, and I've never played fairer than I did with Zorbach.

I warned him. Each of my warnings was a test, I grant you, but doesn't that apply to every sin in life? Every cigarette packet threatens us with death, yet we're also aware of the intoxicating effect of its contents. Every warning is a simultaneous temptation. Like Alina, my blind visionary, whom I sent to see Zorbach on his houseboat. His mother betrayed its whereabouts to me. Not personally, of course, because she's incapable of speech. The diary on her bedside table, from which Zorbach read aloud to her whenever he found the time to visit her, contained a detailed account of the day they happened on the secret path through the woods. I borrowed the book when visiting my grandmother at the sanatorium.

It's certainly no accident that my granny was transferred from the old folks' home in which she was treated so badly to the sanatorium in which Zorbach's mother is also a patient to this day. After writing my article, I ensured that she was moved to an institution whose patients received better treatment. It was there at the Park Sanatorium, as I knew from my research, that Katharina Vanghal, the nurse who so badly neglected my grandmother, had been exposed and dismissed on the spot – months before she was re-employed by a negligent personnel manager and left my grandmother to putrefy until her bedsores were open right to the bone. I repaid Vanghal in kind by gaining entry to her house, sedating her, and wrapping her up in plastic film. At the time it was merely a pleasurable, cathartic form of revenge. I had yet to learn that her own putrefaction would eventually acquire significance within the context of my great game.

When Zorbach and Alina asked me to get the parking ticket checked, I sent them to Vanghal's bungalow. That was the bait. At the same time, I expressly warned Zorbach not to go inside. I even signalled to him with the scrolling electronic sign on the door, which I was able to alter with a simple SMS.

Once again he had a choice: to carry on or give up.

And once again he decided in favour of the game and against

his family. Even though his child was sick – even though it was Julian's birthday – he ventured into the darkened house. Once again he behaved no differently from all the other fathers who desert their children for months on end, forget their birthdays, and leave them to brood on the question that torments them in their lonely beds at night: 'Does Dad still love me?'

You see how fair I am? I played straight into my pursuers' hands by revealing my true motive in an email I sent to Zorbach's computer. I even planted a piece of incriminating evidence on his mother's bedside table: a photomontage of my brother with a vital clue on the back! Last of all, I put a stop to Scholle's foul play and sent Zorbach back on to the field.

Why, you ask? The answer is quite simple: yours truly, the Eye Collector, doesn't want to win. I believe in love – in the love of fathers for their children. By putting them to the test I give them a chance to prove it to me and the world at large. I'm happy only when I lose! That's why I help my opponents, and why I ensured that Zorbach made a personal appearance at the all-important finale in Grünauer Strasse.

And, once again, it was his choice alone which way to go: forwards to destruction or home to his son, who was hoping for a birthday present from him.

Hohlfort got one thing right: I'm a tester, not a collector. I test the love of fathers for their children. I do it again and again, in the hope of an outcome that differs from the one I experienced myself.

Luck or fate?

That question, which has always intrigued me, will never let me rest after the latest developments.

Was it luck or fate that made Alina bump into me at police headquarters, where she'd gone to make a statement about the Eye Collector only hours after I'd enlisted her professional services as a physiotherapist, having pulled a muscle when dragging the Traunstein woman out into the garden?

What could a blind woman know about the Eye Collector, a man no sighted witness had ever seen?

I had to find that out before she spoke to a detective, so I led her into an empty interview room, where I disguised my voice and pretended to take down her statement. People put their heads round the door from time to time, but to an outsider my 'interrogation' must have looked like an entirely normal proceeding.

After that I sent her to Zorbach, my intention being to put him to the test again. His mother's diary had told me where he went to earth when he wanted to be alone and needed a place to think, and I realized he would go there as soon as I panicked him with the news that the police were looking for him. He could have sent Alina packing and remained in his lonely hideaway. Better still, he could have gone to see Julian and helped to celebrate his eleventh birthday.

For all that, I have to confess that I can sympathize with Zorbach's bewilderment when Alina disclosed my bizarre ultimatum.

The more I think about it, the surer I am that there must be a logical explanation for all that happened. How about this?

I was tired that day in Alina's physiotherapy practice. While I was waiting for her to massage me, my eyelids drooped. Perhaps I dozed off, lulled by the gentle strains of her chill-out music. Did I talk in my sleep? Murmur a number?

Forty-five hours seven minutes...

Alina may possibly have read or heard something about the Eye

Collector shortly before, and was thinking of it when she stubbed her toe on the urn. The pain overlaid every other sensation and made her forget what her subconscious had picked up.

Forty-five hours seven minutes...

The bizarre ultimatum.

But how could she be so sure that I was the beast everyone was hunting?

Luck or fate?

I'll admit it. I don't know. I'm not even sure I'm still in command of my own actions. Did Alina foresee the predestined course of events, or did she only put the idea into my head?

What is certain is that I originally had quite a different plan in mind for Julian. Then along came this blind girl, who kept talking about a game of hide-and-seek during which the child would disappear. To me, this story had a touch of genius. What an analogy! What symbolism! I would kidnap a child during a game of hide-and-seek and continue the game on a new, more existential plane! It would be a game within a game!

I naturally had qualms about selecting Julian as my next victim, right to the very end, but I construed it as an omen when Zorbach rejected his son for the last time and deputised me, of all people, to take him the watch. Julian came running out to meet me when I parked in front of Nicci's house. He knew me – Zorbach had taken me there for a meal on one occasion – so I certainly wouldn't have found it hard to get him to talk his mother into a playing a game of hide-and-seek. But I didn't have to, because – this struck me as rather uncanny, I admit – they were already in the middle of one! Although I suggested he hide in the tool shed where I later anaesthetized him, I can't rid myself of the idea that he would have chosen that hiding place without my intervention. Or that Nicci would, of her own accord, have uttered precisely the words Alina had attributed to her hours earlier:

"Sorry to call you, but I'm rather worried. I was playing hide-and-seek with our son, and the crazy thing is, I can't find him anywhere.'

Was this really all *predestined,* just as Alina envisioned it?

Or was it *chance,* for what else would a mother have said in such circumstances?

I don't know what to think, because each alternative seems even more unlikely than the other. The only certainty is that Alina's last 'vision' has given me a good idea. I can't use the good old lift again, alas, so I was initially at a loss to know where to take Julian. My identity must be public knowledge by now, so a mobile hiding place would seem considerably more logical this time. A ship, but one that will not be found so soon.

I know what you're thinking, but remember the sticker on the dashboard of my granny's car: *It's easy to foretell the future when you shape it yourself.*

Alina never could see into the past and I doubt if she can genuinely see into the future. But, one way or another, she has helped to create the template for my future activities, and I confess it gives me great pleasure to stick to it for the most part.

Luck or fate?

I don't know, but isn't that one of my reasons for playing the game? To discover whether the fathers will manage to alter what I myself have predetermined?

Will Zorbach succeed again? Will he manage to rescue his son now that my future course of action is known to him? Will I manage to diverge from Alina's predictions and influence my own destiny?

I'm not sure, but I'll find out.

Time goes by.

The game continues.

Have fun.

Yours,

Frank Lahmann

PROLOGUE

ALEXANDER ZORBACH

Didn't I warn you? Didn't I warn you against stories which, like rusty fish hooks, embed themselves ever deeper in the minds of those compelled to listen to them?

Perpetuum morbile... A story that has never begun and will never end, because it tells of death everlasting.

I strongly advised you not to read on.

These pages – God knows how you gained access to them – were not intended for you. Nor for anyone. Nor even for your worst enemy.

I told you I speak from experience.

Well, now you know it: the story of the man whose tears oozed down his cheeks like drops of blood, the man who embraced a contorted lump of human flesh that had breathed and lived and loved only minutes earlier – the story you have just read is not fiction.

It is my destiny.

My life.

There is a man in this tale who was forced to realize, just when the agony within his mind reached its peak, that the process of dying had only just begun. And that man is me.

1

(45 HOURS 7 MINUTES TO THE DEADLINE)

The search has begun...

ACKNOWLEDGEMENTS

I normally begin my acknowledgements by performing a virtual bow to the people who matter most to any author: you, my readers. On this occasion I'd like to mention some of you by name, because I've never received so much help from so many of my readers as I did when writing *The Eye Collector.*

As soon as I tweeted, early in 2009, that a prominent role in my next novel would be played by a blind physiotherapist, I received some responses from blind persons familiar with audiobooks of my work. They offered me help with my research – coupled, in most cases, with the following warning: 'Books and films purvey so much nonsense about us, please don't make the same mistakes.'

This warning, which I took very seriously, prompted me to remain in regular contact with blind and partially-sighted persons from the start.

I began my research by compiling an interview questionnaire designed to help me conduct a preliminary exploration of their world which was so unfamiliar to me. What are the most common, erroneous clichés about the blind? How do they dream? How do they cope with everyday life at the computer, on the phone, doing their laundry, etc.? You can find a selection of their original replies on **www.sebastianfitzek.de.**

In order to avoid any glaring errors, I based my Alina Gregoriev character on a real, live person: Mike May, who was also blinded by an accident at the age of three. Should this book whet your interest in his fascinating life, I recommend you to read his biography by Robert Kurson, *Crashing Through: A True Story of Risk, Adventure, and The Man Who Dared to See* (Random House). May cycled for miles unaided as child, acted as a school 'lollipop man', and skied downhill at 105 kph – a world record for the blind! His achievements are so remarkable, I had to tone them down a little in Alina's case, or no one would have believed in her.

I gave the relevant chapters of this book to a group of blind and partially-sighted people to read prior to publication. Special thanks are due to Uwe Röder, who organized several group telephone chats, and to Jenni Grulke, who volunteered to read the chapters aloud to all concerned. The group's feedback enabled me to steer clear of some obvious mistakes. For instance, a guide dog in unfamiliar surroundings would never have snoozed as peacefully as I described in my first draft. I discovered that some blind people use make-up and sport tattoos. I also learned a great deal about their fears, their concerns and the incomprehensibly thoughtless and hurtful treatment to which they're sometimes subjected by sighted persons.

For these and countless other valuable insights I should like to thank, in addition to those already mentioned: Feeodora Ziemann, Andrea Czech, Petra Klewes, Günther Sollfrank, Christine Klocke, Sahre Wippig, Roswitha Wagerer, Niels Luithardt, Helge Jörres, Anke Mädler, Nuray Gürler, Andreas Heister, Brigitte Rieger, Fanny Holz, Karina Scheulen, Johanna Sopart, and Victoria Amwenyo.

I've been quite overwhelmed by the helpfulness and candour of all the people listed here. I've learned so many interesting things in the last few months, I couldn't possibly incorporate them all in a single book. That's one of the reasons why I'm toying with the idea of featuring Alina and Zorbach in another thriller.

However, I must also admit that it's frankly impossible for a sighted person like me to enter fully into the world of the blind. In spite of the most intensive research, hours-long interviews and conversations, and personal experiments in dark restaurants, and even though my blind consultants read the draft in advance, I probably haven't succeeded in eliminating every error from my story (for which I, of course, bear sole responsibility).

This is because *The Eye Collector* is purely a work of fiction, not a textbook, and because Alina Gregoriev's 'gift' naturally makes her an extraordinary case. Nevertheless, I hope it is clear from my book how much I admire and respect those who run their own lives without the benefit of eyesight. My respect for them grew with every word I wrote.

In particular, I should like to make a point of mentioning

Lisa Manthey. A young lady of sixteen, she answered all the questions I asked her about a blind teenager's school routine.

Well, now it's time to introduce the rest of the gang. I don't know how it is with you, but to me most acknowledgements resemble the final credits of a feature film. We don't watch them because we don't, in any case, know the names that go scrolling past so swiftly.

To avoid this, I always say a few words about the people I'm indebted to. (A mention in a book comes cheaper than an invitation to a meal. Besides, some of the screwballs from whom I derive my inspiration aren't exactly the kind you want to be seen with in public – right, Fruti?)

Let's start with my publishers. I must once again make special mention of Hans-Peter Übleis and Beate Kuckertz. They have an unerring feel for a good story and – something that never fails to give me special pleasure – wonderful signatures. That of Herr Übleis always looks particularly handsome on my contracts.

Two more names deserve to be printed in extra bold type: those of Carolin Graehl and Regine Weisbrod, my editorial dream team. You appended precisely 252 comments to my first draft (I counted), though six of them, at least, were favourable. I must have a masochistic streak, because I still love you. A thousand thanks for once more making the best of my book.

The production department, too, excelled itself again. Many thanks, Sibylle Dietzel...

Over 100,000 new books are dumped on the market each year. If mine tend to land nearer the top of the pile, I owe it to two world champions in the art of book-lobbing (aka marketing): Kerstin Reitze de la Maza and Christian Tesch.

I've a terrible memory for names, so please take my thanks to the following as a thank you to the entire Droemer team: Susanne Klein, Monika Neudeck, Iris Haas, Andrea Bauer, Konstanze Treber, Noomi Rohrbach, Georg Regis, Andreas Thiele, Katrin Engelberger, and Heide Bogner.

Not to be forgotten under any circumstances, yet again, are my discoverer, Frau Dr Andrea Müller (who has rejoined the Droemer fold), and Klaus Kluge (who is still playing the 'renegade' ;-)).

My list of unofficial helpers continues:

Roman Hocke – you're the man who found me a publisher when so many others had rejected me. My thanks go also to the rest of your crew at AVA: Christine Ziehl, Uwe Neumahr, Claudia Bachmann, and Claudia von Hornstein.

I'm surprised that my list of good friends doesn't get shorter from book to book, given that writing leaves me less and less time to cultivate a social life. Despite this, Zsolt Bács, Oliver Kalkofe, Thomas Koschwitz, Peter Prange, Dirk Stiller, Andreas Frutiger, Arno Müller, Jochen Trus and Ivo Beck regularly get in touch, if only because I've failed to return their DVDs or skipped a root canal appointment on some flimsy pretext – right Uli? (Ulrike

Heintzenberg, the world's finest dentist!) My thanks to Simon Jäger for his wonderful voice, which enhances my audiobooks, and to Michael Treutler for his fantastic efforts at Audible.de.

My thanks, too, to Gerlinde, with whom I've been able to give some terrific readings, and who also has the makings of a novelist. Your story is great – it's high time you put it down on paper. Go on, take the plunge...

Thank you, Thomas Zorbach, for your wonderful surname, which I was privileged to borrow, and for your invaluable help in implementing some crazy ideas with your boys and girls from vm-people. By the way, your photo makes you look very well preserved for a man of fifty-six!

My gratitude to Manuela Raschke, whom I always introduce as my brain, but who looks a great deal nicer and has managed my entire life, goes without saying. (I would also mention Barbara Hermann in this regard.)

Manu, I mustn't praise you too fulsomely, or your husband Kalle (Rocky Graziano's one-time personal trainer) will stick me in a punchbag the next time we meet.

Two people whom I can't possibly leave out, and who have been there from the outset, are Sabrina Rabow (the woman for you if you want to get your name in the papers) and Christian Meyer (the man for you if you want to get it out again).

My thanks to the family Fitzek, Clemens, Sabine and Freimut – guess which one is my father? – for their professional, but primarily emotional, support. The family plays an important role in all my books, and not without reason; but I, unlike my heroes, am lucky enough to possess one that is still intact. It also, of course, includes Sandra, who contrives to share her life with a madman who'll break off in the middle of a sentence because another thought has just occurred to him...

... erm... were was I? Ah yes... the police!

Thank you, Detective Chief Inspectors Ingo Dietrich and Michael Adamski, for some fascinating insights into criminal investigation.

Finally, I must introduce you to the person who first gave me the idea for *The Eye Collector*: my physiotherapist Cordula Jungbluth, who has been putting me through the shiatsu mill for the past four years. She surprised me after every session by coming out with some accurate diagnoses of my life and psyche which she claimed to have 'read' from my body during treatment. At first I was merely amused when she told me I'd been an outsider as a boy (who wasn't?) and that many unresolved conflicts were still warring inside me (you don't say!). But then I thought, 'Hang on, if mere physical contact can really enable her to see into my past, what if I were a serial murderer? Could she tell if I'd murdered someone in my cellar just before she massaged me?' And that gave birth to the idea. (Not of going down into my cellar, of course, but of sitting down at my desk...)

I should add that, while giving me a massage me not long ago, Frau Jungbluth broke off to say (not that I'd ever told her anything about *The Eye Collector*), 'Asphyxia plays a prominent part in your new thriller, am I right?' She explained that she'd felt short of breath while manipulating me. I doff my virtual hat to you, Frau Jungbluth, and look forward to my next appointment!

Well, I now conclude as usual by expressing my gratitude to all the booksellers, salespersons and librarians who saw to it that this book ended up in your hands.

If, after these marathon acknowledgements, you still have the energy to send me your opinion of *The Eye Collector*, you can reach me in the following ways:

ichfandssuper@sebastianfitzek.de
(for compliments, requests for autographs, proposals of marriage, etc.)

or:

kritik@wandertindenspamfilter.de
(for criticisms and complaints, etc.)

fitzek@sebastianfitzek.de
naturally functions as before

Keep reading and best wishes from
Sebastian Fitzek
Berlin, March 2010